Itzig

AN HISTORICAL NOVEL
1900-1935

LONA FLAM RUBENSTEIN

Dust Jacket Design: Ty Stroudsburg
Book Design: John Laudando, JV Advertising & Design
Jacket Photo: Jessica Mackin

Published in the United States by Arete Press Inc.
20 Park Place
Suite 430
East Hampton, New York

WEB SITE: www.Itzigthenovel.com

PUBLISHER'S NOTE: This is a work of historical fiction. Names, characters, incidents, places either are the product of the author's imagination or are used fictitiously and any resemblance to actual persons, living or dead, or events, is entirely coincidental.

For

Msgr. Donald J. Desmond
1938 – 2007
Clara Frankel
1874 - 1966

Acknowledgements

Vay David, Editor, patient, creative, diligent; Ty Stroudsburg, her unique dust jacket design and tireless story editor, as well; John Laudando, JV Advertising & Design, book design, particularly his font research to complement the novel's content; Jessica Mackin, dust jacket photo; Marijane Meaker, mentor and booster, celebrated author as M.E. Kerr and founder of the Ashawagh Hall Writers' Workshop; Barbara Bologna, educator and friend, irreplaceable, gone too soon and sorely missed; Amy Ruhle, editorial assistant and talented jack of all trades; Isabel Carmichael, for her most professional text proofing; Lynda Wolter, reader of many early manuscripts with invaluable suggestions; Sammy G. Nakhla MD, Medical Editor; Eric Kruh, Professor Emeritus, Long Island University, Humanities Division for valued help in reviewing translations; Eleonore Fischer, excellent work on German Edition, Hans-Gunter Richardi, author of the most helpful *Dachau, A Guide to its Contemporary History;*

and,

Andreas R.Braeunling, *Stadtarchiv Dachau*, for his exceptional generosity in sharing his extensive knowledge of place, past, people, and language.

For any errors, the author must take all credit.

Itzig

Chapter 1
The Family Luftmann
1900

Born *Chaim Itzig*, Christian Luftmann, rotund, pink-cheeked, of medium height, was a thinking but practical man with piercing, deep-set intelligent eyes shrouded by dark, bushy brows.

Steeped in Talmud and Torah, he was raised an enlightened *maskilim*, a practice of the new Orthodoxy, thanks to his mother's (*may she rest in peace*) modern family. He had once hoped to be a physician healing others but, suffering a congenital affliction, seeing always the dimmer courses of history, spending his life trying to dodge them, he had devoted himself instead to his own survival.

He had understood what many Jews did not. With citizenship, they lost their *Schutzbrief*, special letters of protection granted in return for their unique talents — understanding money and somehow being able to put their hands on it.

His penny-pinching father, with his Eastern European roots, had told him that in 1810 alone no less than 80 percent of the more than two dozen German states were financed by their Jews.

Breaking with tradition, he studied secular knowledge prodigiously, what all German students studied. He had a crusade of his own: to find the recipe for *Bildung*, self-improvement — the statutory condition for civil rights granted Jews after Germany's unification. Self-improvement meant to become more German-like, fit in with the remaining 99 percent of the country's population.

Bildung! Perfecting one's self. He had trusted the concept, as long as the Germans believed it could be done. So, Chaim Itzig would start his transformation. First appearance and education, then a new name.

He couldn't be German without a German name, certainly not with his own. Given to his paternal grandparents, German clerks with a sense of humor had found it amusing to assign the last name *Itzig* to their newly emancipated Jews, who now needed surnames for citizenship, because *Itzig* was German slang for jewboy.

He shaved his beard (better a Jew without a beard than a beard without a Jew, he told his orthodox father), wore German clothes, discarding the long black coat, the fur-trimmed hat, the daily religious appurtenances. He read German books from front to back, not back to front, spoke the German language, learned *Hochdeutsch* (the universal tongue needed to overcome his own provincial Bavarian dialect), abandoned the Yiddish spoken at home, wrote from left to right, not right to left, using the German alphabet, not Hebrew — because his people before emancipation hadn't done any of these things, not even those who arrived on German soil some 1,500 years earlier with the Roman conquerors to help them colonize their new territories, civilize their primitive populations.

He read the great German thinkers. In Kant and Fichte, with their anti-Semitic treatises, Chaim found little that was hopeful for survival, let alone improvement. In Herder, however, he found a seemingly benign notion, a new idea, asserting that each nation had an unchangeable essence residing in its people (much like the Holy Spirit), an immutable inborn cultural soul, a national *Volk*.

That disturbed him, shook his confidence in Bildung's workability.

Herder did not propose that one Volk was better than the other (that step was lurking just around the corner, Chaim thought), only that each was permanently unique and different, "an assortment of flowers in a garden," and that was that. Continuing his garden metaphor, and because they had no country to call their own after almost 2,000 years of wandering, Herder described the Jewish Volk as different; without a country, a kind of vine that wrapped itself around the roots of the other flowers.

With all respect to Herder, Chaim knew the germ of the Volk idea was neither original nor new. A 4th-century Talmudic commentary insisted Jews were a nation dispossessed that practiced Judaism: a tribe, a race, essentially different, well, actually better (wrote the Rabbi) than those idolaters in whose lands they dwelt. To make matters worse, a prominent 19th-century Jew had written: Jews are a nation first, last, always, whether they have a country or not.

It did not augur well. How could Jews, a nation, a *race* residing in each of them, become good Germans? he reasoned; how could they be German-like, when they were Jewish-like?

Besides scholarly works, Chaim read popular German novels about villains called Itzig who swindled hard-working German Christians. He read about a Judas Jew betraying a German King of Naples. He saw a play that showed Jews could never become good Germans. Why? Because they were Jews.

That was enough!

Bildung had to be impossible; one nation couldn't become another nation.

Germans were Germans! Jews were Jews! Emancipation was another of God's tricks. Freeing His people from second-class status, He in return demanded the impossible.

Chaim had to move quickly. To become a good German, education, appearance, name changing were not enough. He must cease to be a Jew before *they* discovered he couldn't.

With his new wife, one Chaya Frankel — a Nuremberg orphan raised by cousins, a marriage arranged years earlier by his father — he left Munich, moving to Catholic Cologne after carefully planned stops in Berlin and Hamburg to visit distant relatives many times removed in the very different north. He converted to Catholicism at Cologne's Koelner Dom, taking the name *Christian* and petitioning successfully for the benign surname *Luftmann*, an airman, a man without roots.

Luftmann was a safe choice, not triggering the name theft legislation passed after emancipation due to the Jewish stampede for good German surnames. (There was a scandal his Berlin relations had ignited when they tried to change their Itzig brand.)

He had put in place a safety net as well, that Chaya — now Charlotte, called Lotte — described as, "Too clever! Safety net? Foolishness! Too careful!"

"In this world, you can never be too careful," he proclaimed.

Lotte, guileless with an edgy humor, plain except for thick blond hair and blue-green eyes — a genetic courtesy of Crusaders in heat a few hundred years earlier — became, to his chagrin, a sincere believer in her new faith; once an observant Jew, she was now a devout Catholic living with her husband's somber visions, his drastic chess-move plans.

"It is a good thing to believe in what you are doing," Luftmann said to his young wife while they still lived in the small Cologne rooming house. "But it is hard to grasp your ability to change so sincerely and so quickly."

"I believe in God, Christian. And this merciful, loving, and forgiving God is easy to have devotion for. The Bible was difficult to understand — all the family problems, brothers killing brothers, stealing birthrights, everyone smiting, killing for nothing. No, these Christian beliefs suit me. Though I do have fear often of that vengeful God that puts plagues on firstborns and may not like that I prefer mercy over justice."

"I think He is too busy, Lotte, to keep so close an eye on you."

"Don't joke, Christian! I was raised by a strict family who spoke about a God of vengeance, a God who demanded obedience, whose name we couldn't say, and who was jealous. *Thou shalt have no other gods before me*, He said. And here I am with my Trinity and all the saints."

"Trust me, Lotte, He will have other matters on His mind."

"I trust and follow my husband because I know he is smart and kind and took in this poor orphan without dowry and looks out for me. I will not mention these unsettling suspicions again. And I will pray."

Luftmann gazed at his compliant wife, thinking, so she can talk too, this little woman, have opinions. He liked that. "My father picked well for me, Lotte," he said.

To continue on the road to acceptability, they settled in Catholic Dachau near Munich, a small Bavarian town of maybe 2,000 residents, where they were not known. No Jews were known in Dachau, their presence prohibited over the centuries, except for cattle traders passing through. His spinster sister Gretl had unexpectedly joined them just last year (the Munich cholera had attacked the Itzig family, leaving her homeless), rounding out their Dachau household. Soon Lotte was with child.

Dachau served Luftmann well. Strangers blended in better than in other towns. Luftmann had thought so because of Dachau's somewhat transient and varied population: visiting artists who painted landscapes in the seductive light of the *Dachauer Moos*, tourists viewing the medieval *Dachauer Schloss*, European laborers that manned its paper factory.

He had become a Dachau *Buerger* by meeting the new citizenship criteria — buying a house, declaring a profession (investment banking), paying cash, trying always to acquire more property. His penny-pinching father, with the help of his remote but more assimilated north German relations, had left enough of a fortune, had made prudent investments in banking and shipping lines like the Hamburg American. He had even inherited a blind mortgage holding in Dachau from Reb Itzig's wheeling and dealing with the Hamburg bank.

Through this process, Chaim Itzig turned himself into Christian Luftmann, and Chaya into Lotte, both swearing oaths before God never to talk about these matters again.

In the last stage, however (these Germans with their primitive mystical relationships), he learned he needed to go one step further to be considered a real German. He needed *Eigentum*, an ephemeral quality of oneness with community that all Germans had, to prove he really belonged.

Community through soil was a unique and traditional kind of belonging, an umbilical connection once automatically part of *Buergerschaft*, but since emancipation it was no longer implied. One didn't need to be born in a town, have roots in the land for citizenship. One could buy it! He could be in the category of "citizen from the outside." Clearly that was not as valued, not true belonging, rights awarded or not.

So, in Dachau, Luftmann gave generously to *Der Land Arbeiter Bund* and bought real estate, even many acres of wooded property in the Wuerm forest near the river (now referred to as the *Luftmann-Land*, unclear whether through admiration, resentment, or ridicule for a useless purchase), hoping that through sheer quantity of earth, the quality of Eigentum would take seed.

But it couldn't. The German tradition of Eigentum was not for homeless wanderers! He could, however, have made believe, faked it, have had the appearance. Not now, not any longer. *Anti-Semitismus*, race and this seductive notion of inborn Volk meant you couldn't be both a German and a Jew, let alone connected to the earth.

Schver tsu zahn a Yid, hard to be a Jew, he recalled the Yiddish lament. But harder still, Luftmann thought, to become a German — education, appearance, name change, conversion, and property ownership notwithstanding.

What to do? Can anyone ever become what they're not?

Chapter 2
Baptism

Christian Luftmann, a Buerger in good standing, that morning had stood in Dachau's towering St. Jakob's Cathedral overlooking the clear blue River Amper, renouncing Satan for his infant daughter, Fanny, as *Herr Pfarrer* Goetz chanted the baptismal rite.

After Mass, sitting in the large kitchen near the coal stove, comfortable and self-satisfied, Christian read the *Amper-Bote*. Lotte, with Gretl's help, was preparing both a second breakfast — *Weisswurst, Schwarzbrot*, with both *Weissbier* and *Dunkles* — and the day's baptismal feast.

The editorial EPIDEMIC IN MUNICH caught his eye.

Epidemic?

Wearing a deep frown he leaned forward in the cushioned white ladder-back chair to read the respected Dachau newspaper spread on the linden wood table — a rectory table, white and rectangular, without ornate carvings.

EPIDEMIC IN MUNICH

The mass migration into Germany of Eastern European Jews, Ostjuden, for the past 25 years due to Russian and Polish government-approved pogroms, has poisoned our Reich. Once here, they become peddlers, beggars and prostitutes, a blemish on our Country, on our cities. They are an alien race of Orientals, unclean, a contagion of disease carriers bringing plagues like the recent cholera and over-running our Country. In Munich alone we have added several thousand over the last 100 years. Get rid of them! The epidemic must be stopped.

It was no secret that enlightened German Jews felt the same way about Ostjuden as the editorial writer. His mother's family always had looked down on them and on his father, blamed her for marrying Reb Itzig in the first place, a miserly good-for-nothing rag peddler with eastern origins who turned pawnbroker, studied Talmud, and stashed money away — God knows where — while their daughter led an impoverished life.

And he understood well what it felt like to be outcast, to be misunderstood, to be blamed unfairly for misfortunes that had nothing to do with him. His mother, a cold, self-centered woman, associated him with all bad luck. A difficult breech birth, her son, preferring the safety of the womb, fighting tooth and nail and upside down to stay there. She lamented throughout her lifetime that his *bris*, the circumcising rite of separateness, consecrated the Jews' decline.

Two sisters born later, both slow in thinking and oversized from a yet-to-be discovered genetic flaw, were deemed his fault as well. In his brief residence there, he had toxified her womb.

Moreover, he was born the year the *Gruenderzeit* bubble burst, 1873, when the economic collapse of the new capitalism was so severe its debilitating impact lasted until Luftmann reached adulthood. The brief *Gruenderzeit* years, with their frenzied rush to speculation and the accumulation of wealth, simply self-destructed. Jews were blamed for the modern and greedy get-rich-quick schemes, where ordinary hard-working Germans had invested — in railroads never built, industries never started, stables without horses — and lost everything. His mother counted that catastrophe against him, too.

Yes, Christian understood outcast, but now, in black and white in a mainstream respectable newspaper *an alien race* not an alien religion — race, Volk, marginal ideas were concepts supported in the *Amper-Bote*.

Luftmann stopped rocking the cradle that was at his side and looked slowly around the kitchen. What he saw as décor was duplicated in almost every other room in the elegant three-story house bordered outside by shade trees, flower gardens, picket fences, and statuesque poplars — one of the more prominent homes on Freisinger Strasse in the Burgfrieden District, where the self-described *real* citizens of Dachau lived.

There was a crucifix on the wall, Holy Family gatherings on the mantelpiece, saints on shelves, hand-embroidered prayers, a framed picture of a rosy-cheeked Mary looking oddly Bavarian, but this rash of religious relics no longer counted for becoming more German.

Baptism, generously offered to Jews by both Luther and Rome, would not expunge their longstanding rejection and contempt for the ridiculous worship of a Jewish man-god troublemaker, born of a Jewish virgin (Hah!), who had a dozen other Jews in sandals following him around all the time. It no longer erased their own exclusion of Gentiles, their centuries of self-imposed separateness that had later mutated into state-imposed segregation, the ghetto.

Baptism would no longer save them, belonging was beyond reach. The final nail in the coffin: they could not escape blood. *If a horse was born in a cowshed, it was still a horse, gell? Gell,* that punctuating Bavarian word meaning a question wasn't really a question.

If Germans thought it was in the blood, it *was* in the blood. That's how the world worked. "When it comes between you and the world, Chaim, bet on the world," his father had told him.

Furthermore, these racial theorists had Darwinian science and Mendelian laws of heredity to bolster their case. A special Volk gene! He looked down at the sleeping baby in the cradle. How would he secure her future? His grandchildren's future? Who would his Fanny marry? There were no other converts in Dachau. It had not escaped him that converts seemed to marry only other converts, ending up all Jewish anyhow.

"We thought to fool them. We are the fools. The joke is on us!"

"Are you talking to me, Christian?" asked Lotte, looking up from her cooking.

"Just thinking out loud," he mumbled.

"So tell me," she said, seeing from his deep frown that something was bothering her husband. Wiping her hands on her apron, red from slicing cranberries and onions for the *Kartoffelpuffer*, she sat down at the table with him. "I make potato pancakes, your favorite. Give a smile and tell me what joke?"

"It's no joke! Bildung is a farce! We can't improve, Lotte," he declared. "*Blut!* It is in the blood."

"Blood?"

"This Volk, this *who-you-are, what-you-are* can be passed along only by blood. We can neither become good Germans nor achieve Eigentum, despite citizenship," he said, his sigh so deep it was almost a groan. "We are in trouble."

"I do not understand. You are already a Dachau citizen. A member of the parish. A generous man in the community. What is this silly 'land-closeness' business? First, Bildung, now this . . . this . . . Eigentum," Lotte replied with a shrug, "What next? Work on the Golden Rule! Loving our neighbors! Right, Gretl?" she turned to her sister-in-law. "We do what we can."

Peeling potatoes, Gretl, a heavy, squat woman with pendulous, bloated breasts, responded. "Only do what we can," she mumbled with a grin and a nod, as she always did when Lotte showed her kindness, treated her as a person.

Though Lotte was a few years younger, it was as if Gretl had found in her sister-in-law a loving mother. So often when Luftmann was away on business, Gretl would climb into their large bed at night — fit for a king or queen — to sleep next to Lotte, to hold her hand.

"I don't mind at all," Lotte had told Luftmann. "The poor thing needs love and gives it so generously."

"Yes, well, it's good she doesn't try that when I'm in the bed with you, my dear, good-natured wife," Luftmann had said.

Gretl helped prepare for today's party, though she had been absent from the morning service. She had accepted being left home when they went to Sunday Mass, a decision made after that first bizarre experience.

To establish her in Dachau, Luftmann first made immediate and speedy arrangements with Father Goetz for Gretl to join the parish and to be baptized Roman Catholic. She had worn that same grin, Luftmann remembered, during the entire baptism rite executed hastily upon her arrival in Dachau, straight from the Munich hospital.

"She is Lutheran," Luftmann had lied to the priest, knowing that neither his assimilated German mother of the Mosaic persuasion nor his orthodox Eastern Jewish father had ever changed their faiths.

The ceremony was private, very private! Almost secret! Both he and the priest had feared fellow Dachauers would be terrified of the woman as a plague carrier.

Christian, satisfied and grateful for the secrecy, called her Gretl Luftmann. That is what he wanted. In getting the information for St. Jakob's baptismal record, Father Goetz had also asked Gretl her full name when talking alone with her before the ritual. It was his custom to make sure the person, unforced, understood the conversion process.

"Another way to reach God," the priest had told her. "And you want to do this, Gretl?"

"I love God," she answered with a smile. Father Goetz took that as a *yes*.

As to the only Mass they attended, Luftmann remembered vividly that first experience at St. Jakob's. Who could forget his taking the grown, oversized woman with the child's mind to Sunday Mass the first time? And the last! Thank G-d they had been in the back pew!

(*G-d!* Even when I think I still cannot think His name! See it! Is that what the seventh commandment really meant? Not to say, not to write? He sighed. It becomes imbedded, this childhood orthodoxy.)

When Gretl was told they were going to church, her face had gone blank.

"Where God lives," Lotte had explained, simplifying, not wanting to confuse her that God was everywhere and with them always.

Gretl understood, having gone to temple with her father to talk to God.

After the reading of the Gospel by Father Goetz came the responsorial psalm and Gretl's confusion when the congregation prayed aloud. She began to recite the *Shemah Yisro-ail*, the only prayer she knew, the only prayer her father, Reb Itzig, made sure she knew. The only prayer a Jew had to know, proclaiming God's oneness.

She prayed loudly. "To make sure He hears me," she had said as a child, which was acceptable in the noisy orthodox synagogue. Reb Itzig would plant her behind the curtain in the women's section. As was their way, the men and the segregated women all chanted noisily, but not in unison.

In the large cathedral, Gretl never got past *Adoshem*, when Luftmann had rushed her out the back door, dousing her with holy water from the font as they exited.

A memory and a half as his father would have put it, Luftmann thought, watching his sister peel potatoes, helping Lotte. He still blamed himself for not thinking of it before it happened.

He was ignorant of the fact that he had more to blame himself for when it came to the handling of his sister's baptism. If only he could have read Father Goetz's thoughts before the priest was alone with his sister, if he had known what Father Goetz would ask her. If he had not been in such a hurry, Luftmann would have known he had to coach Gretl. But he was unaware, just wanted to get it done.

The priest, however, was focused on his freshly inked parish record kept safe in the rectory. Words ran through his mind: *Luftmann* was *Luftmann!* Let Cologne's cathedral deal with that, but Gretl? *Gretl was Itzig!* She had told him so. And when he looked doubtful and asked again for her full name, Gretl had pulled out and given him her small identity tag from the hospital.

As Gretl peeled the potatoes, Frau Luftmann's attention was glued to preparing today's special Sunday meal.

"Lotte, listen," Luftmann insisted, reciting the newspaper's attack on Eastern European Jews. "You can give me a minute, *gell?* This is important. Those naïve *Ostjuden* going to their promised land, as they call our *Kaiserreich*, where they believe everyone loves Jews? Hah! Not even German Jews want them."

"Very unChristian," she said, listening, but continuing to flour the bread pan.

"Lotte, don't you see? If they, too, despise *Ostjuden*, calling them an unwanted element — and that was before the cholera — if our own people," he whispered, "join officials at border stops, de-licing, stripping, scouring, using sealed trains to ship them directly to ports, making certain they leave the Reich, if they act this way, what will happen when the others join in? Will they say only *Ostjuden*? Why not all *Juden*?" He rattled the newspaper in the air. "We are in trouble."

"A lot of *ifs*," Lotte exclaimed impatiently. "We are Christians!" she added, banging the pan on the countertop.

Luftmann was taken aback. She was not a short-tempered woman, his wife. And he knew his forebodings often disrupted Lotte's desire to be immunized against external events. He realized he'd pushed the subject too far. But how could he explain this race notion to her? Convince her of the seriousness? She told him often enough she was a *Hausfrau* and that she was an orphan raised by cousins — some Nuremberg Frankels — without a home of her own, so she enjoyed every minute of being only a homebody.

"Trust in God and let me be. Be grateful for our daughter. Stop looking for trouble, Christian. *Seek and thou shalt find*, sayeth the Lord."

Luftmann said nothing. Be grateful for their baby girl, Lotte had said. Would baby Fanny be grateful? He worried before she was born, hoping his child would belong, would live a normal German life. It was one thing to grow up fearful about something you had done or not done, the way you looked or the way you didn't. That could be altered. But to be afraid always because of who you were? That was a curse, a life sentence. A Jew by gene, a racial Jew. And if there were racial Jews, there were racial Germans, as well! The only real kind!

What's more, the Gospel of the *Alldeutschen Verband*, that right-wing Pan-Germanic League, was spreading like fertilizer. Jews, they preached, baptized or not, were a mortal threat to Germans and Christians by nature — cosmopolitan materialists living off interest and speculation, making money not earning it, thriving off their neighbors' hard times. Such notions were gaining currency on their own without the help of mainstream newspapers branding them an "alien race."

Would they be denied Christianity as well, despite convert sermons Father Goetz gave about welcoming the return of prodigal sons, about bringing Christians closer to the Second Coming, about one people under God?

Granting them citizenship was not popular in the first place, Luftmann knew. Back then, Bavarians had actually petitioned their government not to do so in writing. *It's not the Jewish religion we hate but Jews themselves.*

They were on to something!

"You're still frowning, Christian, and we are still celebrating our daughter's baptism today," said his wife, carrying the last tray of kneaded brown dough to the black tile oven, finally seating herself next to her husband.

Giving another long sigh — a tragic sigh, that said he had known this could happen, a sigh that had seen Herder's flower garden of national souls, the flower garden beset with parasitic vines, had seen *Volk* and *Antisemitismus*, all coming to no good — Luftmann put away the newspaper. For the meanwhile, he surrendered to his wife's stubborn complacency, offering some levity for all her hard work.

"Do you not think it strange, Lotte? One of His tricks? German Jews do their best to disappear into good Germans and more and more foreign-looking Jews appear — an endless supply from the east. It is like the Jew Offenbach's *Tales of Hoffman* — remember we saw the opera in Berlin? — out one door, in the other," Luftmann joked.

She gave an unsympathetic chuckle for those who behaved so badly to their own kind, calling themselves *Germans of the Mosaic persuasion*, praying in German, even celebrating their Sabbath on Sunday. "Maybe God is laughing at them, Christian. Maybe? When they told Him their plans."

He smiled then gave a shrug, releasing weight from his shoulders. His face wore a wry look, eyebrows relaxed, brown eyes surrendering their worried squint.

Wiping her hands on her heavy linen apron, Gretl joined them, but not without giving the baby a quick kiss, eliciting an infant coo and half-smile, and not before dropping the pot of potato peels on the spotless white tile floor. For a second, she looked terrified, frozen where she stood, her face pinched, about to cry.

"Come, Gretl. Anyone can have an accident," said Lotte gently. Then turning to Luftmann, she added. "Your sister is such a help, Christian, so kind and loving. Baby Fanny already has a special attachment for her. She's a gift from God."

Gretl relaxed. Despite her awkward bulkiness, she got down on her knees, searching for scraps. Lotte, for a moment looked as if she were about to help, but decided to let Gretl do it alone, handing her a damp cloth to wipe away any stains.

"You know, Christian, we should be thankful, not look for things to worry about, things we cannot change," Lotte said, patting him on his now relaxed shoulder.

"Sometimes I push too hard."

She nodded, then said, "Come sit with us, Gretl. The floor is fine. Let us pray in thanksgiving for this breakfast, this child, for today's celebration, for our being together."

Now Christian nodded. His wife meant that despite all the issues he had raised, they were not born slow, clumsy, and mentally dull, limited from so many joys in life as both his sisters had been, one of whom had tragically succumbed to the filthy epidemic.

A medley of lingering aromas filled the kitchen — the distinctive cabbage fragrance for salads, rolls, stews, always there; and a diced pork belly melted in fat (culinary proof of conversion, Luftmann called it). Scents of simmering beer soup, baked wheat flour rolls, pretzels, and sweet apple strudel prevailed as well, preparations for later meals.

"I do find comfort in the smells of your kitchen, Lotte," he said. "No one can say they are not true German."

Lotte gave a contented smile as she intoned the prayer of thanksgiving. Gretl grinned, Fanny slept, Christian's mind wandered elsewhere. He had an odd thought. Maybe he could join the Army. A new route to belonging. German by patriotism? Outlandish! Military service wasn't doing the French Jew Dreyfus any good, poor soul! In any case, it didn't matter. For it to work, to be authentic, he would need a war.

Chapter 3
The August Days
1914

Die Reichskriegflagge was everywhere held high, waving among the animated crowd assembled on Munich's Odeonsplatz, iron cross and eagle with its sun-shimmering gold on the stark red-white-and-black, die Reichskriegflagge, the flag of war.

It had been declared by the Kaiserreich against Russia the day before. Still both the multitude and the intensity of their fervor in Munich's Odeonsplatz was unexpected. Passion-filled with a newfound ardor, the crowd chanted patriotic mantras that resonated off ornate, elegant Rococo buildings, fortresses defining the oversized square.

"All the fanfare! A regular picnic," Father Goetz whispered.

"Europe's family picnic," Luftmann added, wryly referring to Austria's Habsburgs, Russia's Romanovs, the Reich's Hohenzollerns, and Britain's Hanovers. All were British Queen Victoria's brood one way or another. "This time the cousins go too far! Spoiled, squabbling children playing war games as if the map of Europe were their backyard. Risking lives not their own, sacrificing those who have nothing at stake, it makes no sense!"

"When you're privileged and powerful, Christian, you don't have to make sense. Only six weeks ago, relatives together mourning the Habsburg heir at the Archduke's funeral; now, declaring war on each other."

"They'll end up killing everybody!"

Luftmann was not exaggerating. France was expected to join Russia and declare against the Germans, her traditional enemy to the north. And, despite the Kaiser's hopes that Great Britain would stay neutral (after all, King George and Kaiser Bill were first cousins), she would declare against the Reich, too, provoked by its Imperial Army's shortcut through Belgium to surprise attack France, ravaging the neutral country on its way.

"And today we see a frightening spectacle, I'm afraid. Right here in Munich. Those who may die, may lose sons, brothers, fathers, are overjoyed at the sacrificial prospect. Cheering!"

"Can you think of a better place than Munich?"

Suddenly aware of people within earshot, the priest warned, "We should exercise caution. If overheard in the midst of this patriotic zeal, we could end up on the cross."

"But what better place than Munich for this magical hysteria?"

Father Goetz gave it some thought. "I can't think of one," he finally said.

Munich! Her cavernous beer cellars, art galleries, opera house, green tracts of parks, gardens, the magnificent Ebersberger Forest, grand boulevards, remarkable edifices in ravishing Rococo and pale stucco, fountains and statuary, her River Isar spanned by graceful bridges, and the soaring 15th-century Gothic cathedral, *Frauenkirche*, two towering domes like arms stretched high, blessing it all. But most important, Munich was steeped in both pagan myths and Roman Catholic mysticism, a potent, receptive brew.

It was, indeed, an epiphany more than a rally, a congregation more than a crowd. And in the frenzied exhilaration of a brand-new war, a people was born, resurrected. Yes, it was natural for Bavaria's esoteric capital to be the manger of Volk, of a Deutsche spirit revealing itself.

On that August day, in that Odeonsplatz, a cord of Germanhood materialized and connected every citizen in the Kaiserreich. Uncharacteristically, not historically natural, everybody was equally German. Class hierarchies, religious differences, traditional divisions, provincial loyalties, for the moment dissolved like sugar cubes in a cauldron. What Bismarck had failed to do with his imposed fragmented unification was made real.

"WE'RE HAVING A WAR! EVERYONE INVITED!" a summons might have read. There was one German voice, one German heart, one German spirit, sharing a bundle of embedded Germanic virtues, among them fidelity, patriotism, obedience, readiness to die for an ideal, to slaughter for a belief.

A communion by sword, not wafer, there was an eerie undertow of intangible spirituality. On the non-Teutonic Munich altar, the pending war was first worshipped and revered — not Hamburg nor Berlin, not Prussia nor Saxony, all of whom thought Bavarians just two letters away from barbarians. Let northerners say Munich was crass and tacky, but here a Deutsche Volk had triumphed once and for all. It was a religious experience.

And it was in the name of the Father, the Son, and the Holy Ghost! German churches, Roman Catholic and Protestant, both voices of God, gave blessing and consent to fertilizing battlefields with death and holy water, to incense of decomposed flesh and carrion wafers, suspending the Sixth Commandment. The custodians of conscience, Germany's cowled cheerleaders, granted God's permission, proclaimed sure victory, declaring God was on their side.

Within the massive and single-minded crowd, ecstasy mirrored on their faces, one could feel the powerful currents, the surge of elation as they rallied for a sacred cause, a war above all wars, noble and blessed.

On the other hand, at least one Dachauer chose not to celebrate. Lotte Luftmann was not there rejoicing with the masses, not there with her husband and their teenage daughter, Fanny. She chose to stay quietly at home as she had done a day earlier, not attending the rally on Dachau's Schrannen Square either. Gretl kept her company because of a profound fear of crowds.

"The Lord said not to kill," Lotte had told Luftmann. "He didn't say it was all right if they were enemies. No one would want to kill friends anyway," she had added in her commonsense kind of way.

Clearly, Frau Luftmann took the sixth commandment more seriously than Christian religions, Protestant and Catholic. And indeed pious people at Munich's mass celebration were cheering a war that was hallowed, sanctified, and righteous.

"Our war is like Christmas, holy and sacred!" a familiar voice called out from the crowd.

Fanny Luftmann whirled around. There was Sepp Hofer standing behind her. "That voice I recognize anywhere. I searched for you, Sepp, at the train station. Where were you, looking so military and handsome?"

"I stopped first at the academy," he replied, "to pick up the flag."

He was in full-dress *Kadettenkorps* uniform — red, white, and black, colors of the Kaiserreich, navy blue and brass, epaulets, polished buttons and belt buckle.

"I see the Reichskriegflagge. I wish I had one to wave."

Sepp greeted Herr Luftmann and Father Goetz, then handed his flag to Fanny.

And wave it she did. "Do you feel it, Sepp? Feel the glory and wonder? Look around you! The people! Our city! Inspired! We'll not forget this August day. Never!"

Luftmann heard his daughter's passionate enthusiasm. He listened to the noisy crowd. Perverse! It seemed there was nothing like the spectacle of war to get these people's blood rushing. He studied Sepp and Fanny. They were quite a pair, he thought, the teenager and the young cadet several years older. How fast go the years!

Fanny was tall, but Sepp was taller, a wiry, clean-faced young man with a strong look, an honest look actually, and comely despite the thin scar across his cheek. Joking, smiling, sharing the day's exuberance, Luftmann could see how comfortable they were with each other.

His daughter, blond, slender, strong even features, was an unexpected ideal of German womanhood. A veritable miracle, Luftmann thought. Fanny always stood out while his enduring concern had been more about her fitting in.

"She takes after me, has my blond hair," Lotte had said.

Luftmann had laughed. Couldn't help himself. "You are barely five feet!"

"A gift then from a great-great-grandfather?"

"I think perhaps further back, *gell?*" he gently suggested. "Some sturdy crusader, *gell?*"

She was a fine athlete, too, and a scholar, a favorite of the Sisters at St. Jakob's School. Her independent ways threatened no one, yet kept most of her peers at a healthy distance. The exception was her closeness with Sepp Hofer.

Like some only children she was precocious, more a woman beyond her fifteen years. And like some only children, she was oddly naïve at times, and believing in something or someone, she was reluctant to give it up. Luftmann shrugged, Fanny was no more of an enigma than anyone else, he supposed.

His privileged daughter, bolstered by her father's affluence and Burgfrieden standing, was gifted at lawn tennis, an elite and noble sport for the wealthy. Fanny was more than welcome to practice with a small advantaged group from Munich who were starting a tennis club that she probably would not be able to join because of traditional restrictions on women members. She was invited, as well, to play on private courts in Dachau — just south of the old town near the clear blue Amper River — that belonged to the affluent owners of the Mueller Brewery.

Luftmann knew that how he earned a living was a mystery to his daughter. Growing up she had asked him from time to time what it was he did, watching him pore over books and numbers in his study. Once at night when he was storytelling, she confessed that sometimes she felt a strangeness she couldn't explain, a fleeting tickle.

"Is it the dark, Fanny?" he had asked.

"No, I'm not afraid, Papa. It comes sometimes when I'm alone with you and Mama. As if you want to say something, but don't."

He had told her it was an active imagination or the singularity of no siblings. "Don't waste good time making up mysteries or fairy tales, Fanny. *Die Brueder Grimm* have already done that." The next day Luftmann came home with the authors' collection.

Today Fanny did not worry about old mysteries. There was no unexplained tension. Today at the Odeonsplatz, dressed in colorful native smock and blouse, she sang *Soldatenlieder* along with the crowd, her voice ringing out the martial hymns of Germanic valor and, loudest of all, *Deutschland, Deutschland Ueber Alles*, the Deutschlandlied, their anthem.

She cheered each shouted patriotic axiom, feeling no fleeting undercurrent, gone the way of a lonely child's imagination. Her strong, sweet voice rang with emotion.

It was a glorious day, a day for the Kaiserreich to stand up for itself, to restore respect among nations after years of humiliation over imports, exports, navies, territories, finances, treaties, all things powerful that royal cousins held dear and fought over.

In the crowd, the air brimmed with good thoughts, pollinating seeds of unity and togetherness. Strangers embraced, warmly greeting each other, saying *Gruess Gott*, that special Bavarian hello, waving, clasping hands.

Today all were one! It really felt that way. It really was!

Even Luftmann was thinking he could overcome his outsider feelings, thinking that Germans could abandon their pathological fear of "otherness," their desire for keeping people grounded in the safety of sameness.

But then his nature was always to worry, his self-imposed charade rife with anxieties, traps, pitfalls, always turning something that looked good inside out to see what might be lurking there. Like the Frenchman Dreyfus, for example; when he was saved from Devil's Island, Luftmann said at dinner, when the news reached Dachau, "Reinstated so the Kaiserreich will have a chance to kill him if there's a war!"

"If he fights for the French, then he's our Reich's enemy, Papa. How odd your thinking is! Mother's right. You are forever worrying, seeing things for the worst."

Worrying? He had to be perpetually on guard, on the lookout for possibilities of imminent exposure. Yes, it was a drain. It was not easy to be what you weren't.

"Come, Papa," Fanny called out above the din of the crowd. She slipped her arm though his. "No frowning today! A time for happiness, *gell*?"

He got his war, but it came too late. He couldn't serve because of age, couldn't use the military to become a true German by patriotism. Yet, Luftmann thought, maybe, just maybe, it didn't matter, wouldn't matter. Not after today. If things go well. It was clear a unified people was born in the ecstasy that blanketed the Odeonsplatz, feeling in the blood rush of war what they couldn't in the serene flow of peace. Inclusiveness!

"Look at that gentleman," Sepp said, pointing at a man with a funny mustache.

The stranger was wild-eyed, seemed spellbound, both hypnotized and hypnotic, giving the now-recognizable Alldeutschen Verband Pan-Germanic League stiff-armed salute as he bellowed patriotic slogans.

"A new world order!" he called out, in a voice, a voice very much like Munich, much larger than himself. "A new world order."

It was contagious, hard for them to take their eyes off him.

"I would march into French machine guns tomorrow with the Deutschlandlied on my lips," Sepp blurted, the thin scar on his cheek turning pink against his fair skin. He noticed other stiff arms raised, some belonging to people from Dachau. He awkwardly gave the same salute as the mustached man.

"Why, Sepp!" Fanny chided. "What are you doing?"

Sepp ignored her, taking back the Reichskriegflagge, holding it high for all to see.

"Why, Sepp!" he mimicked her reproach, a frown darkening his face. "The League is a serious movement, Fanny. There are fanatics among them. Easy for you to dismiss, perhaps, but I worry for my mother, for our family position."

Sepp's father, Ludwig Hofer, was both outspoken and left-leaning. He was labeled *die Pest*, a known instigator at the Mueller Brewery where he worked. In this climate of war, patriotism, a geyser of intoxicating nationalism, Luftmann thought Sepp had a right to worry, despite his wearing a uniform. Fanny, in her position, could well afford to say "Why, Sepp!" She wasn't in his shoes. After all, his daughter had both her Burgfrieden belonging, with its specialness and insulation, and her talent.

But others who desperately needed an exceptional and distinctive feeling, as if they too belonged, could have it from the Alldeutschen Verband, through the League's doctrines, without doing a thing, not having to prove themselves. It was only birth that determined who they were, rather than where they lived or what they did or how much they had.

Luftmann and Father Goetz had discussions about what was once a fringe group that seemed to be catching on more and more.

A day earlier, Father Goetz and Christian Luftmann had observed the war's inception at the Dachau rally.

"They act as if the Kaiserreich had already won," Father Goetz had said.

"Hubris," uttered Luftmann. "Something about pride and falls, *gell?*"

"So, my friend, you too question the Kaiser's promise of a short war?"

"Promises can lead to disappointments. They should just do it!" Luftmann said.

They were friends — as much as a priest can have a friend that is part of his flock.

Because of Gretl's inability to attend church, Lotte Luftmann had asked Father Goetz if he would celebrate communion for her at the Luftmann home. That's how it started, the regular visits where, afterward over tea in the parlor, he and Luftmann would enjoy at first intellectual discussions then, later, political ones.

Father Goetz told Luftmann about *Sankt Raphael,* a small clergy group helping German émigrés after the mass exodus caused by the *Gruenderzeit* upheavals.

"Does your Bishop mind these outside activities?" Luftmann had asked.

"It is easier to beg forgiveness than to ask for permission," answered Father Goetz with a twinkle in his light-blue eyes.

He admitted that his restless and scholarly mind's eye, refusing to deny what it saw, landed him in Dachau's St. Jakob's instead of Rome's Vatican City.

Sometimes they invited Fanny in to listen with her sharp, inquisitive intellect coupled with being a keen observer and listener all her life, the skills of an only child. She couldn't help overhearing the conversations anyway, unless they shut the parlor door.

He complained about the Church's silence in the face of so many Protestants embracing the new virulent nationalism, the spreading dogma from the Alldeutschen Verband, worshiping a national Volk, instead of a universal God who imbued humankind with His Holy Spirit through baptism. He warned about that League's anti-Semitism and profane whispers of an Aryan Jesus.

He confided, "Our people, inch by inch, are becoming more good Germans than good Catholics," adding, with a smile, "When I tell the most reverend bishop these things, he says I behave like neither a good German nor good Catholic."

Sucking a sugar cube, sipping black tea, Luftmann listened most of the time.

Fanny had been there when Father Goetz talked about the League, its Volk dogma and its dangers. She asked, "Why are Volk and Trinity at odds with each other, Father Goetz? Why can't the Volk spirit that makes one feel special dwell side by side with the Trinity that makes one feel holy?"

"Volk and Trinity? We cannot serve two masters, my child. The Church is for all, universal. All can receive the Holy Spirit. Volk separates, excludes. It is an unChristian notion. *The Lord is merciful to all and hates nothing He created,*" Father Goetz quoted scripture. "We are all one under God.

Remember that! It is sinful to believe differently!"

Yes, the priest had strong convictions. And today, amidst the manic throng, enveloped by an energy-laden aura, Fanny simply hadn't wanted her dear Sepp to expose himself to sin and retribution with his Voelkisch League salute.

The Munich Rally winding down, Sepp had been quiet since Fanny's outburst.

"Sepp, I am sorry. Forgive me?" Fanny whispered sincerely, realizing he was upset. "To make up for my transgression," now she teased to change his mood, "I have a special secret for you. On the way back to Dachau we can talk."

"I have something special to tell you, too," he said, a smile returning to his face.

Chapter 4
Fanny and Sepp
That Evening

They didn't talk on the train. Too many people, too few seats. So Fanny told Sepp her news back in Dachau that evening when, brimming with energy from the Munich rally, they hiked in the Wuerm Forest near the river on her father's land. Rolf, Sepp's German shepherd, an energetic black-and-tan puppy, padded along after them, barking occasionally when he caught the scent of a deer.

"So! You look like you are bursting."

"With joy! I've been invited to try out for the Berlin Summer Olympics! Can you believe it?"

"The Olympics?"

"Yes, they have introduced women's tennis to the games."

He hesitated, then asked. "But will the war interfere?"

"I think not. Didn't the Kaiser promise a short war? Maybe a month. Like the last one with France."

"Yes, well — "

"Don't be a spoilsport. You remind me of my father. Looking at the bad side."

He smiled. "Fanny, that is wonderful. To represent our country. I am proud of you." He gave her a hug. "Will you make the team?"

There was no reply. She just gave him what Sepp called *the Fanny look*. Self-confident and persevering.

"Hah!" he laughed. "Those other girls don't have a chance."

"And you, what did you want to say."

"Nothing as exciting. Just some thoughts about a meeting I attended."

"A meeting?"

"Yes, the Alldeutsche Verband! I had to put those Volk people at ease, Fanny. I said no to too many of their invitations. This one came direct from Mueller — "

"Mueller? Marius? He belongs? I heard Father Goetz say those people were troublemakers."

"He belongs. The brewery boss is a big shot in that League. I had to go to defend myself, Fanny, because of the Wuerm incident, you know. The Alldeutsche Verband did not approve. Comrades from the Kadettenkorps who are members told me."

"They have such members, young men training for war and so loyal to our Kaiser?"

"Training for defense, too, Fanny. But the League seems to enlist cadets with ardor. They favor the military-minded. So I went to their meeting in Munich."

"And?"

"It was scary, as if people were drunk from ideas. That's why I did the salute."

"I am sorry for jumping on you, Sepp. We are good, right? I have to say sorry again."

"That's over, Fanny. One sorry was enough."

"Hmmm! Ideas that make you feel drunk? I prefer the fresh air here in the forest," she said, breathing deeply. "Do you smell it, Sepp? The summer mixed with the hint of fall? It's delicious here. So beautiful! So peaceful!" She scampered ahead of him on the narrow trail, her gait that of a graceful athlete. Then she spun around. "Tell me! How do you find time for meetings in your last year at the academy? Besides, you and meetings! I know you too well. Not a fit!"

He smiled but said nothing. Something of a loner, Sepp had become good friends with Fanny — close friends even though four years her senior — after Rolf ran loose in this forest and Fanny found him wandering near the stately firs and pines.

"Mueller and who else? Dachau people?"

"You'd be surprised. Some from our parish. More from the county, rough around the edges. But those from Dachau, except for Herr Mueller, are not Burgfrieden, as you are, Fanny."

Living in the fashionable Burgfrieden part of town made a difference. Social classes that branded you like cattle, though cordial with each other, were strictly separate. Fanny understood how much being in the exclusive district meant from her father's talk.

Burgfrieden people, the self-anointed true Buergers, had something that her father wanted but felt was missing for him. Living in the district was not enough. It was *something more* he needed, something fundamental which, unlike her father, she somehow took for granted.

Sepp, on the other hand, lived on Burgfriedenstrasse on the fringe of the select neighborhood, its right side that was the wrong side, the working-class side.

He broke the silence. "These ideas they preach are like strong *Schnaps*. Ideas of Volk! Of wonderful traits German people everywhere are born with."

"Born with? Like blue eyes? Which I have and, let's see," she looked at his face with an exaggerated peer, "Hah! You do not."

(It had surprised Christian Luftmann that according to Mendel's new genetic science and its breeding laws, he had recessive blue-eyed genes to match up with Lotte's to produce a blue-eyed Fanny. Mendel! Of all things, a priest dictating breeding laws? Ironic! Recessive genes? Where else could blue eyes come from? From an old brown-eyed Jew like himself? And how? Deposited by some Crusader rape in the Middle Ages on his way to the Holy Land to kill infidels? So he was not a pure Jew, after all. He laughed. Go tell that to the Alldeutsche Verband!)

"Don't mock me, Fraeulein," Sepp replied to Fanny's teasing. "You, the perfect German maiden. The League members believe Volk is what makes them German, blue eyes or not. A German-ness needing protection from non-Germans. They use Gypsies as an example: once pure, now contaminated, mongrelized. They talk of un-German traits."

"What does un-German mean? I don't understand."

"Inferior! Not voelkisch! Talk against Gypsies, Slavs, Bolsheviks, Jews, especially Jew cosmopolitans, as a threat to Volk — more than the old *Die Juden sind unser Unglueck*. They whip up a storm. It sounds like a sermon in church."

"The Prussian who said Jews are Germany's misfortune also said our Catholic Church was a vampire on the German people. Father Goetz explained that in his sermons," Fanny reminded him. "Besides, we have no Jews in Dachau."

He stopped and looked up at the sky. "I cannot believe that I talk so to a fifteen-year-old," he blurted. "How can you be only fifteen and know so much?"

"Don't go by years," she said wisely. "My father says I'm precocious. And look at my dear aunt! Looks old, a child at heart."

"They mentioned Gutmann the Jew *Haendler*. He moved into the Kraisy

Inn. Some Dachau people are talking."

Fanny gave a laugh. "Cosmopolitan? Samson Gutmann, the cattle trader? A misfortune? He makes *no fortune* from Dachau," she joked. "Hmmm! He does have that bright silver auto, needs it to get around the countryside, I suppose."

They had stopped at a favorite spot on the riverbank where a cluster of white pines towered over the clear blue water. Sepp picked up some pebbles and tossed one from time to time, watching as they skimmed the water's surface.

"They speak badly of the Jew *Haendler's* cheating hard-working Germans. They say Gutmann is the most dangerous kind because he doesn't look like a Jew."

"More like Goliath, a giant of a man," she quipped. "Smart his parents named him Samson! And what should a Jew look like? And what does this have to do with anything? Anyway, Father Goetz teaches we need Jews to return for the Second Coming of our Lord. Maybe we can convince Herr Gutmann and get one step closer," she said, only half joking this time as, slipping off her shoes, she gathered small rocks at the water's edge.

"Have it your way. But this idea of the special German soul captures people's imagination, makes them feel good. I saw it in their faces. Even I could feel some stirrings," he admitted. "Hard to resist emotions that are uplifting."

Fanny handed Sepp a few pebbles, keeping one, as she gauged the water.

"What do you think about this idea of races? Of racial purity?" Sepp asked. "Races among people, pedigrees, like breeds among animals? Creating mongrels when mixed together? A provocative notion, don't you think?"

"I don't think about it at all," Fanny answered honestly. "Father Goetz said it was wrong. Sure, people are different. Each of us is. So are we each a race? Aren't people more alike than different?"

"Not what the League preaches, making some kind of sense, too. Another view could make as much sense, I suppose," he added.

"Another view! Like what we learn in church, nations yes, but human beings all? Invited or not, I don't know why you go to such meetings. Wasting your time. And your mind! And exposing your soul to bad things! No more of this, Sepp!"

He took Fanny by the shoulders, turned her to face him, then gave a deep breath, biting his lip as if about to confess something.

"What?"

"I am joining up; I signed for early duty, Fanny," he exhaled. "That is why

I was not there to meet you this morning. Some paperwork at the academy. They give me an automatic commission in the Bavarian Regiment because of the Kadettenkorps; that was my real secret. That was my good news, not this talk about meetings."

Although she had suspected it would happen eventually, Fanny looked stunned, her face dropping the everyday safe expressions one wears.

"You go to war! An officer!" she exclaimed. "Oh, Sepp, I am proud of you. An officer, a patriot! That is better than the Olympics. But now, I shall worry to see that you come back safe. A short war is still dangerous." She was serious, pondering his news. She went on, eyes brimming. "I will not look at dark sides like my Father. When do you leave? I will miss you so."

"Soon, I think."

"Well then, all right. Now is now! Watch," she said, composure restored as if nothing would ruin this great August day for her. She drew her arm back, giving a big smile. "Watch me, Sepp! I'll show you how to skim before you win the war for the Kaiserreich single-handed."

"*You* show *me!*" he said, playfully, wearing a challenging expression, holding her eyes, walking toward her. "Skim or swim, Fraeulein show-off?" He began to pull her toward the water.

Fanny grabbed his leg, and both, laughing uncontrollably, held on to each other as they slid into the shallow River Wuerm.

Δ

Secrets shared. Good feelings restored. But Fanny remembered the new ideas that Sepp found intriguing. And what Father Goetz had said about it in the parlor at the Luftmann home.

All the next day, Fanny worried for Sepp's exposure, not only to the Reich's enemies in the war, but also to ideas Father Goetz had called unChristian. And she had felt so good at the Odeonsplatz rally and about her Olympic invitation. Finally, by early evening she had to escape these unfamiliar anxieties, leaving the house for a bicycle ride, disappearing into a crisp autumn-like twilight, the sky's light blue a background for swaths of purple, pinks, and aqua.

A sliver of yellow moon was fixed above fading green hills; rich yellows and browns of the Dachauer Moos were muted. Clusters of the New Dachau School artists, visiting landscape painters who loved the Moos, collected their canvases and easels as the distinctive Dachau light dimmed.

The distant blue Alps became shadows of shadows, trapped in the darkening azure sky, white caps barely catching the last rays from the setting sun.

Always exercising to keep her lean body fit and strong (striving for excellence by nature and also from long ago finding activity an antidote for uneasiness), she bicycled through Dachau's cobblestone streets, lined with stone walls and abundant poplar trees. They were so lovely with their spire-like branches, and so delicious, too, was the fragrance from the linden shade trees unmistakable scent.

She cycled past red tile roofed houses, shops, town buildings. And always, surrounding her, there were the distant foothills, pillowed against the vaguely outlined Alps, like ideas of mountains. She gave a friendly wave at the night watchman as she passed him. Oh! How she loved her sweet Dachau.

Fanny had cycled all the way home, circling the district, waving again at the night watchman, and, releasing tensions, felt the better for it, calming her, restoring serenity.

Sepp would be protected in battle with a merciful and understanding God taking care of him. About that she was certain. They had a promise, after all, that the Noble War would be a short one, with God on their side. But she prayed daily anyhow.

Chapter 5
The Wuerm Incident
A Year Earlier

Christian Luftmann felt responsible for the Wuerm incident. After all, it was he who allowed the Gypsies to camp on his forest grounds when they passed through town. The townspeople didn't like it; no one liked it.

Several weeks after Oktoberfest, walking along the river in the Luftmann-Land, Sepp had come across local bullies from the county. There were three, about his own age, sturdy looking, out of school, probably farm workers. They were chasing a young Gypsy boy, a child, maybe 10 years old. It was hard to tell. He was small, dark-skinned, dressed in rags, shoeless though autumn chill promised winter snow.

One was allowed to have fun with *Zigeuners*, Gypsies, at their expense, a warning to keep them out of Dachau, out of Munich, out of Bavaria. But these roughnecks were going too far.

They had caught up with the lad, were swinging him in the air and, as Sepp approached, tossed him into the icy cold waters of the Wuerm, laughing and shouting all the while.

The boy was screaming in a tongue Sepp didn't understand, but sounds for help require no language. Sepp recognized the desperate cries. Bobbing helplessly, arms flailing in the water, the child could not swim.

Pulling off his boots, Sepp yelled at the taunting bullies who all the while were laughing on shore. "Get help, fools. Don't stand there!" he ordered, and jumped in the frigid waters.

Sepp was a strong swimmer. Approaching the boy, Sepp shouted over his shrill sounds of panic, "*Sei still! Beruhigdich! Ich will dir helfen!*"

The Gypsy, however, had no German, understanding only Romany. Catching Sepp by surprise, he lashed out at him with a knife strapped to his wrist, like gloves for young children to make sure they are not lost. Clearly the boy thought Sepp was there to drown him, to finish the job.

Razor sharp, the knife sliced a gashing wound across Sepp's cheek.

Treading water, the clear blue turning crimson, Sepp blocked the child's arm that had the weapon. With a single blow to the neck — a maneuver learned in military school — he dazed the boy. It happened in seconds. Sepp could now grip the child under the chin, side-stroking his way back to shore, a bloody trail in his wake.

The county bullies were nowhere to be seen.

Wet, chilled in the November air, blood streaming down his face, Sepp carried the child toward the forest, going to the tribe's camp alone, at some risk. Now the situation reversed. When the Zigeuner men ran to him, Sepp was not sure of their intentions.

A needless worry. The Gypsies understood.

As he sat around the fire, shivering, wrapped in thick, coarse blankets, while they dried his clothes — someone had retrieved his boots at the river — an old Gypsy woman, face wizened and prune-pinched, ignoring his protests, put hot, foul smelling herbs pressed in broad leaves on Sepp's slashed cheek. It stopped the bleeding without any need for stitches and would leave him with a neat, thin scar.

A man wearing a red-and-purple bandanna across his swarthy forehead, thick mustache, rough-bearded, a wide red belt around his waist, unstrapped the knife from the boy's hand. He walked over to Sepp, presenting it to him with a broad smile, showing uneven teeth, surprisingly white.

It was a small but sharp hunting knife with ancient Romany symbols etched on the distressed copper handle; its centerpiece, encircled in black, was a captivating cross, arms bent up and down at each end at right angles. A child's weapon, not a man's.

Drawing an imaginary line across his own cheek with the blade, the Gypsy man pointed across the fire to the whimpering boy, embraced by a big-bellied woman — obviously with child — who was rocking the terrified lad in her arms, humming softly.

"Milosh, Milosh," said the bandanna'd man, nodding his head at the child. "Milosh," he repeated, his grin broadening, then patting his own chest to show that *Milosh* belonged to him.

Δ

He couldn't say he hadn't been warned about letting the Gypsies' camp there.

"When you want to be of the community," Father Goetz told Luftmann, "you must be for the community. Not much room for individualism. Our people don't want Zigeuners here in town."

"For you, a man of the cloth, to preach that?"

"I don't preach that, but then I'm a member of a larger community, an accepting and forgiving one," the priest reminded him. "Eigentum, Buergertum, do not haunt me."

Even Lotte questioned her husband's judgment, given the townspeople's hostility to Gypsies. "They fear the Zigeuner, as born criminals, a threat to their homes, to their families, to their town. Dirty, terrible hygiene, uneducated, everything not German."

"Perhaps unfairly branded?" said Luftmann. "Have we ever seen them do harm?"

"Whether true or not, that is what they think. They don't like strangers, Christian. You know that. And worse, Gypsies! Police look the other way when it comes to acts against Gypsies but watch *them* like a hawk. That Munich registry they keep, counting Zigeuners passing through the district; they're considered alien, a nation within our nation, bad-blood Asiatic wanderers. You know all this, Christian, yet, you of all people give them space to camp in Dachau."

"Of all people?"

"Someone who wants so much and tries so hard to belong is what I mean."

"Destitute nomads, homeless drifters! Yes, me of all people! After 2,000 years, we — of all people as you put it, Lotte — certainly understand dispossessed wanderers, people without a country of their own."

"Yes, yes, I know, but couldn't they find someplace else to camp?"

"They come and they go," he had said glibly. "No one gets hurt."

But Sepp Hofer had gotten hurt. He had the scar to show for it.

Δ

Though everyone in town conceded to Sepp's bravery, both rescuing the boy and going to the Gypsy camp solo, nevertheless, there were rumblings of displeasure, from annoyance to serious disapproval at his helping Zigeuners.

"What next? Will he be inviting them into his house?" was said and oblique references made to how "Godless Bolsheviks" think, referring to Sepp's father, Ludwig the instigator, Die Pest.

Sepp told the police he had warned the Gypsies by gesture and language — "*Raus, Raus!*" — to get far away, reminding them about what they already knew: They were neither popular nor welcome in Dachau.

His mother had heard what people were whispering about the Hofer family. She was genuinely frightened, not wanting scandal. So he had to go to that League meeting.

In late June, when war fevers were running high over the Habsburg Archduke's assassination, this last invitation to attend the Pan-Germanic League meeting had come to Sepp. This one in a note from Marius Mueller.

That had surprised him, Mueller's involvement, from the owner of the brewery where Sepp's father worked. Mueller lived in that same exclusive Burgfrieden District as Fanny.

He had to attend. He knew from classmates it was about the Wuerm incident. Powerful enemies were not good in a small town. Especially with a pending war and intense feelings.

His decision was on target, despite Fanny thinking that he was wasting his time.

The July League meeting was held in the high-ceilinged hall at the Buergerbraeukeller, one of the larger Munich Bierstuben. This particular beer hall near the Gasteig district was where right-wing groups and other dissidents felt most comfortable. It was dimly lit and had the smell of malt. Pitchers rested on dark, shiny counters. There were rows of plain tables, decorated collections of beer mugs on shelves, floor-to-ceiling dark wood paneling. It had the cavernous feeling of no world existing outside it.

The mostly working class and lower income audience were well behaved and attentive (they had not yet had their beer), prominently sporting the Alldeutsche Verband pins on their lapels. Some wore Lederhosen with white, lace-collared shirts and colorful vests.

Marius Mueller looked especially right, tall, lean, hard, dressed as well in the traditional Bavarian costume. He stood straight-backed at the lectern, a soft light focused on him. He was the honored speaker. He didn't address the Gypsy incident until near the meeting's end, building up to it by talk of races and un-German ideas, Bolsheviks and Jews, their infectious contagion, a disease, a plague for all Germans.

"Even in Dachau, we have the Jew cattle trader Samson Gutmann. He has already invaded, moved into our Kraisy Inn. When one Jew peddler comes, the rest are not far behind! And if Jews peddle rags, Zigeuner live in them. Coming from India centuries ago, they show the contamination and blood defilement of mixed breeding, the dilution of an Aryan race turned into filthy wanderers, thieves, swine. Do we want this infection to invade our German Volk? Do we protect those who would debase us?" Marius Mueller's knife-cutting voice was sharpened by sarcasm. "Hofer the hero? Hah! Wasted bravery! Misplaced compassion!" He turned to Sepp. "Our so-called hero is here tonight, finally accepting our long-standing invitation."

There were some angry noises from the captive group. And loud supporting, "Here! Here!" for Mueller. After all, he was just promoted to the

War Ministry in Munich. They were honored he was their guest speaker. After a moment or two of restless movement and mumblings, Mueller stilled the audience.

"Nevertheless, my fellow Germans, we give him a chance. That is the German way! We hope he will learn who and what needs protection. But he deserves no credit for saving a Gypsy. He should apologize to those patriotic young men who were doing their racial duty. He should save his bravery for defending our Kaiserreich!" Mueller said, hinting at the then-imminent war.

At that, the audience cheered.

Sepp did not apologize.

He was not allowed to speak, except to answer questions from the members. When asked why he did it, he said, "It was natural, my friends. My good German training at the academy to save lives. My training for military service."

He repeated that phrase often, "good German" values, training, habits.

"Where is the apology?" came an angry voice from the audience.

"Good Germans, strong Germans don't apologize for being German," he replied.

The crowd didn't quite know what to make of it.

Then as a good faith sign, they wanted him to join the League. Part of him wanted to, these countrymen, their dedication, their national pride and patriotism. But something put him off. Not comfortable with all their ideas, under scrutiny all the time. Eventually having to deal with his father's leftist leanings, since he knew *that* would happen. Mueller had repeatedly emphasized the Bolshevik enemy, looking directly at him each time.

So he put them off, telling them he would be going to fight in the war that loomed over them, and his first duty was to his country, to pay attention to that mission.

Some in the crowd gave in, mumbling that he would soon fight for the Reich. But he had seen the quick and terrible look on Marius Mueller's sharp-featured face. It was an expression Sepp recognized from the military, the brittle and bullying bravado of a man who was not fit to lead but was not accustomed to being disobeyed.

When he left the meeting wearing a deep frown, Sepp was not sure if he had helped or made things worse. But he was sure of one thing. Not a good enemy to have, Herr Marius Mueller.

Sepp shrugged. What is a good enemy? At the academy he had learned the only thing worse than a good enemy was a bad friend.

In any case he was spared further contact by the war that was declared a few weeks later, the war he and Fanny had celebrated at Munich's Odeonsplatz.

Chapter 6
Satan's Homecoming
Nine Months Later
May 1915

A wave of shock like an electrical current jolted St. Jakob's congregants at Father Goetz's pronouncement in his homily: *Bald wird Satan Deutsche sprechen!*

Then there was an audible gasp, as if the many were fused into one when Marius Mueller, seated in a pew reserved for the prominent, the Burgfrieden, stood up at attention, turned, and marched up the aisle out of the church.

Father Goetz repeated, "*Bald wird Satan Deutsche sprechen!* as if he were unaware of the diversion. Frau Mueller, seated beside her son, seemed unaware too, until there was an appreciable buzz among the congregation. Some looked again to find the homily theme, rattling the two-page weekly Mass letter identifying the ill and those who had died. It was boldly printed on the liturgy page. *We Become What We Do.*

Many were aghast, not only because of Marius's behavior, but by what had triggered it — the priest's remark, SOON SATAN SPEAKS GERMAN! A few followed Mueller in protest as the priest, impervious, continued saying what they wanted neither to hear nor believe.

"We become what we do! Inescapable! Disappointment with the stalemated war, anger at broken promises, hurt for severe casualties are not an excuse for silence in the face of wrongdoing. Two atrocities!

"Silence sanctions the Kaiserreich's unprecedented use of poison gas at Ypres, 6,000 men trapped in the Belgian trenches breathing death in ten minutes. I know you understand ten minutes, always looking at your watches while I speak. But do you understand 6,000?

"Silence sanctions the Kaiserreich ally's onslaught against innocent Christian civilian populations in Turkey, the Turks' savagery against its Armenian minority."

Again, there were murmurs. The congregation looked confused. Father Goetz could see their *what-do-we-have-to-do-with-Turks* expression worn alongside *we-didn't-order-the-poison gas.*

"Choosing to be silent is as much an act as choosing to speak," he went on. "We become what we do. Poison gas, a violation of international law and that of our Lord's, making lethal the air of life He gave us to breath in Creation! Slaughtering the innocent is barbaric! The Ottoman Empire, Turkey, our ally blames civilian men, women, children, for a lost battle. Our ally authorizes extermination, deportation, death marches, atrocities. Barbaric! But our civilized Kaiserreich does not condemn these acts, nor is there an outcry from our citizens, a profound sin of omission, making us partners to their act. Yes, partners!"

Father Goetz looked up from the lectern, letting his eyes scan the congregation.

"I see your faces, heads shaking, saying, 'No not me!' I say yes. We, who pride ourselves on law, honor, and advanced culture, are partners to evil in our silence.

"An alarm rings. These two murderous events, gassing and savagery, occurred on the same day. An accident? Two events related to this *blessed* war because God was on our side? A challenge? Satan's challenge. A moral test! Can we expect God still on our side? The philosopher says and Aquinas repeats: *We are what we do. Excellence, then, is not an act, but a habit.* And what we do not do, as well.

"In countenancing the slaughter of the weak, in cheering barbaric war victories, in celebrating chemical battles against humanity, in honoring the chemist creator of mustard gas, the Reich is choosing Satan. Turn your eyes to Lord Jesus, the Christ standing by your side. He is there. Do not abandon him. Speak out! And pray for those afflicted and for those who would inflict such evils."

For the remainder of the Mass, the congregation was uneasy. People fidgeted. More left, joining Marius Mueller outside in the square, many were Pan-Germanic League members or sympathizers. Mueller awaited his mother who, red-faced, confused, and unsure of herself, had remained until the service ended, getting up, sitting down, getting up, and finally sitting down for good.

After the final blessing and the formal recessional, Father Goetz, as was customary, waited near the cathedral entrance to greet parishioners as they left the church. Many walked right by him.

The Luftmanns went to the priest, Christian tipping his hat, making a barely perceptible bow to Father Goetz with exaggerated respect, hoping to influence by example some hesitant congregants who seemed unsure, off balance.

"You were stern today," said Luftmann. "Difficult for some. Interesting quote from Aristotle, Father. But nevertheless, you take a chance."

Staring hard at Luftmann, the priest said quietly, "We all are or become what we do. At some point to which we are blinded, by doing or not doing, by breaking promises, or making evil ones, we become someone else, my son, someone we never intended. "

"Let's go," interrupted Fanny. "Herr Mueller is coming. I don't want to see him. Not after his disrespect to Father Goetz."

Luftmann saw Mueller approaching, his mother tagging after him. She appeared a bit unsteady. Luftmann walked over, offering her his arm for support.

"Herr Mueller, we can take your mother home with us. Perhaps she comes for second breakfast? Maybe we can prevail on Father Goetz to join us as well. Of course you are welcome."

"I would like that, Marius," said Frau Mueller tentatively to her son, as if needing permission, voice wavering but not disguising her refined Berlin accent. She was a handsome woman, dark-haired and full-bodied, who, Luftmann thought, must have been a great beauty when she was younger.

"As you please," Marius said curtly. Turning to Luftmann he added, "I must decline, sir." As they left he confronted the priest, "You talk like a traitor, Father. We allow only one mistake like that."

"Herr Mueller, it is not your *we* who judges me and to whom I am accountable."

"We shall see who's accountable to whom," Mueller snapped, walking away.

That afternoon, Mueller leveled an official complaint to the diocese from the Munich War Ministry, where, after assigning his work at the brewery to a trusted foreman, he had been deputy director for all of Bavaria since the war's beginning.

It did not take long for the archbishop to summon the Dachau priest to Munich. In fact it was the very next day.

"You criticize a war we sanctioned and whose progress the Protestants embrace and cheer? You want to return to the *Kulturkampf* days when the Church suffered under Prussian rule? When our people were persecuted? Thank goodness Herr Mueller interceded for us with the War Ministry. Those Prussians were calling your sermon Roman treachery. Questioning our loyalty. Be silent on these matters, Father," he warned. "Wartime is not peacetime. Opinion becomes sedition. And Roman Catholics are a distrusted minority in the Kaiserreich."

"There is a City of God and a City of Man. Where do I, in good conscience to our Lord Jesus, put myself, your Reverence?"

"Don't quote St. Augustine to me! Where to put yourself? In the pulpit, behaving like an obedient parish priest, according to your vows, protecting your flock, their Church and the Church's interests at all times. The City of Man is in man's hands."

"May the Lord help us," Goetz whispered, crossing himself, taking his leave.

Having declined Luftmann's invitation to second breakfast the previous day, Father Goetz dined with the Luftmanns that evening on simple but robust potato soup with dark bread and cabbage salad.

"A difficult sermon for my flock," Goetz said.

"You are right, of course. These acts are obscenities! Fritz Haber! A scientist! The father of chemical warfare? Violating the Hague Convention!" said Luftmann in judgment, words spilling from his mouth, referring to the chemist behind the mustard gassings. "Civilized nations and the international scientific community condemning him and the Reich. And Haber replies, *It doesn't matter, death is death, by whatever means it is inflicted!* He says those words! That the *how* doesn't matter? What kind of person says that? Six thousand suffered death in minutes."

"Now 6,001 casualties! Herr Professor Haber's wife killed herself after he supervised deployment of the gas cylinders in person during battle at the frontlines. He actually went to the front to make sure it was done effectively! A thorough scientist," Father Goetz said wryly. "Haber made a chart measuring exposure times to cause death!"

"There was no news about the wife. Are you sure?" asked Luftmann.

"It was kept quiet. I learned from my sister. She has a friend who works as a servant in the Haber home in Berlin."

"And no reference to Haber in Mueller's speech before the League yesterday, the speech published in today's paper."

"Fritz Haber is a Jew," explained the priest. "And so was his wife, a chemist in her own right. The League doesn't celebrate Jews, Christian. Even those commended by their Kaiser. And the War Ministry is full of League members and sympathizers."

"*Death is death, it makes no difference how inflicted,*" Luftmann whispered, his face turning crimson. He blurted, "Another Jew trying to show he's a good German!"

"Another? Who are the others? I can't believe you said that. Bad-mouthing people in front of Father Goetz!" This from Fanny.

Luftmann seemed not to hear her. "Poison gas, outcasts among the nations."

"If it brings Sepp and our soldiers home quicker, how wrong can it be,

Papa, saving other lives? German lives."

"What? A believer in the greater good no matter how it is gotten? Poisoning air. A sneak attack? Did you not hear Father's sermon yesterday? We become what we do?" Luftmann said angrily.

"Christian, calm down," said Lotte.

"The soup is good," said Gretl. "Good soup." She was getting confused with the unusual commotion at the dinner table, a vacant look replacing her usual dull one.

"Gretl, you need to go?" asked Frau Luftmann.

As if a light lit her otherwise dim expression, Gretl got up as quickly as she could, turning over her chair. Lately she had become incontinent when upset.

Lotte immediately righted the chair, saying, "Please excuse her, Father."

Fanny defended herself. "Papa, Sepp fights in those trenches, too. It can help him. Shorten the war finally so everyone will stop killing one another."

"And what if the Allies come back with their own poison gas, Fanny?" asked Father Goetz. "Now they have a license, you see. How is our Sepp then?"

"Eat! Please, everybody. It is not our business," said Lotte. "These discussions at dinner are not good for digestion. You get too excited, Christian."

Nevertheless Fanny asked, "Is it really true what the Turks do to the Armenians, Father? To the women? To the children?"

"The Turks do not have a good history among Christians, Fanny. An old story. Last century they promised to stop treating non-Muslims as second-class citizens. Islam despises us for the Crusades against the infidels. Hate breeds hate," he sighed.

"Maybe they would have despised us anyway," Christian muttered. "People like to hate! But this poison gas, a product of science, from a learned man," his voice trailed.

Father Goetz put a finger to his lips. "We can talk later. You are overwrought, Christian. We need not give Haber another casualty, gell? Frau Luftmann is right. Let us please our hostess, my friend."

Yes, Luftmann was overwrought, stricken because Fritz Haber was a Jew. A belated baptized Jew of the prestigious Kaiser Wilhelm Institute, a Jew credited with creating and promoting the lethal chlorine concoction. A Jew acting like a good German, if not a good Christian.

But he wasn't the German he thought he was. And he never would be. With the war going differently than expected, gone like a blink was the inclusiveness, the brotherly love for all so evident that day in August in the

Odeonsplatz a year earlier.

Was Haber fooling himself while killing thousands with his invention? These German Jews! Didn't they understand? I know who I am, Luftmann thought. A man in a masquerade! But do some of them really think they are changed with baptism or that they are Germans who just happen to be Jewish? Have they convinced themselves?

He gave a sardonic laugh. Where do they keep hidden their thoroughly Jewish set of relatives whose mere physical appearance might put an end to their promising careers? Like my own father! Like Reb Itzig, who kept his name, his faith, his beard, his Sabbath, and every extra penny he earned. Haber deludes himself! *A horse born in a cow shed is still a horse, gell?*

Luftmann's face was now beet-red. "I must say one more thing. Worse for God and good for the Devil, our U-boats today sank a civilian passenger liner, American, the Luisitania, a neutral ship, more than a thousand dead, few survived."

"How do you know this, my friend?"

"The newspaper, Father. The United States is sure to join the war. And us? Are we Germans or barbarians? Now we are like the Turks, killing civilians."

"It's not our business," cried Frau Luftmann, getting up from the table. "Throw away all the newspapers."

Chapter 7
Lebkuchen and Lawn Tennis
August 1915

Nostalgia weighed heavily in the air that sun-washed August day. She had memories of last year's rally at the Odeonsplatz with Sepp, everyone cheering, blessed by their churches, because they would win a noble war in thirty days with God on their side.

Like most Germans, *God on their side, thirty days, with God on their side* kept spinning in her head.

But it was now 365 days and God had apparently left their side with the poison gas atrocity. Father Goetz was right about that. Sepp was still in the trenches, casualties mounting. The tightening noose of the British North Sea blockade prevented supplies from getting to the Reich. There was no end in sight.

Fanny had told her father that morning after breakfast, "This month I am sixteen years, but I feel a hundred."

"The war, your worry for Sepp, the arguments about warfare. Your youth is another wartime casualty, Fanny. I fear there is very little *girl* left in you, my child."

"There is tennis left. And today, I am playing at the Muellers'. Did Mother tell you?"

"No, but I thought you didn't care for Herr Mueller?"

"Yes, well, there is distaste for some of his opinions."

"Opinions?"

"All right, his rudeness, too," she conceded. "But he can give me information about Sepp, I hope, about the battles, about how much longer? He's in the War Ministry, he should know. All I have besides the newspaper are your forecasts about a long, hard war, Papa. They're frightening, bleak. Maybe from Marius I will hear something better."

Once upon a time she had looked forward to seeing Marius Mueller even though Sepp had told her he was part of the League and about that harsh meeting he had attended. She was flattered by the attention of a man perhaps ten years older and darkly handsome in a severe sort of way.

His distant ways had seemed interesting. He was demanding, spoiled maybe, but, she reasoned, everyone in town knew his father died of the cholera from the Hamburg epidemic when Marius was a child and that he grew up with only a doting mother.

She admired his self-contained intensity, foreign to her, but which, as far as tennis was concerned, Fanny felt impeded his victory. Winning was more important to him than playing well. If he concentrated on playing well, he might win, she often thought.

Fanny tried to ignore his condescending, class-conscious attitude. She had a glimpse of that disdain before the war at the memorial service for some relatives on his father's side who were lost in the tragic sinking of their transAtlantic ship when it was hit by an iceberg.

For the service, the Muellers had used two adjacent community rooms at St. Jakob's, a wide arched opening between them. The brewery workers were in the larger space. The other was for the Burgfrieden and town notables. Each could see the other, but they did not mix, as if an invisible gate prevented them. Frau Mueller, however, had gone into the workers' room. She was talking with the Hofers when Mueller had intervened.

"Don't pay me any false kindness, Hofer," he said to Sepp's father, Ludwig, Die Pest, ignoring Frau Hofer whose eyes stared at the carpeted floor. "You godless Bolsheviks don't believe in religious services, so why are you here? You think you get a promotion?" Before Hofer could answer, he walked away, saying, "Come, Mother, don't waste your time! What are you doing in this room anyway?"

Young Fanny had heard the interchange. There was an instant hush in the room. Others had heard it, too. Mueller didn't seem to care, seemed to want to humiliate. She had turned to her mother and said, "He insults Frau Hofer! He is lucky Sepp is not here."

"What was that, Fraeulein? What about Sepp Hofer?"

Fanny was embarrassed. Mueller had sharp ears. "Uhh . . . yes . . . I said only . . ."

"Twelve-year-olds should be seen, not heard! It is not your business, Fanny," interrupted her mother, whose only business was what went on in her kitchen. She wanted it that way.

"Be careful with your opinions, young lady," whispered her father.

Fanny at one time had rationalized Mueller's condescension and harshness to those outside the Burgfrieden district and to those who worked at the Mueller Brewery. Being so rich could do that to a person, she thought, and an employer's austere manner with employees was to be expected.

When they played tennis, Fanny won her matches with Marius. Not that it mattered to her. He was good practice. But, she thought, he couldn't really like it. So competitive and serious. There is such a thing as too serious. It can hurt one's game, she told her father.

In any case, regardless of his behavior, despite his disrespect, rudeness really, for Father Goetz, Mueller was with the War Ministry and might be able to tell her about Sepp, who was always on her mind. So she'd accepted the invitation to play.

On impulse, Fanny decided to take her aunt along. Summer was ending; who knew when she would again have a chance to give her aunt a rare treat? Aunt Gretl had never seen her play. How could she, at home all the time?

Fanny loved her aunt. Growing up an only child, in Gretl she had a kindly older sister who adored her, a willing playmate at any time. Now Gretl was more like a worshipping younger sister. Fanny was her idol.

The medical facts of the matter were that Gretl got younger as she got older. Her condition worsened each year — a little heavier, more limited in mind, more difficulty expressing herself in words, and, just recently, an unfortunate incontinence when she was frightened or confused.

She was a five-year-old in a forty-year-old body and looked more like fifty. Once her capacity had been that of a ten-year-old. Fanny didn't remember if at any point they were ever at the same age together.

The weather was glorious this August day, sun bright and warming, the air bearing a hint of cool September. It was a short walk that her aunt could manage. Once there, benches and lawn chairs were scattered among the shade-giving linden trees surrounding the court. Gretl would be able to rest far enough away so she would not be self-conscious.

Surely, Marius would have no objection. Her aunt was no bother to anyone.

"Mother, do we have *Lebkuchen* for Aunt Gretl?" Fanny asked. It was her aunt's favorite, gingerbread so light it melted on the tongue. Gretl could nibble as Fanny played.

"Fresh-baked this morning. It is wrapped and ready."

"You make the best," said Fanny.

"Why not? The recipe from my hometown! Nuremberg's invention! For which we will always be famous."

Bending over, Fanny gave her mother a quick kiss, taking the package.

"Are you making more? I want to send some to Sepp."

"There is enough. I saw Frau Hofer at the market. When I asked after Sepp, she shrugged, saying she supposed no news was good news."

Fanny's face darkened. She had not heard from Sepp in the past two weeks.

"His mind must be on his duty," Fanny said unconvincingly.

"Don't give your aunt too much," Lotte warned. "There is enough Lebkuchen for the Muellers, even though the mother worries always about her figure." She added with a sly smile, "Greetings to Frau Mueller, if you see her. And if she *sees* you!"

Now Fanny gave a genuine laugh.

Frau Mueller, apologizing to Fanny's mother after passing her one day without greeting, had confided to Lotte, "I don't wear my spectacles. They are thick and ugly; I look ten years older. But it is hard to see. Say nothing, I beg you."

"Such a handsome woman! Too bad vanity makes her walk around half blind! Berliners have such airs, but with Frau Mueller I do think it is vanity and not that northern nonsense. Thank the Lord I don't have the problems of aging beauties."

"You are beautiful, Mother, and you make the best gingerbread," said Fanny. "Come, Aunt Gretl, we are off. Maybe we'll go to the river afterward if you are up to it."

"We take Rolf?" Gretl asked, petting Sepp's puppy entrusted to Fanny before he went off to war. ("My father doesn't like dogs," Sepp had said. "A luxury for the rich, he rants. It should just be for a month or so, Fanny. Will your parents mind?")

"I think you care more for Rolf than Sepp," Fanny teased.

"I like my friend Sepp," Gretl said in a childlike manner, blushing. "I love Rolf."

Gretl didn't ask for much. Fanny was attached to the dog as well. She had promised Sepp that his puppy — now over sixty-seven pounds — would get good exercise.

"We take him!" Fanny declared.

She thought of Sepp each day, especially when knitting scarves, baking cookies, crocheting winter socks for soldiers fighting a not-so-easy war at the front, a war that was never supposed to last so long, a war now fought with poisoned air.

When last year's Odeonsplatz jubilation had worn thin with the shocking failure of the "short war" Schlieffen Plan despite God's being on their side, she thought about her country's young men off fighting Russians in places with strange names like Galicia, Volhynia, Belorus. She thought about Sepp, off fighting the French, in harm's way, a *Frontsoldat* with the Bavarian Infantry Leib Regiment in the stalemate trench Battle of the Frontiers, Sepp fighting in foreign places instead of going on to Munich University after his Kadettenkorps graduation.

"Fanny," called her father from the parlor, interrupting her thoughts. "If you go to the square, please stop by Wittman's. Herr Wittman has some books for me."

"Give my regards," added Lotte, as she tied a large fleece shawl over Gretl's shoulders, whispering. "You had better do your business before you leave, dear."

Fanny grabbed her racquet from the brass umbrella stand near the front door and hooked the lead to Rolf's collar. Screws from the racquet's wooden press snagged in Gretl's shawl.

"I need to go," Gretl said, trying to pull away, making a tear in the large scarf.

"I will fix it, Aunt Gretl. No one will notice. But do hurry," Fanny urged. "Herr Mueller does not approve of tardiness."

"Remember the books!" Luftmann called out.

"There is mail on the front table," Fanny called back.

They did arrive a few minutes late. When Marius walked toward Fanny with an angry expression on his face, she heard Rolf growl from the bench under the linden trees where he crouched next to Gretl — his raised hackle growl. Not a good beginning! Marius could be unpleasant, twice offended, by their tardiness and the dog's behavior.

She decided to quickly get through the playing, not ask about Sepp at all, then take Gretl down to the riverside, where they could throw pebbles and wet their toes.

Chapter 8
Letter and Lynchings
Another Promised Land

Luftmann's study faced the flower gardens in his backyard and also the gazebo where Fanny had played as a child. Often they would read together there, the TALES OF THE *Brothers Grimm*. Gazing out the window now, he was thoughtful, picturing Fanny, with Gretl lumbering along, on their way to the Mueller tennis court.

They were an odd couple, clumsy and graceful, short and tall, broad and slim, no resemblance, but a powerful bond of love between them. Gretl had relieved the loneliness of an only child for Fanny; Fanny in turn, gave Gretl a brief experience of maturity. It was a singular attachment.

With a sigh, he removed the rimless glasses that sat so comfortably on his slightly curved nose, leaving a red mark to show they were there, as if to reserve a place for next time. How do things happen in this world, he wondered?

He a Dachau Buerger; Lotte a devout Catholic, Fanny, a rag-peddler's grandchild with *Ostjuden* roots, invited to play lawn tennis on the private court of the wealthiest family in town. Lawn tennis, mind you, a sport of those who rank high in society, have a superior place, are stylish and aristocratic. His daughter invited to represent her country — *her country* — in the Olympics, at least to try out! Yet, she put on no airs.

He was proud of Fanny, her beauty, her considerable talent, her fine mind, her demeanor. And he was sad that a war had prematurely turned his precocious teenager into a woman.

The Kaiser had completed the new *Deutsche Stadion* for the 1916 Berlin Summer Olympics, calling the world-class competition *Games of the VI Olympiad*. Assuming the war over quickly, the organizing had continued after 1914. Yes, God laughs when we tell him our plans.

Once war had been declared and the rest of Europe invited, taking one side or the other, Luftmann had known it would be a long struggle, had known the Berlin Olympics would be canceled, had known Fanny would not compete. Nevertheless, he had no regrets with his decision allowing her to pursue Olympic goals rather than continue her education. There was, after all, little future for university women in the Kaiserreich.

He knew she would be disappointed. But Fanny could deal with adversity. Survival was in her genes. Hah! This new biology had him talking about genes. Thousands of years of wandering and they survived. Yes, facing adversity was in her blood, despite the fact that she had led a charmed life so far and looked nothing like a Semitic nomad. (For one instant the anomaly occurred to him: if there were genes carrying *survival*, how could one argue against genes carrying Volk? But he moved quickly from that detour.) As to her education, she read so much, enjoying books and knowledge as he did. She would be educated.

Books! Luftmann shook his head with a smile, thinking of the looks the bookseller gave him when he placed his order for de Gobinau's *An Essay on the Equality of the Human Races* and Chamberlain's *Foundations of the Nineteenth Century*! Sacred Scriptures for the Pan-Germanic League — spouting a venomous racial ideology.

Father Goetz had mentioned them, decrying their content as counter to Christian teaching. They had not been part of Luftmann's enlightened maskilim education as Kant and Fichte and Hegel and Herder had. Pan-Germanic ideas were gaining currency, the priest had said. And who better than a priest knew what people were thinking?

He liked Father Goetz, enjoyed his company, had dared to tell him, jokingly, the problem for Roman Catholicism was that their best people did not reproduce. The priest had laughed.

"It is good to laugh with a friend," Goetz said. "Laughter is scarce these days."

Luftmann gave a sigh, rolled the high stool away from the worktable, shut his ledgers. He would visit the kitchen. There was the unmistakable fragrance of Lebkuchen coming from that part of the house. Lotte would not have given all of her delicious gingerbread away to Gretl and Fanny.

And Fanny! He reminded himself she would have another disappointment in addition to the canceled Olympics when he told her his plans for her forest. There would be no tennis court built for her there as he had promised, his first broken promise to his daughter. He would tell her today, get it over with.

Useless land when he acquired it, buying so much, trying to capture the ephemeral Eigentum. But now those woods would serve a purpose after all. The government needed a place for another gunpowder and munitions factory. The one at Ingolstadt was not large enough.

He had donated the Luftmann-Land — his major real estate holding in Dachau, true, but it was for a good purpose on many levels. He still held on to the blind mortgage inherited from his father on that other Dachau property. It was income-producing.

The war he had needed to become German by patriotism had not come quickly enough. He could not serve in the Landwehr because of age. He had settled for home defense. So, in a surge of self-serving patriotism, Luftmann quietly offered a gift of the forest land near the River Wuerm for the Kaiserreich's use.

The War Ministry accepted. Offered quietly, but sure to be announced as his gift.

Maybe a medal? A better way than Haber's with his poison gas! On the other hand, the factory might produce the death-carrying cylinders! Was that collusion?

But for Fanny, like the canceled Olympics, it would be another wartime setback, not having her own promised place to practice and surrendering what she had come to enjoy so much, her forest, cycling the secluded paths, running through familiar woodland trails. But she had the survival gene, after all.

The scent of Lebkuchen beckoned him. It was irresistible.

Passing the entry table near the front door, he stopped and flipped through the mail. A guttural sound, like a growl, escaped his throat when he saw the letter. If Luftmann had hackles like Rolf, they would have been raised in attention.

Stomping into the kitchen he barked, "Since when do you get letters from your cousins in America? A return address to Frankels? A Jewish name. Sent to *Frau Christian Luftmann*! How did they know how to reach you, Lotte? Where? To whom? We agreed, from the beginning, no more family connections. We can't be too careful! I thought you understood how careful, watchful, we must be."

Caught off guard, Lotte shot back in her own defense, "And Gretl? Not a family connection? Showing up from nowhere? With your rush to baptize her?"

"An unexpected exception! Was I to let them put her in their asylums? Where doctors discuss racial hygiene and worse? Argue about costs the healthy pay for lives not worth living? *Minderwertig* lives they describe them, these men of science? You think I could do that to her?"

"Bite your tongue! Of course not! My cousins in America are also an exception. If someone wants to reach somebody, they figure out how. Would you rather they mailed to Chaya Itzig? Or Frau Chaim Itzig? I let them know in that Georgia place where they settled how to write and please only to write in an emergency."

"Emergency? What could you do for them in an emergency? They are there and you are here." He was beginning to talk louder. "What kind of emergency!"

"Open the letter, Christian! Maybe you find out. They would write only if important. Lower your voice or you will be making the very announcement to the world with your shouting that you fear from this letter. Open it! Open it, please."

He ripped open the plain white envelope, not using his ornate sterling letter opener, then pulled out one sheet of lined paper, written on both sides.

"At least they didn't write in Yiddish," he said with some sarcasm. "But look here," he snapped. "They start Dear Chaya, then cross out, then write Lotte, and then have the nerve to say forgive the cross-out, it is hard to get accustomed! That is what I mean, Lotte. Suppose we lived in a place where they opened mail, not just where the postmaster idly gossips about who is getting what from where!"

"Read the letter, Christian!"

Exhaling his disturbance with a loud whooshing breath, Christian began to read.

20 August 1915

Dear ~~Chaya~~ Lotte, (forgive the cross-out, it is hard to get accustomed)

> *I had to write about the nature of this country we went to. This promised land of freedom. You are living in a promised land of freedom for all, and rights for all. We are with barbarians, primitives, animals.*

> *On 17 August, this very week, here in the American State of Georgia, in the City of Atlanta, they lynched, a mob lynched . . . that is American for took him out to hang him from a tree — a Jewish businessman, Leo Frank, in whose factory we are employed. A respected member in this American community (like all of us he was so called 'restricted,' their way to keep Jews out of private clubs and schools, but so what, we didn't want to be with Goyim anyway!) Still Leo Frank, a respected community member everyone knew was innocent, yet with cries "Kill the Jew! Kill the Jew!" heard from people marching through the streets since they arrested him and more when they changed his death sentence to life imprisonment.*

> *People, ordinary people, applauded and sang when they saw him hanging from the tree. They lynch black men all the time in this place — we have little to do with those people, they are kept separate, very strict by law, much fear of racial contamination, a few years ago they lynched seven at once — but such hatred for an innocent Jewish businessman, a benefactor of the community.*

Ach! That could never happen in our Kaiserreich *where Germans are not barbarians like these Americans in Georgia. Even their courts of justice! All refused to step in to save a Jewish man unfairly convicted of a terrible crime.*

So this letter is a warning. Don't ever come here, Lotte. Stay where people are civilized. If we could, we would return to Nuremberg. Not enough money. Why is the world so much against us? I understood with the Negroes — they are a different color — but why does God let people hate us everywhere? Why is He so angry with us to punish us so?

You were wise to remain in the Kaiserreich *even though we urged you to leave, to go to America. You had the money then, I know. But you both were smart — whoever made that decision.*

Anyway, no need to remind me not to write. But if we do get back to the fatherland I will inform you, dear cousin. With best wishes and God's blessing to keep you and your husband safe, we hope you win your war with a speedy victory.

Your cousins, Bella and Gustav Frankel (And Wolf and Abe)

P.S. One last request, could you send, some time, your Lebkuchen? American ingredients are not as good as German, let alone Bavarian. We have the same recipe, you and I, but mine does not taste anymore like home. We did stop our name change request just in time. Since we were here working for poor Mr. Frank. His Brooklyn uncle Moses Frank, a German Jew, from Darmstadt referred us to his factory as bookkeepers. We were changing Frankel to Frank. We thought it smart. These animals would have hanged us, too! No more. No more. For us, Frankel good enough. One thing, it is easy here to name change. They have no Name Theft law. (They have fewer old names in this new country!) We remember the Itzig scandal from your husband's Prussian family.

Christian put down the letter, rubbing his eyes.

"They remember the Itzig scandal, but lynching those colored souls is all right with your relatives! For Negroes, no masquerading as we do — "

"Masquerading?"

"Yes, masquerading, being what we are not, hiding what we are. For Negroes it's impossible. Their skin is their country. Their identity badge faces them in a mirror each day. How can your cousins care about one murder and not the other? Answer the letter, Lotte! Tell them never to write again. I will mail it from Munich."

"Yes, Christian, I will," she said tears filling her eyes, hurt by his anger. She thought sometimes she was fed up with this masquerade, but she didn't say it.

But one sentence from her cousins' letter would stay in her mind. Haunt her. *Why is He so angry with us to punish us so?*

Chapter 9
Brand Names
The Itzig Scandal

Luftmann was not yet finished with Lotte's cousins. The Lebkuchen that had drawn him into the kitchen forgotten, he sat at the table tapping his fingers, still upset with their letter.

"A good memory about my family, your family has."

"Well, it is true. All that trouble over a name. Why?"

"Because a name is everything, Lotte. It announces who somebody is, what somebody isn't, where he comes from."

"Christian, how come you, an Itzig, didn't have trouble when you changed your name as your Berlin relative did?"

"Your husband tries to be careful, a trait you ridicule sometimes. That northern Itzig made mistakes from the beginning. Little things that grow into big things."

"You always say that. Little things turn into big things."

"Acorns and oaks should teach us something," declared Luftmann. "He picked the wrong name: Goetz, a German family name; he applied in the wrong place: Prussia. Prussian name-theft law prohibited the squandering of good German names on Jews."

"But I thought Bildung was about Jews becoming more German."

"Not so simple, Lotte. Our countrymen want to know whom they are dealing with, a true German or non-German hiding behind a German name."

"So those mistakes caused the commotion?"

"Itzig had a wrong attitude. He thought that since he was a citizen and a convert, a baptized Lutheran, equal to all, he could say whatever he pleased. The judge told him it was an un-German trait, this rush to name changing among Jews — "

"You just said he was Lutheran," she interrupted, saying Lutheran with some disdain, like a good Roman Catholic.

"He was a Jew. A baptized Jew! The court treated him as a Jew. When the judge scolded his un-German ways, denying his father's name, he was arrogant. He told him 'You think like my father about keeping a name! You are welcome to it, if you believe Itzig so wonderful.'"

"He should have turned the other cheek," said Lotte, for some odd reason.

"He should have kept his mouth shut," Luftmann snapped. "Scandal! One hundred and sixteen Goetz families throughout the Reich filing name theft petitions against him, stories everywhere, cartoons, anti-Semitic pieces, editorials praising the judge's admonition! What did it get him? An H: *Hitzig*. The H for his given name Heinrich, Heinrich Hitzig, a scathing gift from the judge who, in his decision, praised Heinrich's father as a good Jew!"

"All that disgrace for nothing."

"There's more?"

"More? Wasn't that enough?"

"The Berlin family became outcasts, humiliated by his behavior. A much younger sister, a change-of-life baby, a delicate child they called her, barely survived taunts and ridicule by other children of all ages. Damaged! Collapsed! Hysteria, the doctors called it, a temporary blindness or some affliction brought on by nerves. Heinrich's older parents, the Itzigs, went to America, but at the last minute could not get a visa for the sickly child. A convent took her. The parents hoped to send for her later!"

"A convent?"

"Once things go wrong, they have their own wheels, Lotte. They say, and it's just a rumor by the way, that by the time the parents sent for her, they couldn't get her back."

"Oh no!"

"They say the nuns had baptized her. They could do that then. You didn't need anyone's permission, you know. In any case that's the story I heard."

Lotte crossed herself, and sighed. "Who can understand His plans, Christian? Maybe for the better? Did this Heinrich Hitzig marry into that family that insisted he change his name?"

"Of course. They were converts as well. Him a successful businessman, they would have relented, anyway."

"So much trouble over a name!" she shook her head.

Luftmann shrugged. "Hitzig had a son who became the first Jewish Lutheran minister in all of Prussia."

"A Jewish Lutheran minister? You joke."

"The horse in the cowshed again. Both parents were Jews, Lotte. Converts maybe, but not a drop of pure German blood, as some would say today."

"You met this minister?"

"Never had the honor," Luftmann replied, with sarcasm. "Not on our trip up north. Remember that journey, Lotte? Before Cologne?"

"That trip I would like to forget! They were so rude. Couldn't wait till we left!"

"Hitzig's son, the pastor, changed his name, I heard. Hard to preach to Gentiles with that last name and the scandal attached to it."

"Enough, Christian! No more! The judge was right! So many names, those people, you don't know who's who."

"The idea behind it all was not who's who, but who's *what*. Lotte, I'm sorry I yelled before. But we live on the edge of a slippery cliff and must walk carefully every step," Luftmann apologized. He stopped tapping on the table. "So, now for your Lebkuchen. That wonderful aroma! That is why I came to your kitchen in the first place. Do I smell apple cake and doughnuts, as well? Do you ever stop baking, Lotte?"

"Do you ever stop eating, Christian?" She smiled.

Chapter 10
The Other Letter

"Why so late? I worried," said Lotte, when Fanny returned that afternoon with Gretl. "You played all this time at Mueller's?"

"No, I didn't stay there long at all. We stopped at Wittman's and by the river, too. I'm sorry to cause you concern," Fanny apologized. "Here are your books, Papa. Odd! They were wrapped, like a gift."

"Yes, well — " Luftmann began.

Lotte interrupted. "And here's a letter for you, Fanny. Hand delivered just a while ago," she pointed out, trying not to sound impressed.

"Hand delivered!" The tan linen envelope had an engraved MM on the back flap. "From Marius, I see. Perhaps for your Lebkuchen, Mama. But then why not to you? It was not a good day. He was angry we were late. Rolf got upset, too. Decided not to like him. He did not lose well. Maybe an apology!" Then she added, while opening her message, "You have Sepp's Lebkuchen?"

"Wrapped and waiting."

"Good," Fanny said, pulling out the brief note. As she read it, then reread it, her hands began to tremble.

"He walked toward Gretl to retrieve a ball. Rolf was only protecting her. He yelled at Rolf; must have scared Aunt Gretl," she whispered, before dropping the missive to the floor and running upstairs to her room in tears.

Retrieving the note, Lotte read:

Fraeulein Luftmann:
    Please, never again bring your relative uninvited to our courts if you wish to continue playing as our guest. The person, with the dog accompanying her, relieved herself in the bushes behind the linden trees. That dog went for me twice! I should have taught him a real lesson! As for your minderwertig relative! Not only no value, worthless and disgusting, but a shame to call her German.
                                           Marius Mueller

"She was foolish to take the dog, let alone Gretl, without asking," Lotte said, while Fanny was upstairs weeping. "His note was not right. But Fanny wasn't thinking."

"True!" agreed Luftmann, sipping tea with the pastries, hiding from Lotte how affronted he was by Marius's note. No sense in fueling the fire with an already upset wife. One day, he thought, would be his turn with Marius Mueller, a way to even the score for Fanny, for Gretl.

"Is that all you have to say?"

"We forget she is only sixteen. Always ahead of herself, but still only sixteen years."

"That is not how we raised her, Christian."

"True! But that man never appealed to me. His looks, Lotte, give him away. Like Shakespeare's Cassius, lean and hungry."

"What do I know from Cassius?"

"Mueller is handsome in an austere German kind of way, but to me he looks cold and distant. He may even be smart. He has had all the benefits of education. But he is mean-spirited, I think."

"Mean-spirited? Why should he like Rolf growling at him on his own property? Come, Christian, it was not a good situation."

"Rolf was protecting Gretl. Dogs have a good sense of people. He sensed bad feelings coming from Mueller."

Fanny walked in the kitchen announcing she was going for a bicycle ride to the forest. She never called it the Luftmann Land.

Ah, yes, the forest! Luftmann reminded himself, thinking he couldn't tell her today, after all. Not another blow. Besides it isn't happening in a minute. The news of his gift to the Kaiserreich can wait, he decided.

"Feeling better?" Lotte asked.

"I'm better and will be more so once I get fresh air," said Fanny.

Certain that Fanny had gone, Lotte continued. She was the type that had to finish what she was saying.

"Yes, well, Rolf is lucky to be around. Marius Mueller could have complained to the police. A mad dog ready to attack him. And with his connections, who knows? Lucky Fanny called him off in time and had Rolf sit with Gretl as far away as she could."

"His note was so unnecessarily insolent."

"The man was upset because the caretaker must have seen both Gretl and the dog doing what they shouldn't and doing it on his property. Your sister gets worse, Christian. She does not have much to make her life interesting here in Dachau. At least before, in Munich, she could go to the synagogue. Talk with people. And, of course, until the cholera, she had your sister, may eternal light shine upon her, to keep her company. Gretl must miss her. She never talks to me about family. For her everything is Fanny and, of course, Sepp's dog. Does she talk to you?"

"Hardly ever. Between Fanny and Rolf and maybe a short memory, my sister hardly talks to me at all."

"Hmmm! That's not so good," Lotte said, taking the apple cake from the oven, giving a satisfied nod over the results, the cakes a nice golden brown. She put in two more trays of doughnuts, one the carnival kind, superfine sugar waiting on the counter for covering the warm ones. With Sepp in the war and all the other young men in harm's way, Lotte religiously sent baked goods for those fighting at the front.

The trays had Luftmann's attention. "More doughnuts for me, I hope."

"Yes, Christian, more doughnuts for you."

She sat down with him at the table after checking the other cakes and cookies in the oven. Her changed expression showed she was pleased with herself and the baked goods she would have for the soldiers.

"So, Christian, small mistakes are dangerous. Like your daughter with the Mueller visit, bringing Gretl uninvited? Will that small thing turn into something big, too?"

"It could, Lotte. Anything could. People aren't careful enough. In this world — "

" — you can't be too careful," she finished the sentence for him, as people long married often do.

For no reason at all, his thoughts went to Lotte's letter from her cousins. To the part that mentioned the Itzig scandal. Luftmann suspected Father Goetz knew of the name scandal; he had the Goetz name, after all. But he could not know those Itzigs were Luftmann's relatives. He worried for nothing, he told himself.

Actually Luftmann would worry more about Fanny's overt attitude toward Mueller the following weeks and her outspoken exchange with him at St. Jakob's a month later. That would be of more concern than the regrettable August incident, the accident at the Mueller tennis court. He strongly suspected Mueller was a vindictive man.

Chapter 11
Friends and Enemies
September 1915

Marius Mueller's harsh reaction to her aunt and disrespect to herself offended Fanny. Other than a cool nod at church on weekends, she did not speak with him until this last summer Sunday in September, when he approached her.

"Pardon," Mueller said to the Luftmanns, with a faint bow. "I need to speak with the Fraeulein, please."

Mouthing a "*Gruess Gott*," Lotte moved on.

Luftmann stepped away, saying nothing but staying within hearing distance, knowing his daughter's lingering animosity.

Mueller's straight-backed air of self-assurance was particularly evident.

"Why do you not speak with me, Fraeulein Luftmann?" he asked.

"I sent you a note apologizing for the incident, Herr Mueller," Fanny replied switching to the impersonal *sie* rather than their customary and friendlier *du* that Mueller had used. "My aunt had no intent to harm. I find your attitude toward a helpless Dachauer neighbor unacceptable."

His mouth tightened. He switched pronouns as well.

"The neighbor you refer to may indeed be helpless, but she is not a Dachauer at all, Fraeulein, not from our town. Frankly, I am not sure what she is, except maybe useless, a *minderwerteges* life, not worthy of living, some might say. But that is not the topic for discussion. For my part, I accept your apology. I would like to continue our competitions. You are a challenge. Shall we play again? I will be here a few days. And soon we lose the weather." He then added in a stern tone, "It is an honor to be invited to try out. And it could be reversed, that invitation, once we finish this war. Remember your duty to the fatherland to perform well."

"My father says there will be no Olympics in Berlin next year."

"A defeatist, your Father?"

"A realist, Herr Mueller."

Fanny's face paled. Calling her father names, daring to tell her about her duty! She recoiled at the word *useless* for her sweet aunt. There was the true injury. So comfortable was he with language, insults rolled off his tongue. Was it because he had the name Mueller, because he was rich, because he was part of the Burgfrieden? Was it inborn or was it because he was a spoiled child raised only by an adoring mother that made him think he had license to say anything?

Asking her to play? She turned an angry crimson. Angry with herself, as well. What she had once taken for admirable independence was unfeeling coldness. What she thought was his admiration was from weakness and ego on her part, nothing else.

"Shall we play, then?"

"That would be impossible, Herr Mueller, Auf Wiedersehen," she said curtly and walked away. She did not use the customary *Pfueati*, the friendly Bavarian farewell meaning *May God protect you*. (Was it worse to be insincere and say it? Or to have the absence of good feeling and show it? She would ask Father Goetz.)

"Fraeulein," he shot back as she walked away, "do not rely on good looks to excuse rude behavior." Then he muttered, as much to himself as to Fanny, "Looks are fickle. Ask my mother!"

Luftmann did not like the exchange he overheard. Fanny had shown the man what she thought of him. A mistake! Why reveal that to anyone? It was not as if it were the confessional. And maybe, which Luftmann would never say nor admit, you couldn't be too careful there, as well.

For his own visits for the sacrament, Luftmann had little to confess other than the masquerade, the lie he lived each day, which he could not disclose. He made up things — mean to his wife, envy for neighbor, failure to pray daily — things that he thought Gentiles confessed to their priest. He wondered often if the priest was satisfied.

Mueller asked twice more before November, days when the Alpine Foehn wind warmed the crisp autumn air, sending notes which Fanny ignored. Then it stopped. He no longer greeted her at Mass.

As Luftmann predicted, there would be no 1916 Olympics in Berlin. The war lingered on. And Fanny felt almost as bad for her country to lose the prestigious event as for herself. It was generous, he thought, given her excited anticipation.

"I will try for 1920," she told him after some moments of silence. "I will be 20 then, perhaps maturity will help my game. No matter, I will never have to play at Mueller's again. I will have my own tennis court."

"Yes, well, Fanny, your own tennis court. There is something I must tell you."

Her response to the bad news about his broken promise surprised him. A stunned look, then silence. Then relying on her characteristic habit of exercise and solitude, she ran out of the house to take a short bike ride and digest the disappointment.

Returning home she said quietly, tears welling. "I understand, Papa, you gave it for the fatherland. A noble gesture you make for the war effort! I am so proud for our family name. It can help end this war in victory, bring our soldiers home, bring our Sepp home to us more quickly."

Then she ran upstairs. To have a good cry, Luftmann guessed.

Δ

On Father Goetz's weekly house visit, Luftmann finally brought up the lynchings in America about which Lotte's cousins had written.

"I know of the Frank case," Father Goetz said. When Luftmann raised his eyebrows, he added, "The Church has its own network. I did not hear about the other, the Black people, though I was aware those atrocities happened. A profound racial problem."

"The rabble clearly runs that country! Our Kaiserreich is more civilized."

The priest did not reply.

"You must admit our Kaiserreich is more civilized," Luftmann insisted.

"Did you read the books I mentioned to you?"

"Yes, I did."

"Are those civilized ideas, my friend?"

"I refer now to the lynching, Father. Everyday people in a racial murder frenzy? Applauded! No official intervention!"

"Hah! Intervention? Luftmann, the Pan-Germanic League with its divisive voelkische nationalism thrives. Their influence is strong within the Kaiserreich and the German War Ministry. They influence decisions, spread propaganda, distort information, cleverly naming their opponents as cowards. A war that unexpectedly can go one way or the other, so many casualties, a war promised to end quickly, a war in the name of the Father, the Son, and the Holy Ghost, so many people feeling duped by both God and country — we are dealing with warehouses of stored emotions. The longer this goes on, we shall see how civilized the Kaiserreich is. It is Advent now, yes? Ask me the same question next year, my friend."

Luftmann was quiet.

Fanny, who had joined them, wondered if her father would remember a year later.

Luftmann was thinking about whether to mention the Mueller incident and Mueller's attitude toward Gretl (who had just received the wafer and wine blessed and converted into the body and blood of Jesus from the priest). Was that an official position, he wondered, lives not worth living? An argument in the Kaiserreich for years. When times were bad, the voices got louder. Doctors' voices, economists' voices, even some of the nursing sisters' voices.

Rubbing his forehead, he looked up at Fanny and decided not to share the Mueller incident with the priest; she had probably told him anyway when confessing.

When Father Goetz left, Luftmann considered the spirit of unity, the exhilarating *Volksgemeinschaft*, the inclusive togetherness of the August days, and the priest's words today on discontent and divisiveness. The Kaiserreich had better win this war soon, Luftmann decided. The priest was right.

The uplifting togetherness coming from the Kaiser's Burgfrieden announcement after the Odeonsplatz rally ("I recognize no political parties, no social divisions, only Germans") had not taken long to dissipate. That Luftmann could see for himself.

With the failure of the Schlieffen Plan in the very first month of the war, the plan that had promised quick victory and quick surrender, political factions in the Reichstag were resurrected. All quarreled; all made demands on the Kaiser. And there were reasons for restlessness among those on the home front. Casualties were mounting exponentially, casualties for which they were foolishly unprepared.

Promise to take Paris within 40 days? Thirty days. Whatever! Even if generals thought winning depended on brevity, as he had told Father Goetz early on, why not just do it and not brag about it beforehand? Foolishness, he thought. German arrogance!

A fading dream of unity, acceptance, and victory still lingering, Luftmann had a good feeling when signing over the deed to his forest land for the gunpowder and munitions factory, though he realized, with some misgiving, the construction could be the end of rural Dachau. As to her tennis court, he had told Fanny just in time.

There was already an administration building established with estimates of needed workers. Plans were in place for later construction. Bulldozers were clearing the forest. Tracks were laid from the Dachau train station to the factory site! German efficiency!

He had shrugged, shaking his head in wonderment. Worrying about Fanny's reaction, he had thought too much like a Jew. And his Fanny, it was clear, thought simply like a good German! Lotte, on the other hand, thought like a devout Catholic.

That same night, in the dark stillness of their chamber, an early snow shower outside visible in the moonlight, soft flakes swirling, their dance seen through the arched windows, pine scent finding ways to perfume through the room, Christian heard her praying for him, heard his name.

"What, Lotte? What this time?"

"Your gift! You help with murder, Christian. Munitions factory here because of you. Jesus teaches us to love one another. He gave His life for that," she said. "I will pray daily for your soul."

His head next to hers, their oversize goose-down pillows touching in the large four-poster bed, Luftmann whispered, "Tell me, Lotte! Don't you remember that you were a Jew once?"

"I remember I was an orphan, raised with obligation. Becoming Catholic, a part of me was born, a part that was missing. I discovered God loved me no matter what. There was a loving family that asked no questions — a permanent Father, a Son, and a Blessed Mother of Mercy. There are the blessed nuns at the school whom I call Sister! There is Father Goetz who in confession calls me 'My Child.' Gone is the past, the God we feared and so often asked why He punished us so? I want to forget that God of justice and vengeance. Don't ask again, Christian. I like to believe you found something as well."

He turned over on his side, his head on his elbow; his dark beard, trimmed to obedience, brushed against her thick blond hair. "You have a loving husband, too, my dear. A loving husband who finds you a wonderful wife."

"Yes, well, goodnight, Christian. I still pray daily for your soul," she said turning on her side, away from him.

Δ

Though his generosity to the Kaiserreich had been generally admired for its patriotism among the townspeople, there were those, particularly in the Burgfrieden, those real citizens, who wished his gift hadn't happened and held resentment toward him, whispering that Luftmann had to buy citizenship, wasn't a born Dachauer, but was an *Ersatz Buerger*, not the real thing. Their town would never be the same again with all the non-Bavarian workers, strangers, pouring in, because some outsider needed to prove himself, needed to be a hero!

Chapter 12
Das Eiserne Kreuz
1916

Ludwig Hofer, a chunky but muscular man of medium height, was talking to a few coworkers outside the Mueller Brewery, a three-story pitched-roof building tucked away near the Alstadtberg below the Dachau Castle, directly off Schlosstrasse. A late November snow lined the streets. The four men huddled together, shivering from the cold.

"Another brutal winter," said one, clapping hands and stomping feet.

"Maybe will come a Foehn wind to warm things up," said another without conviction.

They were gathered in the brewery entrance to congratulate Hofer on his son's heroism medal. But Hofer was angry and he was not afraid to show it.

"Two years into the war and only now the War Ministry realizes they need steel helmets. If he had the *Stahlhelm*, Sepp's head injury would not have happened in the first place. Sending men to the front in leather head coverings! What do they care about the working classes fighting their war? The *Pickelhaube*'s ridiculous spike on top was supposed to scare the enemy? It couldn't protect the *Frontsoldaten* who wore them." Turning his head Hofer made a spitting sound. "That's what I think of the Kaiser's Burgfrieden. Class truce? Hah! It changed nothing except giving workers an equal right to die."

For heroism Sepp had been awarded the *Eiserne Kreuz 2. Klasse*. Hofer didn't have to brag about it because his wife had put the medal — the blackened iron cross with silver trim hanging from a black-and-white striped ribbon ring — in the front window of their house on Burgfriedenstrasse. She placed it on white linen in a large, dark wood frame for all to see.

"The Iron Cross! Black and White! Prussian State colors for medals. Those war lovers care little for Bavaria, let alone the working class," Hofer ranted.

"It has Bavarian blue and white added," pointed out an elderly worker. Only the elderly and the very young remained in Dachau; others were serving in the military.

"Come, Hofer, we have to think like one nation now. Bavaria, Prussia — no difference! Where is your patriotism? The kind Sepp showed in battle. Our Bavarian motto is on the brigade's silver belt buckle," said another, leaning forward and more than a little agitated. Younger than the others, his fists were clenched, but not enough to hide missing fingers, a deficiency that had kept him from the military.

"IN LOYALTY STEADFAST, some motto!" again Hofer spit out the words. "*In Treue Fest* to whom? The warmongers? The industrialists? The aristocracy? The churches that blessed battlefields, promised victory? Certainly not to the workers slaughtered daily in this illegal war. We get back at them. One day we get even."

"Wait a minute!" the agitated man argued. "Your Communist Party supported the war with the rest of us."

"A concession, Schtreuk, but no more! Workers die, industrialists get rich. A workers' assembly in Berlin last January, and Frankfurt in May, a workers' strike in sympathy with the party's anti-war rally."

"The Polish Jew's rally, foreign trouble maker!" Schtreuk sneered. "No true German tells troops to run backwards."

"Rosa Luxembourg is a German citizen, Comrade Schtreuk." Hofer threw *Comrade* at him to provoke. He was a reckless man, unlike his son, Sepp, who could be passionate, yes, but with restraint and discretion. "Comrade Luxembourg went to prison for workers like you."

"Not for me!" Schtreuk shot back. "Calling for soldiers to lay down arms. Her Spartacus League a bunch of godless fanatics — extreme even for you Communists — internationalists, preaching chaos and revolution You are not only a Red, Hofer, but a dark Red, a Luxembourg lover along with that other Jew, the Leipzig lawyer."

"So they are Jews! But they know the way to change. Look at Russia, you'll see how to overthrow oppression! The empresses' monk is dead; the czar is at the front trying to win people back; the Romanovs are on their way out!" Unaccustomed to getting so much attention from his co-workers — attention meant for Sepp — Hofer was feeling smug and sure of himself. "I'd like to see the Empress Frau Mueller on her way out, as well, walking around like a queen! We'll get them all, you'll see. Think they are better than us. Without us they'd have no food on their table! Mind my words; look to the east. You'll see how the powerless become powerful!"

"Without Frau Mueller you would be the one with no food on the table. She pays your salary," the first worker reminded him with a laugh.

"A Prussian snob! She looks down her nose at us as workers and Bavarians," Hofer shot back.

He had passed her one day near the Burgfrieden district and doffed his cap. Her spectacles absent, Frau Mueller did not return his greeting. Little mistakes, small accidents, cause big problems, Luftmann would have said if he had been there.

"We are lucky your son does not share your views, Hofer," said Schtreuk, wagging his short-fingered hand at him. "Then he would lay down his arms, betraying the Kaiserreich! He would — "

"How is your boy?" the older man interjected, as if smelling a scuffle in the making.

"Sepp is still in hospital. There was delay in his returning to the front. But he goes back any day, now. I wrote him he was a fool to go back."

Schtreuk was red-faced. "You wrote him that? Not to do his duty! To delay!"

He stomped away, the hero celebration over.

At the end of the day, Schtreuk, a Pan-Germanic League stalwart, reported Hofer's comments word for word — the Communists, the Spartacus revolutionaries, the enmity towards Frau Mueller, urging Lt. Hofer's delay to the front — to the brewery foreman, also a League member.

The foreman reported it directly to Marius Mueller in the War Ministry in Munich, who found Hofer's Bolshevism despicable, to say nothing of his disparaging Mueller's mother to the brewery workers.

Mueller had little regard for Sepp Hofer, as well, because he turned down Mueller's generous invitation to join the League after he disgraced himself with the Gypsy boy. Young Hofer was a favorite of that Luftmann girl who also didn't know her place. Yes! Here was the opportunity to get even, to teach them both respect.

Schtreuk was a good man, thought Marius, seated in his ministry office, desktop clear except for a small, black leather notebook. He opened it to a lined page that read *Schtreuk*, a check next to it, written in his neat, small hand. Now he added the first name Ernst, remembered from the brewery employment records. He slipped the pad into the side drawer of his imposing dark wood desk and locked it. He would have to remember to commend the brewery worker who knew enough to report the matter to his superior.

Mueller leaned back in the leather desk chair. The ministry office was on Ludwigstrasse 14 — his department important enough to be in the same Munich building as the Premier's, though his immediate surroundings were not so grand.

His corner space was large, had wide windows. Portraits of General Ludendorff and Field Marshall von Hindenburg on either side of the Kaiser, all in full military dress, decorated the walls — a must in ministry offices. The furnishings — leather chairs, a square leather desktop, files concealed in matching wood cabinets, were austere enough to suggest authority more than comfort.

Mueller was satisfied with the League's effective shadow chain of command, a network established among members feeling loyalty to Pan-Germanic principles. He was gratified that he had been part of establishing the Munich organization of the Alldeutschen Verband, its discipline and strict standards. Weakness was for women! A picture of his vain and doting mother, childlike, compliant, caring about what others thought, flashed through his mind's eye. Men had to be strong. Mueller had to be a father to himself, losing his own to that Ostjuden-plague before he ever knew him. He had to exercise the firm hand. Power is nothing if not used.

Enough thinking. He had to take care immediately of that Bolshevik instigator from the brewery. Swift and strong the retaliation must be. Swift and strong, absolutely no leeway for the son's war record. He unlocked the desk drawer, removing the black leather notebook. Sepp Hofer deserved some scrutiny as well. If one wasn't scrupulous at all times, he mused, things could so easily fall through the cracks.

Ludwig Hofer learned he was discharged from the Mueller Brewery when he showed up for work the next shift, DEFEATIST smeared across his locker in red paint. Ernst Schtreuk walked him out of the building, seeing that Hofer left only with what belonged to him . . . which was nothing.

When Hofer returned unexpectedly to his one-story house on Burgfriedenstrasse, he surprised his wife, who was washing the linoleum floor in the small kitchen. He told her what had happened at the brewery.

"*Mein Gott*," she cried from both shame for the family that had just been honored by her son's heroism and from worry about money. "Your mouth could get you charged with treason! It's wartime. How are we going to live? Everything expensive! Food prices high, when you can get any! Our farmers give so much of their harvest to feed the cities."

"And who makes them do that?" Hofer asked, as if knowing the answer.

"The state! That hunger strike in Berlin! The state orders them, but what's the difference? We have less and it costs more, Ludwig. What's more, the potato crop will not do well from the terrible frost this year. Then what do we do?"

"Eat more *Bayerische Ruebe!* We have plenty of turnips in Dachau. So, are you finished?" he asked curtly.

"How will we manage? You with no job! Who in town will give a troublemaker work?" she began to cry again.

"Stop your tears!" Hofer snapped. "I will work at the new munitions factory. Better for me! Workers from all over, less provincial, less brainwashed by the state and the church. I might be able to enlist them."

"They give you work there? With your reputation?" She was amazed. "Dachau has changed that much?"

"Luftmann intervened," he gave a sneering laugh. "Sepp is a hero. And the priest vouched for you as a parish member, telling the factory administration that he prays for me. Hah! Enemies of the people — one rich man fires me, another rich man gets me a job, and a man of religion recommends my family."

"How can you talk with disrespect about Herr Luftmann? You should be grateful."

"Herr Luftmann? Do you see him work for a living? How does he live so well without lifting a finger while men work long hours and their families still starve? I owe nothing to people like Luftmann."

Frau Hofer gave a long sigh. He was such a miserable man. But she was right about Dachau. There was still the same small-town gossip, but Dachau had changed. Anyone could see it if they knew the town before the war, knew it before the gun powder and munitions plants.

By 1916, the *Koenigliche Pulver-und Munitionsfabrik* — the *Pumf* as it was called by locals, had brought a 40 percent population increase, over 2,000 strangers packed into the tight-knit community, like locusts, overrunning the once rural town. So much beauty and serenity the town sacrificed for Luftmann's patriotic gesture.

Gone were the quiet and safety of old streets and lanes, the quiet evenings with lazy moonlight shimmering on the Rivers Amper and Wuerm, owls flying over the broad Dachauer Moos in soft brown twilight, landscape painters gathering in the clean-air purity of Dachau light, putting on canvas raven flocks across blazing red sunsets.

Sacrificed was the once agricultural town with skilled workers. The Pumf had changed it all, had added polluting smokestacks and chaotic diversity to the former cohesive community of Eigentum-imbued citizens. The Pumf added a mass of strangers for Herr Hofer to convert to workers of the world.

"He brings shame to our family," Frau Hofer apologized to Lotte Luftmann after Mass the following Sunday, walking alongside her on Augsburgerstrasse. "Thank Herr Luftmann for speaking for my husband's job."

"How could we not speak for a neighbor? And Sepp has brought you honor. Thank the Lord it is a wound that can heal," she crossed herself. "So many young men are dying every day at the front."

So when the Iron Cross Class 2 on white linen framed in dark wood disappeared from its post on the Hofer Burgfriedenstrasse window, there was talk throughout town.

Parish members knew there was a shrapnel wound to Sepp's head not protected by his inadequate leather Pickelhaube helmet. There was some degree of what Father Goetz had called cerebral concussion, whatever that meant, from the shell's explosion.

They had been told by Frau Hofer that when the battle started, her Leutnant son, an officer leading a Bavarian Platoon — nine squads, each with eight soldiers — was in harm's way because of constantly checking a wounded soldier, a young Ingolstadt lad defenseless in delirium, calling out for his home.

According to Frau Hofer and also to Father Goetz, Sepp had diligently protected the wounded youth from trench rats grown bold and fat with human flesh, rodent onslaughts drawn to the endless carrion food supply barely below the dirt and muddy surfaces, the burial grounds of the trenches.

For that heroism, he was awarded the Iron Cross Class 2.

There was more to the story.

Across the dugout lay another body, half naked from nibbling rats, genitals exposed, *beschnittener Schwengel* — the dead giveaway — circumcised, *a Judensoldat*, long dead and bloated exposed to that August day's sun, a very different kind of August day from the Odeonsplatz only two years earlier.

Only one month after the inspirational rally on that other August day, Sepp had awakened rudely to a harsh reality. Victory promised by the much-touted Schlieffen Plan and its high priests was neither swift nor forthcoming. Mostly unspoken, those who had believed in a short quick war, like so many at the front, knew they had been deceived, fooled by the state, misled by men of God.

The Imperial Army's horse-drawn trains were inadequate for transporting supplies; bare-chested men were helpless against technological weaponry; prideful cavalry was obsolete when others had tanks. It was not the war they thought they had entered. The Lord was not on anyone's side. Why were they fighting in the first place? Because cousins could not get along and wanted one another's toys and space? Because munitions makers wanted to get richer?

Yes, the Deutschlandlied remained on their lips, but to keep themselves awake, not to storm French machine guns as they had bragged when war was declared. Faces dust-smeared, uniforms ragged, they marched the miles-long trench frontier, the soil soaked in blood. Gone was the lightning flash of a new world, the *Volksgemeinschaft* of righteous souls unified, cleansing mankind. In its place was a gnawing emptiness, a vacuum demanding to be filled. Born was a lonely *Frontgemeinschaft*, a communal bond among those tied together by the horrors of war.

Maybe his father was right, Sepp thought. Or were his promises a litany of lies too? Cynicism replaced idealism. Maybe one side was no better, the other side no worse, after all.

Was he thinking these thoughts when the explosion flung him across the dugout, his face striking the distended abdomen of the August-sun-baked corpse? No matter! No time for thoughts then. The most horrible sensations of taste and smell filled him. Sepp realized the collision had ruptured the poor Judensoldat's swollen carcass.

"*Mein Gott, Mein Gott,*" he mumbled in a deathly croak, trying to spit a hideous substance from his mouth before he lost consciousness. "*Nicht mich, nicht mich!*" he gasped. "*Die Eingeweide, der Mut*! On my tongue! *Die Faeulnis*! Rot in my mouth."

The next thing Sepp knew he was on a stretcher, moving. There was the smell of pus and urine. He heard whimpers and moaning, then realized they were his own. He opened his eyes. There was a beautiful white horse grazing near a ditch. He blinked. No, there was the horse! But then he saw that an artillery shell had torn away its right foreleg. The horse grazed peacefully but, at the same time, slowly, as if in an unspeakable grief, swaying the bloody stump of a leg to and fro.

"Finish the horse off," he commanded, dragging the sounds from his broken body, a body that was approaching having had enough. "Finish the horse off," he cried.

A soldier that Sepp couldn't see, perhaps walking alongside the stretcher for protection, replied in a battle weary voice Sepp had come to recognize, "I can't, Herr Leutnant, I can't! I don't have the heart!"

His brain shut down. That was what Sepp could not forget, what pushed him beyond the bearable — not rats feeding on carrion, not the rat whose head protruded from the dead Jew soldier's mouth, not even the decomposed entrails dripping from his own chin, but the exquisite agony of a beautiful white horse and the soldier in wartime that could not obey an order to kill.

The wound healed, but not the lingering *Kriegstrauma*. Shell shock, they called it, tremors, screaming nightmares, fainting spells, a disease brand-new, apparently affecting the nervous system. Or was it a pseudo-disease, malingering, conjured-up symptoms displayed to avoid battle? This latter notion was an orthodox Pan-Germanic conviction creating a skepticism that influenced the entire War Ministry.

When he returned to duty at the front, Sepp was much shaken but seemingly cured. Then, on first seeing the horses on the battlefield ripped apart by shells, eyes bulging out from empty red sockets, he broke out weeping uncontrollably, followed by a vomiting attack. Later the grisly images would trigger convulsions as well.

Unnerving his men, Sepp felt a terrible gnawing shame that weakened him further. His dreams caused him to awaken pouring with sweat and screaming — thus endangering the lives of his platoon, calling attention to their position in the trenches.

Sepp was removed from his post and sent back to the hospital, where the symptoms subsided without special treatment.

The War Ministry, prodded by Marius Mueller, revoked the medal. Four uniformed men had come one dark night to the Hofer home to take it back, banging on the door, awakening Frau Hofer, who came hurriedly in her nightdress. That was how the Iron Cross 2nd Class disappeared from its post on the Hofer Burgfriedenstrasse window.

Then began the investigation.

Chapter 13
Scrutinizing Sepp

They checked his background. They discovered the father's troublemaking record in Dachau. They found the letter Herr Hofer had written to his son in the hospital saying: "You're a fool to return to the front." They examined the medical records. They reviewed his post-injury performance in the trenches.

Even without his father's left-wing provocations, the charges of malingering, cowardice, non-performance as an officer, made Sepp a candidate for court-martial. Already Germans, as did the British on the other side, admitted to executions for cowardice and the avoidance of duty. This Kriegstrauma, this shell shock, not an injury automatically recognized by the War Ministry, was questioned more and more as a malingering ploy by weak-hearted shirkers.

Deputy Minister Marius Mueller, from his office in Munich, sitting behind his desk, spoke for the ministry when he wrote his opinion on the Hofer case: "The person that is not willing to fight and die if need be for his country has no right to life."

Mueller could have gone after the father as well for subversion and inciting, but the timing was wrong. Ludwig Hofer had garnered some following among workers in the Pumf — disillusioned laborers and their hungry families, angry lapsed Catholics and Lutheran strangers, replacing Volk and God with Bolshevism. They need not be provoked into action for some foolish cause, making Hofer a martyr.

Sepp went from hero to villain. Mueller knew that brand was acceptable. People who had sons fighting and dying would turn against those not willing to carry their load. And though begged by Frau Hofer in person and by Fanny Luftmann in writing, Mueller would not reverse himself. It was Christian Luftmann who again helped the Hofer family.

Luftmann did not intercede solely for Fanny or for the Hofers. He knew Sepp was courageous just as he knew Marius Mueller was cruel and mean-spirited. Who could forget the Zigeuner episode and Sepp's bravery three years earlier, an episode for which Luftmann still felt responsible?

Mueller had tried to cause trouble for the boy over the Wuerm incident and his refusal to join the Pan-Germanic League, but the war and his pending military service had saved Sepp. Whatever the opinion about Gypsies, whatever the opinion as to whether Kriegstrauma was an illness, people in Dachau knew Sepp Hofer was no coward. But maybe a traitor, influenced by his rabble-rousing father?

It was not, however, an easy time for the Dachau community to express compassion or dissent: competing political loyalties, strangers as neighbors, new ways versus proud insular traditions.

When Mueller would not help the Hofer family, indeed wanted to do Sepp harm, Luftmann went over Mueller's head, going directly to Berlin to the same War Ministry Department that had accepted his gift of land for the Pumf.

The Imperial War Ministry building, so Prussian in its attempt to impress and impose, was Greek Revival in style, with massive exterior stone columns. Inner archways were interspersed along stone-walled hallways leading to the Deputy Minister's office. There Luftmann found again the soaring high ceilings, draped paneled walls, marble and cherrywood floors, imposing wall paintings of the Kaiserreich's leaders that were even more imperious this second time around than Luftmann had remembered.

They know how to put on a show, he thought, a show designed to imprint on the brain the distinctive Prussian sense of austere privilege, severity, entitlement, power, and an interior strength that gave no quarter. Taking a deep breath to regain composure, Luftmann knew he could surrender his bargaining position through any sign of timidity. And that he could easily be overcome by the building itself.

He needed to shore up resistance to that feeling of intimidation, which was exactly what all the pomp was meant to arouse. It was a show, only a show, he reminded himself — as he was a show — pulling himself together, knowing it was helpful for him to think that way. He took another deep breath, straightening his back, stiffening his shoulders, regaining his poise.

"This is the last time," warned the senior minister, seated behind an oversized desk, much like Mueller's desk in Munich. He was a wiry man with a paper-thin artificial smile. "It cannot be a habit, doing you favors, making exceptions. No court-martial for the Leutnant, but there will be a censure," he added, reaching for a brown legal-size envelope on the desktop near Luftmann.

Luftmann edged the envelope closer to himself. "No censure, Herr Minister. The officer committed only the crime of suffering an injury. He should get the medal back for saving the life of that wounded soldier."

Clearly the official looked as if he were unaccustomed to disagreement. His whole body stiffened, at once appearing taller though he remained seated.

"You are a skilled Haendler, Herr Luftmann; you know how to negotiate deals! You could even teach those Jews a few things." Then his thin lips tightened, the smile was almost lipless, a sadistic kind of look. "Maybe I should ask you to pull down the *Unterhosen*?"

It took Luftmann aback, yet he concealed his feelings, trained never to show his hand. That was a given. But he had to be careful. To think like a German.

He became indignant. Standing up as if ready to make an exit, he said, "That isn't part of the deal! *Ein warmer Breuder? Nein!* I trust you are no homosexual either."

Haupt's face lost its color. Luftmann had made the right move in that little chess game. Deviance, homosexuality, were not welcome in the Kaiserreich, let alone in the War Ministry.

Now to soften it and let it go. "Sense of humor, perhaps?" he added, sitting down.

Something more was expected because the minister was waiting, waiting and watching. He remembered Father Goetz telling him the ministry was full of right-wingers. He decided casual disdain in response to the Jew reference.

"Jews! Hard to teach those people anything, let alone change their ways, Herr Minister," he said, with a we-all-know-that shake of his head. He gave a small laugh and now wore a pleasant smile. "But deals Germans make with Germans are trustworthy."

The testing expression on the minister's face disappeared. After moments of staring at the pink-cheeked man facing him, the official returned to the Sepp Hofer issue.

"Yes, well, General Ludendorff — the protector of the German Volk, a true believer in the German people, our German destiny, our national strength — demands discipline in our military, restores honor in the face of adversity."

The general's austere portrait on the wall behind the minister alongside the Kaiser and Field Marshall von Hindenburg took on a life of its own, as if spotlighted, a felt presence in the large room. His fierce glowering glare appeared illuminated among the browns, brass, and silver hues of medals, dress uniform, black-and-red Reich's banner almost waving in the still-life painting. Did he really hear the roll of drums, Luftmann wondered, the pounding of footsteps, a baritone chorus singing Soldatenlieder?

Imperceptibly, Luftmann pulled himself back to reality, cleared his throat. Returning the minister's intent gaze, he kept his own pleasant smile, didn't budge at the Voelkische reference, keeping his hand lightly on the envelope.

"Honor, discipline, and justice, too," he countered.

It was the War Minister who broke eye contact. "A standard discharge for the wounded," he conceded.

Luftmann moved the envelope forward, looking up, waiting for more.

"Do not push! We keep the Iron Cross, Herr Luftmann," he said, the pasted smile gone. "We do not countenance cowardice and malingering."

Luftmann frowned, his thick dark eyebrows meeting each other. "The boy is a good boy, Herr Minister. He was wounded, *Das Verwundetenabzeichen*, the medal for the wounded then?"

"He is not a boy, but an officer in the Imperial Army, Herr Luftmann, an officer who shirks his duty. He keeps that medal. He had the head wound. The Kaiserreich is honorable and also remembers those like yourself who are generous for our war effort. But do not take advantage of our memory." Taking the envelope, the narrow slit of a smile appeared on his face once more. "We accept this gift as a voluntary act of patriotism for the Kaiserreich, a confidential gift," he added. "It will of course be delivered properly to the ministry office in Munich. Or maybe not? Too sensitive!" he smiled as he accepted the lucrative Dachau mortgage holding for the Reich. "Strange you should have this to give? May I ask how?"

Now Luftmann gave a forced laugh. "Business secrets held as closely as military ones, *nicht wahr*, Herr Minister?"

"No matter! Was it known to the owners, your position?" His cold tone changed to intimacy.

"Anonymous payments are made to a Hamburg bank as the document instructs."

The minister's face was blank again. Familiarity over. Lips pursed. He was dismissing the gift-bearer.

Nodding, Luftmann got up from the chair, leaving the envelope on the desk.

Once outside, the trade done, he gave a sigh of relief. That reference to Unterhosen, circumcision was a problem! The giveaway. He was as careful as he could be concealing his penis. Yet, if it ever came to that, would they believe the concocted Balantitis infection of the foreskin caused by a soap allergy story? That it required the operation before he married so that he could service his wife? He had chosen the name of a doctor, long dead, so that records could not be researched. Would the War Minister have believed it, if he had pulled down his pants?

Luftmann gave a shrug, the oh-well kind. You try to be careful, it works or it doesn't. For today, there would be another page in his ledger stamped *das Ende*, another Dachau holding to the state, this one income producing as the

Reich more and more needed substantial resources to fight the war, the British blockade a severe impediment.

But, the real value of the gift selected carefully by Luftmann, this holding that he inherited from his father Reb Itzig, was its personal appeal to the Berlin minister. It was a Mueller Brewery mortgage, which to the War Minister would be another weapon over Marius Mueller, his competitor for power, his adversary within the ministry, Luftmann had the feeling its potential advantage would be stored away by the thin-lipped official for future leverage.

Two birds with one stone, he smiled. Helping Sepp and perhaps, as to Mueller, evening the score for the insolent note he had sent his Fanny and his despicable remarks about Gretl.

Δ

A few months later, Sepp, still ill, was discharged and returned home. The normally compassionate community, its stability shaken by the effects of wartime and the Pumf, kept a prudent distance.

With the war going badly and so many unpredictable strangers in town (the small Lutheran community had almost doubled though still using only a rented room with a once-weekly visiting minister for prayers), native Dachauers were reluctant to show feeling for a neighbor at home while others fought, a neighbor branded a coward despite his reprieve from court-martial.

"After all, the Cross has never been restored to him," they whispered.

For his part, Sepp refused to see anyone except Father Goetz, who visited the Hofer home, heard his confession, and delivered the sacrament. Remarkably, Gretl Luftmann on her own showed up, sobbing, one rainy day at the Hofer Burgfriedenstrasse home, with Rolf on his lead.

"This for Sepp. His dog home to help him," she mumbled, tears and rain streaming down her heavy-featured moon face. At the same time, it was hard to loosen her arms from around her beloved dog.

Sepp was unable to see her, but Gretl didn't mind. (Fanny was the one who felt shut out by Sepp's seclusion.) Gretl seemed to understand sadness. She no longer accepted the communion wafer from Father Goetz. It was as if she distrusted a God that would so harm her friend. The priest blessed Lebkuchen and delivered that instead.

And in the middle of everything — of what began two years earlier with exhilarating unity, with Kaiser Wilhem's *Burgfrieden*, all Germans, no differences — down from the War Ministry came *die Judenzaehlung*.

The 1916 October Jew Count! A Jew Census! To count Jews serving at the front, Jewish dead, Jewish casualties, to make sure Jews were not shirking their duty, that the percentage of their dead and wounded matched their percentage of population to the whole as compared to real Germans, to make certain that accounts were in balance.

"Things do not go well in our civilized Kaiserreich, *gell?*" said Father Goetz to Herr Luftmann that Advent, a reminder that a year earlier, he had said, *ask me a year from now about how civilized Germany was.* "The genius German Jew physicist Einstein is accepted to the Prussian Academy while the Reich War Ministry announces the October Jew Count to see if enough Jews are dutifully dying at the front or only profiteering and espousing revolution and surrender! Civilized? Not to mention criminal poison gas we introduced against enemies! More civilized here than in America, you had asked?"

Fanny, thinner and pale, was sitting with them in the Luftmann parlor. She remembered Father Goetz saying, "Ask me next year."

"The cattle trader, Gutmann, came to the Rectory last week asking me to pray for his only son, Berthold, who was lost at Verdun. He showed me the War Ministry letter. It read, *Lt. Gutmann was a brave and fine officer, although Jewish.* Then he opened a case with three medals Berthold had won: *das Eiserne Kreuze, die Tapferkeitsmedaille* for bravery, and the *Verwundetenabzeichen* gotten earlier when wounded," Father Goetz said.

"The young man won medals and lost his life," observed Luftmann.

"Gutmann said, 'When the war started all were Germans, our soldiers. Now there are Germans and there are Jews. Do the bookkeepers count my son in their census?'"

"Pardon me, Father," Fanny uncharacteristically interrupted. "I know these are important matters you discuss, but though he does not see me, Sepp sees you. All I can think about is helping him. Wondering how he does," and then she faltered, whispering, "And if he still cares. Can you help me?"

Chapter 14
Sepp and Fanny
1918-1919

It was Father Goetz who brought Sepp back from the dungeon nightmares of the trenches, Father Goetz, with some help from Gutmann the Haendler.

In the military field hospital, after his head injury healed, after he returned there when unable to perform at the front, doctors had ordered the shell-shocked officer to put the trench experiences behind him, to lock out memories, to stop thinking about old battles, the horrors, the past, in order to get on with his soldier's duty. They saw it ultimately as a matter of will.

Their advice did not work.

However, unlike other Bavarian Catholic veterans disenchanted with their church for failing them, for broken promises and false blessings on yet another so-called noble crusade, Sepp remained steadfast in his devotion.

One Nuremberg veteran wrote a letter to his priest published widely in Bavarian newspapers:

> "Promising victory with 'God on our side,' you said it was our
> holiest duty to go to war, to burn villages and towns, to kill people
> who have done us no harm. This was your Christian teaching, only
> good for insane kings and princes who have bled their subjects white."

Sepp held on to his faith as a drowning man gasps for air, struggles to keep his head above water. Through the daily sacrament delivered to him at home, he began to confess his terrifying tale to Father Goetz. Digging deep into the darkness of stored horrors, bits and pieces emerged. From unhallowed burial grounds of his soul, Sepp unearthed slowly and painfully the dreadful awfulness of his experiences.

Father Goetz listened, prayed, and each time imposed penance of prayers, then absolved the tortured man until the day he spoke to him of Fanny.

"Sepp, be merciful, let Fanny visit. She asked that I make this request."

"Fanny asked?"

"An old friend. She worries."

"I could not suffer her pity."

"A true act of charity to see her, Sepp."

Sepp put his hand to his brow, massaging his forehead as if to squeeze out a proper response.

"Do I tell her to visit? Are you ready, Sepp?"

Finally he looked up and nodded.

"When?"

"Whenever," he replied. "I am confused, Father."

Herr Hofer was at the Pumf and Frau Hofer was at midweek Mass praying for his soul when Fanny knocked on the door of the modest Hofer home on Burgfriedenstrasse that morning. She pulled her green knit shawl tight around her shoulders as much from trepidation as from the cool Alpine air. Though early spring, there was a stubborn winter chill and dampness, the air still moist with morning mist, too soon in the day for the returning sun to teach tenacious winter a warming lesson.

Fanny knocked again.

Sepp answered the door.

Though Father Goetz had warned her, she was unprepared for his appearance.

His stark look was that of a ghost, face waxen, pale and pained, eyes wary, a non-trusting, hunched over, withdrawn man. Nowhere could she see the young cadet who had gone off to war, brimming with patriotism and hope. But it was the shock of white that cut a path through his black hair, a desolate narrow seam through the dark forest capping his head that made her gasp.

Unable to move, she burst into tears.

Sepp flinched. Was this the pity he had feared? There was a moment where neither knew which way to go.

She swayed as if about to fall.

Then Sepp — who understood suffering, his own and that of the men he had led into battle — seemed to recognize a friend in distress, a vulnerable friend who needed him. He reached out, grasping her slender wavering body, taking her in his arms, holding her close, all the while appearing to grow taller as Fanny held on to him.

"Oh, Sepp, I love you so," she whispered.

Sepp stood there outside the doorway as Fanny sobbed in his arms. A dark rain-laden cloud appeared in the otherwise clear blue sky, lightly sprinkling the two as it passed, a Dachau spring shower.

"I was so afraid — "

"Shhh!" he said gently breaking his silence. "I know fear. I, too, have been afraid, *Liebchen*, my dear beautiful girl. It has been hard for me to feel love at all. I had forgotten how, feelings frozen solid. Until now, until I see you, until I touch you," he said, holding the embrace a few moments longer before leading her inside.

On that visit, there were no other words shared, just embraces from which they both drew strength.

Δ

In the days to come, slowly, carefully, as if making their way through shards of glass, the two young people restored their intimacy. Hand in hand they took long walks together, silent walks, before breakfast in the early morning or at the dusk dinnertime to avoid people, Rolf trailing along, walks near the Amper, finding a quiet place, the now smokestacked forest near the Wuerm lost to them as a haven, colonies of laborers tramping there day and night to produce gunpowder and munitions for a war desperately needing supplies, fighting on despite the British blockade.

They embraced as if made of fine crystal, not wanting to shatter what they had. But eventually their bodies responded to long-held-back feelings.

On this June day, finding a sheltered spot near the riverbank cushioned by fresh summer grass, oblivious to the clear blue of the water that mirrored the powder-puff clouds dotting the azure sky, they lay together so close, but not close enough, almost fusing into one, yet separate.

Fanny whispered. "Please, oh, how I wish. Oh, how I — "

"Soon," Sepp promised, holding her tightly. "Soon we have each other, when we marry. Once the war ends."

"Soon," she echoed, then a soft whisper, an almost inaudible, "Now?"

Sepp gently pushed his body away from hers, while stroking her long blond hair that had come undone. "You are beautiful. You expect too much from me to be strong for both of us, Fanny," he said, getting up, brushing off slivers of grass. "Who knew such a well-brought-up young woman could feel so, so — you know what I mean?" he smiled a wicked smile, making her laugh and so the danger of the moment had passed. "We don't do this again," he added, this time sternly, in command.

"You are harsh, Sepp! Too obedient to each word! *Lead me not into temptation?*"

"We have kept faith with our church, Fanny. That can't be wrong."

"There are times rules may be made to be broken, *gell?* When old rules are not what's really best? There are times it would seem natural rather than sinful to do what you feel."

"Yes, well, those are exactly the times we must avoid."

Fanny shook her head, giving a small laugh. "You do get better, stronger, I see."

They walked again, along the riverbank.

"You should keep up your talks with Father Goetz."

"The doctors advised the opposite," he confided, his arm about her shoulders.

"They know nothing about this injury," said Fanny, moving away, eyes blazing. "They hardly acknowledge it as an affliction. You must talk it out, not let it fester inside. How can you suffocate feelings from your heart, choke memories in your brain that struggle for air? Tell Father Goetz. He's not judging. Say how you felt. How you feel. Your fears! Say it!"

"Is that an order, Fraeulein General?" he joked, putting his arm around her again.

Through months of daily talks to God, his priest, to himself, within the familiar and safe confines of the Hofer house on Burgfriedenstrasse, safe from seeing horses on Dachau streets, safe from awkward and concealed glances of neighbors, Sepp gradually got his mind and soul to embrace the horrors, deal with them.

In early March 1918, Father Goetz arranged, through the Dachau district associations of the Jewish cattle trader Samson Gutmann, for Sepp to visit friendly stable owners. Sepp needed farms that would allow a total stranger in without prying, indeed that would welcome a veteran of the war. Gutmann provided transportation in his 1914 Daimler four-seater, the sturdy silver touring car bought in better times.

Snow was still on the ground in the treeless flatlands across the countryside as they drove to the village of Karlsfeld, less than four miles south of Dachau, but still in Dachau County and St. Jakob's parish. The three men's nerves were tense by the time they approached the sprawling Kiembock family farm that produced crops, dairy, beef, pork, anything needed to survive.

After stopping at the red-and-white hip-roofed farmhouse, pitched to protect against storms and mountain winds, and after shaking hands with Herr Kiembock, a sturdy, well-built man with a passel of children of all ages surrounding him, eager to meet the war hero, they moved on to the smaller gray-planked stable, next to a cowshed and chicken house, where the work horses were kept.

Each took a deep breath, Sepp, Gutmann, and Father Goetz, before going inside. It was not roomy for visitors, but the four stalls were large enough for each horse they housed to move around. In the first one there was a black horse with its companion goat chewing on hay, resting without concern alongside the steed's muscular legs.

"He was probably skittish at one time or another and the goat is there to soothe his nerves," said Gutmann. "Doing a good job at it, *gell?*"

"Do I need a goat, as well, Herr Gutmann?" asked Sepp, his face pale and tense.

Gutmann said nothing.

Father Goetz knew the cattle trader had been trying to make normal conversation in a very abnormal situation.

The other stalls held only horses. In the last was a whitish-gray stallion that had interrupted his feeding and seemed to look eye to eye at the visitors.

And that did it.

Sepp screamed, then began to weep, a loud, uncontrollable wail.

"Get him out," said Father Goetz.

Sepp's crying and screaming panicked the horse. Neighing and leaping against the stall's sides, it joined him in terror, unlike the quiet suffering of the one on the battlefield with the pendulous swaying of its bloodied stump.

Reflexes running amok, Sepp's tremors worsened, capturing his whole body in spastic movements as if electrified. All the while there was his eerie howl, spittle appearing in the corners of his mouth.

"Get him out," shouted the priest to Gutmann, who was transfixed by the unfolding scene. "Gutmann! Samson! Go! Now! Move!"

Hearing his name must have broken the spell because Gutmann and Father Goetz rushed toward Sepp. When they gripped him simultaneously, Sepp exploded into motion, breaking away, running wildly from the barn.

The older men followed.

"I do not move well," apologized Father Goetz to Gutmann, as he slipped on an icy patch beneath the snow.

Gutmann, a large man, had long strides but not speed. Yet he was surefooted. When Sepp slipped or simply collapsed in exhaustion, burying his head in the snow, Gutmann reached him and, as if Sepp were a child, or perhaps as if he were his lost son, gently lifted him, cradling him in his arms, carrying him back to the Daimler.

Rocking him to and fro, like a worshipper in an oldtime Yiddish prayer house, it was only when Sepp's howls turned to groans and the sobs to whimpers, that Gutmann placed him in the back of the auto, covering him with a fur blanket kept in the trunk.

"You are hurting from the fall?" Gutmann asked Father Goetz as the priest limped toward the waiting car.

"I am fine, Samson. Thank you. We are blessed that you were here."

"Your faith and your dedication give hope," Samson said, softly. "Hope and faith are wonderful things, Father."

They tried again a few days later. Father Goetz suggested Sepp visit the animals alone.

"You might concentrate only on the black horse, the one with the companion. He seems tame, Sepp."

They did this several times, Sepp always appearing pale and shaken after the confrontations. Eventually, Sepp asked to go more often. He had befriended the fine old black mare and the goat. Both enjoyed the apples Sepp brought them.

The whitish-gray horse Sepp left for last, approaching him gingerly, until confidence was restored in both man and beast. It was only after reaching this threshold of acceptance that Sepp returned to St. Jakob's for the sacraments, was ready to face the members of the parish community.

Almost eighteen months after his homecoming from the front, Sepp and Fanny, with Rolf alongside, were strolling near the river after the Easter Sunrise Mass at St. Jakob's that Sepp had attended.

"For the rest of my life I will thank the Lord for leading me from the terror of darkness. Thank Him for Father Goetz and for your patience, Fanny," he said, squeezing her hand. "An unusual patience, nowadays," he teased, giving Fanny a tender but careful hug of gratitude, absent the riptide of passion which grew stronger between them. "Gretl, also. What an act of kindness returning Rolf " — the German shepherd's ears perked up on hearing his name — "at a time when it was hard for me to see good in this world."

"And Herr Gutmann? There when we needed him. Asking only that we pray for the memory of his son."

"How can I forget what Samson did? I am forever obligated to his kindness."

That September, a healed and restored Sepp surprised everyone by asking to be returned to battle. It stunned Fanny, who had hoped secretly for their early marriage once Sepp recovered, not waiting for war's end. The petition was sent to the War Ministry in both Berlin and Munich.

Mueller stamped it DEFICIENT and NOT APPROVED.

However, the Berlin War Minister, the one with the paper-thin smile familiar with Sepp's case, again overruled Marius Mueller, his junior but ambitious colleague in the Munich office.

Mueller had reached some national stature within the power circles of the Reich for his more than enthusiastic management of the Jew Census for Bavaria. The census findings were consistent with those throughout the Reich: more Jews were killed or wounded at the front than their percentage of the population. The resulting outcome of the count was not released to the public.

Luftmann had watched diligently for them. Not good, the results probably didn't serve their purpose, support their myths, he reasoned cynically. He did not share these thoughts with Father Goetz. He couldn't appear too interested in Jewish affairs.

Father Goetz, on the other hand, raised the issue himself during one of their chats. "We don't see results in the Jew Census, Luftmann. Not made public because they aren't what the Pan-German, Alldeutsche Verband fanatics wanted," he observed.

Luftmann nodded. Not good, because German people could assume their government was protecting Jews from findings that showed them shirking their duty. This, in turn, could support rumors of a Jews-back-stabbing-the-Reich conspiracy, which notion appeared more and more in right-wing anti-Semitic publications, a blame bomb waiting to explode if Germany suffered defeat.

In approving Sepp's petition to return to active duty, the Berlin minister sent Mueller an official note, red-stamped, which was duly filed among the ministry records:

> *When we are sending boys and old men to fight at the front, are you devoted to the interests of the* KAISERREICH *and its struggle when you deny a trained officer's request to return to duty? Though blemished, this officer was once proven valiant and received high recognition from the* KAISERREICH. *Perhaps there is some personal consideration between Lt. Hofer and yourself since it came to my attention you are both from the same Bavarian town.*
>
> *— Reichminister Werner Haupt*

Sepp served honorably, bravely — nerves healed — having only one month before the war's sudden end. He suffered a leg and hip injury as he stormed an enemy dugout with his men. By late October 1918, right before the infamous November Armistice, das Eiserne Kreuz 2. Klasse was restored to Lt. Joseph 'Sepp' Hofer, displayed once again in the Burgfriedenstrasse window on white linen framed by dark wood — confusing everybody at the end of its long and circular journey.

In November, Kaiser Bill fled to Holland at armistice time, a strange armistice signed by neither Generals Ludendorff or von Hindenburg, the military dictatorship in command of the Reich those last months of the war, nor including any admission of German defeat. When the Kaiser abandoned his people, the monarchy collapsed. Then, in February, an unfamiliar entity called Democracy, called Republic, autocratically replaced the Kaiser's autocratic rule, imposed and arranged by the very politicians who had surrendered the nation to the Allies.

Meanwhile, when Fanny visited Sepp in the field hospital near Cologne, she learned that Sepp's injury was more complicated than originally thought, something about intricate hip-and-thigh-joint damage. It would take some time "to make him whole," the doctors said.

Marriage would have to wait until Sepp was well enough to return to Dachau. Unprepared for the delay and aside from living for her visits to Sepp, the eighteen-year-old — her years almost the same as the century — would have to find ways to keep busy.

Two months after the controversial November armistice, in Munich in a beer hall near the Odeonsplatz — where five years earlier in 1914 everyone was a good German — the German Workers' Party, *Deutsche Arbeiter Partei*, *DAP* for short, was born. Growing out of various Pan-Germanic groups, it was strongly nationalistic, obsessed with racial purity. It had a small group of fervent believers. Their liturgy condemned profiteering-Jew-stab-in-the-back betrayals as the cause of Germany's wartime defeat and decried the "November Criminals" who secretly signed the shameful armistice and undemocratically imposed a democratic republic to rule the country.

Once again, Luftmann's reasoning had been correct. Without the census release, it was easy for a humiliated nation in shock to accept the anti-Jew idea to explain the defeat of the Kaiserreich and the imperial troops.

Moving away from the goals of emancipation of forty-five years earlier, the DAP now declared assimilation a dirty word. Their ideology embraced a strict xenophobic exclusion for the protection of Germany, for the survival of the German race, indeed for the salvation of German Christendom as well. There were so many converts, German Christianity daily became more Jewish.

The noted sports journalist, Karl Harrer — a DAP founder — to her surprise contacted Fanny that March. In a note delivered via a right-wing Munich sports club where Fanny played from time to time, he invited her to meet with him at Dachau's Kraisy Inn.

It was not unusual, the connection between politics and sports. Almost every sports club, beer hall, trade union, newspaper, youth group, theater, library, even marriages and burials, were political, connected one way or another to the republic's hodgepodge of right or left or centrist political parties.

Sitting that day in the lounge of the inn on comfortable brown leather chairs, a small table with a tray of cookies and black tea between them, Harrer, a slim, compact man with smart eyes and a pleasant face, asked Fanny to join the DAP.

"How do you know me?" Fanny asked shyly. She had thought perhaps the invitation was for a sports interview.

"How can a sports writer not know of the Bavarian girl invited to try out for the Olympic Games?" he replied.

"Yes, but there were no Olympics for me because of the war, and now, for Germans, they say there will be no Olympics according to the peace treaty. I am an old story, a story that never happened."

He answered that gifted and true Germans like her had to unite to preserve what was best in them, that an athlete with her wholesome voelkische beauty and appearance could be a model for all true German women — perhaps a poster — for resisting the abuse, extortion, and manipulation of defeatists, war profiteers, foreign Bolsheviks whose mission was to bring the German people down. The German Workers' Party could bring the fragmented country, could bring the German people, together again.

Fanny thought it flattering that he would go to the trouble to notice her. She admired this dedication to German values in a sports writer, after all. And oh how she longed for unity and order and a way back to the true Germany without all the daily upheavals going on throughout the country. He was persuasive. Why shouldn't I accept, she reasoned, this invitation from so notable a man for so worthy a cause?

"The goals are appealing, Herr Harrer. My close friend, a wounded war hero, fought hard for our Germany. If I could do something useful it might be worthwhile."

"We work closely with the Steel Helmets Veterans Group," he added.

"I do need some time to think."

"I would expect that," he said pleasantly. "Here is DAP material for you to look over, Fraeulein. And the schedule of our meetings."

"In Dachau?"

"No," he laughed. "Not yet. But in Munich and many Dachauers travel to them. You would not be alone."

That same March day at supper, Fanny told her father about the invitation.

"You must be pleased. A woman! Politics! The attention now that women have the right to vote in this new republic. But with that right comes responsibility, Fanny, especially in these shaky times," Luftmann said carefully.

"You need to examine the beliefs of this German Workers' Party, of any party for that matter. The DAP make it easy. They have a platform, very clear, precise, the sum of what they stand for."

"You are familiar with them, Papa?"

"To survive, my dear, one needs to know what he can about what goes on in the world. In these chaotic times it is not easy. New governments, new political parties of all hues, pop up like daisies."

"Like weeds," offered Lotte in an uncharacteristic contribution to political discussion. "That German Workers' Party does not like — "

A small dish crashed to the floor.

"How clumsy of me! I am sorry, Lotte," Luftmann lied. "Good, not from your favorite set. It cracked only in two parts, it appears. Maybe you can repair it, you are so handy," he said retrieving the saucer fragments from the floor.

Lotte, her mind on sentences she liked to finish, hesitated, then said, "I will fix."

"What were you saying," Fanny asked. "About the German Workers' Party?"

Looking steadily at her husband, Lotte replied, "They do not like a lot of things."

Fanny gave an imperceptible shudder. That fleeting feeling within, a whiff, a sudden draft, not experienced in a while, visited her again. "Is that what you were going to say? Since when do you care about politics, Mother?"

"Don't ask foolish questions! Your mother does more than the best cooking in Dachau," Luftmann intervened, lightening the discussion. "So this journalist, he gave you their program, Fanny?"

"As a matter of fact, yes," said Fanny. "It's in a packet in my room."

"After supper why don't we look at it?"

"His seeking me out is flattering," she said, with a smile, the fleeting feeling gone as quickly as it had intruded. "To be seen as a model for German womanhood! Me! Especially by someone like Herr Harrer. But, yes, Papa, let's look at it together. Perhaps I will see what two and two adds up to," she promised, in their shorthand way of speaking. "I feel so useless. It is something to do that could be good until Sepp returns."

"Father Goetz announced in church this morning that the infirmary needs volunteers. So many war casualties," said Lotte, who attended Mass daily.

"The infirmary? That's interesting, too. It would be like helping Sepp as well."

"I'm glad you like what I say sometimes." Since she didn't say much, Lotte was only half joking, not looking up as she cleared the table. "I hope healing the leg and hip is not going to take much longer. I thought the Berlin hospital they shipped him to could fix everything. Poor boy, injuries not enough, they send him around like a package."

"They try everything. It must be done right, Mother. That is why they transferred him from Cologne to Bad Neuheim to try the water cure, the salt springs. It did calm his nerves, he wrote, but did not help the hip. We are lucky they sent him to Berlin to doctors who had studied under some famous doctor Trengel . . . Trandel . . ."

"Trendelenburg? The renowned orthopedic surgeon?"

"That's it, Papa! I know you know everything, but how do you know the name?"

"A long time ago, Fanny, I thought about a physician's life, studied a little. But I let it go."

"Why, Papa?"

"There were reasons," he said cryptically.

Luftmann could not explain that prominent Jewish doctors, focusing inexplicably on *ostjuden* versus *westjuden*, were well into the new Darwinian racial hygiene science, arguing which Jew was mentally superior, more fit for survival, publishing arguments for each side, thereby foolishly providing self-incriminating fuel to the growing anti-Semitism.

"Trendelenburg was famous. I thought he died," Luftmann said.

"Yes, well, he is old but still alive. Sepp wrote that he saw him. Trendelenburg spoke with the doctors and they are doing wonders ever since. They may even release Sepp. I could be bringing him home by summer."

"Wonderful news, Fanny," said Luftmann. "Then we wait, yes, and have a real healthy talk when he is here about this German Workers' Party. There is no rush, *gell?*"

"I can work at the infirmary and wait for Sepp. You're right. There's no rush, but I should let Herr Harrer know, shouldn't I?"

"It is the proper thing to do, I would think," said Luftmann. "He went to some trouble seeking you out. I am sure he expects an answer."

Lotte chimed in. "Sepp, home at last. Frau Hofer will be thankful. Maybe she will rely less on sipping, you know," she said, obliquely noting what the entire parish spoke about openly, Frau Hofer's drinking. "I give a prayer of thanksgiving at Mass."

"Please don't say anything, Mother. I am not sure what Sepp writes Frau Hofer. Since his move to Berlin, she has not visited. And the father doesn't go at all. Veterans conflict with his antiwar principles, he wrote. Miserable man. It's his son."

"Have you ever asked Frau Hofer to travel with you?"

"I did invite her, Mother, both times she refused," Fanny said. "Never giving any good reason. Is there a good reason not to visit one's son?"

"You shouldn't judge," scolded Lotte.

Pushing his chair from the table Luftmann said, "So, Fanny! You look over the material first. After all, you are not the child I used to read to after supper."

Herr Luftmann gave a worried smile. Had he succeeded only in delaying a bad decision by his daughter? Or was it put to bed for good? How could Fanny know the complex, mined political landscapes on which the new Deutsche Republik rested, understand the undercurrents? Women had won the right to vote for only a month, after all.

Chapter 15
Luftmann's Weimar World
1919

Politics in the Deutsche Republik, the country's new and official name, was no easy matter. It was led by Social Democrats, the same party whose leaders, many of Jewish descent it was noted in right-wing newspapers, had signed the armistice.

With its constitution devised in Weimar, however, historians were already referring to the new nation as the *Weimarer Republik*. As if a name could change anything, thought Luftmann. Who would know better than he?

There was a plethora of other political parties vying for power: three Communist, five Socialist, two Catholic, six liberal, five conservative, and now the new German Workers' Party that had captured Fanny's interest.

The political cauldron was a boiling stew of competing ideas, with myriad recipes and ingredients, all claiming to result in a perfect world for Germans and Germany and some, like the Communists, for the entire universe.

Their doctrinal menus included pro-worker stances, contra-class divisions, ultra nationalism, rabidly racial rules, restoration of the monarchy, anti-Bolshevism. Above all, however, each shared virulently anti-republic sentiment.

Struggling aggressively for dominance, they were constantly at one another's throats. Each had its own paramilitary groups armed for violence, like the Communists' Red Front League, the Social Democrats' Reichsbanner Red-Black-Gold, the right-wing Steel Helmet League of Front Soldiers, and, reactionary fanatics had the fringe Organisation Consul that thrived on political assassinations and revenge.

The DAP, for their strong-arm force, were using remnants from *Sturmabteilungen (SA)*, the storm detachments, an effective, nasty special force during the war. (How would Fanny know that? Understand it? She was young, impressionable.)

The DAP recruited others as well. Since the war, the concept of storm trooper had developed ideological overtones. The soldier-poet Franz

Schauwecker wrote:

> "A new kind of man,
> a man in the highest exaltation of all manly qualities
> and so harmonized and from a single caste
> that one sees a man in the word *fighter*."

Would Fanny know this poem? Should she see it, confusing her even more? With Sepp twice a war hero, would she sympathize?

This warrior notion, fueled by such tenets as "hatred was manly," "complaining was feminine," "violence a life goal" and "might makes right," was exploited by the German Workers' Party and acted out by their SA Storm Trooper paramilitary group.

Ironic, thought Luftmann, Germany a nation with so many armies, yet according to treaty negotiations in Versailles, they were forbidden to have any.

Added to these offshoot political gangs were the effective and dangerous Freikorps, government-sanctioned yet anti-republic, wanting a return of Bismarck's Kaiserreich. Praised by General Ludendorff, that protector of the German Volk, the Freikorps were heavily armed, recruiting former military and youth. It made no sense that the republic's Social Democrat government employed them, but they were needed to overturn revolutions, to stamp out Bolshevism, to stay in power, to avoid total anarchy.

They knew no bounds, had no rules. Shutting down a poorly executed left-wing uprising in Berlin, the Freikorps murdered radical Spartacists Rosa Luxembourg and attorney Karl Leibknecht after arresting them.

The slaughtered, outspoken anarchists had preached chaos, chanted their antiwar slogans while Sepp was fighting at the front. Fanny must bear them ill will, Luftmann reasoned, as other patriots did. Parading such opinions while German soldiers were dying! He couldn't fathom people who spouted such suicidal provocations, begging for retribution.

The republic had troubles.

There were almost daily revolutions throughout the country. There was street fighting, brutal physical encounters on once peaceful boulevards, ugly disruptions at gatherings, rowdy name-calling sessions in the Reichstag. There were Soviet republics in Germany, Bolsheviks in Bavaria, senseless killings, a lack of food and goods, severe economic reparations demanded for the war's victors. Widespread chaos combined with profound loss, shame, and humiliation.

Fanny was aware of some of those things, he guessed. She did read the newspapers about the disorder. But did she understand what they meant? Having knowledge isn't to understand full implications. Knowing is having the check; understanding is cashing it.

All in all, the peace was harder than the war. Germans could not come to terms with losing the war, blaming those who in November 1918 had signed the Armistice — an unorthodox, irregular armistice without admitting defeat — blaming those who had unseated the Kaiser, destroyed the monarchy, betrayed the army, betrayed the people, those who stabbed Germany in the back, blaming the deceitful November Criminals.

How would Fanny put all of that together, he wondered?

In fact, how could any political party give back a nation, a German nation, to its once-proud people?

Chapter 16
The German Workers' Party
The 25 Points

The infirmary started Fanny with four days a week, assigning her to the overcrowded veteran wards, bed after bed of bandaged faces, tractioned bodies, blood tubes, groans, and intravenous drips. She cleaned their wounds, wrote their letters home, read newspapers and books aloud, and served snacks to those able to digest them. She always encouraged them to talk as she sat by their sides.

She learned to control her emotions. These blind, crippled, mutilated young men were the lucky ones. Out of the 11 million men fighting for the Kaiserreich, six million were gone and still counting. Either dead or lost somewhere.

At the end of day, safely home in her Burgfrieden cocoon, safe from viewing, smelling, hearing the horrors of war in the wards, Fanny would review the DAP package. She knew that she knew more than her father thought she did, and she knew that what she knew wasn't nearly enough.

In her sheltered four-poster bed, large enough for two people, with lace and lilac velvet draped over the domed canopy, velvet bows tied to the bedposts, there was a comforting womb-like safety. Sitting upright, her back bolstered by puffed goose down pillows, Fanny looked at the many religious pictures decorating the pale pink walls. The only family portraits were those of the Holy Family.

She sighed. Taking a deep breath, Fanny was ready to tackle the political material.

She read that the Deutsche Arbeiter Partei was founded in Munich in the hotel Fürstenfelder Hof on the fifth of January 1919.

Then there were pages with photographs of the founders and their short biographies. Among them she recognized Herr Harrer.

At the centerfold, she came to the meat. The meat her father said she had to chew and digest. There was the German Workers' Party 25-Point Platform.

No secret, in plain language and bold print: what they stood for, what they proposed, their vision for a future Germany, there for all to see.

Fanny liked that.

Maybe the DAP was the answer, as Herr Harrer had told her, maybe it could restore order and German values. Were they extreme right, extreme left? Hard for Fanny to tell. Radical nationalists that cared about the working classes? What did it matter as long as what they proposed was good for the people? For the nation? What did it matter, if they could fix what was broken?

It would not be a simple decision. But surely a citizen had to get involved. And Fanny saw the DAP made it easier. They knew where they stood, where they wanted to go. She read carefully the full text of the 25-Point Program.

So many of their doctrines — right to employment, communal department stores, extending the old age pension, a national education program for all classes, prohibition of child labor — were good reforms for workers, the elderly, and youths.

The classlessness particularly meant something to Fanny. Sepp's living on one side of a street making him different from, less privileged than, her in the Burgfrieden made no sense to Fanny, never did. Though the status of Burgfrieden seemed important to her father, that he lived there, for her father it was somehow a matter of acceptance, never an attitude of condescension.

But there were problems. Fanny had trouble with Points 4, 7, 23, and 24. Shuffling the pages, she looked back at them.

Point 4 said only a member of the German race could be a citizen, race defined by purity of blood. Purity of blood? Then, if Jews were a separate race as they preached, Samson Gutmann, whose son died defending the Reich, would be denied his citizenship? Have it taken away? That was troublesome. Was this what they really meant? They didn't say it, but it followed, thought Fanny.

This made Point 7 even more onerous: expelling noncitizens if they had to, for the good of true Germans. Here they referred to noncitizens as foreign elements. Again Samson came to mind. He had told Sepp on one of their trips to the Kiembock family farm that his own family had hailed from Hainsfarth in neighboring Swabia.

Sepp had told her Samson said with pride that Jews were in Hainsfarth as far back as the 13th century and that six families with permanent residence rights were present in the 16th century. Would families such as these not only lose their citizenship but be called "foreign elements" under the German Workers' Point 7? Be expelled?

Could they really mean to apply that to people who had lived in Germany for centuries? It was problematic to Fanny. How could she support this?

Sepp had also told her, "Samson said they had their own synagogue in Hainsfarth built very early, the beginning of the 1700s. I remember because I was surprised with us having no Jews in Dachau all those years. There was a Jewish public school, too. Many left, he said; less than 150 Jews living there now. The Gutmann family produced many doctors and professors that dispersed all throughout Europe."

"Interesting! He knows more about his family than I do about mine. So, with all the doctors and professors, how did he become a Haendler?"

Sepp laughed. "He told me that he was good at making deals and that he recognized excellent products when he saw them. So a talent, I guess. Oh yes," Sepp added with a smile, "he says the good *Schnaps* — *Slivowitz*, I think — he always brings to seal the deal doesn't hurt."

And there was Point 23 eliminating a free and diverse press, a press restricted to true Germans. That position was counter to the way she had been raised. The DAP wouldn't be able to express their own views today without a free press. It was hard to deal with this severe restriction as to who could be journalists and who could publish newspapers. Bad thinking, Fanny judged this point not a good idea. After all, how dangerous was a free press to the health of her country?

Finally, Point 24 about religious freedom and positive Christianity.

Though the Roman Catholic Church declared itself the one true church, it never talked about eliminating others, which was hinted at in Point 24. The Catholic Church mostly prayed for others to see the light. The others, Father Goetz said, were wrong-headed. As for the Jewish faith — though in the past they did bash pagan temples and destroy pagan gods — they were not yet a completed faith until they embraced Lord Jesus as Messiah as predicted in their very own Hebrew Scriptures. He had specifically argued against positive Christianity.

"Positive Christianity," he had said, "fights against the Church's traditional dogma, dismissing our fundamental teachings that Christ was sacrificed on the cross to save humanity and for human redemption in the Kingdom of God."

He had explained that positive Christianity wanted to replace the crucified Christ with an active Aryan Jesus. "Aryan! *Herrenrasse*, the superior German race that Voelkische doctrines hail! They claim the historical Jesus fought against Judaism.

"They oppose the Hebrew Scriptures. It's contrary to all Christian teachings. Omitting the house of David? A Second Coming of our Lord without Jews seeing the light of the cross? Soon we hear from them that He was turned away from the Kraisy and was born in a Dachau District barn!"

Fanny remembered it because it had elicited a rare laugh during the service.

She reread the 25 Points, then leaned back in her bed, the wooden crucifix hanging from the wall above her head, the Blessed Virgin Mother smiling benevolently from across the room, babe in arms. Then she placed the pages neatly on the linden wood night table next to her Bible and the Brothers Grimm.

Shutters were creaking as the late winter foothill winds did not easily surrender to the coming March solstice. Fanny unfolded the extra down quilt and drew it over her. She stretched her lithe body, feeling secure and safe within the confines of her blessed room (it had to be blessed with all the icons, she thought), safe from the nation's stormy chaos, safe from the groans and pleadings of the casualties in the ward.

Well, when Sepp returned, clearly there would be a lively discussion. And she would have things to contribute, questions to ask.

Sepp's return. Another problem.

She had never let Sepp know what was going on in his beloved Reich for which he had fought so valiantly. It was a policy urged by the doctors. Insulated in the hospitals, concentrating only on treatments and cures, Fanny doubted any of the severely injured veterans knew of the instability in their country.

"They need all their energy focused on recovery, on healing," was what doctors told visitors. How would soldiers handle the shock once they returned to their homes? Would the hospitals prepare them?

So much to worry about.

Back to the German Workers' Party. Dozing off, it occurred to Fanny that maybe she should not be on a poster after all. Not now! Those troublesome positions they advocated made her uncomfortable.

On the other hand, weren't some rules meant to be broken, not etched in stone tablets like the Ten Commandments? Weren't some rules, once people realized how harsh they were, what their consequences could be, meant to be discarded? Wasn't it natural to yearn for order and discipline and traditional standards?

She couldn't know she needn't have bothered herself trying to figure it out.

Chapter 17
November Criminals

They were waiting on the platform at the Anhalter Bahnhof, Berlin's gateway to the south, looking more like a coliseum than a railway station. Sepp, in full military dress, his medals and epaulets glittering in the late morning sun, was using crutches. He told Fanny how eager he was to return home. It was the end of summer, an especially beautiful time in Dachau.

"We waited long for this day," said Fanny.

Four men sporting red armbands approached them. Their leader, a stocky youth of medium height, demanded Sepp remove his epaulets, medals, and officer's insignia.

"Who are you?" Sepp asked sternly, looking confused.

"Who are we? We are the Red Front People's Army," replied the leader, who looked too young to ever have seen a bullet in the war. "Remove your trinkets from the illegal war against the people."

"Are you insane?"

"Sepp, be careful," warned Fanny.

"Keep your mouth shut," one snapped. "Or we shut it for you. And you? You call us crazy, huh? We're crazy enough to rip those war ornaments off you."

He moved forward. Fanny screamed for help. The stocky man shoved her. She shoved him back with all her strength. After a brief pause, he slapped Fanny hard across the face. "You'll never do that again, Fraeulein," he said.

"Fanny! Are you all right?" Sepp asked, trying to move toward the man, hobbling on one crutch while waving the other as a weapon, "What kind of men are you to strike a woman so?" he said angrily.

The men advanced toward Sepp menacingly. "We'll show you what kind of men we are."

Sepp tried to use his crutch on the men, but they knocked him down easily. He reached in his pocket, but only the intervention of a railroad official with a loaded weapon who had heard Fanny's screams prevented their stripping Sepp's uniform. The hoodlum pack ran down the platform. From their shouted curses one could tell they were bent on violence.

"We can't keep them away, these left-wing thugs! A plague on the November Criminals who spawned Germans like these," said the elderly railroad man. "It wouldn't have happened in the Kaiserreich! I can promise you that." Then as if remiss, he asked, "Are you hurt, sir?"

"I'm fine. But what are *November Criminals?*"

"He's been in hospital since war's end, sir. Knows nothing about what has been going on," explained a trembling Fanny.

"In hospital so long a time? The November Criminals are the men who signed the illegal armistice and betrayed Germany," informed the station master. "Where did you get your injury?"

"Ardennes, the forest," Sepp told him.

"They act like foreigners, bullies, those Reds, not true Germans." He brushed off Sepp's uniform and returned his crutches to him. "A *vielen Dank, Herr Leutnant,* for your service to the Kaiserreich," he added, shaking Sepp's hand. "We would have won if not for treachery within. A surrender without defeat? What is that except betrayal?"

Meanwhile, the gang had launched an attack farther down the platform on another veteran, one who had lost an arm, his jacket sleeve tucked flat and neatly in his belt. Sepp recognized him from the hospital. A Thuringian fellow from Erfurt. He, too, was in full dress but unaccompanied. Roughing him up, they tore off his insignia and medals as the train rolled in. Sepp watched, helpless to do anything for his comrade Frontsoldat.

The trainman, firing a warning shot, started to run down the platform shouting at the Reds, "*Schweine, Rote Hunde, Schweine!*"

As the gang ran off, the soldier fell to his knees, wailing a duet with the approaching train's whistle. "Mein Gott, Mein Gott! Is this the kind of Germany we sacrificed our blood for?"

Sepp was ashen, his expression an angry grimace Fanny had never seen before. Cemented where he stood on the platform, he clutched the only weapon he carried, retrieved from his pocket, the small Zigeuner knife with the crooked cross given to him by the Gypsies.

Fanny tugged at him to board the train. "I am so sorry, Sepp," she cried. "There was no way to prepare you for the chaos throughout our fatherland. You had to heal."

"Are you sure you're all right? You're cheek is red from the pig's hand."

"I'm sure. I worried for your hip! Let's just think about getting home."

Sepp had hoped for a veteran's welcome of some kind, a redemption to remove the memory of disgrace of his last return to Dachau when the ministry stripped him of his Iron Cross. He had looked forward to a restored standing in his community, not to his medals being ripped off by marauding Red thugs in a Berlin railway station, not to witnessing an assault on a vulnerable Frontgemeinischaft veteran comrade from the hospital, not to hearing about November Criminals signing a bogus armistice.

It was a profound shock, this reception, an enemy attack in his homeland by Germans. He would not forget the events of this August day, that glorious, long ago other one when war was declared erased from his mind. "Are these the kind of agitators my father works into a frenzy?" he asked, disgusted with the men and their behavior.

As they climbed aboard the train, Fanny was still talking, but Sepp was not listening. He decided once home in Dachau to join forces with disciplined groups proud to be German that stood steadfastly against cowardly thugs who desecrated Germany's long heritage of valor and honor. The Steel Helmets for *Frontsoldaten* had representatives come to the hospital, a group supporting veterans in need. He would seek them out, seek their direction.

Once seated, the train's steady roll and drone put Sepp to sleep, a troubled sleep. Frowns rutted his forehead as if permanent. The cap clenched tightly in his lap no longer hid the white-gray streak parting his thick black hair.

Traveling that day in late August — the nation's diverse landscapes of forests and mountains, foothills and pastures, rivers and lakes passing them by — Fanny's thoughts went to the straightforward program of the German Workers' Party: inspiring, nationalistic, flowing with Germanic pride and steadfastness, and, most important, forward-looking, promising hope through ideals and tradition.

Having fought so bravely at the front, why should Sepp be so humiliated at home? It should be the government, a fractured-broken-down government that couldn't govern, that should feel mortified, the Deutsche Reich government, an impotent republic, a disgrace, unable to protect its own citizenry.

As Sepp dozed, his body occasionally jerking in a restless sleep, Fanny reviewed the trials of that terrible year, gazing at but not seeing the fleeting bucolic, serene vistas framed by the train's window as they chugged along home. That Dachauers, in fact all the German people, had gotten through those early months of 1919, was in itself a tribute to German resilience.

What was bad became worse; what was worse became intolerable, the peace harder to bear than the war. The June negotiations in Versailles had yielded a tyrannical treaty, exacting more than its pound of flesh. Everyone who followed the negotiations knew it was coming. (Herr Luftmann gave the family weekly reports at Sunday dinner.) They just didn't know how bad it would be, that negotiations were all on the side of vindictive victors, meaning no negotiations at all.

From the year's beginning, everything had been turmoil, chaos, violence, suffering throughout Germany, hitting their Dachau worst last April. During Easter, the lowest point on Palm Sunday, the Bolsheviks, already installed in Munich, took over their town, establishing a Soviet republic. She tried to avoid thinking about those days in Dachau.

Chapter 18
Dachau Shattered

There were traumatic events in Dachau the winter and spring of 1919. Roaming its streets were thousands of unemployed, displaced, angry Pumf employees recruited from all over the Reich. The treaty outlawed the production of armaments. There would be no jobs at the shutdown facility, never to be reopened as a munitions and gunpowder factory. But still they walked the streets, stranded, nowhere else to go.

Many of the men attended meetings of the Communist Party at the Trade Union Hall that were organized by Ludwig Hofer, now an important figure. The newcomers knew nothing about his reputation among the regular citizens of the town.

Nor did they know the Communist Party was in an internal struggle with the radical International Spartacus Group, outsiders calling themselves Dachau representatives. Many had actually fought in both Russian revolutions, 1907 and 1916. Foreigners! Not true Germans!

Fanny, like other Dachauers, resented strangers, foreigners really, coming and making problems. She quarreled with her father about these troublemakers.

"Not true Germans, Papa," she said with passion. "True Germans don't act that way."

"What exactly is a true German, Fanny?" he said, calmly but clearly questioning her way of thinking. "What is going on is not good no matter who does it."

With all the discord they couldn't even count on Munich. As he was about to resign, leftist Bavarian Premier Kurt Eisner was shot dead in the Landtag, which daily became more a war zone than a legislative body.

Hofer was all over the place, never up to any good. Reacting to the Freikorps murders of Spartacists Luxembourg and Leibknecht in Berlin, he mobilized 500 Dachau laborers to riot against the Dachau District administration.

Another Hofer escapade, Fanny sighed. No wonder Sepp's mother drank so much. In the middle of the night — darkness a spawning time for terror and cruelty — the leftists, led by Hofer, stormed the home of the district administrator, taking him captive, roughing him up in front of his wife and his children.

"We lost our jobs, our pay, we cannot return to our homes, our families are sick worrying over food on the table," were the shouts as they pummeled him.

They released him the next day, not having a clue as to what to do with the terrified man, another Hofer plan having only a beginning – making trouble – but no middle or end.

Poor Frau Hofer could not stand the violence or her husband's actions or being treated as an outcast by her own neighbors and parishioners in her hometown.

"I think she is near the end of her rope," Fanny had told her mother.

Chapter 19
Family Quarrels

That terrible year, Lotte repeatedly reproached her husband, blaming him for the train line from the Pumf to the Dachau station. It made a convenient connection to both Ingolstadt and Munich, fueling the street fighting with replacements and munitions. And those trips had been going on for so long.

"Murdering made easier with your tracks," Lotte had cried. "You feed the fighters with weapons. Though your factory is shut down now, it still brings trouble."

She always referred to the munitions and gunpowder plants as his factory, saying it wouldn't have been there without his gift of the land; therefore the government wouldn't have added the extra tracks to the Dachau station; therefore killers and killing replacements would have had difficulty coming to Dachau.

Today the quarrel had new dimensions. "You are the cause, Christian, of those 8,000 men out of jobs with no place to go, roaming the streets of our town. You had to give the land for that Pumf, why?"

"That is an old story, Lotte. I have heard those words before from you," he said tiredly, slowly sipping his coffee while eating black bread and jam.

"Yes, well, here are more words! Another tragedy! Just yesterday in Munich, a truck of uniformed boy scouts killed by God knows whom," she crossed herself.

Luftmann looked surprised.

"Yes, I read the *Amper-Bote*, too," she pulled it off the kitchen counter, placing it on the table. "What do you think? Your wife's a fool? Each side thinking those poor boys were the enemy. What enemy? They were Germans! We are all Germans!" She paused for breath. "The Reds, the Whites, the whatever color they are, would not be fighting their battles here in Dachau without the Pumf and the railroad tracks that make ways to kill easier and for men to get back and forth to do it."

"That's not fair — "

"Fair? That poor Frau Hofer suffering so! Her husband carrying on, instigating trouble with the men out of work, bringing in people I have never heard of. Dachau a battlefield! Can you imagine? Our Dachau! Frau Hofer, sure she is *betrunken* half the time, but she wasn't always a drinker. You and your Eigentum are a curse, Christian."

"That's not fair, Lotte," Luftmann repeated.

"Fair? Again you say fair? What do murderers know about fair," she shot back.

Luftmann had no response.

Fanny had quarreled with her father, as well, refusing coffee and Schwarzbrot as they sat around the linden wood table.

Earlier, on this Palm Sunday, with no service because of riots in the streets, Fanny had gone to St. Jakob's, concerned for Father Goetz. He was not there. The Reds had taken over the boys' school next door. She passed Frau Mueller's on the way home. The door was wide open! Smashed in! Fanny called out. There was no answer. She went inside. Things were broken, furnishings upset. Frau Mueller was gone.

Terrified, then angry, Fanny returned home to find her parents having a light second breakfast.

"Who would do such things? Violations! First the boys' school! Then Frau Mueller's home! A private home! Mother is right. Bringing in these outsiders to provoke violence. Only strangers! These gangs of Reds! They cannot be true Germans, Papa."

"And the Whites?"

"They are our veterans; the Freikorps are true Germans trying to restore order."

"True German, you use that phrase often, Fanny. Where do you find these words?" Beneath his orderly beard, his round face had turned pale, bushy eyebrows converged, a meeting of concern. "What is a true German?"

"Not these hoodlums the papers report who are disrupting our way of life, who are led by foreign elements," she replied angrily. "Here, I read it to you. 'So many foreign Jewish names at the head, leaders of insurrection.' Then they give names. Mama read them, too. Who are these people? 'Axelrod, Levien, Levine, Luxembourg, Liebknecht, Eisner — ' "

"Luxembourg and Leibknecht are dead, murdered by your Freikorps! No trial, no jury! They were German citizens, Fanny. I don't like their politics, but there are rights!"

"I don't care! They preached sedition and surrender while my Sepp was fighting bravely for the Kaiserreich. They all should have left if they don't like the way we are. They were free to go. Their ways are not true Germans ways."

"You are not thinking straight," he told her.

Chapter 20
Geiselmord
The Murder Scourge

As to the Mueller home and the broken door, with the Freikorps on the march and more than ready to fight them, the Dachau Reds, desperate, led by Ludwig Hofer, were taking "capitalist" hostages.

Hofer and six men from the Red Front gang had broken down the door of the stately Mueller home.

"Marius Mueller, pig, warmonger, enemy of the worker, show yourself!" he called out, rampaging through the house. "Coward! Come out! Mueller, show yourself!"

The aging Berlin beauty Frau Mueller cowered in a corner of the parlor whimpering, hiding behind the long velvet draperies. Not seeing well and understanding less, she answered the invaders.

"Not here," she said, disclosing her hiding place. "He is not here."

"Enough! The struggle won't wait," said Hofer, clearly concerned about the advancing Freikorps. "We take her! The bitch with airs," he cursed, dragging the half-blind, hysterical woman from her home. He loaded her roughly on an open truck with twenty other captives — another woman among them — randomly collected from what the Reds believed to be prosperous agricultural property owners from the Dachau countryside. They were in fact mostly those who were in the wrong place at the wrong time. The Reds had to get even somehow for the Dachau farmers' resistance to the left-wing Farmers' League.

"See your neighbors shutting their blinds? They don't want to know what happens to you, all cowards; no one comes to the rescue," Hofer taunted the prisoners as the truck rolled through town on its way to the Mueller Brewery. "Cowards," he repeated, sitting with his guns and thugs amongst the terrified captured civilians.

There were gunshots. This not from the Freikorps Whites, but from men in doorways dressed in brown with red sickle and hammer emblems. Soviet emblems. A war within a war within a war had started, as well. The so-called real Bolsheviks challenging the ersatz ones.

Amidst all of this, Father Goetz had heard from a parishioner, who watched events from his window across the way, that the hostages were going to the Mueller Brewery and that Frau Mueller was among them.

"I saw her on the open truck, Father. But what could I do? I am one man with a family? I came to you as soon as it looked safe to go outside."

The priest dashed out of St. Jakob's hoping to intervene, which explained why he was absent when Fanny had looked for him there. There was going to be no Palm Sunday service, anyway.

On that eventful 1919 Palm Sunday, the real Bolsheviks overthrew the Dachau Communist six-day regime to establish a true Soviet republic. How would Father Goetz know who to deal with to free the hostages? Nevertheless, he continued on his way to the Mueller Brewery.

When he arrived at the three-story pitched-roof building, Father Goetz did not find orderly captors, only three agitated guards in a huddle standing duty, talking excitedly about the Soviet Reds' counterattack against them. They looked surprised when he entered, hair disheveled, breathing heavily from the run.

"Who is in charge?" he asked.

"Our Comrade Hofer leads us," aggressively answered a burly older man.

"Where is he?"

"Out fighting for the people," came the dogmatic reply.

"What do you want here, Father?" asked the youngest Red, clearly not quite used to the fact that there was no God, therefore no Church, therefore no *Fathers*.

Goetz looked around and decided that was his man.

"Where are the prisoners?" he asked, as if certain they were there.

"What's it to you?" the burly older man intervened.

Goetz looked only at the boy.

"They're in the cellar," he said, pointing to the stairway.

"I need to go there to see a parishioner," he explained while walking to the stairs.

No one stopped him.

He found the twenty captives in a damp, chairless, stone-walled room filled with barrels of fermenting water, malt, yeast, and hops. There was a powerful odor.

Frau Mueller was standing separate from the others in the back, leaning against the wall. It was, after all, her brewery. The others talked with one another, ignoring her. The priest surmised it was due to the fact that they didn't know the Dachau woman, rather than any elevated position she held there in the brewery basement.

There was a hush when he reached the bottom of the stairs, then a unified sigh of relief, clearly because he wasn't one of the guards. Father Goetz walked directly toward Frau Mueller, who was having trouble standing.

Disoriented, when the priest touched her arm, her deteriorated vision as always exacerbated by fear, she started to scream hysterically, scratching and kicking at him, a wild, weak, cornered animal.

"It is Father Goetz, Frau Mueller. Father Goetz, your priest," he repeated several times, holding her off, until she understood and collapsed in his arms.

"I come back," he said to the others, as he carried Frau Mueller up the stairs.

Only the three guards were there. But he heard sounds of a truck and loud noise coming from outside the brewery. Was Hofer returning? Danger, he must have thought at the moment, because he did not plead for the others.

"She is ill," he said authoritatively. "I must take her. A side door?"

The still believing youth automatically pointed the way, as the noise outside became a commotion. Wounded Reds on stretchers, blood everywhere, were carried through the front door.

He heard a voice sounding like Hofer's shout, "Kill them! Bring them up! *Schnell!* Kill them all! The Freikorps attack us. Not the Soviets. They come toward the brewery. They heard about the hostages!"

As slender as she was, her weight was a burden for the elderly priest, who made a speedy exit, barely holding up the frail woman. Once outside, he was able to toss Frau Mueller, like a sack of corn, over his back so he could move more quickly.

"Kill them! Now! That is an order!" Hofer shouted, his familiar speech-making voice blaring from the brewery.

Father Goetz stood still until he heard gunshots and cries, one shot after the other. Tears rolled down his cheeks. He made the sign of the cross, muttering a prayer for the victims he had been unable to save, those he had told he would be back.

He had intended to trade himself for them, hoping a man of God was an attractive catch for the battle-crazed, godless Bolsheviks. Carrying his burden, he trudged back to the rectory, deciding to use side streets all the way.

The civilian hostages? *Geiselmord!* A murder scourge! All executed!

Including the one woman, further provoking the Freikorps efforts for revenge against the "non-German elements."

In her heart, Fanny had welcomed them. The real Germans, Germans who did not kill civilians, Germans who would restore order and respect to her nation. Germans who would honor Sepp for his bravery in the trenches.

Chapter 21
Collateral Damage

Frau Hofer, sipping her fourth cup of Slivowitz, sat in her house on the right side of Burgfriedenstrasse (which was the wrong side, the working-class side).

It was just before dark, but no lights brightened her kitchen. She still wore bedclothes, a dusky gray flannel gown, once white, and a worn red chenille robe. Outside, there were sporadic gunshots and people brawling in the streets.

Dachau, quiet, serene Dachau on the clear blue River Amper, where she played as a child, where her family and neighbors were respectful, friendly, where people knew manners — had disappeared. Part of her life extinguished, in a stupor, she wept, thinking of those better times. She drained the cup of plum brandy made salty by her tears.

When work stopped at the Pumf, Ludwig tried to take advantage of the opportunity to enlist the newly unemployed strangers into the Dachau Communist Party.

Though starving through the turnip years, freezing through cruel winters without coal, civilians and soldiers rioting for peace, the country was still in shock when news of the secret 1918 armistice arrived.

Frau Hofer was in shock, but not her husband. He told her the humiliating defeat was an opportunity and he told her to stop her incessant weeping; it annoyed him.

Ludwig had a captive audience, these disgruntled strangers, at Communist Party meetings he organized at the Trade Union Hall. They were men out of work, hungry, many homeless. But they weren't seen as Dachauers by Dachauers, who labeled them outside agitators. To those who attended, Hofer was an important figure, but not among people his wife had known all her life. To them he was a traitor, not a true German.

In church, she took to sitting in a back pew, alone, not just because of her alcohol odor, but because she imagined great hostility coming from parishioners toward anyone close to godless Bolsheviks. How much closer could you be than married to one? Then, after the Geiselmord, it was no longer imagination. In church she was shunned.

Her thoughts wandered, sitting there in the slowly darkening room. Ludwig was out there. He was a target for getting killed. Or maybe he would kill more people, who knew? Either way it wasn't good. Who would take care of her? Sepp away in the hospital. If only Sepp were home. He would take care of her. He was a war hero.

She went to pour another cup of plum brandy, but the bottle was empty. She got up slowly, looked in the cupboard for more. But like the nursery rhyme, her cupboard was bare. Frau Hofer needed more to drink and she needed to find her husband. Where would she get another bottle, maybe two more bottles to get her through the night?

Did she have enough money? Shops were closed. She would go to the Hoerhammer Inn. There were not enough marks in the jar kept in the kitchen cabinet to pay, but surely they would trust her. She was a Dachauer.

Frau Hofer, carrying two empty bottles in a red, crocheted net bag, teetering from side to side, left her home. Walking in the center of Burgfriedenstrasse, she called out "Ludwig, Ludwig!"

She hadn't changed to outer clothes. Still in nightdress and robe, she appeared more an apparition than a person.

"Ludwig, Ludwig," she called out, the only civilian in the street's center as bullets flew past her courtesy of Reds, Bolsheviks, and the Freikorps

"*Raus, Raus,*" came shouts from all sides as she walked the streets searching for plum brandy and her husband. They held their fire for a moment, but Frau Hofer continued on.

While Sepp dozed on the train home and Fanny looked at the countryside, Frau Hofer finally locked horns and face to face had an encounter with a barrage of bullets. Riddled front and back by piercing missiles as if for target practice, they won the match.

And the Freikorps won, overturning the Dachau Soviet republic, Bolsheviks and Communists alike.

Later Father Goetz would tell Sepp, "She was drinking more, Sepp. Living on the Slivowitz. We warned her to stay off the streets with all the violence erupting. But that day she walked right into the sniper crossfire, as if hypnotized, deaf and blind, just calling out your father's name and carrying empty bottles in her net shopping bag. It was getting dark. We don't know whose bullets killed her."

As the train chugged on along the captivating German countryside and, not knowing the tragic news that awaited them in Dachau, Fanny's thoughts returned more and more to the German Workers' Party. A hunger for hope, order, and respect became part of her being.

Chapter 22
Weddings and Partys
1919

After the shock, the funeral, the period of mourning, Sepp and Fanny posted their wedding bans in late September. Meanwhile the Steel Helmets, who had become more political and more violently active since the days after the armistice, had recommended to Sepp the German Workers' Party, the very party that attracted Fanny.

Their September marriage was a simple service at St. Jakob's. Little fanfare, Fanny did not wear the colorful *Dachau Tracht*, choosing muted hues in her quiet blue smock with her special bridal crown. She had the traditional silver *Florschnalle* clasped at the high neck of her blouse. Sepp dressed in uniform, in defiance and in deference to war casualties, in deference to the Frontgemeinschaft, in deference to those now eight million Germans, according to the revised count, wounded, dead, missing, or prisoners from the eleven million mobilized.

Members of the congregation dressed plainly, too. Bavarians did not have much taste for making merry in their customary lighthearted fashion, Bavarians who had once been derided by the more stiff-necked, serious, northern German states.

For all citizens of Bismarck's vanished Kaiserreich. the world had fallen apart around them. They and their country were humiliated losers left only with a weak left-wing, disorderly, ineffective democratic republic they didn't understand at all.

No, it was not time for a big church wedding. But a smiling Gretl was there for the wedding Mass. Forgetting much of what she had ever known, there was no fear any longer of Hebrew chanting. She might, in fact, have forgotten that God lived in that building, and Luftmann saw no reason to remind her.

"We celebrate our love with our families," whispered Fanny as they walked together up the aisle. "And with the memory of your poor mother in our heart.

Her life was not easy, Sepp. Maybe she is in a happier place."

"I want to believe that," Sepp replied.

"I hoped to do more for your wedding, but things can't be accomplished in a day," said Luftmann, giving them a private space in his Burgfrieden home but thinking about the farms, outside Dachau, nearby but still the country, thinking about food and safety.

Lotte wept and could not speak at all.

Ludwig Hofer, hiding in the countryside, did not attend the religious ceremony, both on principle and fear, no longer a big shot but a wanted man.

There had been no more talk in the Luftmann household of symposiums or political discussions. Living through the Dachau revolutions, the fear and violence, the executions, Luftmann had little faith in any more intellectual deliberations about politics. He watched in vain as his daughter moved further away from him in ideas.

They still mourned Frau Hofer and the manner of her death. How could Sepp argue for moderation, restraint, tolerance, and equality when, unthinkably, his mother could be shot in peacetime walking the streets of her own town? When unimaginably a German warrior, a hero, could be assaulted in public, his valor jeered at, his patriotism mocked? How could he preach moderation and restraint when neither moderation nor restraint was present anywhere he looked?

Unlike the wedding ceremony, the wedding feast was splendid, without restriction, the scarce times ignored — a lavish open house for the parish featured tables laden with herring in sour cream, roast pork, potato pancakes with cranberries, cabbage rolls, plum brandy, an assortment of wines, beer and ales, and of course the *Sekt*, champagne to toast the bride and groom and, as the saying went, for everyone else to live a ripe old age. Frau Luftmann had reluctantly conceded the excess to her husband though reminding him that "people were starving in their land."

"We have but one daughter," he said. "God will allow us to eat and drink well on her wedding day."

That late September night, the young couple's marital union, in that same four-poster bed of her childhood that had waited patiently to be filled by two, was more sober than what they had awaited for so long. In the privacy of the Hofer section of the Luftmann home, they joined together, sweet mountain air wafting through their windows, shutters rustling softly, interspersed by muted gasps of quieted passion and murmurs of everlasting love.

It was only in October of that harsh 1919 year that Fanny and Sepp Hofer went to a German Workers' Party meeting at the Hofbraeukeller in Munich — a much-heralded event since its honored speaker, a new member, had made a strong impression at a meeting a month earlier.

The murder of Frau Hofer and the events at the Anhalter station had made Luftmann's efforts useless, efforts meant to dissuade Fanny and Sepp from participation in such a group. What they wanted was not what he wanted.

On flyers throughout Dachau, Sepp had seen a picture of the guest lecturer. It was the same man who had inspired him to fight the good fight so very long ago on that August day at Munich's Odeonsplatz, the man with the mustache and the hypnotic face of patriotism and love for country.

The DAP meeting was well attended; many people stood until the uniformed brown-shirted SA guards from the party's paramilitary organization brought more folding chairs from a neighboring beer hall.

They weren't the only Dachauers there. Ernst Schtreuk, the brewery worker with the missing fingers, attended. He seemed to be known, to have some standing, judging by many friendly greetings.

Marius Mueller was there as well, giving a courteous nod to Sepp and Fanny, perhaps acknowledging the Luftmann family's concern for his mother after her horrific experience when the Reds were in power those few days. They had taken her in to stay with them until the next government was in place.

Fanny and Sepp sat with the journalist Herr Harrer who, it was announced, was about to become the first editor of the *Voelkische Beobachter*, the People's Observer, a racial newspaper for all Aryans, bought from the virulently anti-Semitic Thule Society. Harrer was applauded, a celebrated figure. Fanny thought Harrer's importance and prominence was the real reason Mueller had nodded to them.

Fanny was leaner now; without play and daily training, the blond poster girl for German womanhood appeared less athletic, looked more like a slender ballerina. It was a different look, a more mature look. She had cut her striking blond braids — schoolgirl braids she called them — in favor of a short bob, more befitting a Frau, a married woman.

Sepp, with the white streak in his shock of black hair, looked more distinguished. His boyishness was replaced by the strength of features that hallmarked character that came to one who had experienced much life in a short time and had lived it well.

Mueller looked exactly the same, thinly Germanic, dark eyes dispassionate, with the Cassius face, the lean and hungry look Luftmann and Shakespeare had once described. He was given the honor of introducing Herr Hitler, whom he called "a man with vision, who can see the truth and beyond."

Adolf Hitler walked to the podium. Fanny had not seen where he had been sitting, so it was as if he had suddenly materialized.

As he stood there before the assemblage, an eerie stillness filled the room. His eyes, his look, his bearing — from this little man with a mustache — were hypnotic, focusing on the audience, making them focus on him, drawing attention like metal to a magnet.

When he started to speak his voice had a quality that drew her closer, into his words, as if they were words coming from her own soul. Fanny never felt anything like it. It was more than religious, more than a sacred homily, the sounds and the words, their meaning, became her whole world. An inspiring epiphany!

Sepp had to shake her to get her attention. "You see what he says about Marxists and pacifist and those Reds, all things he calls un-German?" he whispered.

Fanny just nodded, still in the speaker's trance, tears streaming down her cheeks. Each day she saw the wounded that these non-Germans reviled. And here was a true German speaking as if there were a glow surrounding him, a halo, talking about saving Germans and Germany. He was electrifying and spoke with spellbinding clarity of purpose, a mesmerizing intensity, for the survival of Germans by race. His visions of strength over weakness, internal threats, and racial damage, were compelling. Many of the party's points that had troubled Fanny seemed unimportant now.

"So the strength which each people possess decides the day. Always before God and the world, the stronger has the right to carry through what he wills. We cannot be slaves of the weak!" Herr Hitler exclaimed.

Murmurs of approval stirred the audience.

"The whole world of nature is a mighty struggle between strength and weakness. There would be nothing but decay in the whole of nature if this were not so. States that offend the elementary law rot. You need not seek for long to find an example of such mortal putrefaction and uncleanliness; you can see it in the Reich of today. You can see treacherous and cunning rich Jews, contaminations, holding power by deceit, their scheming uses of money, their lending oppression, enslaving stronger, noble Germans. These elements must be purged for our true German-ness to be restored."

Louder voices from the audience and the stamping of booted feet expressed agreement.

"We are a party that reaches the masses, our German masses, not the godless Bolshevism," — he pounded the lectern — "the Jewish Bolshevism" — again he pounded the lectern — "that poisons the minds and hopes of our people, promoting internationalism, diluting the German race and nation."

Ideas she had read, reread, and dismissed, his speaking them made right, reasonable, as if holy and self-evident. Fanny shivered, feeling chills race through her.

He opened his arms to the group as if uniting a congregation to join a sanctified battle. "We are one! By blood! We are together!"

The workers who comprised much of the audience stood up, shouting approval.

"*Blut und Boden meinen Freunde*, we must struggle as one mind with one body, only through blood and soil are all classes thrown aside." He punched with his hands as if knocking them away right then. "We must struggle against those elements of decay and rot in our Reich that would defile us." Here he lifted his eyes slightly as if in prayer. "It is our noble duty to defend against it."

When Herr Hitler finished, at first there was silence — then as if coming out of a trance, people were on their feet cheering. "Heil Hitler! Heil Hitler!" they shouted with abandon.

"We are one again, Sepp," said Fanny, feeling what she had felt on that August day at the Odeonsplatz. "Do you feel it, too, Sepp?"

"I listened, Fanny."

"Why were you standing at attention at the very end, my dear Sepp?" she smiled, kissing him on the cheek. "Why are you still standing at attention?"

"He is the same as that day I first saw him, Fanny. Inspiring."

"Things can change, those other parts," she mumbled to herself. "When good Germans understand them better."

Herr Hitler stepped off the makeshift podium to shake hands with the crowd.

After congratulating the guest speaker, Mueller, for all to see, immediately walked over to Schtreuk, a loyal party member and longtime widower who had raised his daughter alone. In a loud voice, he invited the working class Schtreuk with his daughter to dine in the Burgfrieden at his home.

"As Herr Hitler said, the German Workers' Party includes all Germans, not by class but by blood, includes all worthy Germans no matter their place in society."

The brewery foreman looked stunned, unprepared for classes to be extinguished so quickly. He said, "I would be honored, Herr Mueller."

If there were any question as to Schtreuk's standing before, it was clearly established by the War Minister's gesture.

People got up to shake Marius's hand as well.

"He spoke well of nature, of feelings," Fanny pointed out, reminding Sepp that things natural can't be wrong, her old hymn chanted to no avail before they married.

Sepp shook his head, but smiled. "If the DAP brings order and respect for German tradition, they do good. I think they mean what they say. This man Hitler wouldn't be with them otherwise."

"They are sincere. I feel it. My father's reluctance, even Father Goetz's about a new unChristian religion, the party can change. Once order returns, Sepp, divisions will disappear. Reasonableness will come back. It's the chaos of the times that creates hatred and envy."

Both Hofers signed up that night. In the alphabetical registry, their names — Hofer, Fanny, born 1900; Hofer, Sepp, born 1895 — appeared below Hitler, Adolf, born 1889, who had joined in late September, and he appeared below Herr Harrer, whose name was inscribed in an ornate special type as a founding member.

By February of the following year, 1920, at a Munich DAP gathering on a cold winter's night, Herr Hitler suggested the German Workers' Party change its name to National Socialist German Workers' Party, add *Nationalsozialistische*, make it the NSDAP, *Nazi* for short. And so they did. National and Socialist had more appeal, the new party leader said. He would not, however, allow them to alter their 25-Point Program by even one word.

"It is only a name change," he declared. "When a horse is born in a cow shed, it is still a horse, *gell?*"

Smiling broadly he showed them a new party flag.

Sepp was startled. "Is it fate?" he asked Fanny. "Is it meant to be?"

The party emblem, the crooked cross, at the flag's center was the same as the design on the small knife the Zigeuner boy had given him. The *Swastika*.

Chapter 23
Farms and Rats
1922

Christian Luftmann, Sepp Hofer, and Samson Gutmann were seated in the back parlor of the red-and-white hip-roofed farmhouse at the Kiembock farm in Karlsfeld. There was a desk, a round table, and straight-backed chairs. It was a room for doing business. They were gathered there because the cattle trader had told Luftmann the farmer was having financial troubles.

Kiembock, a sturdy bald-headed man wearing overalls patched at both knees, looked stiff and uncomfortable. It couldn't be easy for him to talk about money problems, Luftmann guessed. Farmers, let alone Germans, were hard-working independent people.

"Your village is charming, Herr Kiembock. I remember it before the war. Maybe 100 people here, now how many? I would guess over 1,500," he said, making small talk to break the tension.

"Our lakes are pretty," said Kiembock, only too happy to talk about Karlsfeld and not his personal problems. "Did you see the Karlfelder See and Waldschwaigsee? The forests, too? And the fishpond in the village hiding behind the wall of trees?"

"Not all of that," Luftmann chuckled.

"You know the River Wuerm, just a narrow stream here, flows on to Dachau traveling across the Luftmann Land. Your land, Herr Luftmann, before the Pumf."

"I hope that I will get a chance to explore Karlsfeld if we reach an agreement today," Luftmann said.

"You want to take my farm?" Kiembock asked, turning pale.

"No, no, my friend! May I call you my friend? I have something else in mind. Perhaps we can make some arrangement, good for you and good for us."

Kiembock looked surprised at the "us."

"I'm talking about my son-in-law, Sepp, and daughter, Fanny, Herr

Kiembock. Tell me, who owns the large farm next door? It looks abandoned. Is it yours, too?"

"Not mine. The bank owns it and does nothing. The Geiselmord incident! The owner was a hostage the Reds took and killed, but not before raping his young daughter. Thirty of them! The wife and children left Karlsfeld to go I don't know where."

"Cowards! Filthy swine!" Sepp blurted. "I remember their handiwork at the Anhalter Bahnhof."

Kiembock went on. "A farmer's life right now is very hard, Herr Luftmann. To make payments when our goods are stolen by gangs. And the soil weakens."

"Weakens?"

"The gangs hurt us and we hurt the earth. Maybe we stop, they stop?" He said unconvincingly. "But, I try different things. Unhealthy soil makes unhealthy crops."

"Well, a farmer's life is complicated," agreed Luftmann, learning something new.

Sepp again had something to say. "I'm ashamed to tell you, my father organizes the Pumf workers, agitates them, sends them to the countryside to steal."

"They come from the cities, too. About your father, I don't know. But about you, we remember you were a brave war hero. We remember your injuries and how hard you worked to overcome them," the farmer said with obvious admiration.

"There is no protection against these farm thieves?" asked Sepp.

Kiembock shook his head. "My sons want to fight back, but they're no match for ruthless profiteers. And men who are starving fight better then those who aren't."

Sepp took out a card. "Here, I'm a member of the National Socialist German Workers' Party, the NSDAP. Write this name, Ernst Schtreuk. Contact him in Dachau, Herr Kiembock. No one has to live in fear, have their hard labor snatched from them even in this useless republic that doesn't know how to govern. Our party's storm troopers, the SA Brownshirts, will give you protection. In return, give them food for their families."

"Storm troopers, Ernst Schtreuk, I will remember," said Kiembock, pocketing the card. "I gladly give them food, if they are willing to help. It's the same food the gangs would steal from my farm."

Luftmann appeared taken aback. NSDAP, Nazi storm troopers! At the farm? "Can you find out which bank owns the abandoned farm?" he finally said.

"The same one that wants to take mine," said Kiembock. "Hamburg."

That was a bit of luck. Luftmann took a deep breath. He had known he would do this deal before he came to the farmhouse. If it could be done and if Kiembock agreed. He wanted a farm for Sepp and Fanny. Food was the commodity needed in these times and Fanny, with child, should be away from the turbulence in Dachau. He hadn't known a bank where he as a shareholder was the mortgagee. If handled correctly, from both farms there could be food for the family and food left over, as well, and food to give to Father Goetz for those who suffered in the parish.

"I'll purchase both farms, yours and the one next door, and, I'll deal with the bank. Don't look so worried, Herr Kiembock. Though I take ownership of your land, you and your family stay, work it as if it were your own. But there is more for you to do. You need to get us started, to put the other farm to work again for my children." He turned to Sepp. "You want to be a farmer, my boy? Good for you and Fanny to be out of Dachau, away from the violence. Good for your baby that comes soon, too. And we accept your storm troopers help," he added with a sigh, making a concession to the party built on some principles he abhorred.

"Father-in-law, I'd welcome the countryside. I think Fanny would, as well. But I know nothing of farming. I think you put too much on me."

Gutmann piped in. "I'll help, Sepp. I am strong and healthy for a man in his 40s. I know horses. I know Kiembocks. We all work together."

Luftmann looked surprised.

"There is not much cattle trading nowadays," explained Gutmann.

"Your wife will do that with you?"

"Herr Luftmann, my wife has left me." Grim-faced, Gutmann's normally pleasant mien disappeared.

Luftmann probed no further.

"I tell you what! I build a large farmhouse. No! I build a compound, a place for you, Samson. And for Fanny and Sepp and their child, with many extra rooms for extra children," he laughed, loving the making of a deal that was good for everyone. "A place for me and Lotte when we visit. For Gretl, too! Fresh air can be good for her; my sister withdraws in Dachau, where she has to remain inside or in the garden, so dangerous it has become. And I build a guest house for who knows?" he said expansively.

Luftmann could do this because he had bought gold, hoarded it before the war was over, believing that when America entered on the side of the Allies, it could be the end for the Kaiserreich. The farmlands were a good deal. Picking up the mortgages would be dirt cheap, as they say. He smiled to himself at the pun.

"A wonderful opportunity for me!" Sepp exclaimed, taking Luftmann's hand in his own. "Sitting with you working on your ledgers, I am grateful for employment, but I need the outdoors, the air. My body yearns for physical work. I'll talk to Fanny today when she returns from the infirmary. Thank you, Father-in-law." Sepp turned to the farmer. He wore a broad grim. "Now I'd like to visit my friends in the stable if I may, Herr Kiembock. How is my comrade the light-gray steed?"

"You are his only comrade," Kiembock confided. "He is friendly only when you come to visit him. But watch out for the rats, Herr Leutnant," Kiembock warned. "The rats are hungrier these days it seems. Hard to control. Like people, they fight for food."

"You should try the new rat poison," suggested Gutmann, showing he knew something about taking care of a farm. "What is it called? Zyklon something?"

"Zyklon B," said Kiembock. "Too expensive, but you are right, a good rat killer."

Now it was Luftmann's face that tightened, a rare angry look. Any reference to Fritz Haber's poisonous creations set him off. He despised the man. The mustard gas to kill humans as if they were rats made his Zyklon B no surprise. Luftmann would be forever disgusted with Haber for his callous remarks about the terrible deaths experienced by thousands of soldiers from his gas. *Death is death. It doesn't matter how you die.* Incredible! This from a Jew!

"Samson, why don't you go along with Sepp?" Luftmann said abruptly.

"Sepp likes these visits to be private, Herr Luftmann."

"Then go walk the abandoned farm. Familiarize yourself! Herr Kiembock and I have work to do." When they were gone he went over the details.

"You make me a happy man, Herr Luftmann." Kiembock extended a hand.

"Thank Gutmann for bringing your problem to me, Herr Kiembock."

"I was not used to being in such trouble," he said, eyes averted, face turning pink.

"Who isn't having trouble these days, with the Deutsche mark worth nothing and nothing to buy with it anyway?" Luftmann replied. "At least farmers are making food, producing milk, beef, pork, grain. And potatoes! Noble work, especially in these times when so many starve all over our republic."

"We have chickens, too," added Kiembock, proudly, comfortable knowing no one was taking his farm away. "For eggs and to eat! We'll be happy to share them with the men who give us protection. I feed a large brood. There are eight children, from ten to nineteen."

"Eight! Congratulations! I would like to see Sepp and Fanny do the same," Luftmann smiled, shaking hands with Kiembock again, making plans to meet once more.

Driving his tarnished but well-maintained silver Daimler the six kilometers back to Dachau, Gutmann said, "You do good, Herr Luftmann, for me and the farmer. Thank you."

"Take some credit, Samson. You did bring us the deal." Then Luftmann turned to Sepp. "In Dachau the people who suffer most are the Pumf workers, thousands of them, unemployed, homeless because of that rotten treaty. No wonder your father can instigate them. A captive audience! If not him, someone else would. You see them walk the streets, begging, wearing signs saying they'll do any day's work for food."

"You try to make me feel better, Father-in-law. Well, at least they know food is better than money. A wheelbarrow of Deutsche marks barely buys a loaf of bread."

Chapter 24
Later That Year
Unexpected Baptism

"Tell me, Fanny and Sepp. They come back to have the baby?" Father Goetz asked as he and Christian strolled in the garden behind the Luftmann home.

"Fanny wants to stay at the farm. Frau Kiembock's sister is a midwife."

"Just as well, cities and towns are not safe. Tell me about Sepp. He is happy?"

"He works the farm and becomes a farmer, Gutmann reports."

"And the horses?"

"As far as horses, it's not the black one that gets the most attention from Sepp."

"You mean the one with the goat companion?"

"Yes. He says that stallion already has a friend. He is close with the light gray steed. I had Gutmann trade cattle with Kiembock so Sepp could own the two, keep them in his own stable."

"Samson told me you did that. Those were difficult times for Sepp." Father Goetz hesitated as if deciding whether to bring something up or not. He cleared his throat. "And the protection against raiders? Still the same, Christian?"

"The storm troopers from Fanny and Sepp's Nazi Party. They and the Steel Helmets Veterans Group protect both farms, patrolling the area."

"The Helmets just threw out Jewish veterans from membership. Does Gutmann object? After his son's sacrifice?"

"He keeps quiet. I know you disapprove of the SA and the Nazis. At first I was put off by Sepp and Fanny's decision. But they are a help. The Kiembocks and Sepp and Fanny share food with them."

"So much for Jewish Germans who gave their lives for the Reich!"

"How do you continue to look so young?" Luftmann asked, needing to change the subject. The sixty-two-year-old cleric's appearance had scarcely changed in all these years. "You are like Wilde's *Dorian Gray*. You are sure you hide no portrait?"

Father Goetz's looks were typical of certain lanky, tight-featured men. Yes, his pale eyes were a bit more watery, some gray strands were sprinkled through his black hair, but that was all. Whereas Luftmann had become heavier, worry lines etched on his brow, hair receding, shoulders more curved though they had been rounded always from poring over his ledgers.

"How? You ask? Take pleasure, my friend, when you can, in small things, instead of brooding over events that you cannot control. It ages you before your time."

"You don't worry?" Luftmann asked.

"Not about things I can't do anything about."

"So what do you do about those things?"

"I pray."

"Yes, well, I am about to be fifty and I look like your father, Father," Luftmann half-joked. "Yet, today I see something is on your mind. I know you too well. You don't walk with your hands clasped behind your back for nothing. Is it still about the Geiselmord? You saved Frau Mueller. Do you blame yourself for the others?"

"No, I gave that up to prayer. But, you are right, something is troubling my mind. Herr Gutmann is converting to our faith."

"Gutmann? Hmmm! He told me his wife left him. Is that what moves him?"

"I don't think so. Frau Gutmann never adjusted to Dachau, no temples, having to travel to Munich — that alone breaking their law of the Sabbath — then the Munich Rudolfstrasse synagogue she attended was vandalized!"

"The first Munich synagogue to burn was in the 13th Century," Luftmann said automatically.

"Where do you pick up these facts?"

Luftmann shrugged. For centuries Jews had kept track of and passed along to the next generation every desecration, violation, crime, murder against them, a laundry list of grievances for God, and a reminder as to who they were and how separate from the rest of humanity. But Luftmann couldn't tell the priest that.

The priest took on an entirely different tone. "My friend, there is no reason for you to have that information, to know that information, let alone mention it."

Luftmann was alerted. Was it a warning? Did Goetz know something? Or just a comment about what was safe to talk about these days?

Before Luftmann could respond, Father Goetz went on, back to his Gutmann situation. "Losing a son fighting for the Kaiserreich, veterans groups no longer honoring Jews who fought, marching in Munich chanting, "Kill the Jews, they're everywhere. Stop them from breathing German air" — was too much. Frau Gutmann picked up and returned to her family in Poland. She had no use for Germans or Christians."

"The Jew Einstein wins a Nobel Prize for Germany, earning back some pride to our nation after the humiliating war, and they parade in Munich to get rid of men like him! What a world this is, Father! What a world!" Luftmann observed, shaking his head, his face wearing a worn and tired look. He gave a deep sigh and went on. "So, what made Gutmann decide to convert?"

"We prayed for his son. He is drawn to the love and mercy of our Lord, the Christian philosophy. And I think Sepp's devotion and healing influenced him, as well."

"Then what worries you about him?"

"Yes, well, you remember my sermon about Satan speaking German?"

"How can I forget?"

"Well, now I would say Satan has settled in Munich. Does his dirty work from our capital. People flock to our great city bringing their hatreds — a haven for right-wing zealots and Voelkische organizations — hatred for Berlin, its decadence, for the Left, for revolutionaries, for the republic, for Bolsheviks, for Bohemians and freethinkers, and for Jews for all of the above."

"I know Ludendorff has settled in Munich. He despises the republic and he is an outspoken anti-Semite. A popular man with bad ideas," Luftmann sighed.

"The Prussian is not a friend to Rome, either, Christian, worse since the Allies awarded his Silesian birthplace to Catholic Poland."

"What does all this have to do with Gutmann? What troubles you about the Haendler? Come to the point! It is good when a prodigal son returns, *gell*?"

"I need someone to stand up for him at his baptism, Christian. Without fuss."

Christian stopped near a shade tree and sat down on the dark wood bench beneath it. Eyebrows lifted, he gave Father Goetz a wondering look.

"The hate in Munich spills over to Dachau. Our own congregation would not welcome him, I fear. I hear confessions. Jews as a toxic race, blamed for everything, a litany of grievances from before, Christ killers, and now for simply being who they are."

"Dangerous the racial thing. For being who they are. There's no defense."

"Our Dachauers believe Jews have it easy while good Germans, unemployed and starving, struggle against the soaring inflation. They see the few who have moved here since the republic allows them to live anywhere — professionals, engineers, music teachers, one even planning a factory, moneyed Jews who bought Burgfrieden homes from distressed Dachau families and who keep to themselves. Our Dachauers say they are too uppity, think they are better than everyone."

"The townspeople now have empirical proof for their prejudices, Father, if one allows reasoning from the few to the many. Prosperous Jews, poverty-stricken Germans."

"It cannot be taken lightly. There are some in the parish, Christian, who cheered when the foreign minister was killed because of his Jewish ancestry. Parishioners from whom I would never expected it. That's why Gutmann's coming to the faith worries me."

"Bad times make bad people," Luftmann said, a little too offhandedly.

(He wondered if he was one of the bad people, too. Fundamentally misguided. Was this the Germany and Germans he had so wanted to be part of all his life?)

"Bad times! Bad people? Too glib, my friend! The people do suffer. Economic plagues! A helpless government that makes things worse. No value to their stacks of printed money, coffee one price when you enter a cafe and double when you leave!"

"The real story, Father, is four marks to the American dollar before the war; in January it was 17,000; now it is almost 60 million! By the end of the day, higher still."

The priest groaned in despair. "Reds, Whites? Germans killing each other. The French take the Ruhr. The extended blockade. Treaty reparations! What goods we have they seize. People out of work! What crosses we Germans bear!"

"You focus on the secular! Not quite your realm."

"I cannot be blind to anguish in my parish." He reached in his pocket taking out a letter, the name deleted to protect the writer's privacy. "What do you think of this?"

Neatly penned, it read:

> Here in Bavaria, I am in the stronghold of reaction. At night I am awakened by military commands heard from the forests and the march of men, trained by the monarchists, training men to kill other men, training peasants and workers, not the class we usually think of as soldiers. My cousin in Saxony

tells me the same goes on there, but this from the Communists, also to kill their own kind, other Germans. I see no difference between the two, Father. They wait to massacre each other. And the looting, the rioting, and street fighting are regarded as grist for the mill to Communists and reactionaries alike. I am so weary, so destroyed by uncertainty and the impossible costs just to survive. I am ashamed to tell you, Father, I do not care what happens. I do not look to God any longer to help us. I am so tired of it all.

He sighed. "Not quite my realm, you say? In our country now, the City of Man versus the City of God is not an easy separation for the religious."

Luftmann gave an understanding nod. There was nothing to say.

"And Gutmann? What about Gutmann? Are we going to get to the point, finally?"

"Will you stand up for him as he embraces the Christ?"

"Me?"

"Who else? You are understanding and tolerant," said the priest. "Others are hungry, hurting, harbor old grudges. Gutmann likes and respects you, for what you did for the Kiembocks and for him working and living on the farm, Christian."

It was an honor, Luftmann knew. Yet, it was ironic, for a Jew standing up for a Jew to become a Christian.

"Christian, please — "

He looked up, dragged out the moment, then smiled. "Of course I will."

The priest let out a soft sigh, a burden lifted. "Bless you! I worried about this."

"Not like the *Zigeuners*, Father! This time Lotte will approve. She will think one more soul returning before the Second Coming, *gell*? And I would be the Haendler's godfather. Amusing! Quite a large son for a man like me, *gell*?" Luftmann gave a deep breath, smiling, knowing he was doing the right thing. "Small pleasures you say. You have something there, Father. The trees' branches dressed in green protect us from the sun. The flowers perfume the air. Too bad, by Oktoberfest they will be gone."

"Next month we could all be gone," said the priest. "Enjoy the present."

Δ

At St. Jakob's after Oktoberfest celebrations, Father Goetz was anointing chrism on the forehead of Samson Paul Gutmann. Christian Luftmann was at his side.

Sepp and Fanny were there, as were Lotte Luftmann and Frau Mueller,

125

without her glasses. The Kiembocks with their eight children came from Karlsfeld to celebrate the sacrament. Frau Kiembock's sister, Anke the midwife, joined them as well, just in case infant Hofer decided to make his or her presence known that day.

Luftmann could not figure out Frau Mueller's attendance, since the rest of the church was empty, though the baptism had been announced at Sunday Mass.

It was Gutmann who had chosen Paul for his baptismal name after the Jewish Apostle Saul, who had spread the word, the good news, to the Gentiles. At the close of the rite, Gutmann shook the hands of each worshipper.

Father Goetz said quietly, "The others who stayed home today should be ashamed for not welcoming a new member to our faith."

"I apologize for my son's absence, Herr Gutmann," Frau Mueller whispered as the giant of a man held her hand in his. "I don't know why he's like that."

"You are a good woman, Frau Mueller," said Gutmann. "And a beautiful one, too," he added, much to her delight.

1923, November

My Dear Children,

Again, much love, pride, and congratulations for the new arrival. Mother and I enjoyed so much being united with you and Sepp if only for two days and seeing our beautiful grandson Josef baptized at St. Jakob's. Did you receive the crucifix Father Goetz sent for baby Josef? I am glad you decided to stay on the farm longer. Gretl is on her way to Karlsfeld with Herr Gutmann as I write. She becomes more withdrawn and the country air and freedom to roam may do her good. I think she will adore young Josef — I remember how she was with you — and she misses Rolf very much, looks for him in your quarters daily. Herr Gutmann, face all bruised, ran into some trouble, an incident he will not discuss. With the continued unrest, it is best for him — for all of you — to be out of Dachau on the farm. After all, he is my godson! You asked about Munich's failed Beer Hall Putsch and your friend Herr Hitler. We will talk when I see you."

— Your Loving Father

1923, November

My Dear Papa,

Thank mother again for the baby baptism gown she made, so many laces and intricate details. We cherish it and hope to use it for more little Hofers. Tante Gretl united with Rolf before falling in love with Josef. I think she keeps that old dog young! Do not worry about her. Nor about us. The incident with Herr Gutmann was here in Karlsfeld. Emotions were intense after the arrest of Herr Hitler and his comrades, but Sepp had a talk with our guardian SA about Gutmann. They accepted it. So it will be safe. The storm troopers are not really bad fellows. I told you, people can be reasonable with a good meal in their stomachs. They were so helpful when Josef decided to be born.

— Your daughter, Fanny

1923, November

Dear Fanny,

In Karlsfeld? The Gutmann incident? I worry now.

— Your Father

1923, November

Dear Papa,

Do not worry. It is over. Sepp said he is disappointed over the Munich Putsch. Not because it was unsuccessful, but he thought the NSDAP was against revolutions. It is written so in their program. He is very firm when it comes to rules. I reminded him that even our cardinal said this false republic was under the curse of God. As usual, I lost the argument! Sepp replied the new cardinal said the republic was 'under the curse of God, born under the sin of Revolution,' so revolution was a sin. My husband is too smart, gell?

— Your Daughter, Fanny

1923, December

My Dear Fanny,

Father Goetz did send a note welcoming Gutmann to the faith; he can present that to the new priest next year when services start at the Karlsfeld Ludlkapelle. About your new Nazi members? Are you a missionary for your party — bringing in the entire Kiembock family? I saw the Nazi newspaper Voelkische Beobachter in your parlor. You do surprise me. Inflation worsens. Good you are on the farm, and for the Kiembocks, otherwise we all starve."

— Your loving, Father

1924, January

My Dear Papa,

Your eyes miss nothing. Our SA friends bring the party newspaper to us from time to time. The Kiembocks joined because of Sepp, I suppose, their hero, and also for the protection they give us from the gangs. Who do you think our son looks like? He is dark-haired like Sepp, true. But after that I think he favors me. *The Karlsfeld Ludlkapelle will take a little time to adjust to Herr Gutmann. The people remember him as the Jew Haendler. They are not used to strangers. I trust in God it will all work out. The walk to St. Jakob's when Samson couldn't take us was hard for Sepp with the old injuries. The chapel makes it easier. We love the farm. Happy New Year! Do we see you for Easter?"*

— *Your loving daughter, Fanny*

1924, February

Dear Fanny,

You may know about Herr Hitler's trial, in any case, his sentence is five years in Festungshaft — fortress time. He serves the more comfortable punishment at Landsberg am Lech. Tell Sepp that Herr Hitler — what do they call him now? The Fuehrer after that Italian Il Duce? — had the same judge that gave him the easy sentence when he and his troopers disrupted the Bavarian League meeting a few years ago, that brutal beating that blinded the old man speaker, remember? Tell him also that General Ludendorff was acquitted for his role in the Putsch. I hear he may have little taste for the Fuehrer! The NSDAP is banned, Fanny, as are the SA. New developments daily! We try for Easter now that the government may finally stabilize thanks to the currency reform. The Red violence may not disappear so quickly. Take care! By the way, when we visited last you did not get to tell me about that incident.

— *Your loving Father*

1924, March

Dear Papa and Dear Mother,

Sepp thanks you for all the information. Our son gets bigger and stronger every day. Samson pays him so much attention. It is nice to see. He will have to be with a new brother or sister coming before the year's end. Yes, I am with child again. Bringing healthy German babies into the world. Praise God! We are so glad to be here. It saddens me that we — our Nazi Party — are banned from expressing our views in a democracy! Why aren't the revolutionary Communists banned? Doesn't the Deutsche Republik remember the Geiselmord? The Social Democrat Deutsche Republik may not be democratic at all! Do they condone the murder of innocents? It upsets me, Father. We share our food with the outlawed SA. They still protect us from the Reds who are bolder now that their number-one enemies *have their mouths gagged and their leader imprisoned. I miss you. I forever reminisce about the Dachau that once was. We wait to see you at Easter. And you are right; we never did discuss the incident.*

— Your daughter, Fanny

Chapter 26
The Gutmann Incident
Several Months Earlier

Fanny, still swollen with her first child, looked ready to give birth at any time. Yet in her oversize tunic dress with a denim apron and a big, old wool sweater for the early autumn chill, her face had become more beautiful as she approached full term. She continued to work alongside Sepp in the field behind their Karlsfeld farmhouse. Their farm was picture-perfect, verdant fields tucked between rolling tree-lined hills on the village outskirts. A place where the world seemed good.

That was when their guardian SA storm troopers stopped by.

"Well, Leutnant Hofer, all goes well? Those Red Front thugs don't bother you or your neighbor?" asked Ernest Schtreuk, doffing his brown militia cap at Fanny.

His men waited on the dirt road in their motorcycles. His vehicle with its sidecar, stood alone, befitting a leader.

Schtreuk, stocky and powerfully built, had a new air of authority, less brittle and tentative, that came more from his position in the SA, the *Sturmabteilung*, than from the surprise marriage of Marius Mueller to his daughter, an unattractive girl who looked much like Schtreuk but with all her fingers.

Schtreuk guessed that arrangement was more political than romantic, a show of solidarity with the working class by a party higher-up. It was meant, he figured, to thwart the Communists who were gaining ground among the unemployed working class in Dachau. He had confided all this to Sepp and Fanny at the big show of his daughter's wedding at St. Jakob's.

"Mueller marries a Schtreuk! Anything is possible right? My daughter Helga will be comfortable now. Even when he is rude, she is still Frau Mueller, *gell?* Growing up alone in a motherless home she had too much household work. Made her a little sour. But his reasons for marrying my Helga don't matter anyway. Party members have a duty to stop the Bolsheviks and restore German-ness to our Germany."

"I hope they will be happy," Fanny said tersely, still bearing a grudge against Marius.

Schtreuk asked again. "Those Reds aren't giving you trouble, are they?"

"No complaints! We know others in Dachau who do much worse than us."

"Yes, Dachau is worse than the countryside. You would think your father would help protect you from Der Rotfrontkämpferbund, these Red Front gangs, if you don't mind my saying so, Herr Leutnant."

"I do not speak with my father. He has more compassion for workers of the world than for people here in Germany, but we are fine, Herr Schtreuk, thanks to you and your men," Sepp answered, dropping the large shovel to shake hands.

"As my husband says, Herr Schtreuk, we are good because of you and your crew. The Red gangs bother others in the district but leave us alone," said Fanny with a friendly smile, waddling over, rake in hand, hair tied back with a patriotic blue and white bandanna — Bavarian colors — blond wisps escaping against her still tan face.

"It is our sacred duty to stop the foreign Bolsheviks, Frau Hofer."

"Those who have sacred duties must eat, *gell*? May I give you some milk and freshly ground rye flour to take home?" offered Sepp.

"Thank you again, Herr Leutnant. The outlaw Social Democrats and their Jew republic are killing us all just as if they used guns."

"Disorder, even in the Reichstag, I heard from my father," said Fanny, shaking her head. "How can bullets fly in the place where government meets?"

"The government is a criminal one, not German, Frau Hofer. Germans are orderly and obey the law," recited Schtreuk. "Germany betrayed." He looked away as if remembering better days. "My men brought back empty milk cans, Herr Leutnant. So precious is milk. My daughter expects a second child. Even she with her important husband has difficulty."

"Mother Luftmann says all mothers need milk to make milk. We are happy to help all mothers," Sepp grinned. "Bring the cans over."

"Today we need for six, Herr Leutnant."

Schtreuk repeated Sepp's rank, stubbornly insisting on giving military respect when there no longer was an official military. The Allies had finally clamped down on the Freikorps, outlawing them once the Social Democrat government — which never paid them — no longer needed their services to squash the Soviet takeovers that had sprouted all through Germany.

"Samson, bring two fifty-pound sacks of rye flour," Sepp called out toward the barn. "I will get the milk."

Gutmann carried a sack on each shoulder balanced across his broad back, head facing the ground. He placed them near Schtreuk then looked up with a broad grin, wearing the smile physical work had always brought him. His expression changed when he saw Schtreuk's handgun pointed right at him.

Schtreuk had never seen Gutmann working at the farm, only trading cattle among Dachau County farmers.

"I remember you from Dachau. The Jew at the inn! What are you doing here, Haendler thief, preying on hard-working Germans? Herr Leutnant, you know who this is?" He gave Gutmann a hard shove. "Answer me when I speak to you! What are you doing here?" He shoved him again.

Her rake dropping to the ground, Fanny's hand flew to her mouth. Her startled blue eyes opened wide. How could this be happening? Their farm, kept safe by these very men, was a peaceful haven. She was dumbstruck, staring at Schtreuk, her protector, holding the gun on Gutmann, always a friend in need, whose help and patience had made the farm work.

From the loud talking, smelling fear and aggression, Rolf had come tearing out of the barn. His fierce barks brought Kiembock running across the field with his two eldest sons. Chickens were squawking from the chicken house. Pigs squealed, mashing together in front of the feeding trough. Sepp ran out from the cowshed.

"What goes on here?" Kiembock asked out of breath.

"Our duty to defend Germans against Jew treachery. The Haendler makes money off farmers' backs! Over here," Schtreuk commanded his men. "Teach him a lesson!"

The five storm troopers were in their brown-shirted uniforms, wearing red Swastika armbands, even though outlawed, to show their affiliation with the also banned Nazi Party. They left their motorbikes on the dirt road and ran forward, carrying rubber truncheons on black leather straps, holstered pistols and knuckle busters.

With a nod toward Gutmann, Schtreuk's only directive, one of the storm troopers struck the Haendler hard across the jaw with his rubber club, downing him, bringing blood and broken teeth. Joined by the others, he was about to strike again when Sepp moved between them, taking a body blow.

"Sepp!" cried Fanny, finding her voice.

"*Achtung! Aufhoeren!*" Sepp ordered, holding onto his injured shoulder but in command as he was in the trenches of Verdun. "Stop! This man is a friend. He works with us. A good man who helped me recover from my wounds. Who came to my aid."

"To ours, also, comrades," chimed in Kiembock."When we were in need,

Herr Gutmann stepped in for us and helped save our farm."

Fanny, kneeling beside Gutmann, wiped away the blood with her blue-and-white kerchief. "Stop this madness!" she cried at the brown-shirt storm troopers. "He lost a son fighting for the Kaiserreich! He is Roman Catholic, a new member of our faith. There is a letter from Dachau's Father Goetz recommending him. His family on German soil for centuries."

"A horse born in a — "

"Don't give me that worn-out cowshed saying. Gutmann is a decent man."

"Herr Hitler says it is beside the point whether the individual Jew is decent or not, a so-called good Jew is a bad Jew, Frau Hofer. It is who they are," defended Schtreuk, but he put up his hand to halt his men.

The brown-shirt SA troopers were stunned, looking apologetic about clubbing the lieutenant. They turned to Schtreuk for orders, surprised at the Jew's defenders.

At the same time, a stream of water appeared on the ground, coming from beneath Fanny's long tunic, darkening the dusty soil, the flow turning pink from Gutmann's blood.

"Sepp," she cried. "The midwife! I think we need the midwife!"

The gun was back in Schtreuk's holster in a blink.

Fanny's labor began.

Gutmann was still on the ground.

Sepp's shoulder injury restricted him.

Kiembock was on his way to get his sister-in-law.

Kiembock's sons were staring — first the gun, then this?

Schtreuk and his men lifted Fanny gently into the sidecar of Schtreuk's motorcycle. He took her back to the farmhouse where they waited for Kiembock to bring the midwife who was as talented in delivering babies as her sister was in having them.

Meanwhile, Frau Kiembock, a plump, plain-faced woman whose pear shape looked always with child, was called to the scene by her sons. She was at Fanny's side, supporting her as they paced back and forth in the large rustic farmhouse bedroom. It was a pleasant space with beamed ceiling and white walls, blue-and-white cotton curtains, furnished simply except for its four-poster canopy bed, a replica of the one Fanny had in Dachau.

Gutmann, face swollen, teeth missing, was recovering with ice and bandages in his quarters, attached to the back of the main house. The troopers grudgingly had helped the Haendler off the ground with a look from Sepp and a command from Schtreuk.

The incident was over.

That evening, Sepp and Fanny's first child, Josef Christian Hofer, entered the world, his arrival precipitated by blood and soil, a truly German blessing, his grandfather Luftmann might once have said.

In any case, Luftmann had thought it a good choice, a kind of symmetry, for Samson Gutmann and Hannah Mueller (much to her son's dismay) to serve as the infant's godparents at his baptism in St. Jakob's.

Chapter 27
Welcome, Luddy
December 1924

Adolf Hitler, a national figure since his well-publicized trial, was released early from the confines of Landsberg Prison, and Christian Ludwig Hofer was released late from the confines of his mother's womb in Karlsfeld. The birth announcement appeared in the first issue of the new Nazi Party newspaper, the *Dachauer Zeitung*.

From the beginning the round, chubby baby, whose looks favored his grandfather Luftmann's side of the family, was known as Luddy.

Josef, who at one year couldn't care less about Herr Hitler or the newspaper, was not at all happy with his brother's arrival, spitting up on him when his mother first held him over the cradle to kiss the new tenant.

"He protects what he thinks is his. Like our attention. It will change," said Fanny optimistically.

"Oh, really?" Sepp countered.

Yet, Fanny carefully watched over the baby's cradle at all times.

Their great-Aunt Gretl instinctively paid more attention to Josef, petting him, making soft sounds as she did with Rolf. And Fanny prepared for Luddy's baptism at the *Ludlkapelle*. The 19th-century Karlsfeld chapel just this year celebrated Masses and delivered sacraments. She missed St. Jakob's and Father Goetz, but it was part of the same Dachau Parish and its closeness to home made a difference.

That cold December day in 1924, the Luftmanns, the Kiembocks — Herr Kiembock and his wife were honored to be godparents — Gutmann, Hannah Mueller, and Anke the midwife, who had delivered both boys, were there for Luddy's baptism.

Fanny had invited their stalwart protectors, Schtreuk and his SA crew, who had been so kind at Josef's birth one year earlier and who continued to protect them from marauders. The Nazi Party and the SA militia were still banned because of the *Putsch*. The men — more disciplined under Schtreuk's leadership than most SA — and their families were surviving on small party stipends and food from the Luftmann and Kiembock farms. Ever ready to defend, they were seated in the back pews near the door, motorcycles parked outside. They had left their forbidden party flags in the barn at the Luftmann farm out of respect for the church.

There was an unpleasant scene a night earlier. Fanny had promised Aunt Gretl she could attend the baptism. It upset her that she had to renege at her father's insistence.

"It is hard for Gretl to behave," he had argued. "You learned that from the Mueller incident years ago. As to promises, who knows how much she understands or remembers? Why look for trouble? Trouble has a way to find you without any help."

"My aunt understands more than you think, Papa," Fanny said in Gretl's defense. "It's expressing herself that is the problem."

Now, the church was still. The liturgy of the sacrament began.

"What name have you chosen for this child?" intoned Father Ignatius, a young Silesian priest of Polish descent, which, along with the many mysteries of the Church, had landed him in this tiny Bavarian village. "What name?"

"Christian Ludwig Hofer," the Kiembocks replied in unison.

As the priest poured water on the infant's forehead and the baby began to whimper, he pronounced, "I baptize you Christian Ludwig Hofer in the name of the Father, in the name of the Son, and in the name of the Holy Ghost. Amen." Father Ignatius made the sign of the cross. Droning on, he began the final sacred blessing, common to and hallowed by both Christians and Jews.

Luftmann could not help his early background re-emerging. As the priest recited the translation, "May the Lord bless you and keep you," in his mind he heard the original *Yivorechechor adomshem vayismorechor*. He shook his head as if to empty it of Hebrew words. "May He make his face shine upon you and be gracious unto you. May He lift his countenance unto you and — "

Loud pounding on the church door startled the congregation. As one they turned their heads toward the back. A dog was barking as well. The SA storm troopers quickly went outside. They saw a disheveled Gretl, whom they didn't know, and Hofer's dog, Rolf, with whom they were familiar. The parishioners saw Gretl for the very first time.

"They come! They come!" she said, gesturing wildly with her arms.

Gretl was not clothed for the weather, wearing a gray tent-like housedress and bedroom slippers wet from the snow-covered road. She was gasping for breath, her massive body heaving up and down like a carousel horse. A strong stench came from her that the troopers recognized. On the field it was the scent of fear or death. Here at the church, her speech garbled, a grotesque image — *Quasimodo* sans hump — the bedraggled old woman emitted the strong stink of *der Kot*, of shit.

Though younger than Luftmann, Gretl appeared older than her brother, with misshapen features on a too-round face, dull, lifeless eyes, no flexibility in her body.

"They come! They come!" she repeated, pointing.

Schtreuk looked off in the distance toward the farm and saw black smoke rising rapidly against the ice blue sky. He shouted, *"Das Feuer! Schnell! Something burns!"*

He ran to his motorcycle, giving it a loud whirring start. The other brown-shirt storm troopers followed. As they approached the Luftmann farm a truckload of Red Front guards whizzed by, standing in the open truck, rifles mounted, the raised clenched fist and Soviet red star emblem emblazoned on their white flags and armbands. Unlike the Nazis, their party and militia were not banned.

"Rot Front, Rot Front," they chanted, taunting the Brownshirts.

"To the fire," shouted Schtreuk. "Do not engage! Let them go!"

The older Kiembock boys were there trying to extinguish the blaze, struggling against grasping, greedy fire fingers that ravaged the Luftmann barn and cowshed. They were running back and forth from the well pump with buckets. Red sparks splattered, some tailed like comets, airborne in a wild destructive dance. Tongues of flames licked hay, voraciously swallowing anything in their path, livestock were stampeding through the maze of heat for safety. The troopers heard the terrified neighing of horses enclosed in stalls. Forming a water line from the well until the fire trucks arrived, they filled and passed buckets along. Only Schtreuk, dousing himself with water, entered the burning barn.

"I go to the stalls," he shouted. "Wet a path for me."

The trucks pulled in loaded with water tanks and fire extinguishers. Four volunteer firemen pulled down the large black rubber hose aiming it at the barn.

"Our leader is in there," shouted a storm trooper, "trying to reach the horses."

The firemen lowered the hose. The horse neighs had turned to unimaginable screams.

Schtreuk came out leading the black horse and dragging the terrified goat along. The horse's limbs were singed. One of the Kiembocks ran to get liniments, burn oil and salves from their own barn. Schtreuk was going back inside amid a horse's horrific wails. The firemen hosed him down. Gray and black smoke poured out of the barn door. The horse's pathetic, tortured screams diminished, turning to wretched grunt sounds, then it stopped . . . silence.

When Schtreuk emerged, angry tears made paths down his soot-blackened face. He cursed the Red cowards that would destroy animals. "I cannot save the other," he cried. "He is down."

By this time Sepp arrived with Gutmann. He saw and heard. He grabbed the hose, carrying it alone, finding strength beyond himself, and rushed into the barn. He went to the gray steed's stall, drowning it in water, and threw himself on the barely breathing horse, his friend, his final step in recovery.

All the while, he told Fanny later, he had visions of the white horse in the battleground pasture swinging the bloody stump of a half-off limb.

Another truck came, mounting their hose. With water flooding the barn from rafters to frame to scorched floor, the storm troopers, with Samson Gutmann, forcibly removed Sepp from the barn. When the area around the stall was covered in ankle deep water and some scattered cinders, Schtreuk went back. Revolver in hand, going right to the gray horse stall despite the smoke from the smoldering wood and hay, despite the heat, he wept as he shot the gray horse, ending its agony.

Overcome by fumes, Sepp had passed out. Once again as on that long ago day at the Kiembock farm, Gutmann carried Sepp in his strong arms, taking him this time not to the once bright silver Daimler, but to the large farmhouse bedroom with the canopied four-poster bed.

"It was when they saw the flags in the barn, Herr Hofer," the Kiembock boy later explained to Sepp, who sat staring ahead, face and hands smeared with goose fat. "They were just going to take the food and leave until they saw the Nazi flags in the barn. Before the others could stop him, one of the gang stood there yelling right at the Swatstika *fascist pigs this is for my grandfather you beat and blinded.'* Then he torched the banner and, by its staff, tossed the burning flag into the hay."

The other Kiembock boy added, "We tried to get the animals out — the cows and the pigs are safe, Herr Hofer, but we couldn't reach the stalls. The fire grew too quickly," he said in tears. "We tried, God knows we tried. That old lady — a relative? — who lives with you, the one who had been hiding when the truck drove in and the Reds were ransacking the farm, came to see the fire. She screamed and, with Rolf chasing after her, ran to the village. We stayed to put out the fire, Herr Hofer. What else was there to do?"

Sepp said nothing. Body taut, his face stretched so paper-thin his old wound that the Gypsy's herbs had healed so well stood out, a thin curved line across his cheek.

There was a burning hatred raging in him for the Rotfrontkämpferbund and all of their kind. His father's kind. No longer Germans, but foreign savages alien to German values. There were no firemen or trucks or hoses or farm boys that could put out the inferno smoldering in him.

Fanny did not recognize his look. Gretl moaned in a corner of the bedroom. Lotte, after saying it was safer in Dachau, prayed on her knees next to the large bed, Rosary beads in hand, tears cascading down her face. Hannah Mueller tried to soothe Gretl.

Josef was screaming; Fanny had nursed the infant Luddy in his presence. It was not planned that way. The one-year-old wanted his mother's breast; it first was his, after all. Frau Kiembock and the midwife took them both off to the nursery.

"Watch Josef!" Fanny warned. "He cannot help himself."

As Fanny tended to Sepp, using every skill she had mastered working in the Dachau infirmary treating battlefield casualties, Luftmann sat in a corner rocker. Only he — the Itzig he had buried deep inside him with its painful history of centuries of pogroms, stake burnings, synagogue destructions, mass drownings, and other atrocities — understood the abominable and lethal loathing roaring inside his son-in-law.

Chapter 28
Repercussions

It was one thing for the Karlsfeld villagers to get used to the newly baptized Gutmann, the cattle trader, a Jew, not a German, living among them, the very first of his kind. They had reluctantly adjusted. After all, Hofer was a war hero and the Hofers were true Germans, long time NSDAP members.

But now the *minderwertig* woman!

Fanny and Sepp's Kiembock neighbors had seen little of Gretl since she had come to Karlsfeld. Gretl always darted away, hiding herself. The villagers hadn't seen her at all.

Fiercely conservative and Voelkische, what they saw that fateful day of Luddy's baptism was a defective person, a low-quality life, a person against all codes of racial hygiene, an accident needing to disappear to protect their German-ness.

Two racial violations. The Jew and *die Minderwertige*! That they would not countenance. The Hofers were viewed differently. The Kiembocks remained loyal to Sepp, Fanny, and Samson, but distanced themselves publicly, to avoid repercussions.

How to deal with the Minderwertige was brought up more and more since the post-war bad times. Described as a parasitic drain on the healthy, they were a blemish on the German Volk as well.

Father Ignatius tried to explain to Fanny.

"An object of fear, an uncontrollable birth accident, that could happen in their own families. Germans are unable to think about themselves as damaged. They suffered enough humiliation. However, all God's creatures need and deserve grace and absolution, Frau Hofer, united not by Volk, but by the Holy Spirit in each of us through baptism. I bring the wafer for your aunt to your home."

"Thank you, but I think not, Father," Fanny said, knowing Gretl would take only the Lebkuchen.

That spring — a wintry day, a late frost vainly resisting the sun's return north — Schtreuk stopped at the farmhouse. Fanny was there alone, Sepp in the new barn with Gutmann tending the cattle.

"My crew asks questions, Frau Hofer. They remember now that Sepp is the son of a Bolshevik. And that the baptized Haendler is, after all, a Jew living in your home with a Minderwertige, as well. It offends them. They are good Germans. Loyal Nazi members even though the party is outlawed. It would be wise to settle these problems like disciplined party members among yourselves. These doctrinal racial violations need to be cleaned up."

"I love my aunt. Herr Gutmann is a friend. If there is trouble with our staying in Karlsfeld and we have to we return to Dachau, then we will," Fanny replied.

"Abandon the farm? The food it provides?"

"Do we really need this conversation, Herr Schtreuk? It's not what I want, leaving the farm. Everything's going so well," Fanny appealed to the man, not the SA leader.

"The party helps Germany, gives hope, but has its demands, Frau Hofer."

"Well then, we have to work it out, leave the farm for Herr Gutmann to work at least until there is more reasonableness, some flexibility, in the party's rules. Gutmann is a decent man and a good Christian."

"Have it your way. I meant only to advise. You may need to deal with Herr Mueller back in Dachau. He is aware of the incidents. My son-in-law" (he gave a dry laugh calling Mueller his son-in-law) "is not a man who bends when it comes to party ideals and doctrines," Schtreuk said. He was about to leave when he added, "Nor am I a man who bends, for that matter. Our Germany, to survive, needs those with the will to be strong for racial hygiene and racial purity."

"We read the *Dachauer Zeitung*, Herr Schtreuk. And we know Herr Mueller."

"Then you know the Fuehrer has said specifically that "the destruction of the weak and sick is far more humane than their protection" and, as for Jews, I have told you before, he said, as well, that it is beside the point whether the individual Jew is decent or not. And if you know Herr Mueller, well, then, you know him." He tipped his cap. "I can let him know, if you wish, that you want to meet with him when you return to Dachau. Good day to you, Frau Hofer," he said, meaning it.

That night Fanny could not fall asleep. She thought of Samson Gutmann, over and over again and of Schtreuk's warnings, of his comment quoting Herr Hitler that even good Jews weren't, couldn't, be good, because they were bad by nature. How does Samson have a chance if being decent and kind doesn't count?

And Hitler saying killing the helpless and the weak was humane. Her Christian upbringing rejected both ideas, and just as important was her closeness to her dear Aunt Gretl. It was unthinkable to want to kill her because she was what she was.

Yet, Fanny did try to imagine Herr Hitler with his spellbinding voice and gestures delivering those words. Brimstone and fire! Scorching the soul! Inspirational! He understood Germany. For those few seconds only, she forgot about Samson Gutmann and Aunt Gretl.

Chapter 29
The Muellers
1925

As Sepp and Fanny had done, first moving into the Luftmann house, Marius and Helga Mueller had taken up residence in the Mueller home in the Burgfrieden district. The two dwellings were almost identical, as all others there, no one wanting their homes to seem less important or more ostentatious.

"Why not start your own home, Marius? There is room on the other side to build," said his mother.

"Me? You would put me outside the district? Foolish woman! There is just so much I'm willing to do to show that the NSDAP is not class conscious!"

There was enough room in the house so that Frau Mueller and her daughter-in-law could manage to live within the same walls. That was until Helga Mueller learned that in order to differentiate between the two Frau Muellers the townspeople were referring to them as Frau Mueller *Die Schoenheit*, the beauty, and Frau Mueller *Die Haessliche*, the ugly. She was the latter.

"Why can't they just say the elder and the younger," Helga had complained to her husband. They were in their bedroom, dark-paneled, dark draperies, heavy mahogany furnishings, very masculine.

"Why couldn't you be better looking," Marius had replied impatiently.

"You want me to look like Fanny Hofer? Everybody's darling?" she sulked.

"I have no use for Fanny Luftmann Hofer. Just take better care of yourself."

"Well, you keep me with child. Is that my fault?"

"It is both an improvement and a duty," he said curtly. "What is for dinner?"

"Why do I have to cook for your mother? Am I an inferior? I have no help to take care of Alf. And now another one coming. I thought I was finished being housekeeper."

"Why would you think that?"

"Papa told me so."

"Papa," Mueller said derisively, "had no authority to tell you anything. *Kirche! Kueche! Kinder!* All you need to remember," he said dismissing her. "I am going into my study. I do not want to be disturbed."

"He treats me like a maid with his church, kitchen, children," Helga pouted to her father that week when he visited young Adolf, so named by Marius for their party leader. "Stop rolling the ball and playing with Alf and listen to me," she said irritably. "He treats me like a maid and a broodmare!"

"With Mueller you should feel lucky the child you lost was a girl. Do better with the one you are carrying. And don't whine where your mother-in-law can hear you," Schtreuk snapped.

"That is everywhere in this house," Helga complained, ignoring her father's command. She moved her bulky body from side to side, unable to find a comfortable place on the stiff leather couch.

The child's ball rolled behind the couch. He started to cry.

"The boy whines just like you."

"My husband treats me as if I am beneath him, ridicules you behind your back," she lied. Wanting her father to side with her, she would say anything to convince him.

Schtreuk got up and got the ball for his grandson.

"He insists I address him as Herr Mueller."

"And what does he call you?"

"Frau Schtreuk-Mueller," she said. "As if he wants me to remember he married beneath his class. I don't care for that arrangement either."

"No one cares what you care for, Helga. Don't you understand?" He tossed the ball at the three-year-old where it was hard for him to reach. "Now get that one yourself, Alf," he ordered. Then he said to Helga, "Herr Mueller is your boss and my boss. And he is a good German."

"This talk makes my head ache."

"Then talk about something else."

"The Hofers are back from the country," Helga said. "She invites Alf to visit with her sons. My mother-in-law takes him. At least some time for me."

"She is barking up the wrong tree to solve her party problems if she thinks it will do her good with Herr Mueller to pander to his son," Schtreuk mumbled, again tossing the ball to Alf.

"What party problems?" Helga's carping tone and dull mien were suddenly animated.

"Not your business. She just has to find her way. A good woman."

"Yes, well, she might as well play tennis with Marius as she did when she was younger, the only way she can win points with him," Helga said with a superior air. "Marius has no use for her."

"How do you know?"

"He told me so, himself. Besides they are not staying, just visiting her parents."

"I thought they were here for longer."

"They want to go back to the country. She is with child again," whispered Helga, with an air of superiority. She could tell her father a few things.

"And how would you know that?"

"My mother-in-law told me. Frau Luftmann told her. So you see, you can learn some things from your daughter."

Chapter 30
Play Time

No matter how Frau Mueller *Die Schoenheit* tried — playing the piano, singing a song, even marching around the nursery playroom with toy instruments — it wasn't working out.

Though her grandson Alf, at a year older was a bit of a bully, young Josef Hofer mobilized all his protective instincts and used them on his four-year-old guest. They didn't talk with each other; it wasn't name-calling. They were toddlers. Josef's brother, chubby Luddy, barely walked.

Josef knew one word, *unsrig*, ours, about everything that was his or Luddy's. Alf tried to push Luddy away from Luddy's rocking horse that day and got a bite in the leg from Josef for his effort. Despite being bigger and stronger, Alf ended up crying while Josef sat on him, pinning him down.

Fanny pulled Josef off his guest. Frau Mueller was not quite sure what happened, Alf cried and whined so often.

Luddy merely observed.

Luftmann came in and watched the end of such a scene. "Maybe when they are older they will become friends. Josef has this stong inclination about what is his and Luddy's and who may share it," he explained. "Come, have Kaffe und Kuchen with me and Lotte, Frau Mueller. It is time for good coffee and cakes. Sweetens our spirits, *gell*? They can't kill each other for another half-hour together?" He looked at Fanny.

"They can only kill me," she laughed. "I will take them to the garden for a little exercise. Go, enjoy with my parents, Frau Mueller."

"So join us," he said, offering the beleaguered grandmother an arm. "Afterward, I walk you back to your home?"

Sitting with Lotte and Luftmann in their large kitchen, the tray of cookies and cakes and Lotte's fragrant brew set on the table, Frau Mueller confided, "It's not easy in the house with a daughter-in-law. I don't blame her, so pregnant all the time, about to give birth once more, right after losing the girl child. It's difficult for Helga, I am sure. Makes her especially cranky. I try to stay out of her way. But I am always there, or else she thinks I'm there. It's hard for both of us I guess."

"And your son?" asked Lotte.

"He seems not to care. Maybe not to notice. I don't know," she shrugged, hands raised upward. "He is busy with political matters. That's what gets his attention. Not much left for his wife." Then, surprising everyone, Frau Mueller began to weep. "Excuse me, excuse me," she cried. "So hard to live without love."

"Christian, I have an idea," said Lotte. "Why doesn't Frau Mueller visit the farm for a while? She can go back with Sepp and Fanny. Fanny could use an extra hand, God willing."

"Lotte, I know everything comes under God's will, my Dear. But all we are doing is inviting a friend to the farm? Do you really think He has time for that?" said Luftmann, impatient with her accelerated and intensifying religiosity these days.

"Do not blaspheme, Christian. Who are you to tempt God?"

"No intent either to blaspheme or tempt, whatever that means, just to be reasonable. But let us get back to your excellent idea, Lotte." He turned to Frau Mueller. "You could take a holiday. The farmhouse compound is big. Almost completed. There will be a guesthouse. And there are rooms in the main house, meanwhile. And if you like the outdoors Sepp will put you to work."

"It could be a help to Fanny with the boys. You understand. That news we spoke about," Lotte said whispering, "I do not say, with child, bad luck, taking His blessings for granted. I shouldn't have even mentioned it to you, God forgive me."

Luftman looked as if he had enough. "Jesus is a forgiving and loving God, Lotte. You said so yourself," he reminded her. "So what do you think, Frau Mueller?"

"Maybe fresh air can make me look younger again," Frau Mueller said, tears halted. "Of course I need to check with Marius. I would love so much to get away."

"I'll discuss it with Fanny. They leave soon. And now," he turned his head, "with all the screams we hear from outside, we should go help her out. Let us gather young Alf, wrap some cakes for Helga and Marius, perhaps sweeten them to this proposition?"

Getting up to leave, Frau Mueller said, "Thank you so much. You are true friends. A gift from our Lord. And from the Blessed Virgin Mother, who has always watched over me, a child without parents. I'm feeling better. Why would Marius say no?" she added, full of hope. "I overheard he will see Fanny and Sepp. That is friendly. A good sign."

Frau Mueller the beauty didn't hear much better than she saw in this case. Marius had refused to see Sepp and Fanny "until they cleansed themselves of the Minderwertige and especially the Jew Haendler living with them. As if a few sprinkles of water changes what he is!" he had told Ernst Schtreuk.

Δ

Fanny and Sepp had hoped to work things out. "With the membership starting to grow — remember they had only 190 stalwarts when we joined? — you would think they could afford to be reasonable," Sepp had said. "These matters need to be discussed."

Fanny tried to contact Herr Harrer, but he was helping organize the party branch in Nuremberg. So they would soon return to Karlsfeld, their mission incomplete. Nothing had changed that Schtreuk had told her the party wanted them to alter.

Before they left, Schtreuk's grandson, Bernd Mueller, was born, a large baby, added to his brother Alf; Helga needed help. Frau Mueller was afraid she could not go to the country with Sepp and Fanny, after all.

It was Fanny, paying Helga a polite call for the new family addition, who suggested that maybe Anke the midwife, Frau Kiembock's sister, could visit and play nurse for a while.

"Naturally she would have to return in time for my own delivery, but that's months away. Perhaps Anke could make it easier for you, Helga. She's a party member, too, with the rest of the Kiembocks. That should satisfy your husband."

"You don't like Marius, do you," Helga said offhandedly, then added, "I like the idea. Better than having my mother-in-law around. That way she can go visit with you."

Gutmann arrived in Dachau with the midwife and left for the countryside with Frau Mueller and Sepp and Fanny. Gretl and Rolf were there to greet them.

Chapter 31
Everything Legal
1925

Fanny and Sepp had arranged a meeting with Herr Harrer, a party founder and a friend. Their party problems, like Damocles' sword, hung ominously over their heads. They had returned to Dachau that morning to meet with Herr Harrer, driven there by Samson Gutmann. That over and done with, their business finished, they all planned to return to Karlsfeld late that same afternoon.

Now, with Father Goetz and Gutmann, they were lunching at the Luftmann home before the drive back to the farm.

"So Herr Hitler learned something at Landsberg, after all, giving up revolution as the way to power," Luftmann said, holding a copy of the Nazi leader's recently published *Mein Kampf.* "And this is only volume one, the *rest* of his driveling nonsense expected next year."

"Neither drivel nor nonsense, Papa! It was important to Sepp and maybe to others that the party renounce revolution. Un-German! And Herr Hitler did that."

"His book is probably more dangerous than foolish, Christian," suggested Father Goetz. He turned to Fanny. "Have you and Sepp actually read it through?"

"I haven't yet," said Sepp. "But I did hear about everything done legally for the party to do its work."

"I haven't read it either," admitted Fanny.

"I have," said Gutmann, surprising those at the table.

"You have what?" asked Fanny.

"I have read *Mein Kampf*," said Gutmann.

"So?" asked the priest. "What did you think?"

"I prefer not to say," Gutmann replied, carefully.

"You should read it, Sepp. He is a terrible writer," said Father Goetz. "Boring! But not his thoughts."

"Dangerous drivel! What do you make of equality only for those who have German blood?" Luftmann gave a laugh. "What is German blood? A different color?"

"No politics at the table," commanded the boss of her kitchen, as she served *Mittagessen*, the midday meal. Because of Sepp and Fanny's pending departure, Lotte prepared dishes out of the ordinary. There was beef in thick sour cream gravy, and an assortment of fresh-cut dark breads and vegetables. There were *Radler*, a refreshing-but-low-in-alcohol drink of beer and lemonade, and wine.

"Even when the Fuehrer was in prison the Nazis won 32 seats in the Reichstag election last year," said Fanny.

"In December, only 14. Not very successful, my child. The Communists won over three times that. And of course our Social Democrats surpassed both. Germans are coming to terms with their new republic as has the Catholic Centre Party."

"This year the people voted the first time for a president, Father-in-law. The winner, not pro-republic. You can't select only the facts that please you," Sepp pointed out with a smile. "We have a monarchist president at the helm in Field Marshall von Hindenburg."

"A small margin, but yes, a victory," Luftmann conceded. "Intimidation, violence all over Germany at the polls. Four people killed, I read. Many more injured. Your party's SA was involved, Sepp."

"The Social Democrat *Republikanischer Schutzbund* and *Reichsbanner Kampfbund* also had their thugs out in full force," Sepp replied, "with the *Rotfrontkaempferbund* as well, all militia of one kind or another. I agree with you there, not an orderly German way to run a country. We desperately need order!"

"Yes, well, Munich voted for the winner! And for order!" interjected Fanny. "Our women's vote is supposed to have won the election for the field marshall."

There was a loud clang from the pot cover Frau Luftmann crashed against the stone countertop. "No politics at the table. Fighting over things that make no difference because you make no difference! We make no difference. I couldn't even vote for president with all those political gangs at Town Hall attacking women, men, young, and old."

"I thought you had voted in the runoff, Lotte," said Luftmann surprised.

"You thought! You thought! Just talk, talk, talk. That's all it is. And in the house, this politics all the time, it's your fault, Christian. I hold you responsible."

"I should have gone with you."

"I would have taken you, Mother Luftmann," said Sepp. He was angered by the bullies and the intimidation of voters the republic generated, if not allowed. His still-raw memories of the Anhalter train station and the attack that killed his horse were more festering wounds than scars. "Democracy!" he made a spitting sound without actually spitting. "To attack women!"

"I asked you to go with me, Mother," interjected Fanny, seeing how angry Sepp was. "I had no idea you went."

"Yes, well, all of you think all I know is the kitchen. And I tell you, that is all I need to know, because here I can control outcomes."

"Even without your vote, Mother, women made a difference."

"You get the right to vote from the democratic republic constitution, then, in the first direct election for president, you turn around and vote for a monarchist! How the world works is strange, yes?" Luftmann sighed, then — after a disapproving glance from Lotte — again gave abject apologies to his wife.

An unfamiliar quiet embraced the dinner table, a silent vacuum pleading to be filled by their customary animated talks. It couldn't last.

"More Protestants in town, do you notice? With the influx of Pumf workers and their families from all over. The prayer room they use in Fruehlingstrasse, overcrowded. Soon they need a regular minister and a regular church," remarked Father Goetz. "Pastor Heinrich was telling me just this weekend."

"Dachau is still Catholic, Father," Luftmann observed. "This Pastor Heinrich? A good man of God? Except of course misled by Luther."

"That, Christian, is not for the dinner table either," Lotte said.

There was another pause in conversation.

"Those backward Americans," Fanny said, raising a new topic. "Find a teacher guilty of teaching science, in these days. Hypocrites! Not so advanced or free to speak in that democracy. The Monkey Trials? They are the monkeys, *gell?*"

"Darwinian Science, his theory of evolution," Father Goetz said softly. "Some who believe seriously in the Bible are offended, Fanny."

"Are you saying — "

Luftmann interrupted. "The children nap. We should enjoy our meal in peace. Lotte is right. I notice no one says anything about my wife's cooking.

Delicious, *gell?*"

"As usual, Frau Luftmann. The best meals in Dachau," Father Goetz agreed. "By the way, how is Frau Mueller enjoying the farm?"

"Well, she didn't accept our invitation to visit Dachau with us today. That should say something," observed Sepp.

Δ

After lunch, Fanny took her father aside in his library.

"Herr Harrer helps with Gretl and Gutmann, Papa. He makes a deal for us. I want you to know so that you don't make trouble for us thinking out loud with your opinions."

"So we are not allowed to think in my house? Who stops us?"

"Well, Mother is the censor at the dinner table, for one," Fanny reminded him. "However, we're not in Berlin. Munich and Dachau do not share your democratic views."

"I will not address that, Fanny. What deal? You gave away the right to think?"

"I will not address that!" she shot back. "It's good for the family. Herr Harrer, bypassing Marius, is arranging for Sepp to be offered a commission in the new security police for the Fuehrer. It is for true and best Germans, like our Sepp."

"Yet one more paramilitary to deal with when no military is allowed," he said in a tired voice. "And what are this special police called?"

"*Schutzstaffel! The Protectors. SS* for short. There are only about 200 such men, Papa. An honor, really. They work only for Herr Hitler. Just as the Imperial Guard protected only the Kaiser. The party strictly checks backgrounds in order to belong. One must be racially pure. The same uniform as the brown-shirts SA, but with a black tie and a cap with a *Totenkopf* insignia to separate them."

"A death head their symbol? That's very nice, Fanny. Let me be now. Mother is right. We should not have politics at meals or in this house."

"We made a deal. If it works well, they forgive Sepp his Bolshevik father, Papa. They don't bother us, thank God, with that Minderwertige talk or about our friendship with a baptized Jew living on the compound."

"For now!"

She ignored her father's skepticism.

"Sepp may be working less on the farm, Papa, if at all. But I wanted you to know we dealt with that party problem we were having. It's important to us."

"Fanny, were you really going to argue with Father Goetz at the dinner table? A priest bound by his theology? Creationism versus evolution?"

"I'm not talking about Father Goetz, now. I was only trying to make table conversation. I think I was helpful in this deal, protecting my aunt from scorn and our friend Samson. Meanwhile Sepp is given an honor, as well. His studies at the military academy and his heroic record in the war give him deserved recognition in a field that has been his first choice. As you would say, a good deal, everybody happy!"

Luftmann seemed distracted. He massaged his bearded chin, as if not listening. Something Fanny had said earlier stuck in his mind.

Looking up, he asked, "They check backgrounds, you say?"

Something else to worry him. A test of his masquerade.

Chapter 32
The Last Laugh
1926

With his son-in-law's background check, his safety net strategy was being put to the test. What Lotte had called his foolishness, laughing at him.

Naturally they — whoever *they* were and whatever they were checking — would look into Sepp's wife's background as well, Fanny's background. Clearly, on matters of racial purity, this minority party was very thorough.

Father Goetz had told him they came to St. Jakob's asking for baptismal records. He had no qualms about sharing them, though the men weren't public officials of any sort. Why raise any kind of suspicions by hiding the harmless, Father had explained.

"Suspicion about whom?" Luftmann was again on the alert.

"About me, of course," said Father Goetz smoothly.

Fanny Luftmann's record he gave. After all, he had baptized her at St. Jakob's. As far as her parents Christian and Lotte were concerned, for those records he directed them to Cologne's *Koelner Dom*.

From Cologne, when shown the Luftmann's baptismal record, it clearly stated that they had converted, indeed, but from Lutheran to Roman Catholic, as Christian knew it would, because it was true.

Those trips, those unpleasant visits to Berlin and Hamburg before they married that Lotte wanted to forget, were planned by Christian, part of his clever transformation game. They would marry in Hamburg, but not until they had become Lutherans in Berlin.

He went to his father's distant relations — the Lutheran ones — for direction in both northern cities. The assimilated relatives had already left the faith, loved Luther, loved everything about him including Luther's medieval treatises on *The Jews and Their Lies*. Whatever it was, they loved it, defended it, or feigned ignorance.

Back then, the distant cousins in both places, Berlin and Hamburg, were in a hurry to get the foreign-looking provincial relatives, Chaim and Chaya, on their way out of town. The former Itzigs were sensitive to non-Prussian looks.

Chaim and Chaya were altered, altared, and shipped out as quickly as those *Ostjuden* who were sealed in trains going directly to the seaport, after the de-licing. That process also arranged and observed carefully by waiting and terrified German Jews at the eastern border. They had to make sure their exotic, eastern, non-European-looking brethren didn't land in the Kaiserreich as their final destination.

So, like the *Ostjuden*, Luftmann and his new wife were out of Berlin and then Hamburg before ever meeting the rest of the family, including the family 'jewel,' their Lutheran minister. Luftmann's safety net ploy was a brilliant move, however; farseeing, but not entirely original. He could not take all the credit. But who cared as long as it could mislead nosy people?

Christian Luftmann nè Chaim Itzig had read about the Moses Mendelsohn offspring, children and grandchildren, almost all of whom had abandoned Judaism, unlike their respected philosopher father and grandfather. Moses, remaining loyal to his Jewish orthodoxy, was still the only philosopher footnoted in Kant's writings. The convert grandchildren were not impressed.

Most became Lutherans then later moved on to the Roman Church.

It had been a puzzle. Why had they done this, employed this mechanism? Clearly he didn't believe they accepted Jesus in the first place. He knew better than that; this wholesale Mendelsohn family move was not an epiphany of faith, but a yearning for German-ness, for acceptance. So why two different kinds of Jesus religions?

Then the answer had come to him. A security measure, Lutheran to Catholic, to move them one more step away from their Jewish roots. That was why! Luftmann was pleased and wore a broad grin. The Nazi background investigators checking out Sepp for this new job would have to work a little harder to find Jewishness in Fanny. And maybe they wouldn't get there. The Mendelsohns must have understood in this world one can't be too careful. And what other world was there?

He had a brittle smile on his face, his heart pounding, when Fanny ran into his library, great books pressed together on their dark wood shelves, titles jumping out, authors' names emblazoned — Dostoevsky, Shakespeare, Chaucer, Goethe, Aristotle, Plato, Sophocles, Euripides, Homer, Virgil, Voltaire, Dante — so many books, so many great minds he would never have known without the Enlightenment, without emancipation, without the advent of the *maskilim* well-rounded education his mother had chosen for him and his father had allowed.

He pushed his chair away from the desk. Fanny looked intense, flushed. He couldn't tell why.

"So?" he asked his daughter. "What news do you bring on this unexpected visit?"

Fanny blurted, "We passed, Papa. We passed!" Breaking into a broad grin, she gave him a hug. "Everything went well. No bother to us anymore from Marius Mueller, no more annoyances about Aunt Gretl and Herr Gutmann. No more questions about Ludwig Hofer. No more mysterious fleeting tickles inside me. All arranged through our mentor, Herr Harrer. Sepp is now officially accepted to that elite Schutzstaffel group; he's in the SS. We can all happily await a new healthy baby for our nation's future. What a joyous family Christmas we will have this year."

Chapter 33
Lisle
1926

Right before Christmas, Sepp and Fanny Hofer's daughter Lisle was born. The child was premature, six weeks earlier than expected.

Frau Kiembock helped with the delivery. Anke had not gotten back from Helga's home in Dachau in time. Lotte, there on a Karlsfeld visit with Luftmann, was too nervous to be useful. She prayed a lot instead.

"It is a girl, Frau Hofer," said the farmer's wife, cutting the cord, setting aside the afterbirth on old newspapers.

She wiped down the tiny infant with goose oil before wrapping her upper body in brown paper. She covered her with a flannel blanket and handed her to Sepp. Farmers' families knew the healing powers of drained fat on lungs and breathing that plagued premature infants. Then she burst into tears and ran out of the room.

"What is the matter, Sepp?" asked Fanny. "Ten fingers? Ten toes?"

"Yes my love, ten fingers, ten toes."

"Then?"

Lotte entered the room with Luftmann trailing. She saw the child. Her face turned gray. She began to shudder and moan as if a torrent of pent-up dark doubts, primitive fears, and punitive portents flooded through her.

"What is going on?" Fanny cried. "Let me see my baby."

"Fanny, *Liebchen*, dear wife, prepare yourself," said Sepp, bringing the child to her side. "Our daughter is not right. She resembles your aunt. She looks more like Gretl than Gretl does."

Standing in the middle of the room, Lotte swayed as if she might faint. Luftmann caught her in his arms, holding her upright, trying to soothe and placate his distraught wife. Nevertheless, something had already snapped inside her.

Chapter 34
Secrets
1927

It was early morning feeding time. Through the nursery window, farm fields spread before her, damp crops budding in the rising June sun. In the distance, Gutmann, the Kiembocks and some extra farmhands were out feeding the livestock, milking the cows. Fanny knew Luddy and Josef were performing their chores in the noisy chicken house, tossing feed and collecting eggs. Sepp was just getting up, washing, shaving, dressing for the day's work. He had returned home in the early morning hours from an assignment in Berlin. Gretl was roaming around somewhere with Rolf.

Sunlight danced on pastel walls decorated with sheets of pink, yellow, and blue paper. Fanny sat in the cushioned rocking chair, a gift handmade from the Kiembocks when Josef was born. The baby in her arms, she was nursing her daughter.

Fanny and Sepp, accepted in Karlsfeld once again because of their Storm Trooper protection and political connections, stayed at the farm now as much to keep prying eyes away from their daughter as to get away from a turbulent, changed Dachau.

She hugged her seven-month-old to her breast. A lovable child, their Lisle, often laughing, smiling to herself as if in her own world. Even Josef and Luddy were affectionate, amused by their tiny sister's expressions and sounds. Gretl worshipped the baby, Gutmann took her for short drives, and Rolf was fiercely protective.

"Come, come, my darling Lisle, take the nipple," Fanny coaxed. "Don't you want to grow big and strong?"

The baby alternately gurgled, giggled, grunted, moving her head, and looking away. Feeding was never easy. Mostly, Lisle was nourished from mother's milk. Her diet was the simplest of pureed foods because she had difficulty swallowing.

She was so undemanding. No trouble at all, Fanny was thinking, when

Lisle stiffened like a board, her expression frozen, unblinking opened eyes transfixed. It was all in a few seconds. As Fanny screamed for help, Lisle began to spasm, jerking movements here and there. A foamy spittle ran from her mouth. The episode lasted a few moments before she went limp like a rag doll and nodded off, too weak to make a sound let alone suckle.

"Sepp," Fanny screamed. "Samson! The baby! A doctor! Hurry."

Fanny had heard the Karlsfeld doctor was a war veteran like Sepp, feeling the *Frontgemeinschaft* communal bond, as all the Great War veterans did who had been *Frontsoldaten*. And many of his patients benefited from the SA and steel helmet protection of the Luftmann farms. He would be discreet, as were the Kiembocks.

It seemed like forever until he arrived, a large man, tall, looking more like a wrestler than a physician. After his examination, as if understanding all concerns, he said quietly to Sepp and Fanny, "There is strict patient-doctor confidentiality that I honor." He went on. "I have sedated your daughter. Having had one such episode you need to watch carefully for others."

"You think there will be more?"

"Herr Hofer, with brain disruption, one event gives opportunity for a second." He turned to Fanny, handing her a liquid medication from his small black satchel. "A strong drug to calm the brain activity, Frau Hofer. Three times a day. She will sleep more."

"Is she epileptic, Doctor?" Fanny asked, a mother's anxiety rushing to the worst possibilities.

"I cannot tell. This is the first you notice, you say. It was a mild seizure. I believe she has a loss of lateral vision as well," said the doctor, after he swung a bright ball on a cord back and forth before Lisle's eyes. "A minor loss, but not encouraging. Yet it could be temporary, Frau Hofer. Is she growing slowly for her age?"

"Slower than the boys," Fanny admitted. At seven months, Lisle could not turn over, let alone sit.

"Remember, watch her carefully for seizures," he said, ready to leave.

"I was a volunteer during the war and afterward at the St. Jakob's infirmary, Doctor. I learned to follow instructions."

"You must have seen a lot. I am sure your baby is in good care."

Noting the frontline badge in the physician's lapel, Sepp asked, "Verdun?"

"Ypres, third battle."

Sepp gave a half salute, then shook his hand. "Thank you for coming to the house so quickly. Samson drives you back, *Kamerad*."

The next day, Fanny was reading the *Voelkische Beobachter*, the Nazi newspaper published again since Herr Hitler's political ban was lifted earlier that year. Just last month he had started speaking tours in Bavaria.

She was sitting in the feeding rocker in Lisle's room, on watch all night following the doctor's orders about close observation. Gutmann, who had brought the paper, offered to relieve her, but Fanny had to do it herself. The child was sleeping. It was another delightful June day, the perfumed scent of summer in the air. Fanny was exhausted. She wished they could be outside.

Yawning, she glanced at the front page. It showed the Rotfront-kaempferbund, parading through the streets of Berlin led by Ernst Thaelmann, their losing candidate in the 1925 presidential runoff. He looks smug, thought Fanny. They all look smug with their brown uniforms, high boots, and red armbands. She searched for her father-in-law in the photo of these marching Communists. She and Sepp had neither seen nor heard from Ludwig Hofer since before Lisle was born.

Lisle stirred. Fanny quickly got up. The child was still asleep but was trying to move her body to another position. Fanny sighed, gently turning her over, then went back to the rocker and the *Beobachter*.

On page three there was a story that caught her sleepy-eyed attention:

NSDAP RESCUED

"The Nazi Party had its financial troubles in this deflationary period. Without Herr Hugenberg, the Industrialists, and the Junkers bailing us out, our party would have gone bankrupt. The rank and file, working class, and farmers suffering so under this criminal republic couldn't support the party. The party couldn't afford to fund our SA or SS anymore. Those respected wealthy Germans helped keep the party alive."

Fanny was surprised.

Sepp had never worried her about this party crisis, never shared it with her. If the party had failed, his military life would have been *kaputt*, done for, with all of his hopes and dreams for their nation. Yet knowing how vulnerable she was since Lisle's birth, he had protected her from his troubles. Again she fell in love with the husband she adored.

But it was the next headline in the centerfold that woke Fanny up, reached her where she was most sensitive.

THREE GENERATIONS OF IMBECILES ARE ENOUGH!
AMERICAN SUPREME COURT DECISION FROM CHIEF JUSTICE OLIVER WENDELL HOLMES

The article said the respected American jurist made that statement in upholding the American State of Virginia Forced Sterilization Law, forced sterilization of what in Germany was called the Minderwertige. What they called Gretl. What they might call Lisle! Unworthy lives.

The Nazi Party talked often about racial fitness and hygiene, about controlled breeding and eugenics at meetings she attended. Their views were bolstered by books on race, written by respected authors. Always piled neatly on a table in the front of the room, they were available to members on loan. Separate flyers cited references and quotes from them, promoting racial purity, protection, and preservation. There was one authored by a Jew named Goldstein.

No surprise, Fanny thought. For centuries Jews religiously kept to themselves, flatly rejecting Martin Luther's invitation to join his reformed Christianity — everyone knew that. They had practiced what now was called controlled breeding by marrying only other Jews, mingling with non-Jews forbidden by their laws, their laws now used against them! Were the tables turning?

In the worst economic times, the issues at party meetings referred to the wasted spending on Minderwertige by state and ecclesiastical asylums, as well as the genetic elements of racial hygiene.

Using charts, guest lecturers showed draining costs to the healthy to support the weak and inferior, showed that poor workers and families could starve, lose their homes, while incurable imbeciles and cripples had food and shelter. The posters revealed the construction costs of asylums as six million marks, then estimated how many homes for sturdy and strong German families could be built for that money. Lastly, they argued, healthy young Germans died on the battlefields while defectives were cared for and protected.

With the assumption of limited resources, Fanny was torn between compassion for the helpless versus the deprivation and drain on the healthy.

The Nazi lectures made their point, repeating American policies (thirty American states had forced-sterilization statutes) and praising Denmark, where unofficial forced sterilization had been going on for years. "As in Sweden, our tiny Nordic neighbor to the north, with no misplaced pity, also knows how to protect itself, dares to serve the strong in their nation," said the guest speaker, who happened to be Marius Mueller that night. He was becoming one of the party experts on racial issues.

"But some German writers and authorities have gone further than sterilization," he had said, holding up a new book. "They write about euthanasia, like authors Binding and Hoche in *The Destruction of Lives Not Worth Living*."

At that meeting, the party distributed brief summaries of the controversial book; Fanny had thrown hers away once she got home. But her memories of these discussions became more important after Lisle was born. These ideas were no secret. They appeared often in *Voelkische Beobachter* and *Dachauer Zeitung* articles.

The book's summaries had included a standard one-sheet flyer — that page Fanny saved — telling how advanced Greek and Roman civilizations were destroyed by inferior races. It warned that could happen to Germans as well.

"We must thoroughly understand and use racial engineering," read the flyer. "We cannot depend on Darwin's natural selection for the survival of Western civilization. We need selections controlled by humans based on right genes, eliminating wrong ones in whatever way necessary to accomplish the task."

Fanny had showed the sheet to Father Goetz for an opinion.

"The destruction of Western civilization! Hah! A compelling bit of reasoning," he had said. "Reasoning that, itself, can cause the destruction of Western civilization." Then he added, "What is troublesome is the part about elimination. In whatever way necessary? Dangerous thought!"

Fanny hadn't argued with the priest, but Greeks and Romans, superior races, *were* overrun by barbarians, by less civilized aggressors. (The party sheet had not identified which barbarians, however — namely, the Goths, Huns, and other East Germanic tribes!)

Today, the *Beobachter* wrote in the Justice Holmes article "Americans, by upholding forced sterilization of the genetically inferior agree good environment cannot pass health to future progeny, only good genes, hence the science of Eugenics."

Fanny had often heard Father Goetz and her father talking about these matters. They had been under discussion ever since the new 19th-century sciences of Darwin and Mendel. The Catholic Church from the beginning was outspoken in opposition to forced sterilization, let alone euthanasia.

"We cry out against human breeding selections versus the will of God the Creator. We pray daily that God's will be done, not ours," Father Goetz had said in one of his many sermons against this Nazi policy. "A sign of civilization in a nation and in people is altruism and their treatment of the helpless."

Frau Mueller, a highly emotional and fragile woman all of her life, tears welling up, had said to Fanny after that particular Mass, "To think they might have killed me, an abandoned child who couldn't see, whose nerves broke down, as they called it. Thank the Lord for the convent and the caring sisters," and then all her anguish spilling over, she added, sobbing, "And thank them for finding a husband for me, a good man, who had to die too soon. My cross to bear!"

Not knowing what else to do, Fanny had given the distressed woman a hug. She remembered Marius Mueller walking over saying, "Come Mother! Don't make a spectacle."

A spectacle! Was Lisle a spectacle? Her thoughts traveled back always to Lisle.

Fanny dropped the *Voelkische Beobachter*. Hugging herself, she began to rock back and forth. She was painfully aware, as a member of the Nazi Party, that more would be expected from her as to standards of racial fitness.

Given Gretl and now Lisle did she, did the Luftmanns, have their generations of imbeciles? Were there terrible secrets? Did she carry inferior genes? Would Sepp lose his position with the SS? Would Marius Mueller take advantage and destroy all of them?

Instead of rocking in the nursery room chair, Fanny wished she was back in the Dachau of her youth when cycling around the familiar and friendly town had made things better when she was upset.

Chapter 35
More Secrets
1927

Just when the economic climate looked better, improving with the help of American loans and adjustments to the Versailles reparations, the agrarian crisis occurred. It had a domino effect. Government was once more ugly with factions pointing fingers. People were losing their jobs.

Her father had tried to explain it.

"You see, deflated selling prices for farm products while farmers are indebted to inflationary loans cause terrible problems. People are out of work because the demand for farm goods decreases in proportion to the government's efforts to save money, to stabilize the economy, creating even more unemployment."

"I don't understand," Fanny had said.

"You're just like your mother," Luftmann had said.

"Yes, well, what I do know is farmers in the county borrowed many marks when money was worth little and now have to pay back while getting less money for their goods. Pay more, make less. Then starve. That I understand." But Fanny did remember Father Goetz' sermon about hard times, human nature, and the helpless.

"When hardships fall upon us, suffering families are tempted to disregard the weak and helpless. Tempted to abandon our Christian values. Tempted to take extreme measures. I urge you to trust in God."

Ideals were expensive for poverty-stricken, jobless people. There was revived interest in the costs of the Minderwertige and the solutions of sterilization and euthanasia. "That's where money could be saved, not by lowering unemployment benefits and losing job opportunities," Mueller had said at one of the meetings.

On watch in the yellow, pink, and blue nursery for the second day after her child's seizure, Fanny kept visualizing the *Beobachter* headline THREE

GENERATIONS OF IMBECILES. Caught up in her own thoughts, she did not hear Sepp come in the room.

"Fanny, come in the hallway! I need to talk. I don't want to disturb Lisle." He was wearing his SS uniform.

She peeked in the crib before leaving her post and left the door ajar.

"The baby? She is good?"

"She is good," said Fanny. "You're dressing to leave again? So soon?"

"Another meeting. But I have news," he said, looking happy. "I'm told I'm part of the SS group providing security to travel with Herr Hitler and high-ranking party members like Roehm, Himmler, Strasser, even Goering, on an unofficial mission. Outstanding Germans like Ludendorff and even the Kaiserreich War Minister Werner Haupt, go as well. Maybe ten days gone. Imagine, after all we went through, Fanny, your husband is trusted so within the party. And, I can take the boys, as well, if that is acceptable to you."

"The boys? Aren't they too young? Josef not yet five? Luddy about to be four? And such a long trip for them?"

"The *HJ*, Fanny, the *Hitler-Jugend* are going along. They make a film! They invited SS members' children — boys only — to join them. Promotion for future recruits to the party youth movements. That is supposedly the reason for the outing. We go to a resort town. The HJ will have a play bus for the younger children. And there will be nurses along as well."

"Too much, too quick," said Fanny breathlessly. "Where are you going? And when is all this happening?"

"We leave next week, I'm afraid. Russia, France — "

"Russia? Why do they wait to the last minute to tell you? And Red Russia?"

"They didn't wait. But some official matters are secrets. Not to be discussed until the time is right."

"Secrets between a wife and husband? Not like us to be that way," she tried to wheedle the information from him.

"State secrets are different from marriage ones. Don't try to coax me, Fanny. It will do you no good. Anyway, the *Deutsche Republik* did sign a second treaty with the Reds last year, remember?"

"I suppose so. Yes. My father found it funny. No, not funny, what did he say? Ironic, that was it."

"We visit a resort town about 300 miles from Moscow. It's a recreational area so Hitler-Jugend, our Hitler Youth, will see to it that it is enjoyable for the young people, set an example for them, shoot the film about the advantages of the Hitler Youth Movement, while the Fuehrer and company do their work."

"Which is? What? More filming?"

"Again, you try! Naughty girl," he laughed, giving her a pat on the cheek, then, standing closer, he kissed her to make it better.

His hand brushed against her blouse. Fanny blushed. It did not escape Sepp. He looked at her hard, eyebrows raised. A question? An invitation? Slowly she shook her head. Sepp gazed a moment longer, then moved away.

"The army militias go there often. Hitler wants to see what goes on. I think he knows. Otherwise he could just send emissaries to find out."

"Well, if you have to go to Russia, better in June than December. I will worry, but of course the boys can go. It is an honor for them to travel with the Fuehrer!"

"They'll get badges, I'm told. Imagine how they will like that? Feel special. When they're ten, they'll be old enough to join the Hitler Youth junior branch. I think of myself longing to be a cadet, to live a life of honor and duty. That dream was blocked, but the Schutzstaffel returned it to me. It will be good for our sons."

"You know I agree. Friendships, a good influence! Maybe Josef can learn to use all that physical energy in a better way," she said, with a worried frown. "And Luddy, always looking in from the outside, never a part of something."

"People mostly are who they are. I thought you knew this by now, Fanny," Sepp said quietly. "Josef is a warrior by nature, I think."

"But their programs are healthy, the camps, the physical training, Sepp. Mind and body. Self-discipline! Boys grow strong! With character. It can change them for the better, is how I think. People can change! That Rote Jungfront, I read in the *Beobachter* the Reds take their youth to visit the Soviets often. Their leaders should be ashamed, twisting young minds away from German ways. But why France, Sepp? It's out of the way."

"More propaganda! On our way back, a detour. Not so bad! We meet in Lyons to see *Le Faiscea* and their youth. More filming, establish ties. The French fascist group has many of the same ideas as our party, especially about racial purity and foreign elements."

"Too bad wives are not invited on this venture," she pouted in a half-serious way. "A holiday is tempting."

"Well then, you should have one! Take a trip alone. A good time to do so, Fanny. To work things out. I know you haven't been feeling 100 percent." He paused and again looked hard at her. "We can't go on this way."

Fanny knew he referred to her seeming lack of interest in their marital bed — not like the passionate woman he married. If Sepp only knew how much she wanted to be with him as always — like this morning — but she feared having another child. From time to time she pleaded physical weakness and lack of strength.

Lisle's birth was not easy for her nor was the lingering nightmare afterward. Sepp had been understanding and, fortunately, had been away often on duty, protecting higher-ups and their Fuehrer on visits throughout Germany. Yet she knew he was right. They couldn't go on this way.

Sepp was serious, not about politics now, but about their marriage.

"Lisle will be no trouble. As long as she has medication she sleeps most of the time anyhow. Samson and Gretl are here. Frau Mueller can help. She prefers us to Dachau with her son and daughter-in-law. The guest cottage suits her. We could name it the Hannah Mueller House." He looked amused at that notion. "Or if you prefer you could tear Anke away from Helga."

Anke was not an option. Her long relationship with the Muellers, a party member herself. It could raise questions about her daughter's condition. Marius would somehow get involved. No, she dare not go in that direction, but Fanny had plans.

She never wanted to go on a political trip to Russia with Sepp's SS group. By acting as if she was interested, Fanny hoped Sepp would make the holiday suggestion — her getting away alone — because she needed to get away. She had considered such a plan since Lisle was born and had come to a decision, only waiting for when and how. Sepp's trip with the boys gave her the opportunity to proceed.

But first, the conversation with her father. She had been putting it off but could no longer. THREE GENERATIONS OF IMBECILES! Fanny had to ask him about Gretl, about his family, about her mother's, before she took action.

Chapter 36
Talks and More Secrets

Fanny accompanied Gutmann to Dachau the next day on his weekly visit to see Father Goetz.

"Do you go only for confession, Samson? You could do that in Karlsfeld."

"Father Goetz will always be my confessor," he said simply. "And I study, too, Frau Hofer. I still learn the mysteries of my new faith." He pointed to the baby sleeping in the carrying cradle. "See how your daughter sleeps when I drive, always happens when I take Lisle in the car."

"She sleeps most of the time, Samson, since the seizure and the medication. Except when she needs something and I am never sure what it is. A mother should know what her child wants, right?" Fanny could not conceal the despair in her voice.

"You seem sad. If I can help in any way, I am here for you and your family."

"I may ask for your help, Samson."

Fanny could not stop thinking about the new science of eugenics, good genes, controlled and selective breeding. Reasoned Fanny, where there's good, there would be bad. Bad genes. Dangerous genes. Genes that promoted racial degeneracy, degraded racial health, bled the nation's financial resources! Controlled *not-breeding*, then? Sterilization?

Arriving at the Burgfrieden Luftmann home, Fanny deposited the cradle with the sleeping baby in the kitchen with her mother. Frau Luftmann took little notice, eyes focused on her work. Busy cooking as usual, thought Fanny, grateful that her mother didn't ask her standard question of late. Are you with child again?

Lotte's kitchen today was as Fanny recalled it from the past. It had the same comforting aromas — as if part of the plaster walls. The apple cake was safely warm in the kitchen's tile oven, waiting for the coat of whipped cream added at the meal's end — a tasty desert! Simmering softly on the stove top, releasing seductive, mouth-watering fragrances, there was seasoned potato soup and potted meat, stewing in onions, turnips, and greens. Clearly she was planning for Fanny to eat with them. And there was enough for Samson, as well.

"Is that Lebkuchen you make, too?"

"I send some back for the boys and for Gretl. Enough for her to have for a while."

The delicious scents wafted into the study where Fanny and Christian sat together, the way she remembered Father Goetz sitting with her father on his weekly visits to deliver the sacrament to her aunt.

"Mother works too hard, all that cooking. She does not look well. She acts strange, she's so quiet. She should come to the farm."

"Your mother has built a shrine to the Virgin Mary in the bedroom. When not working she prays there many times a day. I ask if she feels ill. I tell her to see a doctor."

"At least she didn't bring up my having more children. That is obsessing her, and with Lisle not yet a year old. But something is wrong. There is a fine physician in Karlsfeld and mother could rest at the farm. It would do her good."

"That woman has a mind of her own. I tell her to rest. Instead she works harder. Finds things to do. Scrubs on her knees and prays more. Tells me we have plenty of time to rest when we die. Maybe you talk to her," he sighed and gave a helpless shrug. "So, tell me, the baby is well? No more episodes?"

"Still listless, Papa, but that could be the medicine." She waited a moment and said, "We need to talk."

"Then we talk," Luftmann said.

"There was another one, too, another sister besides Aunt Gretl, wasn't there, Papa?" she asked, knowing it was a clumsy way to start a conversation.

"I beg your pardon?"

"There was another sister," Fanny repeated.

For a moment Luftmann remembered his own mother's lifelong rejection. Old and foolish superstitions. He remembered how he was blamed for his sisters' abnormal conditions, for toxifying her womb, for all Jewish troubles. The thought triggered old feelings, childhood feelings of sadness.

Clearing his throat, Luftmann said, "Yes, there was another sister. She died in the cholera plague."

"Was she like Aunt Gretl? Were there any others like Aunt Gretl? Were there others before them?" She fired one bullet after another from her arsenal of questions. "Are there secrets I need to know about your families, yours and mother's?"

"Do not upset your mother with such questions!"

"I know that. I am asking you."

"Family members either died from the epidemic or emigrated during the *Gruenderjahre* panic, Fanny, when over two million other Germans left the Kaiserreich in order to survive the economic catastrophe."

She hesitated, looking around the room, taking deep breaths, building up courage for the next question. "Why did you and Mama have no other children after me?"

"That is all there is to tell, Fanny. Finished! Is that why you are here? To interrogate?"

"Justice Holmes in America's highest court announced that three generations of imbeciles are enough!"

"They should check your leader's family then," he snapped.

"I will forget you said such a thing about Herr Hitler, Papa. Why are you so angry? Don't you understand? I worry about my family."

Luftmann stared at the beautiful woman in front of him. A woman that somehow came from him and Lotte. She worries about what could be upcoming, prospects and expectations, he thought, realizing for once his daughter was taking after him.

"I do understand," he said quietly, regaining his composure.

Fanny worried for her child's future and their present, hers and Sepp's. If she had bad genes, the alternatives were to practice birth control, which was marriage abuse in her church, or, forgoing sex, which was unnatural, or trusting in God, which was dangerous, or being sterilized.

Forgoing sex and physical love with her husband was not normal. Marriage abuse was a sin — though practiced by many Catholics, especially returning veterans after the war. Their weakened confidence in their church was coupled with economic hard times discouraging large families. Sepp would never agree in any case. Trusting in God was too much to ask of her. Suppose He had other plans?

Sterilization remained. That she could do. A sin by intention, yes, irreversibly preventing conception, but she would not tell Sepp. He hadn't worried her about the party's financial problems; she would protect him now from sinfulness. He would have no decision to make, she rationalized. It was the only way. Her decision. Now was the opportunity, when Sepp and the boys would be away.

She had to have a Jewish doctor, a foreign Jewish doctor. He would have no Christian religious constraints, no probing inquiries, no possible connections to friends, family, or the National Socialist German Workers' Party.

The *Beobachter* had praised Denmark in that article. They were sterilizing defectives for years it said. They have the experience. What did they call it for women, she tried to remember? Yes, tubal ligation, that was it. Denmark!

One such child, Fanny could manage and hide. But several? She crossed herself and prayed to the Blessed Virgin Mother for mercy because she had heard Father Goetz say, begging for forgiveness was easier than asking for permission.

She would go to Samson. He had offered help just this morning, she thought with a wry smile, not having any idea how soon a request would be made for his services. Samson was a safe choice for many reasons.

He was a Jew or had been. Had doctors in the family dispersed throughout Europe, he had once told Sepp. Maybe some were in Denmark or some could send her to a Jewish doctor in Denmark. She wouldn't have to tell him why. He wouldn't ask out of respect, she knew. And he was closemouthed; a Catholic Jewish German who had been a Haendler all his life had to be careful about everything now.

Frau Mueller and Gretl and Gutmann could watch Lisle. Sepp was right about that. She could not ask her parents. They would ask questions. At least her father would.

Her decision had other consequences that bothered her. How would she ever go to confession again? Would she dare not admit what she had done? Receive the Eucharist when her confession was defective? Another sin! Or would she confess the truth? Could she trust the sacred privacy of the sacrament? Trust the discretion of Father Goetz?

And what about her mother, acting so troubled now? Telling her to have more children. A good Catholic wife. What would she think of her darling Fanny if she knew?

Feelings more basic churned inside her, shame for hiding her child and guilt, guilt for that shame and for what she felt she had brought about. She, who was so perfect, a model for German womanhood, just invited to the 1928 Summer Olympics in Amsterdam as the women's lawn tennis coach. Herr Harrer, so esteemed in the party and still an influential sports writer, had arranged it.

Fanny had kept this Olympics secret from Sepp. But did Sepp know? Had Herr Harrer told him? Is that why he suggested a vacation trip? A substitute treat for her?

The 1928 games was her nation's first participation in the Olympics since before the Great War. She declined, of course. The training, the practice, the event itself — Fanny could not leave Lisle for so long a time. And clearly she couldn't take her along. Would they laugh and call her Germany's future generation? Tears gathered in her eyes.

She, Fanny Luftmann Hofer, had created an imperfect daughter to whom she gave none of her outstanding traits or talents. She had wished for an athlete like herself, a daughter whom she would teach the skills of lawn tennis and of competing, to fulfill her own aborted dream!

So confident most of her life, now she was tormented by an unfamiliar feeling of helplessness, of not being able to do anything for Lisle, for her child. These emotions ripped her aching heart, tore her apart, a disfigurement of her very soul. Alone in her room at the Karlsfeld farm she looked at herself in the mirror, the poster maiden looked back. She threw herself across the wide four-poster canopy bed and wept.

That same week, through Gutmann, she made an appointment with a Dr. Held in Copenhagen. Sepp had been delighted Fanny was going off to some renowned Danish spa near the seaside for rest and recuperation. That is what she had told him.

Gutmann offered to drive her on the mysterious thirteen-hour trip, but Fanny needed him at home on the farm. Besides, journeys by rail could have a calming effect. If it weren't for the incident at the Anhalter station she might have enjoyed the ride back to Dachau with Sepp in that long ago time.

As for Sepp's SS trip to that Russian resort, once there, Sepp wrote reassuring her that the boys were fine. They enjoyed the journey, the songs, the marching, the games, and wore their gold-and-red Swastika honorary youth badges prominently on their jackets, looking up to their happy and robust hosts, the Hitler Youth

He still could not reveal more. He could not tell her Lipetsk was the spa town they visited 300 miles from Moscow. Nor that he saw the Junker airplane factory and training school for test pilots where anti-republic, high-ranking Germans — in a secret deal with the Soviets — practiced flying and built new war planes because they were forbidden to do it at home, that it was the reason why the airman war hero Goering was along on the trip.

He could not tell her that he overheard War Minister Haupt tell Ludendorff, "We have other undisclosed armament facilities here in Russia. No French treaty, no criminal Deutsche Republik, can leave Germany defenseless."

Chapter 37
Prognosis and Pedigrees

"Unlikely in your case, but what you describe does resemble Tay-Sachs, Frau Hofer," said the Danish doctor in his spotless examining room a day after the surgery. "Though from the physical features you portray it could even be Down."

"What is Tay-Sachs?"

"A congenital disease, but again I say unlikely."

"Why is that, doctor?"

"Your pedigree, so to speak." He stroked his clean-shaven face. "Tay-Sachs is a degenerative disease found mostly in Jews of Eastern European descent. There are exceptions of course. Are there others like this in your family?"

"Of course not," Fanny lied. "Is there a cure?"

"I'm afraid it is neither treatable nor curable. The afflicted do not survive long."

"Only children have this?"

"There is adult onset as well. They deteriorate as they get older. But they do get older. Anyway, I would have to see your daughter to make a diagnosis. Now, about you," he switched the topic, seeing how worried she looked. "Good news! The ligation procedure went well. I strongly recommend you stay in our recovery facility for a few more days until we are sure there are no complications. It is comfortable there, more like a spa than a clinic."

"That works well for me, doctor. Thank you."

"Good, then that's settled." He smiled then and added, "You don't have any Eastern European Jewish genes floating around in your ancestry, do you?"

"I beg your pardon!"

When he saw by her expression that he had misspoken, he quickly said, "Sometimes you Germans have no sense of humor. I joke, Frau Hofer. I saw your National Socialist Party badge on your jacket. No Jews floating around in that group."

He walked to a desk, shuffled through a stack of newspapers, taking one.

"Here is our latest German language newspaper. Reading material while you rest, if you get bored. The American industrialist Henry Ford, probably bowing to public opinion, apologized to all of us Jews for his support of the forged and disavowed *Protocols of the Elders of Zion*. It's in the paper. You know about that false document, *The Protocols*?"

"Dr. Held. I am a member of the Nazi Party. As you said, I wear the badge. An accident! I did not mean to have it on. Believe me! But I prefer no politics, please."

The short, rotund man with spectacles stopped what he was doing. "I apologize for any affront. It was not intended, Frau Hofer, and also for my poor joke about Jewish genes. Here in Denmark we sometimes joke about politics."

"Yes well, Denmark, Germany, horses of a different color, yes? And how do you in Denmark feel about sterilizing the helpless, leading the way in Europe?"

"Most often it is with their permission."

"Permission? From the feebleminded? Hah!"

"Yes, yes," he admitted. "How real is permission from people in that condition? A nagging question. Yet, soon Denmark passes a law institutionalizing an involuntary policy. Nordic nations take race protection seriously, despite joking about politics. But, I'm a doctor, not a politician. I prefer we not discuss these matters either, Frau Hofer."

"So, we have an understanding," she smiled. "And this Down you mentioned?"

"Also about genes but different."

Jewish genes? Congenital diseases! There was the fleeting tickle in her throat that had been absent for so long. Then Fanny remembered. Of course! There was nothing to worry about. They had all passed the background check for Sepp's admission to the SS, including her parents. There could be no Jewish genes.

It was an aberration, this disease. Whatever it was. The doctor admitted he had not actually examined the child. One small seizure! The possible loss of side vision? A little — well, more than a little — difficulty swallowing? Was that enough to give a child a death sentence? She was slow and didn't have a right appearance. Fanny could deal with that. Give the child love and care on the farm, far from curious eyes. As long as she knew there could be no more. And there could be no more; that was taken care of by Dr. Held.

Relieved on that score, she dismissed the idea of Tay-Sachs disease.

The good doctor arranged for a fully recovered Fanny to have a horse and carriage tour of Copenhagen — the parks and gardens surrounding the castles. Gustav the driver was a talkative Dane, conversant in German, who, by rote explained and described the sites they were passing.

He stopped at a stunning red-and-gold brick church. "Roman Catholic?" Fanny asked. "It is beautiful, so different from the other stucco buildings."

"Yes," he nodded.

"The same architect who designed the Great Synagogue about a century ago designed the church. It is called *Sankt Angars Kirche*. Saint Angars to Danes is the Nordic Apostle," he smiled. "Inside is beautiful and colorful, to match the exterior. And the statues of the saints are a scene to behold. You are Roman Catholic, too, Frau Hofer?"

"Yes, I am."

"You should go in. You will be inspired, I think. And all services are both in Danish and German. Maybe you see Father Martensen. Very popular here in our city. A friend," he said proudly.

When she entered the church, Fanny was struck by the large stained-glass windows not visible from the outside and the elaborate paintings of angels and saints and the Holy Family on the flat ceiling and arched nave. The statue niches were truly overwhelming, the interior, with its frescoes and murals, was more colorful and decorative than Dachau's St. Jakob's.

On a wooden announcement board at the atrium entrance, there were scheduled confessions at this very time. An act of God to bring her here, she thought, finding her way to the confessional. There were only a few people before her. Father Martensen was her confessor that day.

"Your sin is grave, my child. As to your penance, you must make a good confession to your Father Goetz at St. Jakob's."

"You know our Father Goetz?" She couldn't help herself for asking.

"We work together in a priest organization, Sankt Raphael," he explained, then went on with the sacrament. "He will be our Lord's instrument for you. Confess to him, my child. I see and abhor the decision you felt you had to make. But you are in a different country from ours, that surely made everything more complex. However, you took the easier road. Laying down your cross, not bearing it. Do you accept the penance with a contrite heart?"

"Yes, Father."

"May our Lord and his Blessed Virgin Mother watch over your child, keep her safe. I deliver His absolution in the name of the Father, the Son, and the Holy Ghost."

"Amen! And thank you, Father," Fanny said through falling tears, tears that needed to escape.

She waited until the priest finished delivering the sacraments to other penitents and introduced herself face to face.

"I am Fanny Hofer," she said. "The woman from Dachau. You have a beautiful cathedral, Father. Shall I give any special greetings to Father Goetz for you?"

The tall, craggy-faced cleric said. "Do tell him he is in my prayers."

On her way out, Fanny stopped at the church shop and bought picture postcards of Sankt Angars for those waiting at home. At the end of the sightseeing tour, there was a brief cruise on the Copenhagen coast, Sealand they called it, which she found relaxing.

Fanny thanked Gustav, paying him extra for bringing her to Sankt Angars. then she went back to the recovery complex to pack her belongings for the daylong trip by rail to Karlsfeld, to normal married life with her husband, and to a session with Father Goetz.

Chapter 38
Gutmann, Goetz and Gets

Samson Gutmann's weekly visits with his priest, after confession, were not limited to confessions and discussions about the mysteries of the Roman Catholic faith. Once he had gotten past the Virgin Birth, Samson had faith in all mysteries.

"Look at it this way, Samson," Father Goetz had said, "You have accepted from the Hebrew Scriptures the parting of the Red Sea, the plagues on the Egyptians, an aged Sarah's giving birth far beyond normal fertility for a woman. Moses on the Mount getting the tablets from the Father himself. Even the Creation! Why not the Virgin Birth of our Lord? They are all miracles done by the same hand, the hand of God."

"I see what you mean," he had said. "Accept one, accept them all, right?"

Father Goetz had given a sigh. "Yes, well, that's it more or less. A package deal, take them all *grosshaendels*, wholesale, your people would say."

But today's problem was different. They were in the rectory at St. Jakob's, Father Goetz sitting comfortably in the black leather armchair.

Gutmann leaned forward. "It is hard to talk about such things with a priest," Samson started. "But who else gives me guidance? So, you know I am a man, a normal man. I am not yet 50. I am strong. I work hard on the farm for the Hofers. And to get to the point, Father, I miss having a woman. I need having a woman. My body yearns for a woman!" He gave a relieved sigh. "So there, I've said it."

"Well, that was a mouthful, Samson! We may be celibate, but we deal with human nature and urges all the time."

"There's more. I think I have found the woman for me."

"Samson, did you divorce before you were baptized into the faith?"

"Yes and no," Samson replied abashedly, turning red.

"What does that mean? Either yes or no! One or the other!"

"My wife, my former wife, comes from the east, Father. An orthodox family. We were married there by a rabbi and we were divorced there — I gave her the *get*, the divorce document with three rabbis present following our law. A woman cannot divorce a husband, he must divorce her. But my wife wanted one. As is the custom, we had a *sofer*, a religious scribe, write it on the proper parchment with the proper language. I said *I put you aside* three times and that was accepted by her voluntarily, a must according to Jewish tradition. So we are divorced."

"Then what is the problem?"

"Yes, well, the problem is we were never married in civil courts, so never divorced there. Everything, as it had been done for centuries in Poland, was under the authority of the *bet din*, the rabbinical court. So you understand my *yes and no*, now? We were never properly married under German law."

Father Goetz gave a sigh, looked to heaven, arms akimbo, asking, "What else, dear Lord?" Then he said, "Samson, this was all before you were a Christian. And was completed without controversy. The mother of your son, may eternal light shine upon him, has left Germany. You are a free and single man, cleansed by baptismal waters; you may marry. You may not engage in relations without marriage. That is sinful. So if your thinking does not go in the marital direction, I suggest you pray a lot for help controlling your natural urges."

"Do you want to know whom I have in mind," said Gutmann, now smiling broadly, a free man with a way to resolve everything.

"If you want to tell me."

"Hannah Mueller!"

"Frau Mueller? Marius's mother?"

"Yes, Father, Frau Hannah Mueller. A little older than I, but a lonesome and beautiful woman with a kind and soft heart. She stays at the farm. She enjoys the boys, with Fanny preoccupied with Lisle. She is a help. Frau Luftmann doesn't visit much anymore."

"I worry about Frau Luftmann," Father Goetz mumbled in a momentary detour. Then he asked, "Frau Mueller doesn't stay at her Dachau house?"

"No. With Anke there and the three boys and Helga with child again, there's no room, or desire, I understand, for Frau Mueller to be there."

"Good Catholic childbearing family, the Muellers, but I fear Marius has the production of good Germans more on his mind."

"Sometimes I drive Frau Mueller for visits with her grandchildren. We get to know each other, slowly. I know I am beneath her, but Father, she never treats me that way. So, do you have an opinion?"

"You and Frau Mueller? You Marius Mueller's stepfather?" The priest got up from the rectory chair. "I still suggest you pray a lot, Gutmann, my son, more than a lot," he chuckled. "And," he added, "get the poor woman to wear her glasses."

There was one more parishioner waiting to receive reconciliation.

"Forgive me, Father, for I have sinned. It has been weeks since my last good and true confession," said Fanny Hofer, performing the penance imposed by the Danish priest at Sankt Angars Kirche two weeks earlier.

Chapter 39
Mercy, Forgiveness and Reparation

Father Goetz listened to it all, what the penitent withheld, why the penitent did what she did, those for whom she thought she was doing it, her need and connection to the Nazi Party, Sepp's future happiness — the reasons, the rationalizations, the excuses, and the remorse for having made such a decision, which she still could not regret except for the sin against Jesus.

Rearranging himself on the confessional bench, he was quiet for a long time. Sterilization in and of itself was not a sin. The sin was in the intent, sterilization as permanent birth control. An egregious sin, a final form of marriage abuse, and one could even say killing all the future babies that might have been. Permanent abortion before the fact. He thought about all these things, and he was saddened that a Catholic woman dealing with the City of Man had found that she had to make that decision despite the precepts of the City of God.

As he thought about these implications, he heard Fanny weep.

Finally he spoke. "Once your child heals, you are to volunteer at the Eglfing-Haar Asylum, near enough to Munich for you to get there, to work in the children's wards and those of the aged and the incurably ill. Devote yourself to them."

"I heartily accept the penance."

"*Te absolvo*, my child, for this grave and serious sin. Think of the penance imposed as a gift to your Lord into whose coffin you have pounded another nail in acting so against his spirit."

After Father Goetz recited the absolution formula, Fanny dutifully said "Amen," ending the sacred cleansing rite.

Breakfast was on the table, the traditional sausage, dark bread, and coffee. Luftmann as usual enjoyed his wife's cooking, but Lotte had no appetite to eat.

Their elegant home on Freisinger Strasse in Dachau's Burgfrieden district seemed too big for two Luftmanns, empty without Gretl and Fanny living there. At one time Sepp and Fanny lived there as well, in separate quarters Christian had designed for the married couple. And even the lumbering Rolf had made his presence felt in the family home, barking at the postman, protecting any member of the household. Now it was just the two of them.

Lotte's behavior was getting worse. She prayed all the time and ate less. She was not herself. Luftmann wanted her to go to Munich to see doctors.

"Trust in God, Christian," she said. "That is your problem. You never trusted Him, always tried to take matters in your own hands."

"Forget my problems, Lotte. You lose weight and are so silent nowadays. What is troubling you, my dear?"

"Nothing," she lied. "I go out today to vote."

"Vote? But you don't feel well," he objected.

"I missed votes since the terrible 1925 experience. I go today to do my duty."

"You are stubborn. But I will take you this time. I need to vote, as well."

"Do as you wish," she said.

"I lay down the law, Lotte. You will go with me tomorrow to Munich to the doctor. Gutmann will drive us. It is his day to come to town from the farm."

"I wish I could go to the farm and help Fanny more. But there are things I must do here. And she has enough help. I hope Gretl is useful. Hmm!" she mumbled. "I wonder if I need to make more Lebkuchen for her."

"Fanny says she plays with the boys in the fields and roams the farm with

Rolf all the time. Amazing the dog lives so long, *gell?* Gretl has fewer accidents. Nothing much frightens her on the farm. Not since the Reds burnt down the barn and stable. So Gretl is good and bothers no one. It seems there is a purpose, a place, for everyone. At least you used to think so, Lotte. And you were right."

"I wish Fanny would have another child. Yet she doesn't conceive. It is a punishment." She took out the Lebkuchen dough from the icebox and began working it, preparing it for the flat buttered pan sitting on the counter.

"Punishment? Since when did you start talking punishments? Forgiveness is what you admired so. What is she being punished for, our Fanny?"

"Maybe for things others did," Lotte said cryptically. "Lisle more helpless every day takes all her attention. I see the child failing steadily when Fanny brings her to visit. Sepp is away so often. At least Frau Mueller is there. And Gretl. And Gutmann, God bless him, tending the farm with the help of the neighbor's boys."

"What do you mean for things others do? I don't understand you, Lotte."

Lotte looked away, brushing back her blond hair, now streaked with gray. "We go now to vote, Christian. I need my sweater and cap." She went to the oven, placing the tray of Lebkuchen inside.

"The dark bread is baked. The doughnuts wait for you to eat. The Lebkuchen will be ready to give to Gutmann to take back to the farm."

"And what about for you? You hardly eat anymore."

"Penance," she muttered.

"What? Penance? Not eating? Father Goetz gives no such tasks. Have you lost your appetite, Lotte? Is that it? I ask you again, are you ill?"

"I leave the potato soup on a low flame. It cannot take us long to walk to Town Hall, vote, and return," she said, not answering any questions.

The next day it was reported that the left — the Social Democrats and the Communists — made the most gains in the fifth federal election of 1928. The Nazi Party got only 2.6 percent of the vote with a mere twelve seats in the Reichstag. Dr. Goebbels, the Berlin Gauleiter, a regional director, the article went on to say, was among their delegation.

"He, this Dr. Goebbels, has a tendency to make a lot of noise, convincing noise. I have heard him on the radio. Persuasive," said Luftmann to his wife as they waited outside their home for Gutmann to get them for the drive to Munich.

"Is he a doctor?" asked Lotte.

"He has a Ph.D. But the Nazis refer to him as Doctor Goebbels. How they write about him. He is a little man; they give him stature."

"Well, we are impressed with doctors," said Lotte.

"It looks like they didn't do well, Lotte, but the once-banned Nazi Party had a victory to be on the ballot with the sixteen other choices. Fanny and Sepp will be disappointed at the showing, but they should see the accomplishment. The party grows. They are now 108,000 strong in the Deutsche Republik. When Fanny joined eight or nine years ago, what? Did they have 200 members?"

"I voted for the Catholic Party."

"The Catholic Centre Party."

"Whatever you say, Christian. That's all I need to know. Not all your numbers and figures! Your head will explode with all the information you stuff into it. And I get a headache. Which doesn't matter because God will take care of everything as He sees fit."

"We must take care of some things ourselves, Lotte. You begin to sound like a fanatic." Luftmann sighed. Whatever troubled her, Lotte wasn't interested in the goings-on of this world.

"Our neighbors are coming," she said. "The Mueller tribe! I wish our Fanny could make children so easily."

He looked up and saw, walking toward them crossing Freisinger Strasse, Helga Mueller, Anke the midwife, and Helga's assortment of boys. Helga's father, Ernst Schtreuk, was with them as well, policing the older boys and talking in a loud voice — over the children's noisy squabbling — about the election.

As they approached, Luftmann overheard the conversation. He couldn't help but!

Said Schtreuk, "I don't understand. The Nazi Party represents the workers, German workers, more than the international Communists, more than the Social Democrats, too."

Anke, holding the baby, Marius and Helga's fourth boy, said, "I voted for the Nazi Party, Herr Schtreuk. My sister and brother-in-law in Karlsfeld voted for the party, too."

Now the two families were face to face.

"*Gruess Gott*, Herr Luftmann, a beautiful spring day for an outing," observed Schtreuk. He tipped his cap to Lotte, then again addressed Luftmann, "I was telling my daughter I don't understand the results of yesterday's votes."

"There are a lot of things I don't understand like why my husband insists on my going to Munich to see a doctor," interjected Lotte, an unusual complaint to a stranger.

"The doctor examines us both. I told you that, Lotte. Two birds with one stone."

"You are lucky. Frau Luftmann. After all these years. He must care for you very much," said Schtreuk.

"The Lord cares for us all. May He watch over your grandchildren, Herr Schtreuk," she added solemnly. "Protect them from our sins."

Schtreuk looked surprised and gave Luftmann a questioning glance.

Luftmann shrugged. He was careful not to show his feelings about Schtreuk because of that years-ago Gutmann incident, the beating of the Haendler on the Karlsfeld farm. He made himself remember, instead, that Schtreuk had protected his family and his goods from raiding gangs.

"Christian, I have to see Father Goetz," she announced unexpectedly. "Maybe you invite him for second breakfast this Sunday. Then I go to Munich today with you. The ride will be nice, after all. And I need to talk to you, as well."

Now Luftmann looked surprised. "Of course I will ask him to join us, my dear. And surely we can always talk."

"No! That is wrong! I'm not thinking straight, these headaches. I see Father Goetz in the confessional, Christian. Do not ask him for breakfast. But you? We do need to talk. We must trust in God no matter what. Beg forgiveness for our sins," she mumbled, more like a mantra than a point of discussion.

Schtreuk, confused about the Luftmanns' back-and-forth conversation, went on with his own agenda. "What do you think, Herr Luftmann, of the results of our election? So many of our party's 25 Points — profit sharing, right to work, prosecuting usurers, communal department stores, extending the old age pension system, a classless national education, no child labor — make *us* the working class party not those Communists."

"You recite them like a schoolboy, Father," Helga snickered.

"Insulting me won't change your life, Helga. My daughter is not happy," he explained to Luftmann. "Always complaining. Her boys are wild, no discipline. No wonder Herr Mueller treats her disrespectfully. Though between us I don't approve. If he did better, maybe she would too." He shrugged his shoulders in a who-knows kind of gesture in this rare intimate conversation. A lapse!

"Everyone picks on me," she whined, sounding as if she would cry.

"Emotions often are not controllable after birthing, Herr Schtreuk," said

Anke, in Helga's defense.

Schtreuk ignored both women. "What do you think, Herr Luftmann? Why do workers vote for them and not for us?"

"Well, I can tell you my Fanny agrees with you on those principles. What do I think? What I think, Herr Schtreuk, is that you can never tell what the German people will do," he smiled, adding, "My respects to your husband, Frau Mueller. Congratulations to both of you on your fourth son." He nodded at Anke as well. "We must leave. Here comes Herr Gutmann to drive us to Munich."

"Oh, Christian, I forgot the Lebkuchen for Gretl. I run back to the house. Of course I baked enough for everybody. The Kiembocks, too. I will be right back."

As Lotte went to get her package, Schtreuk said, "Very broad-minded of you to make the Haendler part of your family, Herr Luftmann, if I may say so." It was not a compliment.

"Samson is a farmer, now, Herr Schtreuk, and he is my godson," Luftmann asserted. "And a good son indeed. Good day to you."

Samson pulled up. Christian climbed into the car. A few minutes later Lotte joined them.

"People never learn," said Schtreuk to nobody in particular, as he watched the tarnished silver Daimler pull away.

Seated comfortably in the back of the long car, Luftmann turned to his wife. "So Lotte, what do you wish to talk about? Finally I hope you can tell me what bothers you lately. You have not been yourself. I worry," he said gently, taking her small hand in his.

"I need to talk about our secrets, Christian. God is punishing me," she whispered. "Having two lives in one person."

Luftmann pulled his hand away. And in his harshest low voice, rarely used, for only her to hear, said slowly, "We have no secrets. You understand that? We have no secrets. Remember our pledges. We have promises, oaths on children's lives, never to talk again about those private and confidential matters between us. *Verboten*, forbidden, restricted! Never! You understand, Lotte? Never!"

And to Gutmann, he called out, "Turn the car back, Samson. No Munich! Take us back to Freisinger Strasse. We go home."

"The Lebkuchen! Remember to give the Lebkuchen, Herr Gutmann," Lotte reminded him, when they reached Freisinger Strasse, and Samson was returning to Karlsfeld.

Chapter 41
Lotte's Confession

Once back in the comfort of their home, Lotte pleaded. "I try to work things out for myself and with the Blessed Virgin. Give me more time, Christian. You are right. I promised you once when we first married not to speak of certain things. And I have honored that promise. Don't be angry. Just give me some time."

"Remember Lotte," he warned, his voice still harsh, "verboten, forbidden, never!"

Lotte took to her bed. Some days later, when she felt strong enough, she went to St. Jakob's. "I will have my confession, Christian," she told him before she left. "But I will not violate our oath."

The first rambling words she said to Father Goetz, after asking for forgiveness were. "The Father is stronger than the son."

"What father? What son, my child?"

"God the Father overpowers His son. Vengeance rules over mercy. I made a terrible mistake that my grandchild is paying for."

"Paying to whom? Our Lord demands no payments, only love and compassion."

"Father, I tell you I made a mistake."

"What mistake disturbs you so? Are you well?"

"Only the headaches, Father, for my sins. I cannot speak of my mistake."

"You talk in riddles."

"I tell you I angered the Father."

"You cannot separate God the Father from the Son nor from the Holy Ghost. They are a Trinity, a fundamental mystery of our church, inseparable, except in words."

"The God of Vengeance punishes. Sins of the fathers are visited on the children."

"My dear, you punish yourself for no reason. God is love. Unconditional love. God is mercy. God is forgiveness."

"I pray daily to the Blessed Virgin. I do penance by fasting often. But he is stronger than them all. The child dies slowly before my eyes. Each day worse."

"What child?"

"My grandchild. My daughter Fanny suffers. And she cannot conceive."

"Maybe that is the way of the Lord," said Goetz quietly, thinking the poor woman blames herself for something Fanny has brought about!

"They are paying for my sins. I am a sinner. Punish me, not them!"

"My dear child. Do not take so much upon yourself. You cannot be the cause for an absence of conception in another. It is sinful to believe you have that power which belongs only to the Almighty and His ways, which we cannot understand."

"I am the sinner. They pay for my sins," she insisted.

The priest came out of the confessional. There was no one waiting.

"Let me take you home, Lotte. You are not well. God loves you; we love you."

"I am so afraid, Father," she whispered.

"Stop! Stop right now!" the priest said gently. "*God is light and in him there is no darkness at all.*" He quoted the apostle John. "You are serving the devil, not God."

She quieted down, "The devil? The devil you say? Yes, the devil! That's the answer! You know I can't think straight when the headaches come. I don't see things right. I must find my way. Lamb of God, Mother of Mercy, Holy Father, help me!" she implored as together they left the empty church.

That day, Lotte pushed aside her conflicts between Gods, Fathers, and Sons, accepting the tensions and discords to be satanic, as Father Goetz said. So she was left only with her headaches from time to time.

Chapter 42
The Lebkuchen Incident

The economic situation for all Germans felt better in 1928 than those earlier nightmare years where people saw no end in sight to their suffering. More good news for Germany also came that August. Fanny was reading it to Sepp from the *Beobachter* at supper. Hannah Mueller and Samson Gutmann were there, as well.

"The NSDAP didn't show much in the June election, Sepp," she said.

"Because things are settling down somewhat in the *Deutsche Republik*," he said.

"But listen to this from the newspaper. Something we all can be proud of:

> Despite the *Deutsche Republik* governed by the November Criminals, our German athletes overcame all obstacles winning ten gold medals in Amsterdam, 31 medals all together. Second only to the United States and number one for all of Europe.

"And one of them won by a woman!" Fanny continued. "The women's foil event! Helene Mayer from Offenbach am Main. The *Beobachter* describes her as a privileged half-Aryan from her Silesian mother, saying the Aryan side of the blond, square-faced, blue-eyed athlete had won it for her! Hah! What does it matter the *Goldene He* — what an honorable nickname for her, *gell?* — our *Goldene He* won the gold for our country!"

(Fanny had looked further. There was no mention of the women's lawn tennis team.)

"It might have been *Goldene* Fanny, if the opportunity wasn't lost because of the war and its penalties after," said Sepp. "She will always be my *Goldenes Maedchen*."

Fanny gave him a loving look. It had been what she was thinking.

"Sit still, Josef, and stop playing with your food," Fanny said, leaving yesterdays to yesterdays.

"Why don't you tell Luddy to stop? He's kicking me under the table."

"I tell you both to behave. Is that better?" Fanny smiled.

"Grandpa Luftmann thinks I'm a fine fellow," Josef said proudly.

"Well, Grandpa Luftmann is a very smart man. Just stop playing with your food. Remember this great news for our Germany. You will be proud of our athletes. Gold medal winners. Maybe one day you, also. Who knows?"

This was a happier Fanny, on old familiar terms with her darling Sepp, having confessed and received absolution, making peace with her faith and herself.

Upstairs, Lisle began to cry on and off.

"I do, I do," Gretl mumbled, lifting her heavy body, leaving the table, before anyone else could. Rolf, lying near the oven, got up instantly and raced up the stairs, following her.

"Sepp, I'm afraid my aunt has taken your dog from you," joked Fanny.

"Breathed life into him!"

"Aunt Gretl has a way with Rolf and with Lisle. Our daughter stopped fretting."

"Lisle sleeps less, doesn't she Fanny? Still no more episodes" said Hannah, adding, "thank the Lord."

"Gretl, also more life in her since she came to the farm and the baby was born. You see how she manages to lumber up the staircase?" observed Samson.

While Fanny went on reading the names of the gold medal winners, upstairs Gretl was feeding the baby Lebkuchen crumbs from Lotte's cakes, which she kept in her pocket for nibbling. Lisle savored the delicious gingerbread bits on her tongue, lining her mouth, making happy gurgles that prodded Gretl to give her more and more.

The baby savored it but was unable to swallow. Lying flat on her back, they gathered in her throat, first gagging then choking her. The sounds became raw, grainy and coarse, ugly and unrecognizable.

Rolf began to bark furiously. Had it been Lisle he was protecting when he followed Gretl up the stairs? Had it happened before?

Gretl rushed from the nursery grunting words of help as loud as she could over the child's raucous gasps. Then, relieving herself, causing a putrid odor, she fell in a heap at the same time, hitting her head on the banister with a loud thud.

Sepp, his chair crashing to the floor, dashed upstairs, followed by Gutmann.

Fanny was frozen, her hand clutching the *Voelkische Beobachter*.

Hannah cried out, "What can I do? What can I do?"

No one thought of the two boys, Luddy and Josef, who slipped themselves under the table. There they huddled behind the draping linen tablecloth, gripping the white border so hard, china and porcelain and unfinished food scattered all over the kitchen. Camouflaged in the brightly patterned tent, they held each other in a fearful embrace.

Sepp and Samson found Lisle in her crib, Lebkuchen vomit staining her clean white sheets, crumbs scattered over the bedding. The child was blue-gray, eyes fixed, immobile, moribund.

Sepp shook her, held tiny Lisle upside down. Samson put fingers down her throat, attempting to clear it. Nothing! So quickly, she was gone. In the doorway, Fanny stood, transfixed, then fainted.

Luftmann was awakened by the Dachau Home Police, who were notified by their Karlsfeld counterparts. He went to St. Jakob's, got Father Goetz, then found Schtreuk at home. Schtreuk, with his sidecar motorcycle and the help of the SA storm troopers who always stood guard, got them both to Karlsfeld.

Lotte, alone in her Burgfrieden bedroom, standing naked, tore at her hair, struck her body repeatedly with Luftmann's leather belt. She had heard the policeman's detailed story. It was her Lebkuchen! Her Lebkuchen the instrument of death. The devil or Him? Her head was throbbing. When would He stop punishing her for abandoning Him?

Gretl, soiled clothes changed by Hannah Mueller, body washed and powdered, a bump swelling on her large head, went into her bedroom, cascades of tears flooding her round, vapid face. She retired more from the world that night, a giant step back, rarely speaking, often hiding.

Hannah quietly cleaned up the mess using pages of the *Voelkische Beobachter*, then scrubbed the floor with strong soap to get rid of the odor, as they had taught her to do at the convent.

Later Hannah said to Samson, "Perhaps Gretl should stay in the guest cottage with me for a while, until, oh, until I don't know what."

The next day, quickly arranged at Luftmann's request, Father Goetz presided at the private funeral mass held at the gravesite. There was no wake.

To everyone's surprise, Ludwig Hofer showed up to pay his respects. Lord knows how he found out or where he came from. He disappeared after the burial.

The Kiembocks, husband and wife, attended.

Marius Mueller and his wife Helga were not present. They were having lunch and, as usual, not speaking a word to each other.

Lotte was there, her black veil covering her pained and guilty face, fiercely holding Christian's arm to keep her frail, bruised body steady. Luftmann had warned her to behave, not carry on, if for nothing else in deference to their daughter.

Fanny collapsed in Sepp's uniformed arms when the tiny coffin was lowered at Dachau's Guttesacker Cemetery.

Chapter 43
Times Have Changed
1930

Luftmann muddled about in his library, pacing the floor, radio tuned to the *Deutschlander* station, waiting for the result of the Reichstag election. There had been a forum on the air, representatives from the thirty or so political parties of the Deutsche Republik, major and marginal, nasty and combative, with agreement on one point only: America's Wall Street Crash had devastated Germany.

America, by calling in all loans extended to the crippled nation to help them overcome their severe postwar economic difficulties, pulled the rug out from under their feet. German banks collapsed. Chancellor Bruening's leadership was a disaster. Only his Centre Party defended the Catholic chancellor's obsolete approaches to the modern catastrophe.

Over three million Germans were unemployed.

All factions blamed the Social Democrats, the November Criminals, for their failed, unwanted democracy, turning Germany into a divisive nation without leadership. Thirty political parties! Made no sense! Luftmann worried. It was a perfect time for extremists, left or right.

Said the Nazis, "Hard-working Germans, begging on the streets for food for their families, for jobs. Never before have Germans begged! Where is our strong leadership?"

Father Goetz had said this week at Mass, "A second Gruenderzeit collapse! Worst than the first! We must be strong. Have faith! Trust in God and pray for His help!"

On the radio, the Harmonists, a popular male vocal group, were singing their hallmark comic melody *Veronika*, filler entertainment until the election results were in. Abruptly the song was interrupted. Luftmann turned the volume up. Dr. Goebbels was on the air, the Nazi Reichstag Gauleiter, a small man, yes, maybe five feet, but with a big voice, Luftmann thought.

"Achtung! Achtung! All Germans! A stunning victory today. Two years ago less than a million supported us gaining only 12 Reichstag seats. Today over six million winning 107 seats. 107 Seats! We are second only to the Social Democrats. There is backing from all Germans loyal to Volk and Rasse! Laborers, shopkeepers, farmers, white-collar workers, small-businessmen, professionals, bourgeoisie, young voters, all see the hope and promise of a strong leader, a racially pure German nation with its rightful place in the world. Ein Volk! Ein Reich! Ein Fuehrer! Heil Hitler!"

Luftmann switched off the set and went into the kitchen.

"Well, Nazis won many seats," he said to Lotte. "Your daughter must be happy today."

"MY daughter? All of a sudden?" Lotte said. "What did you expect? Things are so bad people would vote for anyone who promised them better," she said shaking her head.

"Yes, well, I go over to St. Jakob's to visit with Father Goetz. I'll probably have supper there, Lotte," Luftmann said leaving the Freisinger Strasse house.

"That would be good, Christian. I feel a headache coming on," she said.

Δ

"You heard?" said Luftmann when Father Goetz greeted him at the rectory.

"I heard. I'm still listening. Let's go into the kitchen, the radio gives results. So far the Reds and the Nazis win. Nazis more, representing themselves as Christians to win moderates. But their God wears a Swastika. On the other hand, the Bolsheviks have no God at all. Extremes!"

"Remember that poem before the war? *Der Krieg? Aufgestanden ist er, welcher lange schlief? He has arisen who was long asleep.* Did German-ness awaken? Is the true German Volk, their inborn cultural soul, emerging?" asked Luftmann, sitting down in the plain, whitewashed rectory kitchen.

"Times have changed. Times! Not people! Forget that foolish Volk talk. Germans are good, bad, smart, dumb, weak, strong — no different from others. You know that! You said it yourself once, bad times make bad people. Bad times lead to bad choices, desperate decisions, too."

The table was set for supper, a red-checkered place mat over the linen cloth to protect the wood finish as Father Goetz brought out black bread, marmalade, and brown mugs for the brewed black tea.

Luftmann carved a slice of dark bread from the center, spooning raspberry jam on one half and apricot jam on the other. Father Goetz joined him, breaking off an end piece. "I prefer the apricot this evening," he said, smothering the crusted bread.

"The size of our Communist Party now is second only to the Soviet Union. Did you know that? The Church watches carefully. They'll shut us down as they did in Russia if they ever win the hearts of Germans."

"What if Chancellor Bruening forms a government with the Social Democrats? Do road government projects, creating jobs, like Adenauer's Autobahn in Cologne. Bread on the table might stop both Nazis and Bolsheviks. Remember, they won only twelve seats two years ago when things looked better, before this Wall Street Crash turned the whole world upside down. Bruening should make a deal with the Social Democrats while there are still Social Democrats."

"You're dreaming, Christian. Bruening's a conservative monarchist. He wants to get rid of the Social Democrats, not work with them. He wants to shut down their Deutsche Republik once and for all. He runs the country like a dictator. And our democratic constitution allows it! What good is a republic whose rules allow anything?" Father Goetz threw his hands up. "Anyhow, 50 years from now, people will say who's Bruening?"

When they finished eating, the men sat quietly digesting the light supper and the day's election results. The setting September sunlight, streaming through a stained-glass arched window slightly ajar, painted light shadows on the cherry-wood floors. The last breaths of summer-scented mountain air were refreshing and sadly comforting, like a farewell embrace.

The silence didn't last. Strains of the *Horst Wessel* song and the pounding of footsteps in unison broke it. "Not more marching! Is there no peace?" said Luftmann, getting up to look outside.

> Clear the streets for the brown battalions,
> Clear the streets for the Storm Divisions.
> The Swastika's already gazed on in full hope by millions,
> The day for freedom and bread is at hand.

Luftmann opened the door to watch. "It is a cadre of Hitler Jugend, Father. Lord help us, my grandsons can't wait to join the HJ.

"Are they old enough?"

"One has eight years, the other nine. Soon they go to the *Deutsche Jungvolk*, then comes HJ. One way or another they kidnap our young early, mold minds and build bodies."

"Yes, well, the Church practices capturing young minds, too. We start earlier. And the other political groups, not just the Nazis, do the same."

"The Kiembock and the Mueller boys, by privilege, are HJ. Did you know the Hitler Jugend have now enlisted over 25,000 boys fourteen and over?"

"Enlisted?"

"HJ uses that word."

"What? Are they building an army for the future?"

"Irony! They are very democratic, despite the lingering class consciousness in the republic. Any able person can get ahead, merit not class! They have the *Jungmaedel* and *Bund Deutscher Maedel* for girls. If Goebbels is right about their widespread support, they will have covered all grounds."

"Not all grounds! Not Catholics, thank the Lord! There'll be no Lateran Concordat like the Italian fascists made with the Vatican! Some of our German bishops prohibit Roman Catholics from joining the Nazi Party. But on the other hand, they watch out for the Bolsheviks."

"The Mueller boys come by the farm often with their grandfather Herr Schtreuk when he picks up food for all the unemployed SA storm troopers."

"Schtreuk is good to his men. And they, though unemployed, are dedicated! I hear they put their own few pennies to help their cause when they can. It's like what the Church used to be in bad times."

The Hitler Youth began to sing the Storm Columns song.

> So stand the Storm Columns, for racial fight prepared.
> Only when Jews bleed, are we liberated.
> No more negotiation, it's no help, not even slight:
> Beside our Adolf Hitler we're courageous in a fight.

The noisy revelers passed down Augsburger Strasse, turning into the working-class side of Burgfriedenstrasse.

"Sinful!" he blurted. "Politics nowadays depresses the soul, let alone the mind. So tell me, what you do now? Have you been hurt by the Crash, too, Christian?"

"I have gold and farmland, so there is food and money."

"The banks?"

"I released most of those holdings beforehand."

"Lucky or clever?"

"A little of both."

"Do you spend time at the farm?"

"Samson takes care of the farm with the Kiembocks. I go there for my grandsons while Fanny volunteers at Eglfing-Haar.

The parade noise was now in the distance. The two men sat back down in the darkening room. Father Goetz did not switch on the lights. They sat for a while watching daylight disappear behind the mountains. The priest hesitated, then asked, "I often wonder why they stay?"

"I beg your pardon?"

"I wonder why they stay."

"Catholics?"

"The Jews. Their soldiers who sacrificed for the Kaiserreich thrown out of veterans groups. Memorials erased! Marches in the streets singing anthems calling for their blood. If the Nazis ever win more seats, come into power, it can only get worse. They can leave. Why do they stay?"

As the room's shadows merged with the sun's disappearance, Luftmann sipped the still warm tea from his mug, then said quietly, "They stay because they think they are Germans."

Chapter 44
Bad Influences

On that cold December Sunday afternoon at the Luftmann Burgfrieden home, they were seated near the warm fire in the front room, on the soft upholstered chairs placed around the circular marble-topped table.

Luftmann looked pleased that his wife seemed to be enjoying the guests. Hannah Mueller and Samson Gutmann were visiting, Hannah to inquire about Lotte's health. Samson wanted to speak privately with Luftmann.

Hannah had brought *Christbaumgebaeck* for the Luftmann Christmas tree, the delicacy shaped like stars, bells, and angels. Lotte provided her special coffee, black tea, and sugar wafers.

The same day, the Dachau Nazi Party held a meeting at the Mueller brewery.

Said Samson, "We saw at least 150 booted men in brown-shirt uniforms with red, black, and white Swastika bands arrive in Town, five trucks, two cars, a brass band trumpeting their presence. A big crowd at the brewery, bigger than the one they had last year. Did you hear them? They were singing the *Horst Wessel.*"

"I don't listen. The marching nowadays seems never to stop. It hurts my head," said Lotte, opening the cheerfully wrapped package brought by her guests, decorated with red-bowed wreaths and pine trees. "My goodness! These are lovely, Hannah. Not all Bavarian style."

"A mix of North and South," Hannah said softly, shy at the compliment from so accomplished a baker. "Recipes from here and from the Berlin convent."

"So when are you two posting bans? You are so good for each other."

"Frau Luftmann, we both decided these times are not right. But we will," said Gutmann. "Hannah promised."

"Don't wait too long," Lotte advised. "Life doesn't go on forever."

Hannah blushed. "You are looking well, Lotte."

"You need to put your glasses on, Hannah. I look terrible. Sometimes feel worse! My Fanny is still not with child. Two years now since the accident. It does torment me," Lotte explained as she poured coffee from the heated silver pitcher. "Tell me, how are your dear grandchildren?"

"Yes, well," Hannah tried to respond, but her voice choked up.

Gutmann answered for her. "Marius will not allow their grandmother to visit them. Hannah is a bad influence on the boys, he claims."

"Oh, my dear friend," Lotte consoled. "How sad!"

"A bad influence? How?" asked Luftmann.

"Me, I'm afraid. Consorting with a baptized Jew Haendler. Promoting race defilement, whatever that means. Herr Mueller does not want his mother to go against Nazi Party rules. He is becoming important in their party structure."

"Narrow-minded!" said Luftmann, "They have one grandfather Schtreuk and one grandmother Mueller! The children should be enjoying both of you!"

"But I do see them once in a while," Hannah was able to say, tears in her eyes.

"Herr Schtreuk lets me know in advance when he comes to Karlsfeld with the boys to pick up food for his men. 'Politics is politics and family is family and you are a good and true Christian German,' he tells me. 'Just, like a woman, making terrible choices'."

"A helpful person, does good acts, yet a lover of Hitler, an anti-Semite, and a follower of that squat and ugly, scar-face man who breathes violence. Doesn't seem to mix! Schtreuk is a puzzle," observed Luftmann.

"Aren't most people?" Lotte muttered, putting plates out for the cookies and cake.

"What scar-faced man, Samson?" asked Hannah looking perplexed.

"Ernst Roehm. The SA leader who enjoys clubbing people's heads."

"I know nothing about politics. Just a silly woman, says my son."

"I hope your son realizes the errors of his ways, keeping you away from your grandchildren, Hannah. And I admit Herr Schtreuk and his men helped me, too, in Karlsfeld, protecting the farms. He was good to Fanny, too."

"About Karlsfeld, may I speak with you alone for a minute?" asked Samson.

"We leave the women and go into the library," Luftmann replied.

Once there Gutmann said, "The HJ youth tease your sister Gretl mercilessly. Schtreuk shouldn't bring his grandsons when he picks up the food for his storm troopers. The Mueller boys go after Luddy. They are worse than the others. I didn't want to say it in front of Hannah. It would upset her. Hannah's grandsons are bullies with Luddy. Say he looks like a jewboy, call him an *Itzig*! Josef, to his credit, defends his brother, telling them to shut up or they'll get what for. They start in on Gretl with the other HJ boys. Call her a *nutzlose Esser*, a useless eater. Shout it where they think she hides. Make fun of her handicap!"

"You know, Samson, handicapped can't join HJ. They wouldn't let Goebbels in with his club foot! Did you know that?" Luftmann countered with a dry laugh. "A Jew-hater. Yet, at Heidelberg, his PH. D. mentors were Jews. The Nazis are the bad influence, not you, not Hannah!"

"What happens to these people? Like Goebbels? What makes them turn so?"

"As my wife would say who knows why people do what they do!" He got up to go back and join the women.

But Luftmann worried about Luddy. How could he help his grandson who looked more like Christian's own father, Reb Itzig, than like Christian? He was built like Christian, soft, round, shoulders beginning to curve. Luddy, the quiet observer who Luftmann suspected collected injuries, warehoused insults. Would he forget nothing for some future retribution? Luddy, the angry outcast whom, Luftmann admitted painfully, was hard to trust.

"Thank you, Samson, for making me aware. Let's go back into the front room. If we stay too long, my wife has a nose for trouble, though she doesn't want to know about it."

"Just in time! Is anything wrong? Don't tell me if there is!" Lotte greeted them.

"Then why do you ask?" said her husband, bringing some chuckles among the guests.

"I was just telling Lotte how much I enjoy staying at the farm, Herr Luftmann. I am grateful to you for letting me use the guest cottage. Lotte should come to Karlsfeld more, spend time there. It would help Gretl, too, I think, if you don't mind my saying."

"I love poor Gretl. I miss her here at home. She was good company for me, because she is a good person. It's better for her in Karlsfeld, I know. She doesn't want to come to Dachau, you see. So she stays with Fanny who, blessedly, convinced her the past is the past. They were always close, Fanny and her aunt. When we do go, Gretl will stay with us during our visit," Then Lotte added, "And, of course, my grandsons, I want to spend time with the boys. They grow up so quickly."

"Your Josef is so handsome, Lotte. His dark black hair and fair skin, people say he resembles me. Imagine!" And tossing a smile at Luftmann she added,

"Luddy, I think looks more like his Grandfather, at least your side of the family, *gell?*"

A brass band was heard again, stomping boots in the distance, bypassing the Burgfrieden, marching in the workers' districts, loudly singing "*dann musst du lauter schreien Freiheit! Freiheit!* Freedom! Freedom! Then rolling drums introduced another song, *Arise ye workers! From your slumber, Arise ye prisoners of want* the words echoed loud and clear.

"Hard to ignore the noise! New songs, I think! Which ones are they, Christian? National Socialists?" asked Lotte.

"The Reds! They sing the *Internationale!* Their anthem! Baiting the Nazis at their rally. Dachau is a perfect place for extremes, hit so hard by unemployment and the economy."

"Your dreams! Eigentum, buying forests, donating land for the Pumf. Why? To bring in all those people to work who for years have no jobs, some no homes? Your responsibility, Christian."

"You are starting to sound more like your old self, Lotte," he smiled.

From the other direction, the storm troopers, the drums, and chanting, were going back toward the trucks that had transported them to Dachau. Supporters followed the brown-shirted Nazis, singing the Storm Columns song along with them, trying to outshout the Reds.

"Will it ever stop," said Lotte, holding her head.

Luftmann shut the windows. "I wonder if Fanny and Sepp were at that Nazi rally."

"Sepp is away and Fanny is at the farm. There is a more important assembly next month in Munich which she hopes they can both attend," informed Gutmann. "I promised I would watch over the farm and the boys while they were in Munich."

"Next month? January! That's next year! 1931 already! It doesn't seem like a dozen years since the war. Hard times have never left us," said Lotte. "Over three million unemployed, Christian tells me. How do you count three million?"

"There will be more," Christian predicted. "Much more!" He went to the window. The winter sun was going down as the Nazis passed by.

Random beams highlighted the demonstrators' faces, their exhilaration and passion. Luftmann saw that several neighbors on Freisinger Strasse displayed Swastika flags. Where on earth did they get them, Luftmann wondered? Had they hidden them in their basements?

Chapter 45
The Meeting Was a Riot
1931

"Again violence surges among rival paramilitaries on the streets of the nation. Warring parties that put away machine guns in 1924, replace them with rubber truncheons, blackjacks and knuckledusters. The worst confrontations — Steel Helmets and the Reichsbanner groups participate — are between Reds and Nazis.

"They began in Berlin, the Babylon of every thing non-German — sexual deviants, bars, honky tonks, whores all ages and genders, the Kurfuerstendamm an avenue of perversions leading to hell.

"The rest of the republic follows. Since the Wall Street Crash, the western world's economic meltdown triggering chaos, marching chanters disrupt Germany's cities, brown-shirted storm troopers, red-banded Communists. For every crisis only the Nazis repeatedly blame Jewish financiers."

— *Amper-Bote, March 1931.*

Sepp, sitting in the Karlsfeld kitchen while waiting for Fanny, put the newspaper down.

The paramilitary disturbances bothered him. He was a loyal and true believer but always an adherent of German order, discipline, and obedience. Last year, he knew, the country's political casualties had multiplied. Germans against Germans. Each side claiming victims.

"Violence and disorder are the mood in this republic," he said when Fanny came down, ready to go.

"Once we win, it will all change, be civilized again," Fanny said fervently.

The special Party gathering, once scheduled for January, had been pushed back to March by Marius Mueller. Mueller was now the Munich Kreisleiter, county official specializing in matters of race, just below rank to Gauleiter, regional director.

Gutmann gave Sepp and Fanny his Daimler to use for the drive from Karlsfeld, saying, "Don't worry about the children, they and Gretl will be safe. Hannah and I see to that."

"Aren't the new black uniforms smashing?" asked Fanny. "Sepp looks so distinguished and handsome." She thought for a moment, then added, "And severe all at the same time."

"At least it separates him and his disciplined Schutzstaffel from the brown-shirt rabble," observed Gutmann.

"Be careful with that talk, Samson! We can save you from Herr Schtreuk and his SA men only once," Sepp said. Then he smiled, changing the warning mood and patted the giant of a man on his back. "I go with the most beautiful maiden, *gell*? My wife has not changed since she was a girl. We'll see you later, my friend."

The meeting was held in the same beer hall near the Odeonsplatz where the German Workers' Party was born. The *Alte Kaempfer*, those old campers who had joined the party earliest, in recognition were given the best seats, near the front of the large basement meeting room.

Mueller had changed the date because of a special, high-ranking guest speaker, very special, none other than *SS Gruppenfuehrer* Heinrich Himmler himself, Munich born and, like Sepp and Fanny, an early member of the party.

There were rumors that the Communist paramilitary Rote-Front League planned to break up the well-publicized meeting. Police attended, presumably to ensure order. The press would be there. It was a great opportunity to establish strength in these bad times when people were yearning for leadership, before the next year's elections.

"They wouldn't dare! Not in Munich," Mueller had dismissed the reports.

However, the Rote-Front League attended and they were armed.

After the singing of the Deutschlandlied punctuated by three stiff-armed Heil Hitler salutes, a tall handsome man with a strong craggy face got up to speak amidst the Swastika and Fuehrer posters plastered on the walls.

"I am a Navy man," said Richard Krebs, "and I am a Red Front leader. I have brought with me tonight over 100 dedicated Red Front fighters to this beer hall. Workers join with us. Now is the time! The Nazis deceive you, big industrialists who gorge themselves while your families starve, who profit from your labor, are their backers . . ."

There was a buzz from the crowd, like the swarming sound of agitated bees. People moved around, restless in their seats. Himmler, in his redesigned black SS uniform, small, stature unimpressive, wearing clerk's round eyeglasses, rose immediately and gave an order in a lethal but quiet voice, *"Raus! Raus mit dem roten Schwein!* Throw the Red pig out."

Though less than imposing in appearance, with his large head, short back, receding chin, pencil mustache and pudding-basin haircut, the command and his demeanor were subtly menacing. They triggered respect, fear, and action.

The Brownshirts lining the walls of the hall rushed to the center, facing the interlopers as if opposite partners in a country dance. But it was a dance of war. They clashed! Both the Reds and the Nazis fought with total disregard for those civilians assembled to hear the SS Gruppenfuehrer speak. It happened so quickly. Sepp and Fanny were caught in the melee before either could act.

Blackjacks, brass knuckles, clubs, heavy-buckled belts, and bottles crashed on the heads, backs, faces, groins of the fighters. Fragments of glass, pitchers of beer, chairs, hurled over the audience. Men from both sides used chair legs as bludgeons. Women fainted in the bedlam of battle.

Sepp and Fanny were jammed in the crush of bodies falling, bodies trying to escape, bodies trying to push back, bodies climbing over those downed. Dozens of heads and faces were bleeding, open wounds, gashes. Clothes were torn, ripped apart, as the more experienced fighters dodged about amid the terrified but helpless spectators. Sepp, a target in his SS uniform, could do nothing but use himself to protect Fanny from the tornado of hurled projectiles, symbols of hatred flying through the air, crisscrossing the room.

The storm troopers fought like lions, ruthlessly, as if violence were their reason for being. They pressed Fanny and Sepp toward the main exit. The band struck up the Storm Columns. And Heinrich Himmler, with Marius behind him, stood calmly on the stage, his fists on his hips as if ready to curtsy, looking as though he enjoyed the ferocious brutality and bloodshed.

However, the man who had increased the SS from 290 members to thousands, an elite, independent, disciplined Nazi internal force, never gave his lecture on the connections among race, Jews, the world's financial market collapse, and Germany's now six million unemployed workers, as outlined in the evening's program.

(Unemployment had doubled in one year; Luftmann's dismal prediction had been accurate.)

Sepp was disgusted by the rogue mayhem, an unplanned battle, though the Nazi paramilitaries came out on top. His military training recoiled at anarchic aggression.

Yes, he remembered always what the Red thugs did to his farm, burning the stables with his beloved horse, yet Sepp was disappointed with the bias of the police, meant to put down riots, not watch them. Their unprofessional behavior disturbed him, standing by, doing nothing as the Reds were routed. They had always treated the Red Front as criminals since they were enlisted from poor slum areas that were known centers for organized crime (the Horst Wessel killing by a Red ex-convict only confirmed their prejudice). Still, the police were not doing their job.

He was revolted by the Red provocateurs and the brown-shirt ruffians, both of whom offended his strict schooling as a *Kadett*, which stressed the Germanic codes of discipline and obedience. Herr Hitler was right. Ein Reich, ein Volk, ein Fuehrer. One nation, one people, one leader. Pride and order.

"Law is law. Their duty is to uphold the law, to bring order back to our nation," he muttered to Fanny as he watched police arresting battered Reds, ignoring the SA aggressors.

After making sure Fanny was not hurt, he said nothing more on their way back to Karlsfeld in Gutmann's tarnished-silver Daimler, his once-new black uniform now torn, ripped apart. Hannah and Samson, waiting to greet them, were shocked by their war-zone appearance.

No words passed between them. Sepp was looking angry — the faint outline of the thin, pink scar on his cheek surfaced beneath the layers of skin. Clearly, he was upset about the direction Germany and his party were going, SA hooliganism and disorder.

In tears, Fanny went upstairs to their bedroom conflicted, emotionally faithful to the Nazis, committed to Herr Harrer, and still believing these bad elements, the parts that disturbed her, could change.

Chapter 46
Altar Boys
December 1931

Father Goetz sat with Fanny near the coal stove, in the warmth of St. Jakob's rectory. An ermine cloak of soft snow dressed Dachau's cobblestone streets, falling flakes like frosting on a cake, matching the white-capped mountains in the distance. The Wuerm was icing over. And the Amper was frozen clear blue.

It had been a year of turmoil and suffering.

The meeting was at Fanny's request. There was no tea, no cookies — these were stark times, with Dachau leading the nation, let alone the Bavarian state, in unemployment, over-crowded living conditions, and school space so rationed that teaching nuns were relieved when sick children stayed home, making breathing room for the others. Dachau's streets were in sad disrepair with no money to restore them.

There were bigger problems facing Germany, as well.

Father Goetz was ashamed that Chancellor Bruening, a Catholic, continued to ignore the Reichstag, violating rights, banning newspapers, misusing the emergency provision in the republic's constitution that permitted ruling by decree. He would not spend a nickel to create jobs, fix roads, help education, or build housing, wanting only collapse of the Deutsche Reich.

The priest would serve no refreshment in such poverty-burdened times. There they sat on the worn leather chairs; the seventy-one-year-old priest was preoccupied with the troubles of his nation and the guilt-ridden mother of two he had known all her life, having baptized her into the Church thirty-one years ago.

Said Fanny, "I cannot go there anymore, Father. I have served my penance faithfully, but can no longer go to Eglfing-Haar. They now put *ballast* inmates, deadweight, the ones they call inferior-quality lives, on display, visitor tours, a circus sideshow of the insane. In the wards, they are letting defective children starve, and the tour guide, the chief of the asylum, once picked up a skeletal young girl like a rag doll, waving her for the visitors to see. 'This is where money goes, wasted on these, when it could be spent on healthier children, on food for our unemployed, on those who are strong for our Germany, not those who bleed it dry,' he said to a gaping crowd. They dismiss me, say mind my business if I try to intervene."

The priest looked pained. Fanny went on.

"When I think that could have been my Lisle," now tears welled up in her eyes, "displayed so before a gawking group of sightseers or other Lisles yet to be born, I have little remorse, Father, for preventing such births. And I know that compounds my sin against the Church, against our Lord."

Father Goetz gave a long sigh that shuddered through his lean body. Didn't he sin as well, longing for the City of God, absent human suffering? Wanting freedom from his obligations to this accursed City of Man that spiraled into the depths of Satan's world? Involving himself in nonspiritual matters. Disobedience! Can the guilty in thought, as he was, deliver moral judgments, earthly punishments to others who are trying to do their best but fail?

"There's more," Fanny said softly, turning her head away, unable to face him. "Gretl manages, thank goodness. She is in our home, at peace with me, but hides from those who tease her so maliciously. But Luddy hates her. I see it. Hear it. Both sons serve as altar boys for Father Ignatius at the Ludlkapelle, both learn Christian values, yet Luddy hates, hates Gretl for the derision he suffers from the others about his minderwertig aunt. When they make fun of her, he joins in, says worse than they do, trying to prove something." Fanny started to cry. "I start to think of my dear Aunt Gretl as a cross to bear, Father. And I am ashamed of that. She causes no trouble."

"When your altar boys joined the HJ they learned about who deserves to live and who doesn't, more than those Christian values Father Ignatius preaches. What did you expect, Fanny?"

"Hitler Jugend and Deutsches Jungvolk do teach discipline and physical rigor, loyalty and cooperation, as the Church teaches spiritual principles, Father," she defended the youth groups.

"You cannot serve two masters, Fanny."

For that there was no defense. Fanny could not reply. Father Goetz had made a point about Hitler Youth and the Nazi doctrines. About Lord Jesus and the Fuehrer.

"I cannot stand to see my boys hurt. I love my aunt. But Luddy is not as strong as Josef. He can't fight back, so he joins. I need your guidance." (She did not tell Father Goetz about the *Itzig* name-calling directed at Luddy and did not know why she withheld it.)

"And what does Sepp say about all this?"

"He says the HJ will build Luddy up, improve his physique, make a man out of him. Then Sepp laughs when he thinks of Herr Himmler and Dr. Goebbels. Those are supposed to be Aryans, he says, and shakes his head!"

"But both of you agreed about their joining HJ. Little storm troopers!"

"Hush, Father! Don't say such a thing." She involuntarily looked around.

He thought for a while, rubbing his chin. "I make a suggestion? Before their minds are turned inside out altogether about useless eaters and low quality lives, let Gutmann bring them to Dachau on Saturday nights."

"But they have to be in Karlsfeld for Sunday Mass."

"Hear me out. They sleep at the house of their grandparents, who welcome Samson each week as a guest, and I will have them serve with me as altar boys for Sunday Mass. This way we have second breakfast together and talk and think and pray. We discuss Gretl. It would be good for your mother, too. Lotte feels more herself again and needs to see her grandsons. I'll clear it with Father Ignatius."

"If you could work that out, Father? It gives me some hope for my boys." Then she whispered, "And as for me? Do I have hope?"

"You have done the penance imposed as best you could. And you come to me with an open heart to admit bad thoughts and weaknesses. Yes, we are only human, imperfect. But now, you must find the strength to tell your husband what you have done to yourself, Fanny, and hope that he forgives you as our Blessed Lord has. I see your sorrow to our Lord for your offense. As for Gretl, she is one of God's children, as much as you or Josef or Luddy or Sepp. But you do honor that, Fanny, and our Lord will bless you for your compassion."

Fanny, tears streaming, fell to her knees and Father Goetz blessed her.

"I'll tell Sepp after the holidays," she promised.

"No, my child, now! Tell Sepp before Christmas, Fanny. A clean and honest celebration then, of the birth of our Lord."

Chapter 47
Confessions
Farewell 1931

"I don't know why Mother and Father bring us here to Dachau and then go for a walk, in winter, in cold, leaving us alone with nothing to do. All *Grossmutter* does is cook. And *Grossvater* works at those big books — "

"Ledgers," informed his brother.

" — or he wants to talk about things I don't," complained Luddy.

They were spending Advent week at their grandparents' home. Josef and Luddy would be altar boys at St. Jakob's for the pre-Christmas services.

"And why aren't we in Karlsfeld?"

"Mother said Father Goetz needed us, Luddy. St. Jakob's is in the same parish, after all."

For lack of anything else to do, they were looking through the shelves of books in their grandfather's library while he worked at his large desk in the room's corner.

"At least it's good to get away from old Aunt Gretl."

"Quiet, Luddy," whispered Josef. "Aunt Gretl is Grandpa's sister."

"I don't care. It's good to be away from her."

"And why is that?" asked Luftmann sternly.

"I told you to be quiet," said Josef. "Now see what you've done."

"I tell you why, Grandfather! She makes me ashamed. She has disgusting accidents. And she's useless and so is that useless dog that never leaves her."

"That was your father's dog," said Luftmann.

"They do make fun of Luddy about Aunt Gretl . . . and other things. It isn't easy for him, Grandpa," Josef explained, always quick to defend his brother, who couldn't defend himself.

"And who is *they* that matter so much?" He turned to Luddy. "Why do you not call me Grandpa like your brother? I am no stranger."

"Because I don't feel like it," Luddy said, and sauntered out of the room.

"Don't mind him. He has a hard time fitting in, Grandpa, and he wants to so badly. It's not good not to belong. Makes him feel . . . feel . . ." Josef searched for a word.

"Like an outcast," Luftmann finished his grandson's sentence, removing his glasses and massaging his brow, remembering well that same feeling.

"Yes, outcast, a good word, Grandpa. Like an outcast! How do you always know so much?" Josef said. "And where are Mother and Father?"

Δ

Fanny and Sepp, dressed for the winter cold, were walking on the trails in the Wuerm forest as they had when they were younger. The closed munitions factory still stood, but the forest around it had grown back.

"It feels like old times," said Sepp, holding her gloved hand in his pocket. "How many times we did this, Fanny. I remember the day you, a schoolgirl, found Rolf for me. No Pumf, then. No strangers in town. And the forest belonged to your father."

Fanny's cheeks were red, her blond hair hidden under the fur-trimmed hat. "We can't go back to those days again, Sepp. I think I already loved you then, so handsome in your cadet's uniform, so proud you chose me for a friend."

"A friend?" he laughed. "It was more than that, my dear girl. I just had to be patient."

They were approaching the river. Fanny stopped walking. Took back her hand and turned to her husband whom she loved so much. "I need that patience now, Sepp. More than patience. Your love. Your forgiveness."

Brows furrowed, Sepp looked perplexed.

"I must confess something to you."

"What? You have left the hospital? I know that already. I know why, too. I hear what goes on there, Fanny. Frankly I'm surprised you stayed so long."

"No, Sepp! Let me speak." Tears were forming in the corners of her eyes. Fanny brushed them away with her red Christmas scarf.

The woods had gotten so quiet, no whooshing winds, no crackling branches, no rustling dead leaves. There was a hush, a prelude pause, like that magical concert moment when batons are raised expectantly in stillness before ushering in a thunderous symphonic movement.

Sepp went to put his arms around her, but Fanny backed away. She took a deep breath.

"Sepp, when our Lisle was born the way she was, I thought of my Aunt Gretl, and also of another aunt, Gretl's sister who had died in the cholera epidemic. I asked my Father and learned for certain that other sister was the same way as Gretl.

"There was no eugenics in those times, no talk about racial hygiene and lives not worth living. But I had to ask my father about his sisters and were there any more afflicted in the family. Was I carrying bad genes? Genes that undermined a healthy German race? Genes that our party warned against as weakening Germans and Germany, breeding those whose care and institutions took money away from healthy Germans in need?

"Lord forgive me, I feared bringing any more like Lisle into the world. And Lord forgive me, if I carried bad genes I did not want that to hurt your position in the SS where you were so happy, a military career well-deserved. We were party members, held to the strictest standard." She paused for breath. "I had myself sterilized, Sepp. There can be no more children."

He looked as if her words at the beginning were just starting to sink in. With a bewildered frown, it appeared he was trying to understand what his wife had revealed to him.

"I couldn't tell you, Sepp. So devout you are. Avoiding conception in the worst and final manner. It could only offend you."

"Where? When?"

"On my trip to Denmark. When you took the boys with you on the Hitler Youth excursion to Russia. I saw a Danish doctor, a Jew, modern, who had no religious constraints, who didn't judge, only performed, having done these operations for years."

He reached out and pulled Fanny to him. There was some resistance, at first, but Sepp took her in his arms, held her close.

"Fanny, you think you married a saint? There is no concern you had, no thoughts, that I didn't have also. I worried about Lisle, about Gretl, about family connections. But my background had been checked rigorously by the SS. And I didn't want to insult my wife by asking about her family. So I kept quiet and you carried this burden alone. Father Goetz told me, in my anguish about such thoughts, to pray to our Lord for His mercy. Now I ask Him for forgiveness, must pray for it, for letting you suffer alone through these trials."

"Father Goetz heard my confession, Sepp, as did a priest in Copenhagen."

"Before?"

"After. A beautiful cathedral. The one on the postcards I brought home. Father Goetz said he knew the Danish priest."

"My poor, brave Fanny, what you went through."

Unsteady, Fanny leaned against him. She wept, burying her face in Sepp's embrace.

"I love you so," he whispered. They clung together, in the woods, near the Wuerm River, on the old Luftmann Land, in the forest, with the vacant Pumf buildings beyond them.

Fanny relieved of her burden of secrecy was first to speak. "God bless Father Goetz. Let's stop at St. Jakob's, Sepp, and bring him home with us for supper. He loves my mother's cooking."

At dinner that night Lotte asked why Fanny's face appeared swollen, "Were you crying?"

Sepp answered. "It was the cold wind near the river. We got away from there quickly."

"You would think you two would know better," said Lotte.

"Did Aunt Gretl always live here in Dachau?" This from young Luddy.

"What was that, Luddy, dear?" asked Lotte, ladle in hand, serving in large bowls the pungent potato soup rich with onions, turnips, and greens. "The black bread is coming warm from the oven."

"Was Aunt Gretl born in Dachau?"

"No, dear. She was born in Munich."

"Why do you answer him, Lotte?" Luftmann said abruptly. "It's time to eat, not talk about people who are not here."

"Why can't Grandmother answer me? I'm not doing anything wrong. You pick on me for nothing."

"Luddy, I'm surprised at you! Apologize to Grandpa," said Fanny.

"Why? Did he snitch to you about what I said to him in the library before?"

"I don't know what you're talking about, Luddy. And don't refer to Grandpa as *he*. Such rudeness! You can't like yourself being that way. It's not who you are."

For a second his hardened expression collapsed, as if his mother knew a better part of him. Then, a chilling coldness returned. He said to her, "Nobody knows who I am!"

"What does that mean?" asked Fanny.

But Lotte went on, with her own unfinished conversation. "Aunt Gretl was baptized here at St. Jakob's like your mother and father. Remember Gretl's baptism, Father?"

"Yes, of course. It was a quiet ceremony," the priest recalled.

"Why wasn't she baptized as a baby in Munich if she was born there? And was she confirmed? And what about our other grandfather? The one we never talk about?"

"He's the one we never talk about," Lotte laughed.

"That's no answer," Luddy shot back.

Fanny gasped.

"Ludwig, enough! Listen to your mother! Don't make me ashamed of you," ordered Sepp. "Apologize!"

There was a look of contempt on his face, rare for a ten-year-old. Luddy despised his grandfather as well as Aunt Gretl. Blamed them both for his being ridiculed, for being treated like a nobody — comparing him to his grandfather in looks and to his aunt in brains. He did not think he looked like his grandfather, but he knew, with his curved nose, narrow shoulders, and a soft, pear-shape build, he didn't look like his brother, Josef. His curly blond hair did not buy him any relief. Josef looked like an HJ. He did not.

From the time Luddy realized he looked different from his neighbors, his brother, his parents, he saw a bleak future for himself. He grew up in a German world that demanded German-ness. Its first sign was appearance. The ideal? A long square face, the short blond hair, blue eyes, athletic build were the criteria — the Nordic-Aryan look.

But he wasn't really different, basically different from the Kiembock boys, the Mueller boys. He had the same values, goals, beliefs. His parents were Nazi Party members like theirs. His father was in the elitist SS. He spoke the same language, read the same books, had the same opinions. Why did they make him feel like an outsider?

When they laughed at Gretl, derided Minderwertige, his voice was the loudest, his name-calling the meanest. When they sneered at Samson Guttman, his loathing and derision were merciless. "Scratch a convert, find a Jew! When a horse is born in a cowshed, it is still a horse!"

But like his blond hair, cut short to hide its non-Germanic curliness, nothing counted. He was different because they treated him so. He was an outsider. Outsiders were not welcome in the Nazi Party. He sensed that different led to worse, and worse would lead to inferior. It had already started.

Knowing all this was not enough, he had to do more than the others, more than the party demanded when he was in the HJ. He had to call attention to his loyalty, zeal, obedience, no matter the consequences. He could not weaken to sentimental appeals. Then they would see that round-faced, curved nose, pear-shaped Luddy Hofer was a true German. No, they'd see a person who excelled in his German-ness, a somebody, not a nobody at all. That was his mission.

Those bullies, the Mueller boys calling him that nasty word *Itzig*. Others teased and taunted, too, but Alf and Bernd Mueller and their sidekick brother Fritz pushed him around when Josef wasn't there to defend him and when their Grandfather Schtreuk was busy getting meal and milk to bring back for the unemployed, unpaid SA.

"Ludwig!" his father said sternly. "Apologize!"

"All right! Sorry," he mumbled.

He was quiet for the rest of the meal. So was everyone else at the table, where oddly, Sepp rose from time to time to kiss Fanny gently on her swollen cheeks.

And Luftmann and the priest yielded to Lotte's order not to discuss any more politics, after Luftmann had observed that Chancellor von Papen was following in Bruening's footsteps, stifling the press, ignoring the Reichstag, and ruling more and more by executive decree.

Father Goetz had apologized, "Yet, another Catholic, I am afraid!"

After dinner, the children gone from the table, Luftmann asked, "Your father, Sepp?"

"Still in Moscow."

When Luftmann gave a respectful nod at Sepp's precise information, Sepp added, "We keep track of our enemies in our SS."

"He is returning to seek a seat in the Reichstag in next year's elections," said Father Goetz. "The Bolsheviks make a big push." Now they all looked surprised, so he added, "The Church keeps track of its enemies as well."

"Does Herr Schtreuk know? He pledged to get him for the Horst Wessel tragedy? And for the hostage murders."

"If he doesn't, he'll find out. Schtreuk does his job with some dignity, Fanny. But Roehm's Brownshirts are wild, untrained, and unreliable. They are bullies, not soldiers," Sepp said with contempt.

"From what we've seen here in Dachau, I also think Schtreuk's men are better trained than most SA. Remember their ranks are suffering, too, almost all SA in Germany are out of work. To themselves they justify their violence. With six million workers unemployed — "

"Six million, Father!" gasped Lotte. "Dear Lord! How do you count six million?"

"Yes, a number hard to contemplate, to picture, *gell?* Now is a golden opportunity for extremists to expand. The Reds are not stupid," observed

Luftmann. "Parading like the National Socialists, singing a call for workers to unite in their Internationale!"

"Herr Hitler, in 1928, predicted economic disaster with this criminal republic. Nobody listened. They considered him a fool and agitator. Now they will see how clever he was," whispered Fanny, putting a quieting finger to her lips as the boys returned to the dining room.

Chapter 48
Seek and Thee May Find

On Advent Sunday, Josef and Luddy were altar boys at St. Jakob's. Lotte and Christian, Fanny and Sepp attended the Mass. Each in his own way was proud of the boys and the honor Father Goetz bestowed on them.

Father Goetz digressed from the regular readings. He chose one from the Prophet Isaiah about suffering insult and shame and becoming outcast. *"Yet the lover of God stands steadfast as does the Lord for the lowest among us, reviving their hearts."*

The second reading he selected was from Matthew, about betrayal and disloyalty making people hate the day they were born. Fanny was certain the selections were meant as messages for her son, for Luddy, to give him hope and strength through faith and God's love.

After Mass, the adults left quickly to prepare for second breakfast, waiting at home for Father Goetz and the boys to join them. Fanny said that gave Father more time alone with them, to get to know each other.

Inside St. Jakob's, Josef was relieving himself in the small water closet in the hallway. Father Goetz was busy talking with a parishioner near the lectern. Luddy was alone in the sacristy, where he removed and stored his vestments along with the chalice and host and other items used in worship.

He took off the white linen surplice draped over his red floor-length cassock, the red worn by altar boys on special holy days. Unfamiliar with St. Jakob's, he was opening drawers and doors when he discovered a narrow stairway just beyond a side entrance. It led to the basement beneath the nave and chancel.

Luddy looked around. No one was there. Switching on the light at the head of the stairs, he tip-toed down. It was cool, but surprisingly dry in the wood-paneled cellar, with twist-and-turn hallways to many rooms.

One such room had RECORDS painted on the door. He looked around again. Seeing no one, he tried the door. It was unlocked. He entered. There were record books labeled as baptismal and confirmation documents. The books were in chronological order, a white sticker in front bearing dates in large capital letters written in thick black ink.

He was excited. It was exactly what he wanted. It was as if they had found him, these files. Maybe God's will, he thought cynically. He would look for Aunt Gretl's records. All the fuss at supper that night over his simple questions might mean something. Why wasn't she baptized as a baby in Munich?

Grandfather didn't want him to know the answers, didn't like the questions when all Luddy wanted to know was how Minderwertige were treated by the Church. He knew his sister, Lisle, had been baptized in Karlsfeld. But confirmation? How could Gretl, who peed her pants and shit her clothes, declare a willingness to be Catholic? Be voluntarily confirmed?

Maybe he would find something in these files, something secret, something worth reporting that could make him shine, stand out, be accepted by the others. He took a book labeled 1880-1920 and opened the alphabetical index.

"Can I help you?" said a severe voice.

It was Father Goetz.

"What are you doing, Luddy? You don't belong down here. And clearly you should not be looking through materials not your own. We do not lock our doors or our records in God's house. We count on honor and respect. You violate our trust. What is it you seek?"

"Just looking around," he lied, unnerved and frightened at getting caught by the priest.

"Those records belong to the church, Luddy. Not to be tampered with. And you are not permitted in the basement. What were you looking for?" The priest repeated, seeing the index page L opened.

"I confess, Father, I wanted to see the Luftmann records."

"Then why didn't you ask rather than sneak around when you thought no one was looking?"

"I didn't think I'd be allowed," Luddy answered honestly.

"Good Lord, son! More reason to ask!"

Father Goetz guessed he was looking for Gretl's papers. Hadn't Fanny told him about the boy's problems with his damaged aunt? And, he noted, all of those questions at supper during the week.

At that moment, it occurred to the priest that Luddy Hofer was vindictive, capable of betrayal. Hoping to find a way to get rid of his aunt. Not for thirty pieces of silver, but all for wanting to belong! The boy needed help. Still Father Goetz gave an inner sigh of relief. Luddy would never have found the document under L. Gretl's baptismal record was buried under the letter I.

He thought about Luddy, his wrongful act. Had he not interrupted him, Luddy would have seen that Gretl's baptismal record was not under L with the other Luftmanns, his mother's and the ones from Cologne, his grandparents. That alone could have made the boy suspicious! Father Goetz thanked the Lord for bringing the opened sacristy door to his attention, for helping him decide to investigate, therefore allowing him to interrupt before any damage was done.

He looked up at Luddy and saw a frightened child who had not moved.

"Your brother waits for you. Go upstairs! Finish changing and we go to your grandparents for second breakfast. About this episode, however, we need to talk alone. Rummaging through things not your own is a serious matter. When you think no one sees you, Luddy, God is watching all the time. Remember that! You cannot escape His eye."

When Luddy went upstairs and Father Goetz heard the door shut behind him, he checked his I FILE. Yes, there it was in the back, not upright, but lying horizontally under others, as if it had slid down.

The baptismal document read: Gretl Itzig (called Gretl Agnes Luftmann, according to her brother's information). But Gretl had given him that other name and her hospital identification tag that long ago day when they talked privately, just before her baptism.

He had kept the record, following the rules; kept it but hidden it.

He had done the same with the M FILE, as well.

There had been no need to do more or to do otherwise. He wasn't breaking any law, God's or man's.

The two men were in the Luftmann library. Lotte, who was not feeling well, had prepared a simple meal of potatoes with cream cheese and caraway seeds and retired to her bedroom.

"Another headache, Father. I must excuse myself."

"You should see a doctor," advised the priest.

"I try to tell her the same thing, Father. But I am just her husband."

"It's all right. They come and they go, like unwanted visitors," she joked.

With Lotte gone, the two friends, as was their habit over the years — certainly when there was an important election — were waiting for results, predicting them, analyzing them afterward.

"Only you, Christian, know the secret of my worldly interests," Father Goetz once said.

"I feel privileged, Father, except there are so many elections in this Deutsche Republik! Elections, runoffs, changing political appointments — I think it makes the people crazy. Harder and harder to know what's going on."

"The July Reichstag election is barely two months away."

"Chancellor von Papen, leading your Catholic Centre Party, follows Bruening's autocratic style. He, too, is 100 percent against parliamentary government."

"With President von Hindenburg's blessings, I'm afraid," said Father Goetz.

"Every few months another chancellor! A regular merry-go-round! Not good for the stability Germans need. Unfortunately, this democratic republic fails them."

"Those in government are doing everything to make sure it does."

"I know. Executive decrees replacing the Reichstag, more newspapers suppressed. And confusing! Von Papen just this week bans the Hitler Youth! For what reason? My grandsons are upset. Not fair, they say. Other factions' youth programs are allowed."

"As much as I'd like to ban them myself, you see the effective Nazi outcry," said Father Goetz. "Storm troopers creating havoc on the streets, bashing in windows of Jewish stores. I don't know why? Von Papen's not a Jew. The Nazis will cause enough trouble. The ban will be lifted."

The priest was right. Before the July Reichstag elections, the HJ was reinstated.

By July, all over Germany the warring multi-political factions fought in the streets. Large election signs featured a giant, half-naked worker — supposedly depicting the real German people — pouncing on effete, top-hatted, frocked politicians drawn as pygmies.

The two men were in the rectory parlor looking at political posters strewn over the planked wooden floors, bearing vote-seeking messages, an assortment given to the priest from members of the parish.

"They all use that image," said Father Goetz. "As if politicians know that the weaker people feel, the more they want to look strong and yearn for a strong man to put our country back together again."

The Nazi poster showed the giant worker towering above a bank labeled INTERNATIONAL HIGH FINANCE that was bludgeoned by blows from a Swastika-bedaubed compressor.

The Social Democrats portrayed the giant worker pushing aside Nazis and Communists.

The Centre Party carried a cartoon of the giant worker, sleeves rolled up, forcibly removing tiny Nazis and Communists from the Parliament building.

The People's Party showed the giant worker, dressed only in a loincloth, sweeping aside soberly dressed politicians of all the other warring parties.

Even the staid Nationalist Party used the giant worker waving the black-white-red flag of Bismarck's Second Reich.

"The message," said Luftmann, "is for parliamentary politics to end. Stepped-up street clashes and violence at political party meetings are doing a good job against it as well."

"To me, that giant with the Swastika is powerful, shows the failure of the Deutsche Republik, and gives the promise of a new Germany."

"True! With the unthinkable six million unemployed as Hitler predicted, Dr. Goebbels' propaganda machine is compelling. He understands reaching people's emotions, the power of falsehoods becoming truths by repetition, and Hitler promises he'll abolish unemployment, put down the Bolsheviks, eliminate chaos, make Germans proud once again! He's hypnotic when he speaks."

"They are thorough. The diocese tells us posters, pamphlets, pageants, demonstrations are all over. Nazis films in the cinemas show a Red civil war in cities. They spread fearful news to middle classes that the Bolshevik Party in Germany is second only to their Moscow bosses."

"Have you been to Munich lately? Microphones and loud speakers blast out the Nazi message in every public place: Germans we give you a national rebirth. We give you *Gleichschaltung. Ein Reich, ein Volk, ein Fuehrer!* Not make things better, but change everything, from top to bottom. Something completely new!"

"Not completely!" corrected the priest. "Five Austrian intellectuals from Linz with strong German leanings had that Gleichschaltung idea of uniformity forty years before this Fuehrer of ours, Christian. Among them a Jew. Hitler simply expands on it!"

"A Jew among them?"

"They wanted the complete Germanization of Austria, only German-speaking, only German customs and so on."

"How could a Jew be part of that? Against Jews?"

"The Linz Doctrine was aimed at Slavs, my friend, not Jews."

"Always somebody who wants to keep out somebody else. Somebody who thinks they are better by birth or blood. An amazing world, Father, frightening. Clearly the idea failed in the old Habsburg Empire. But the question today is, will our Germans buy Hitler's version of it?"

"We will find out soon enough."

The day after the Reichstag election, Luftmann brought the newspapers to St. Jakob's. Father Goetz was listening to results broadcast on the *Deutschlandsender* station.

Luftmann read from the *Amper-Bote* as the radio broadcast a similar message.

UPSET NSDAP LANDSLIDE
NAZIS WIN, REDS GAIN,
SOCIAL DEMOCRATS LOSE

"The Nazis doubled their vote from 6.4 million to over 13 million, making them the largest party in the Reichstag. There was an increase for the Communists to 89 seats, closing in on the Social Democrats who lost more seats. Support diminished for the parties of the center. The once-marginal extremist groups now lead the country."

Luftmann put the paper near the pitcher of tea on the worn wooden table.

"It needs sanding and new varnish, I know," said Father Goetz. "So does Germany, the people seem to think." He gave a long sigh. "Maybe a new table altogether!"

"They won, the Nazis, because they succeeded with the middle classes."

"They haven't won over the Catholic vote," Father Goetz said, his voice as worn out as the table before them. He lowered the crystal set's volume.

"You seem distracted."

"I'm thinking of the Lateran Concordat, between the Vatican and the Fascists. Do you remember three years ago, we both looked at the front-page picture of the Fascist Mussolini watching as Cardinal Gasparri signed the agreement for the Pope? Remember I said that could never happen here? Now I'm not so sure."

"With the overwhelming Protestant and Prussian support for the Nazis, Father, Rome must fear another Kulturkampf, one worse than Bismarck's anti-Catholic policies in the last century. A treaty is the expedient move."

The priest looked at him, his pale blue eyes glazed over; a worried frown furrowed his brow. "Do you think they will have the sense to get out now, Luftmann?"

"Catholics?"

"No, Luftmann, Jews. The worst has happened for them with this Nazi victory. Now that they have power, more than slogans can be expected. It's been in the Nazi Party platform, out in the open, since its beginnings 13 years ago. In Hitler's speeches since the 1920s, for goodness sake: 'Jews have racial tuberculosis!' 'The Jew stock exchange profits from our economic collapse!' 'Their criminal Jew republic!' 'The bloated Jew and the poor German!' 'Germans work, Jews exploit!' 'Aryans or Jews, only one can survive!' — I could go on and on."

"I told you once before they think they are Germans no matter what the insults. They convince themselves the Nazis are referring to others. And that's alright with them!"

"Aren't they listening? Are they blind? Haven't they read *Mein Kampf?*"

"They are so assimilated, Father, like Nobel Prize-winner Fritz Haber leading our imperial battalions with his mustard gas in the Great War. Like him, they think they're Germans, are convinced they're Germans, and that's that!"

"It's hard for me to understand. A people unwelcome since Luther, no, since the Crusades, yet they remain. They must love our country."

"You know the *Ostjuden* escaping the Russian and Polish pogroms of the last century used to say they were going to the promised land. They meant Germany."

"Yes, well, what once was isn't now. Maybe it never was," said Father Goetz.

"On the other hand, who could anticipate it would go this far?" Luftmann mumbled. "I never was one to ignore warnings. Yet, some things you don't see. Or refuse to believe possible. Why do they stay, you ask? As Lotte says, who really knows why anyone does anything?" He looked back at the newspaper. "There's more news. Herr Hitler is not willing for his party to form a coalition government. Interesting! So we have yet another election soon."

"*Ein Reich, ein* Volk, *ein Fuehrer*, so not surprising," Father Goetz gave a sigh. "Have your grandsons joined the Hitler Youth or their junior group?"

"They have, Father. Not good! There is a problem. The Mueller boys and their friends still pick on poor Luddy. He distances himself from me. It's not just Gretl. I think he blames me for his looking different from his brother and the other boys. Persecution turns him mean-spirited. The sad part," he gave a sigh, "is that he does look different!"

Δ

An incident in August bolstered Hitler's refusal to form a coalition.

SA thugs, still fueled with the high octane of the unexpected July landslide, attacked and killed a German Communist sympathizer of Polish descent in eastern Silesia. Found guilty, the courts sentenced them to death, causing a Nazi rash of anti-Jewish and anti-Communist actions throughout the nation by gangs of Brownshirts. Chancellor von Papen, however, had agreed "objectively" with the court's sentence.

In response to the court decision and the subsequent wave of terror, Herr Hitler declared on radio another reason for his stand against coalition:

> "German racial comrades! Anyone who has feeling for the struggle for the nation's honor now understands why I refuse to enter this government. Herr von Papen's justice can condemn thousands of National Socialists to death. Did anyone think they could put my name to this aggressive action, this challenge to our people? Herr von Papen shows what his bloodstained 'objectivity' is! I want only a nationalistic Germany and annihilation for its Marxist destroyers and corrupters. I am not suited to be the hangman of nationalistic German freedom fighters!"

"German freedom fighters? He endorses storm trooper violence," said Father Goetz.

"Yes, but what's the difference," Luftmann asked, "between the SA murder and the Reds' murder of civilian Horst Wessel in his rooming house? They are all lawless thugs!"

In September, von Papen commuted the condemned men's sentence to life imprisonment. "Hitler scared him off," said Luftmann as they strolled in the rectory garden.

"Von Papen fears the Nazis," said Father Goetz. "What else happens?"

"Here's news for you! The Communists made Ludwig Hofer a Reichstag deputy from Bavaria, using the added seats they gained in July."

"Oh my! Hard for Sepp with the SS?"

"Sepp has established himself, but hard for my grandsons, dealing with the HJ."

They stopped to sit on a sunlit bench in the small garden.

"Especially Luddy, who can't fight back and who shares the same name. He at first denied knowing him, denied they were related."

"That couldn't work!"

"Of course! So he hides and cries. Josef tells me his brother tries to find a scheme that would harm those who hurt him and also make him a hero in the eyes of his attackers."

"I worry about that," said Father Goetz. "but I'm not able to reach the boy."

"Meanwhile, Herr Deputy Hofer still has a big mouth. He was quoted in the *Amper-Bote* saying, "Do not fear the Nazi landslide, my comrades. We are catching up. First Brown, then Red: That is our new slogan!"

In one of his rare prophetic moments, Hofer seemed on course, Luftmann would admit later. The Nazis lost seats in the November runoff and the Communists gained another eleven.

As things turned out, it made little difference.

Chapter 50
August Days Reprised in January 1933

Sepp knew something important was happening when he was called to Berlin in late January. His orders — exceptional ones — said to bring his family, lodging would be provided. He invited Fanny to attend with the boys. It had to be about the nation's new chancellor appointment by President von Hindenburg and his advisors.

The war hero, pilot Hermann Goering, a Nazi insider who loved the limelight, bragged to the papers that he knew the news beforehand and that it was he who revealed it to the lucky man.

Once announced, some foreign journalists wrote the decision was "a product of misguided and incompetent backroom deals, von Papen's Conservative elements overrating their own strength and underrating the Nazis."

Nevertheless, on January 31, 1933, Adolf Hitler was appointed Chancellor of Germany by the aging President von Hindenburg.

General Ludendorff had something to say about the choice, as well. His former chief of staff sent the president a telegram a day before the public announcement.

> BY APPOINTING HITLER CHANCELLOR OF THE REICH YOU HAVE HANDED OVER OUR SACRED GERMAN FATHERLAND TO ONE OF THE GREATEST DEMAGOGUES OF ALL TIMES. THIS EVIL MAN WILL PLUNGE OUR REICH INTO THE ABYSS AND INFLICT IMMEASURABLE WOE ON OUR NATION. FUTURE GENERATIONS WILL CURSE YOU IN YOUR GRAVE FOR THIS ACTION.

In Berlin, Sepp found himself with the SS contingent that would be marching that night in the victory celebration. Fanny and the boys were there to watch. Stage-managed by Dr. Goebbels, disappointing no one, it was an inspirational spectacle.

"Just like 1914," Fanny said to her parents over the telephone the next morning. "You should have come with us. Everyone could have fallen into everyone else's arms in the name of Hitler. Intoxication without the wine, like the August days, remember? It was something to see. A nighttime torchlit parade of SA, Steel Helmets, and SS in Berlin going on well past midnight.

"Can you imagine? The passionate singing as they marched? German voices lifted to the heavens! All the old *Soldatenlieder* — the *Horst Wessel*, the Storm Columns, the national anthem, accompanied by the crashing tread of boots keeping time! There were red-and-black flags, Bismarck's and the Swastika — no more Social Democrat gold. Flickering torchlights on the marchers' proud faces as they sang for the new Germany, so stirring and sentimental. For hours they marched by. Josef and Luddy saw groups of boys and girls no older than themselves."

"Up so late at night!" exclaimed Lotte as Luftmann held the phone for both to hear.

"Tell Mother I heard that. I wouldn't have had my boys miss it, pride for their country, pride for who they are. From Unter Den Linden, to Wilhelmstrasse, to the Kaiserhof, then to the Reich Chancellory through the Brandenburg Gate, we followed them — passing all government buildings, marching as strong at the end as in the beginning. We were so proud of Sepp. You would have been, too, Papa. You should have come with us."

If Luftmann had gone, he might have seen the thin-lipped Werner Haupt, the pragmatic Kaiserreich War Minister leaning out the window of a government building cheering as well. Haupt had managed to keep his office during the Weimar debacle. A shrewd and natural survivor, he had that evening replaced Generals Ludendorff's and von Papen's portraits with one of Herr Hitler's, prominently hung a few inches above von Hindenburg's.

Luftmann could have learned that slipping through the cracks of change, Haupt had secured a low-profile job under the republic while remaining a conservative and a monarchist. Token democratic tolerance. The shrewd diplomat had switched his Conservative Party membership to the National Socialists after the 1932 election. He was hoping for a new assignment.

Fanny did not tell her father on the phone that morning about a marcher who leaped from the ranks and struck a man who was not giving the Nazi salute, making him bleed, knocking him down. She had pulled the boys away so they wouldn't see the man lying on the ground, blood gushing from his mouth, ignored by police and spectators alike.

(Christian read that story later in the *Amper-Bote,* which had also written:

> "The brutality that accompanied the marches throughout Germany seemed incidental to the multitudes of middle class

observers who appeared intoxicated with elation and immune to violence."

Who could have anticipated this from so civilized a people, he had asked himself again?)

Fanny went on, a flood of words rushing from her.

"Papa, do you remember Sepp, on that August day in the Odeonsplatz shouting he would fight French guns for the Kaiserreich? It was like that at this Berlin celebration. A new country, a rebirth. A Third Reich! Germans were holding their heads up high again. I think it made others want to belong to these people. I know it was the magic of the moment, Papa, but I was overcome, as I was in 1914, with a burning desire to escape my narrow life and attach myself to something that is great and fundamental."

Earlier that afternoon — Fanny was not there — the National Socialists German Students League staged its own parade, which ended up in front of the German Stock Exchange, called the "Mecca of German Jewry" by one right-wing paper. The students chanted "Judah perish!" at the emerging stockbrokers. The Nazi newspapers had a field day showing the support of Germany's "youngest and brightest."

The torchlight celebrations were repeated in many towns and cities, particularly when the new Chancellor, on February 1, 1933, by executive decree, dissolved the current Reichstag, setting yet another election in March. People cheered when Chancellor Hitler claimed the body elected in November would not and had not worked for Germany. "We must act as one. *Ein Reich, ein Volk, ein Fuehrer* all working together."

The revelries throughout the Reich became louder, their language more aggressive.

"Twenty thousand brown-shirts in Hamburg," the state radio reported, "followed one another like waves in the sea, their torch-lit faces shone, a religious rite." They quoted an American journalist in Berlin who had written, "Hitler and his party are restoring pageantry, color and mysticism to the drab lives of 20th-century Germans."

People's voices rang out, "For our leader, our Reich Chancellor Adolf Hitler, a threefold *Heil*." A three-year-old, raising his tiny hand in salute, chanted, "Heil Hitler, Heil Hitler-man" again and again, adding, "The republic is shit."

"Death to the Jews," was shouted repeatedly. Marchers sang of Jew-blood that would squirt from their knives.

The August days were remembered by Goering, too, an *Alte Kaempfer* who joined the party back in 1922. Backed by von Papen's Catholic Centre Party, the hero pilot had assumed the presidency of the Reichstag since the

1932 Nazi landslide victory.

"The shame and disgrace of the last fourteen years are wiped out! A second August miracle," Goering's voice boomed. It was broadcast nationally. He was a popular Nazi who had a sense of humor rarely found among his colleagues. Many remembered with pride when he was ordered to surrender the planes of his squadron to the Allies in 1918. In defiance Goering and his fellow pilots intentionally wrecked them on landing. There was no punishment, only cheers.

"He doesn't wear celebrity well," said Father Goetz. "He's getting fat as a pig. And all those medals he packs on. Clearly not a modest man, this Bavarian with a peasant mother. Did you know, Christian, that his godfather and mentor is of proven Jewish descent?"

"I didn't," he replied, munching on one of Lotte's sugar-coated doughnuts.

Sitting in the library of the Burgfrieden house, a silver tray of coffee and doughnuts before them, Luftmann told the priest about Fanny's call.

"Who would guess Germans would act this way? Fanny, my own flesh and blood, ignores last year's unpunished rampages, violence against Catholics, criminal attacks on opposition party members, Red sympathizers, German Jews, violation of synagogues. But worldly things don't have to make sense," Luftmann said philosophically. "In 1914 Germans became a people, *ein* Volk. In 1933, Germany becomes a nation, *ein Reich*. And this man Hitler? *Ein Fuehrer*, completing the Nazi slogan."

"Fanny says nothing about the bad behavior?"

She says, "These things will change. Everyone is drunk now with hope and pride after years of hardship and humiliation. With their dignity restored, sobriety returns; our people will again act civilized."

"Fanny never forgave the Reds for their attack on Sepp," Father Goetz said. "The German Workers' Party was her outlet, Christian. I'm afraid the Church has failed her," the priest said sadly. "And Sepp, what does he have to say?"

"We didn't speak, but Sepp is German through and through, a patriot. However, he holds the random violence, disorder, and lack of discipline of the SA in great disdain."

"Yes, well, I see the Communists' Red flag was banned by the Nazis and Goering outlawed Red newspapers. That should satisfy Fanny."

"Makes no sense. They are all Catholics, these Nazi bigshots — Hitler, Goebbels, Himmler, Goering — yet they're embraced by Protestant masses."

"It's the ultra-nationalism the Nazis offer, Christian, and their anti-Bolshevik tirades. The 400-year celebration of Luther's Reformation in 1917 awakened Protestant fervor, not toward religion, instead making a hero of the monk who singlehandedly reformed Christianity. And Hitler, I suppose, is to them Luther's Second Coming, who will singlehandedly reform their nation, restore German order and discipline. They are Prussian values. He promised full employment. Good for Catholics and Protestants! He and his Nazis present the vision of a promised Deutschland. A new Germany. A Third Reich, this one for a thousand years!"

"Order? The storm troopers represent order?"

"Like your Fanny, Prussians think that temporary. So what next?"

"Race and Blood! Remember the powerful Steel Helmet leader, a Prussian who was part of the back room deals for a new chancellor? He was against Herr Hitler and the Nazis. Too vulgar and disorderly, he said."

"I remember."

"Suddenly it was revealed this powerful man had Jewish ancestry. That was enough to throw him out of the Steel Helmets. Race and blood. The half-century-old *Arierparagraph* used by private groups to keep non-Aryans, Jews, excluded from German life — like the Americans use *restricted* to exclude Jews — could become legal state policy. That's what's next, I think. Either Aryan or you're out!"

"Well, they have kept it no secret, Christian. In their 25 Points! In *Mein Kampf!* In Hitler's speeches when he was released from prison!"

"The Steel Helmet incident, discarding a substantial Prussian based on blood and race, has an ominous message, Father. What I am saying is the question will no longer be whether Jews can be good Germans, but which good Germans are really Jews?"

Chapter 51
The Perfect Vehicle
1933

On the first April Sunday after the Nazi national boycott of Jewish shops and businesses, Father Goetz was ending his homily.

"Using words of His Eminence, we were saved not by German blood, but by the blood of Christ, of which we partake in the communion rite! This Nazi treatment of so called racial enemies is unjust! God always punishes the tormentors of his chosen people, the Jews! Pray for them! And I ask, as well, in the prayers of the faithful, you include in your intentions a prayer for the continued safety for our Sankt Raphael Organization and their century-old mission helping any German emigrate."

"That was a daring sermon," Luftmann said quietly, leaving Church with Lotte. "Foolhardy, maybe?"

"Jewish businesses with brown-shirt bullies standing with clubs at their shopfronts, anti-Semitic slogans painted in red on their windows? At Halpern's small leather goods store they scrawled NO RESPECTABLE GERMAN SHOPS HERE! If people who know better do not speak out, they may as well embrace Satan," said Father Goetz.

As Father Goetz was talking to their grandfather and greeting other parishioners, the Hofer altar boys were changing in the sacristy. Luddy, now a member of the junior Hitler Youth, put on his uniform quickly. He could repeat the priest's inflammatory homily almost word for word.

"Where's the fire?" said Josef as he folded his vestments neatly.

"Please do mine," asked Luddy, leaving his vestments on the floor. "I need to get out before Father Goetz sees me. Why don't you wear your HJ uniform?"

"Because Father Goetz asked me not to. A simple request. No politics in the House of God. He thinks it's political."

"Yes, well, do as you please. But help me out here, Josef," said Luddy. "Don't you ever try to look in the future, Josef? To prepare for it? Think of what can happen?"

"No one can see the future. That's foolishness, a waste of time."

"Easy for you to say with your good looks and muscles."

"We all can only hope for the best, Luddy."

"But prepare for the worst. There I agree with Grandfather. You can't be too careful. What do you want to be when you grow up, Josef? Do you think of that?"

"An easy one, Luddy. I want to be a warrior like Father. A soldier who fights soldiers, with honor and courage."

"You are an idealist! All is fair in love and war, I have heard our leaders say. We cannot be soft. I would like to be in the secret police. Work for my country in other ways, the betrayer not the betrayed. I trust no one but you, Josef. You defend me against those Mueller bullies. But one day I'll get them. You can be sure. I have to go. Thank you for taking care of my vestments," he said, rushing out the side door.

Luddy wanted to get home to write the priest's words down before he forgot and before anyone knew he was doing it. He would store it until he had — what did the youth leader call it? — a 'dossier.'

"It is not a game but a responsibility. A duty to the Fatherland not to be taken nor exercised lightly," the leader had said when they had the first mass assembly after a day in the fields exercising and hiking.

They had all solemnly sworn the HJ oath, a promise to do their duty "*at all times in love and faithfulness to help the Fuehrer — so help me God.*" Then, stomping their boots in time, they sang the HJ anthem " . . . . *we march for Hitler through night and suffering with the banner for freedom and bread. Our banner means more to us than death. Our banner means more to us than death!*"

With extraordinary timing for Luddy's career goals, that same month Hermann Goering created the *Gestapo*, an internal secret police that depended on people turning in people, reporting on enemies within. It was the perfect vehicle for betrayals. The Hitler-Jugend and its junior branch, Deutsche Jungvolk, were told by their group leaders how to use it.

"People, family, teachers, have loose tongues in your presence. They underestimate because you are young. But you are also loyal and smart. Be alert, as well! A noble service for the Fatherland."

Chapter 52
Konzentrationlagers
The Concentration Camps

While Luddy and Josef were changing in the sacristy, the last of the worshippers were leaving St. Jakob's.

Shaking Samson Gutmann's hand and giving Hannah Mueller a big smile — she was so tiny and delicate beside her giant of a man — Father Goetz said, "Maybe we get to talk Samson, you and I?"

"He can't now, Father. The Luftmanns wait for us for second breakfast," Hannah explained.

"I will be at Luftmanns, too. It has become a pleasurable habit. Perhaps after breakfast?"

"Oh! I'm so sorry. After breakfast Samson and I return the boys to Karlsfeld. Fanny couldn't come today. She went to Ludl Kappele. Gretl took a fall, you see, and has swollen knees. And Sepp eats with us but then has business in the new Dachau Concentration Camp, so we're taking Josef and Luddy back to Karlsfeld."

"Yes, well, Samson, we make it for another day. Sometime this week I hope."

"Is something wrong? We don't do anything wrong, Father," Hannah said, clearly sensitive about the long-standing relationship between herself and Gutmann. "Whatever they whisper" — she meant the other parishioners prone to gossip — "I promise you that we follow the rules."

"Don't worry yourself, Hannah." Father Goetz had to chuckle. They were not teenagers, but the dear woman sounded like a child. And people did have busy tongues in his parish.

Finished with his farewells, Father Goetz walked briskly from Augsburgstrasse to the Luftmann home.

Sitting in the Luftmann dining room, sipping their cups of tasty coffee (Lotte always added a pinch of salt to the finished brew, never reheating it, always fresh) their stomachs were full from the warm crisp rolls straight from the oven, the creamy butter, homemade jam, honey, and, always, the treat of doughnuts because Luftmann loved them so much.

Luftmann noticed that Hannah Mueller had put on an Alte Kaempfer badge. First making sure the boys were out in back (two little Nazis, my grandsons, he thought) he said to his guest, "You, Hannah, a party member?"

"A maternal obligation," Gutmann jumped in to explain. "Hannah was among the first hundred thousand members who joined. Herr Mueller insisted for his career. Mothers do that for their sons. The badge is rewarded to true believers, those who signed up before the Nazis' 1932 victory. Herr Mueller tells her to wear it. Meanwhile he rewards her by keeping her from her grandchildren."

"What do they say? No good deed goes unpunished," sighed Luftmann. "They are good-looking pins. Fanny has one. She values it. And you see Sepp's on his uniform. Clever, the red-white-and-black Swastika party badge encircled with a gold wreath."

"People who have it are called Golden Pheasants," Gutmann said with a chuckle. "My Hannah is a Golden Pheasant," he teased.

"Not altogether my cup of my tea, if you don't mind my saying so," Luftmann sighed.

"They might mind, Father-in-law," said Sepp without looking up.

"Warning noted, Sepp, about opinions? But not discussing what happens each day, current events, right? That's permitted?" There was a sarcastic edge in his tone.

Sepp did not respond.

Luftmann turned to Father Goetz. "About your homily today. In the American South, no need for store boycotts. Negroes shop only in Negro stores. Whites only in white stores. Everything between the races is separate in their South by its states' laws. You heard of Jim Crow laws? Based on blood and race? You can look white in America, but if you have black blood in you, you are black and must obey racial laws. In some southern States, the racially white can't play checkers or dominoes in a public park with a racial black, no matter what they look like. You go to jail for that!"

"To jail?" gasped Hannah.

"They had a case where a man was seven-eighths white and one eighth black. That means but one great grandparent, mind you. He challenged his state law ruling him a Negro. Their highest court upheld the ruling. They fear racial mongrelization, a threat to the existence of their white America. Does the theme sound familiar?"

"I see you read everything that may affect life in Germany, and even more," said Father Goetz, trying to lighten the discussion, aware that Sepp looked uncomfortable. "But we are talking about America."

"One can't be too careful in this world, ignore warning signs," Luftmann said. "Jim Crow began as a simple-minded song ridiculing Negroes. Now it is a brand name for all restrictive anti-negro legislation. Are you making fun of me, Father?"

"There is nothing funny, my son, about the *Arierparagraph*, excluding so-called non-Aryans, Jews, from German life."

"As always, we all have to adjust," said Luftmann. "New government, new ways."

Said Father Goetz, "We know Hitler and his party's attitude toward Jews. However, Jews everywhere are known for helping brethren in distress. But were we to follow a 'Jim Crow' trend — which our church watches carefully, by the way — what happens to non-Aryan Christians? To our converts and their offspring? What recourse do they have?"

"None it appears. Trapped in the middle. That would be a shock to many! A terrible situation to find out you are not who you think you are," said Luftmann. "Though they may look like German Christians, think they're German Christians, be raised as German Christians, act like German Christians, not circumcised like German Christians, they would not be seen as German Christians. Always non-Aryans! Blood is blood!"

Father Goetz said, "It's a crisis. You heard about Pastor Heinrich's new allegiance to the *Deutsche Christen* movement?"

Luftmann nodded.

"The German Christian movement wants to get rid of the Old Testament altogether! Destroy everything Jewish! Rabbi Paul! Amens! Allelulias! purged from our own Gospel! Some want to throw out the Gospel! That's how far back the Deutsche Christens would go, not just great grandparents. Non-Aryan Christians are at risk. The Protestants don't want them! As I said, Jews can help themselves with their worldwide welfare organizations, Jews for Jews. But Non-Aryan Christians? Who helps them?"

"There are some Protestant factions that object strongly to this movement. They form a separate Confession, a break-away sect. Perhaps they will help their own non-Aryan members."

"Niemoeller's Pastors Emergency League, their Barmen Declaration?"

Luftmann nodded again, taking a bite of Lotte's delicious doughnuts then washing it down with her splendid coffee. He did love the sweet, heavy pastry.

"Niemoeller's faction objects only to state interference with religion, who dictates who can do what to whom, not to the racial content," Father Goetz admonished, as if Protestants missed the moral point, focusing on the legal. "We are concerned about our own non-Aryan Catholics."

Samson finally said, "Is that why you want to see me, Father? If you worry, I'm not a coward. Not someone who gets frightened and hides or runs away when things aren't going right! That's how we last so long here, we Gutmanns."

"Must we talk about these terrible things at the table? We are with friends, good friends. We eat well. Let us enjoy," said Lotte. "There are more cakes in the oven. More fresh coffee."

But Luftmann went on. "You should be especially concerned, Samson, with Marius Mueller getting more powerful, strengthening ideas of blood, race and ancestry. He is ambitious and will not make it easy for the person his mother mixes with. It is a mark against his getting ahead, Hannah consorting with a non-Aryan Christian, a one time Jew Haendler. You should think of these things. Always good to see what might be coming."

"The Nazis put in a request for Mueller's family baptismal records. An ancestry check. A deep one. They need the Church's help! All the churches. They have no records before 1876, they get documentation only through us and the Lutherans," said Father Goetz.

"He's in trouble, I hope," said Christian.

"Afraid not! I heard he is up for something important," said Gutmann.

"Word does get around, doesn't it," observed Father Goetz.

"Mueller's wife Helga tells her father, Schtreuk, who tells my Hannah, still trying to convince her to stay away from the 'baptized Jew.' Me! He tells her she can be an obstacle to her son's future."

"He gives accurate advice," said Luftmann. "Only this week *The Law for the Restoration of the Professional Civil Service* bars Jews and those of Jewish descent from state jobs. Cutbacks in the medical and legal professions include the same restrictions. Blood and race count for everything!"

"Marius Mueller is not a good person," said Samson.

"Never mind Mueller! Read *Mein Kampf*! Herr Hitler's vision for Germany."

"You forget, I did," reminded Gutmann.

"Read it again," said Luftmann, glancing at Sepp to see if he had gone too far.

"Please gentlemen, please stop. The boys can come in at any time. This is not for their ears," pleaded Lotte, her face turning crimson.

"I just add this, Lotte, then no more," Luftmann said. "What sold poorly, what Mussolini called boring, now sells millions of copies throughout the Reich! People's new bible, *Mein Kampf*! Nazis will deliver on their promises and intentions. It has already started."

"You will excuse me, Mother Luftmann, I must be off to the new camp," Sepp said.

"Of course, Sepp." Lotte, always trying to find the best in things, looked relieved. "The Pumf now a *Konzentrationslager*, *KZ* people call it, a camp for protective custody, right here in Dachau. The first KZ in the Reich, I think, and they choose what once was your land, Christian. Your gift to the Kaiserreich. It is welcomed in town, putting people back to work, bringing in tax money, they say in the shops. The newspaper wrote a good editorial on the KZ lifting us from 'crushing economic hardships'."

"So now you quote the *Amper-Bote*? Miracles do happen," teased Luftmann.

"I need to keep up with my husband," Lotte said dryly. "Reading and doughnuts!"

Sepp, still in the room, added, "Herr Schtreuk with his SA men have the run of the Dachau KZ. The SS tries to change that. We do have barracks in the Camp. You know they arrested my father. Sent him there. He died within a week under 'protective custody'."

"Oh Sepp, I'm so sorry, I didn't know. Couldn't you have helped?" Lotte said, clearly in distress at her blunder for bringing up the KZ.

"I learned after the fact, Mother Luftmann. But anyway, Himmler's SS does not interfere with Roehm's SA. There are boundaries," Sepp replied, turning to the priest. "You know, Father, they have loose-lipped Protestant pastors and Catholic priests at the camp. They use them for slave labor. One needs to choose his words with care in any new government that is trying to establish itself and trying to serve the people."

"I understand, Sepp."

"Did Schtreuk kill your father?" asked Luftmann

"As my father destroyed my Mother?" he said with acrimony. "Of course, Schtreuk. For the Horst Wessel murder. And for the cowardly Geiselmord! They said he was a Bolshevik suspect in the February Reichstag fire, too."

"Do you really think Herr Hofer was part of a plot to burn the Reichstag down?" asked Gutmann, looking doubtful.

"I suspect he was a doomed man," said Father Goetz.

"I was told he went into hiding once the Communist Party was banned and the arrests started," Sepp explained. "His savior Moscow did not come to the rescue. They found him using the workers' barracks at the KZ, posing as a laborer."

"How do these things happen so fast, Father?" asked Samson in wonderment. "A blink and everything changes? I feel like I moved without moving. The nation, a legal dictatorship by that Enabling Act passed after the fire. The Reichstag yes vote to the Act, putting themselves out of business, like Herr Hofer working at his own death camp. Hitler now Chancellor. All in two months! It's hard to keep up. Nothing makes sense."

Sepp got up. "I must take my exit now. Thank you again for the wonderful meal, Mother Luftmann." With that, Sepp left the room without a glance at his father-in-law or Samson.

After he left, Luftmann said, "We all must be careful not to put Sepp in awkward positions. He tries to be fair. He is fair. But he has his duty, too. I forget that from time to time. As for your questions, Samson, with Goering presiding, Reichstag approval of the Enabling Act was an accomplished fact before any vote was taken. And sudden change? Don't you know, you of all people, raised as a Jew, don't you know that bad things happen quickly? Good things struggle, take time."

"And faith and prayer," added the priest.

"Amen," mumbled Lotte automatically.

"They promised this forced unity, one and only one nation, one people, one leader. They give it. They won on that platform, after all," Luftmann said. "We must adjust."

"Did you ever think we'd see respectable Germans of opposing political parties treated as criminals? Arrested and put away in our Dachau KZ for protective custody? I heard fifty 'protected' inmates killed the first week. Not just Herr Hofer! With the law allowing it!" said the priest.

"Repeating rumors can be dangerous, Father." Again it was Luftmann urging discretion.

"I thought the KZ was a good thing, not a place for murders," moaned Lotte. She leaned on the counter to steady herself. "This talk makes me dizzy."

"No one knew what would go on in concentration camps. They warned Father Ignatius many times about speaking against the Aryan clause, or he could visit Dachau as well. Ignatius preaches that laws keeping Jews out violate the Church's mission to bring Jews back to the fold for the Second Coming. They cautioned him, reminding him of his Polish, non-Aryan descent."

"I'm a simple farmer, I mind my own business. A Catholic farmer," Samson insisted. "Can they really hurt me? Us? Hannah and I could marry and live and work on the farm."

Luftmann said quickly "I don't think — "

"That's it! Enough! Eat, Christian! No more talk! I make fresh coffee for everyone. My head aches. We end on hope," ordered Lotte, having the last word.

Closing on hope, it was Lotte's last word before collapsing when an overburdened brain vessel burst from the high blood pressure she suffered, warned by her headaches, yet never treated. The rupture severely damaged her left frontal lobe.

Chapter 53
Old Habits

When she left the Munich hospital, speechless and paralyzed on her right side, half her face drooping like an uneven hem, Lotte was taken to the Karlsfeld cottage, where Fanny hired Anke the midwife to help care for her. Though a nursing home for rehabilitation was recommended by the doctors, Luftmann could not find one that would accept high-maintenance elderly patients. (They did not say useless.)

Living in Fanny and Sepp's cottage, built with so many bedrooms for children that now would never come, Gretl and Lotte shared a room. One morning Anke found that Gretl, apparently hearing her sister-in-law moan during the night, had managed to climb into bed with her, an old habit revived. The aged Rolf, finding some space, joined them.

"I let them be. I used to crawl in for comfort with my sister as well," Anke told Helga, visiting the Schtreuk home on her day off. They had become close, the two women born of the same class, while Anke helped Helga raise her four boys. "So what they sleep together?" she muttered. "A pity! Fanny Hofer now has two inferior, ballast lives, one could say. A feebleminded aunt and a paralyzed mother."

Said Helga, "The energy and money wasted on them could be used to help sturdy but poor German families. Well, not my business; they do what they please. You walked to the station?" she asked while serving a tasty liver dumpling soup for lunch.

"Walked to the station, then took the train. Herr Gutmann offered to drive me, but do you think I would ride with the Jew?" Anke asked, expecting no answer. Both women wore their *Alte Kaempfer* badges. "You know, I think Luftmann's wife could recover. It takes time from such an accident in the brain. But someone needs to keep moving the good part of her body so that ability doesn't disappear. I try to show Fanny. She learns. But there are people trained for that."

"You are a good woman," said Helga, walking over and kissing her quickly and intimately on the lips.

Chapter 54
A Friend in Deed
1933 — 1934

In the early months of 1933, the *Arierparagraph* racial restrictions were applied to teachers unions, pharmacists unions, public health doctors, sports and track and field associations, tax advisers, all Jewish employees in the Army, dentists and dental technicians in public health services, and to the National Association of German Writers. And there was the Law Against Overcrowding, placing severe limits on Jewish children accepted at public schools. All were legal moves under the Aryan Paragraph's new official status.

In May, over one and a half million new German members had joined the Nazi Party. Non-Aryans were not welcome.

Sepp was sitting in one of the extra rooms at their spacious farmhouse, a room once meant for their extra children. He used as it a study, a place to think, to think independently, to see what his conscience was doing. The room was sparsely furnished, an easy chair, a small corner desk with pencils and paper, and a hardwood chair next to the desk. On the walls were family pictures, his family, Fanny, the children, and the picture of his graduating class from the academy.

Sepp understood what was coming in the future. Not just because he was in the elite SS. It was what the Fuehrer and the party said they would do in the first place. Promised to do once in power. So many were blind.

But as an SS Captain, he knew more, knew it first, and he knew what he had to do.

He had to speak with Gutmann. Samson was a good man, a good German, a good friend always. He had saved Sepp's life once, worked his farm, helped Fanny. The conversation at his in-laws' home about non-Aryan Christians was disturbing. More troublesome was Samson dismissing Father Goetz's and father-in-law Luftmann's concerns. Changes were moving quickly. He knew they would. It was the way to get things done before people knew what was happening.

In July, there was the *Reichskonkordat*. The Catholic Church decided to dance with the Nazis, signing a peace treaty with them. Newspapers worldwide carried the story. Rome's approval was a Nazi victory. Sepp was glad peace was made with his Church. There had been an increase in anti-Catholic violence by his party, especially by the storm troopers. The treaty promised that would end.

That same week, however, The Law for the Prevention of Hereditarily Diseased Offspring was passed, making compulsory sterilization legal. Had they blindsided the Pope? Sepp heard Father Goetz attempt to explain it to his father-in-law. Yes, the Church's position had been disregarded, but still the treaty was necessary.

"I know well the sterilization law is a slap in the face in view of the treaty. I know ultimately Herr Hitler favors euthanasia for the incurably ill. I know it could be the beginning of a descent into modern barbarism," admitted Father Goetz.

"And?" Luftmann asked.

"And what? I also know when our bishops banned the party, Goering banned our press. We allowed priests to refuse the sacraments to those wearing Swastika uniforms to Mass; Catholics went to Lutheran churches to receive the gifts. The cardinals — Munich's Cardinal Faulhaber once a member of *Amici Israel* — privately spoke of deals made with the Devil."

"But they made the deal anyway, adjusting. Smart! What we all need to do," Luftmann said somberly. "Adjust."

"Hitler approached our bishops. He said he was only finishing what the Church had started 1,500 years ago but doing it better. He promised no second Kulturkampf, promised the escalating summer violence against Catholics would stop, promised religious schools and no interference," Father Goetz grimly defended his Church.

"Does Rome trust him?"

"No, we're not fools. They have the superior position. The cardinals, however, must hold on to the many that have become more German than Catholic, forcing the Church to follow the flock, not lead it. And we must protect the devout, those who stay more Catholic than German. A double edge, pushing and pulling. As important, we must defend non-Aryan Catholics, like Samson."

"Yes, well, Jesus's church is more practical than He was. So much for the Christ's sacrifice for the good of mankind, for bearing crosses. There would be no church if the Christ adjusted. But we are neither saints nor God. Accomodations are in order."

"Sadly, for us, I must agree. Obligations outweigh lofty ideals, Christian.

It is our job; we must do it. That is the cross to bear. To know better, yet to do otherwise from the obligation to protect our flock."

Sepp agreed with Father Goetz. The Church did what it had to for its people.

Sepp knew his party would put into place all they had promised, swiftly and without exception. His friend, the old Dachau stationmaster, was put in protective custody at the KZ by storm troopers for three months for removing the Nazi Party banner at the depot and replacing it with the Bavarian state flag. But they had pledged conformity, unity, for all Germans. No states, one Reich! They swore they would have the will, the strength, to do whatever was necessary to bring honor back to Germany.

Nobel Prize winner Fritz Haber left Germany. An imperial officer in the Kaiserreich, awarded the highest medals for helping in the Great War, a Jew later baptized, he had not left with honor. He was stripped of his standing, dismissed, and persecuted. That should wake Gutmann up. (It had surprised Sepp that Haber's fate seemed to please his father-in-law.)

By the year's end, the Aryan Paragraph extended to the national railroad company, excluding not only non-Aryans, but Aryans married to non-Aryans. If Hannah Mueller was allowed to marry Samson, she would be an outcast.

All newspapers were placed under Nazi control; non-Aryans could not be journalists. Only Aryans could serve as jurors and work in government. And then, the Army previously immune, in February 1934, they targeted Jewish soldiers serving in the *Wehrmacht*.

Sepp, sitting in his study, safe from the responsibilities and obligations of the outside world, wondered how Gutmann felt about that. His only son, his Berthold, lost in Verdun serving the Kaiserreich, died for the country which he thought was his. Sepp led Jewish soldiers in battle. He remembered well the dead Jew soldier, the one whose innards had ruptured under the scorching August sun beating down relentlessly on the rat-filled trenches.

He would speak to Gutmann. He told Father Goetz his help might be needed for the baptized Jew. "I let my father-in-law know as well," he had said in the confidentiality of the confessional.

"Of course I'll help," Luftmann had replied. "Does he know he needs help, I wonder? Baptized Jews along with Jewish Germans are at great risk. Amazing the Jews do nothing. Do they think they're immune? I see the Third Reich declaring war on all non-Aryans who stabbed the fatherland in the back, who threaten the survival of their Aryan race."

"Be careful, Father-in-law!" Sepp warned. "*Their* Aryan race? Not a smart way to put it."

"You are right. Not a smart way to put it," Luftmann agreed. "But let me ask you this, Sepp! Only 500,000 Jews live in Germany, 1 percent of the nation's population, why do they get so much attention? And now those with Jewish ancestry are noticed as well? Why don't they leave? What are they waiting for? The Messiah? He already paid them one visit!"

"These are not matters I question my superiors about, Father-in-law. Not for discussion! I thought you understood that."

Δ

Father Goetz also promised to help. "I will do whatever I can to assist. The Church must protect its non-Aryan Christians, Sepp."

"I will speak to Gutmann," said Sepp. "Tell him to leave Germany. I have a way, and it is helpful to our government, too."

"And Hannah?" the priest asked. "Samson would not leave without Hannah!"

"That is harder. Mueller would never let her leave with a Jew."

"You would be saving her life. Trust me on that!" He sounded conspiratorial.

"Father, I beg you not to share anything with me I need to report. I am an SS officer who swore the oath, as you are a priest who took your vows."

Δ

Sepp couldn't speak with Gutmann until much later that year. Events got in the way. The summer Roehm Putsch, then, after that, the eighty-six-year-old President von Hindenburg died. In August, Reich Chancellor Hitler made himself Reich President as well, the final act of *ein Reich, ein Volk, ein Fuehrer.*

The Roehm Putsch — falsely accusing the powerful SA leader and his storm troopers of planning an attempted government takeover — was used as an excuse by the Nazis to murder Ernst Roehm along with hundreds of SA loyalists, imprisoning thousands more. It had taken two nights. Once a close ally, Roehm had become a threat standing in the way of Hitler's own plans.

The successful purge of the SA caused conflicts and doubts for SA Group Commander Ernst Schtreuk, yet it resolved conflicts and doubts for SS Captain Sepp Hofer.

Some of Schtreuk's closest comrades were ambushed, killed, or imprisoned. He had been a Roehm loyalist, never thinking he would have to choose between his SA leader and his fidelity to Hitler. There would have been no Third Reich without the early dedication of the SA and its storm troopers headed by Roehm.

Schtreuk knew he escaped death that night as well. Had Sepp Hofer intentionally saved his life, insisting Schtreuk stay in the Dachau KZ? He would never know. That order prevented him from attending the meeting convened by Roehm at Bad Wiessee. The agenda had been to sort out the openly hostile divisions between the SA versus the SS, Gestapo, and Wehrmacht. At the meeting Hitler walked in, brandishing a gun and backed by a cadre of SS. Sepp was there.

Schtreuk wondered, should he say thank-you to the newly promoted Captain Hofer? Then he thought it was better left quiet between them whether or not Sepp had intentionally saved him.

As far as Sepp was concerned, Schtreuk had helped his Fanny. He had protected the Karlsfeld farm against the food raids of violent gangs in the postwar years. Schtreuk had bravely saved one horse from Sepp's burning barn and had risked his life attempting to help Sepp's special steed, something Sepp would never forget. He had no quarrel with Schtreuk. In fact he felt indebted to him. True, Schtreuk had killed Sepp's father, but it was a militarily correct action. Ludwig Hofer had begged for such an end if his enemies were ever in power. He was a traitor.

As to his prior doubts, Sepp's faith in Hitler and the party was restored with the SA purge and removal of Roehm. In the past year, no political parties to pick on, storm troopers would run riot after a night of drinking, pick on passers-by, attack police, be overbearing and loutish, more like gangsters than soldiers. Sepp always had contempt for their lack of military discipline and bully tactics. He was reassured to see that his party really meant to bring back order, obedience, and restraint to his country. As for Roehm, the SS knew he was a degenerate pervert, a lover of men, an undisciplined sadist.

After the Putsch, Fanny was quick to tell Luftmann, as they stood together in the bright sun at the Karlsfeld farm, "You see, Papa, I told you our party would restore order to the Reich. The Bolsheviks gone, and the drunken clubbing-anyone-on-the-streets storm troopers were punished severely. Those left are now under the strict reign of the SS, even the Dachau KZ. You were skeptical! Admit you were wrong! Admit I told you so. Nothing is perfect in this world, I know from Father Goetz, but Herr Hitler and the party have done so much good for Germany. Are you perhaps ready to join us now, Papa?"

"Fanny, sun rays on the gold from your *Alte Kaempfer* badge glitter in my eyes," Luftmann replied.

Meanwhile it was reported that, in 1933, more than 60,000 German Jews had left the country. The Nazi press flaunted their success in the 1934 issues of the *Voelkische Beobachter, Dachauer Zeitung* and *Der Stuermer*, the latter a new, virulent, anti-Semitic Nazi hate sheet. "Our racial enemies can't go soon enough," read the *Beobachter* editorial. *Der Stuermer* had vicious cartoons of Jewish stereotypes, scurrying like rats to cross the border, dragging money, long tails showing through their waistcoats, jewels and furs spilling out of their satchels. "We don't need Zyklon B to get rid of the Jew rodents. Just the voice of our Fuehrer makes them scatter," was one clumsy caption.

"At least some have brains," was all Luftmann had to say to Father Goetz about those Jews who had left. But there was more on his mind. "I must find a good nursing home for Lotte. Fanny does her best with Anke's help, but Lotte desperately needs fully trained attention to recover. Have you made any connections, Father?"

"Not yet, Christian. But I try. So many of our facilities are shut down by the government."

And so, with the SS now running the Dachau KZ, with stability in place after the Putsch, with Hitler as the one true leader of the Reich, Sepp finally spoke some sense to his friend Samson Gutmann.

On a blustery, cold March evening, Father Goetz, responding to knocking from the outside, opened the rectory door carefully and slowly. Looking up and down the street, he seemed satisfied. Then he saw them.

"Ah! Samson with Hannah. What a nice surprise! Do come in! Excuse my hesitation!"

"Good evening, Father. I told Samson we shouldn't come without warning. Did we startle you?" Hannah asked.

"No, No! I thought it might be the others paying me another call."

"What others?" Gutmann asked.

"Police in plainclothes."

"Our police? From Dachau?"

"No, not ours. Secret state police, men from that new group Herr Goering created to fight the enemy within. *Geheime Staatspolizei*, Gestapo they call themselves. They came to warn me. They do not care for my sermons. Specifically, when I discuss the divisive Aryan Paragraph and its conflict with the universality of the Church, of Christ's message for all humanity. They said a complaint was reported to them by a member of the parish."

"From our own church? Hard to believe, Father," Hannah said.

"We do have many in our congregation who take their politics as seriously as they do their faith, I'm afraid. They may often not like what I say, but now they seem to have a place to report it. And of course there are Hitler Youth in our parish ready and able to report anything. They join HJ as puppies and are trained as watchdogs. To turn in anyone! Parents and teachers had better be careful what they say in front of children now."

"And clergy must be careful what they say to their parish, Father," Samson advised. "What did you tell the men who came? Did they threaten you?" Samson asked.

"They try to intimidate. Said they had a dossier on my sermons and acts. I told them, since they wear plainclothes, they were welcome to come to hear my sermons. But I warned them, too, that there are ideas they preach that I am obliged to mention when they violate my creed, my vows. I invited them to St. Jakob's; they invited me to Dachau KZ."

"You plan to go?"

"It wasn't meant to be a visit."

"You play with fire, Father. That police organization must be the one Marius Mueller is up for, the need for the deep background check, asking the Church for records."

Father Goetz looked away, acting as if he were busy with some minor thing. But it was the baptismal records about people the churches had and the Nazis wanted. He had his own opinion of churches in collusion with the state. No better than the HJ turning information over to them. What to do with the M FILE and the I FILE weighed heavy on his mind. Getting Gutmann on his way saved two birds with one stone, he mangled the maxim; take care of Samson and Hannah if it worked out as planned. At least they had come to see him. Progress!

In the stillness of that night, a soft snow was falling. Pine-scented mountain winds whirred through the Dachau streets and forest, swirling white flakes as if a decorative snow globe, encasing St. Jakob's at its center — surrounded by quaint red-roofed houses and cobblestone streets — shaken by God's hand.

"My manners! Do excuse me! Why do we stand here? Poor, shivering Hannah. Come, we sit by the coalstove in the kitchen. I was brewing black tea for just such a night."

As they entered, Father Goetz looked up and down the Augsburger Strasse once again, then he shut the rectory door and locked it.

As Hannah and Samson took off their fur-trimmed coats in the vestibule, removed their snow-wet boots, loosened the scarves protecting their faces from the fierce March wind, discarded their mittens and woolen hats, it was clear to Father Goetz they had been unrecognizable walking Dachau's darkened streets, except for Samson's large size and broad shoulders, a giant of a man. Few would venture out anyway to fight winter's last blast. The priest silently thanked the Lord for the weather and the clothes that masked their identities.

"I know you spoke with Sepp. I know a little of what you spoke about. As Sepp said, better no one knows too much. And he may know more than we think, but he is bound by his life's oath to his SS organization. What times we live in!"

They sat in the plain whitewashed rectory kitchen near the coalstove,

Hannah and Samson rubbing their hands together, warming themselves. The Holy Family gazed down at them kindly from the framed watercolor hanging on the wall opposite. It was guarded by two crucifixes, one on each side.

Father Goetz served the steaming black tea in large mugs. There was honey and hard sugar cubes for dipping. A platter of plain sugar cookies sat on the checkered oil cloth that protected the wooden table. Three Dresden-blue china plates and a basket of fragrant potpourri, a gift from a parishioner, were placed there as well.

"It feels good to be here," said Samson. "Yes, Captain Hofer spoke briefly to me."

"First we give our prayer of thanksgiving," Father Goetz proclaimed. "A special one for good outcomes."

They bowed their heads thanking the Father, Son, and Holy Ghost for the bounty, the warmth, the gifts of friendship, bestowed lovingly upon them by the man-God hanging from his cross on the kitchen wall, blood-spotted red paint on his hands, side, and feet, the crown of thorns on his head.

Hannah, sipping her tea, said she was too nervous to worry about her figure. "The cold makes one want a sweet. I think I will try a cookie," she said, putting two of them on her plate.

"They are tasty. Thank you, Father," Gutmann chimed in.

"Now for the business at hand. Here is how we can help, my children."

Father Goetz told them about Sankt Raphael and its work.

"Sankt Raphael's is a priests' group that assisted German Catholic travelers in the exodus during the Gruendejahre. We stayed in business, as you might put it, Samson.

"Right now it is easy to get out of Germany, emigration offices sprouting up throughout the Reich for that purpose. The Nazis want to force all non-Aryans to leave. One Volk, remember? However, getting in somewhere is a different story. Other countries suffer the same lack of jobs and depression we have. Their quotas are purposely unfilled. In these times, you must have work waiting for you."

"It could be difficult, then? Getting in, let alone having a job waiting?"

"That is what Sankt Raphael can do for you."

Gutmann said, "It is ironic. Things are better in the Reich. Herr Hitler extending the Autobahn, created jobs. Our Voluntary Labor Service — planting forests, repairing riverbanks, reclaiming wasteland — keeps our youth working, puts bread in their families' mouths. Paying women a bonus to leave jobs so that men could work makes our unemployment figures lower than any other European country. People smile again. If there weren't this racial problem — "

"But there is, my son."

Gutmann gave a sigh. "Hannah's unhappy staying behind, following later. But agrees."

"As I said, I do not know the details, Samson. Our job is in the end."

"Time is critical, Sepp seems to think. Maybe he does know more than he can say. But we, too, see writings on the wall."

"So many don't or won't!" said Father Goetz. "Ostriches with their heads in the ground!"

"That's because it's hard to believe this is happening in our homeland."

"We try to work fast." Then he added, "Whatever the plan, Luftmann said to travel by rail and leave your car here, at the train station, to be seen. People think you're coming back if your beloved old Daimler stays visible in Karlsfeld. Sankt Raphael will make arrangements for you once you are out. Sepp takes care of getting you out."

Chapter 56
Plans and Plantations

"Herr Luftmann, may I ask why you never joined the party? In all due respect, with your daughter and son-in-law so prominent and respected, your absence could be noticed. Besides, it is a good thing, overall. You can see what the Fuehrer has done for our country so far," Kiembock said.

The two men sat in the Luftmann farmhouse kitchen. Kiembock wore his *Alte Kaempfer* badge on his workshirt.

"Things are better here. True! However, I am not political."

"In these times, Herr Luftmann, everyone is *political*, as you call it. Unity, one nation, all working together."

"Is that why you came over to the house and pay me a call, Herr Kiembock, to invite me to enter politics?" Luftmann said good-naturedly.

"First I ask, how is Frau Luftmann? My wife visits with her often."

"No nursing home, yet. Recovery very slow, too slow," Luftmann replied, sadly.

"A shame you can't find one," the farmer said. "I won't take much time. Today, I come to ask you to join me and other Karlsfeld farmers to send Samson Gutmann on a mission that interests our Reich. A new way to improve farming methods."

"Samson? Farming methods?"

"Our soil is weakening, you see, the way we do things now. The Nazi Green Section wants to try doing something to make it better. Actually your son-in-law, Captain Hofer, told me about it. Wanted me to talk to the other Karlsfeld farmers. He suggested Samson for the task. A good choice, I think."

Luftmann suspected Kiembock remembered that his farm was saved from bankruptcy because of Samson's intervention. There was gratitude in the man. Clearly he trusted Samson for the job. Samson was smart, had learned farming in the last few years.

"What is the task?"

"Captain Hofer explained to me that SS Reichsfuehrer Himmler, with the Nazi Green faction, has developed an interest in a new form of farming, of cultivating a better quality soil."

"That's a noble goal," Luftmann said. "No one gets hurt."

"This idea, if it works, gets healthier food for our people. It is something called biodynamics! It's a very different approach, banning chemicals, substituting only organic materials in caring for soil. Healthier soil produces healthier crops, which fed to livestock makes them healthier and, therefore, all food healthier for the German people."

"What would Samson do?" asked Luftmann.

"Get information and give it. Speak to farmers among our Nordic neighbors who value their race as much as we do ours. Many there already try this experiment. We can learn from them. Then convince others to do the same in the interests of health and race."

"I'll speak to Sepp, Herr Kiembock. Find out how the government got involved. I never knew the Nazis had a Green Section."

"We have a lot of things. That's why you should become a party member, sir."

When they spoke, Sepp explained to his father-in-law. "Reichsfuehrer Himmler is a serious mystic, drawn to this biodynamics because of its mystical and racial roots. He calls it a spiritual science! Some Austrian philosopher developed a worldview that everything is alive and should be treated as such. It can be applied to farming, organic farming. What matters to us is, does it work? Samson would ask questions. Learn more."

"Interesting, never expected this from the Nazis. That's the truth, Sepp."

"Would it surprise you, Father-in-law, to learn that Himmler has already put experimental organic farms — plantations, he calls them — in several of the KZs throughout the Reich. One was carved out of the peat-rich Dachauer Moos north of the SS Garrisons in the Dachau KZ. They are farmed by prison labor."

"A Nazi Party Green Section, benign and constructive. A surprise," Luftmann repeated.

"If you joined us you might learn more, Father-in-law," Sepp told him, "The healthier produce feeds the SS as we speak. Then we sell off the rest. Make a profit, too! We experiment with existing crops and some medical herbs now imported. The goals are to make the Reich self-sufficient and to build a stronger German race."

"Altruistic! Perhaps, the SS Reichsfuehrer is so interested because Herr Hitler is vegetarian. Doesn't smoke or drink, I understand. No chemicals for his body!"

"It doesn't matter, the whys. It's a good program and it's good to send Samson. Helps his situation," Sepp added cryptically.

So Gutmann, on the Karlsfeld farmers' recommendation, was sent to Sweden and Denmark to talk to farmers trying the new form of agriculture — cover crops off-season, manure and something called compost made from organic materials to feed the soil. He was to convince others to stop the intensive use of chemicals that was depleting farmland. Traveling by rail and with arrangements made by Sankt Raphael, he had followed Herr Luftmann's advice, leaving his vehicle at the Karlsfeld station.

He went first to Varna in Sweden, where a large farm was experimenting with the biodynamic approach, then to the Jutland peninsula in Denmark, where certain farmers were doing the same, the Danish soil already weakened from chemical pollution.

He sent extensive reports to both Kiembock and Luftmann. Then he went on, as planned, to Copenhagen to wait for Hannah at a small hostel near Sankt Angars Kirche, also arranged by Sankt Raphael, where Father Martensen would preside at their marriage ceremony.

Hannah waited a month. With Gutmann gone, she wore her thick spectacles daily, her eyesight unreliable, nerves fragile from the stress, and an unanticipated fear of abandonment she had unconsciously carried within her all her life. The plan was that she was going on a pilgrimage to Catholic Churches and religious orders in the Nordic countries and needed the guide Father Martensen sent to care for her.

Before Hannah left, Luftmann quietly bought her interest in the brewery — they would need money to get started, she and Samson — and, besides, it was a good investment. Germans drank their beer. He recaptured as well, for a tidy sum, the brewery mortgage he had given to the then-War Minister Werner Haupt. He knew Haupt would hold on to it, not donate it to the Kaiserreich, feeling about Marius Mueller the way he did. And he could bequeath the brewery to his grandson Josef, leaving him a note:

> *"I know you want to be a soldier like your father, Josef. You may already be one. But some day there may not be a war to fight or a need for warriors, or you may wish to retire. So the brewery is for you. Do with it what you wish when you are of age to accept this endowment."*

As to his mother's sudden, uncharacteristic trip, Marius was distrustful with Gutmann out of the Reich at the same time. But there was little he could do without calling authorities' attention to the race defilement he wanted to keep secret. Besides, Herr Hitler had loved his own mother. Treated her well. He could do no less without reason.

Once out of the country, Hannah first visited the Roman Catholic cloister at Vadstena founded by Sweden's 13th-century St. Brigitta. It was special. After the Reformation, Catholicism was banned by the Lutheran Swedes.

"Sweden changed that policy in the 18th century," explained Gustav, the all-knowing guide Father Martensen had sent.

Fanny had recognized Gustav when he came to the farm to help Frau Mueller prepare for her journey, remembered him from her Denmark trip and his taking her to Sankt Angars Kirche. She had greeted him warmly, sending regards to Father Martensen and telling Hannah she could not have a better guide and companion.

From Vadtsena, Hannah would go to Denmark, to the magnificent cathedral Sankt Angars, to join Gutmann. But there was an obstacle. Father Goetz had told Sepp there was a problem getting Hannah's baptismal documents, the MUELLER FILE, to Father Martensen, the certificate and records needed for the marriage ceremony. He had to get them there for the wedding and get them back for the government. Those same records were needed as part of Marius's deep background check.

"I do not want to hear about ceremonies or difficulties. You take care of it. You and my father-in-law! I have done my job," Sepp said, uncharacteristically terse.

Because Father Goetz felt he was being watched by the Gestapo, suspected they checked his mail in and out as well, he needed Luftmann's help. Yes, Father Goetz needed assistance, but without disclosing information that would violate his own commitment to Rome and confidentiality to parishioners.

"Christian, I have to get documents to a church in Copenhagen. I cannot send them directly. I think the Gestapo checks my mail. None of their business! Any ideas?"

Luftmann, without questioning why or what, thought for a while and came up with a solution. Noting the Gypsies were in Dachau County, camping on the outskirts of the district, far away from the old Luftmann Land and new KZ, he said, "The *Zigeuner*! the Reich — their old, troublesome *Zigeunerfrage*, like the pervasive *Judenfrage* — wants them to leave as quickly as possible. I get the boy, a man now, Milosh. You remember? Sepp saved him. I gave the tribe land to camp on. They do owe a favor, don't you think? Taking things in or out should be right up their alley, so to speak."

"Very good! Now, how do we get them back? I need them for the state authorities. I cannot put them off much longer."

"What would be incriminating for you to get them, sent from priest to priest? Church to church? Perhaps through diocese mail?"

"Getting this material sent back directly to me would tell the Gestapo that I knew of Samson and Hannah's plans to marry and not return. Marius would go wild! Incriminating, makes me a conspirator by having provided the needed records — and in turn drags in Rome as part of the conspiracy. Then the Gestapo wonders how I snuck them out in the first place, not good for you and the Gypsy."

"It's complicated, isn't it?" Luftmann smiled at the workings of the priest's mind.

"Yes, well, Mueller would seek revenge, having a baptized Jew stepfather with my help! Getting the diocese network involved only makes matters worse. I would be endangering the Church's position. The cardinal scolds me for causing trouble as it is. What I need is for no one to know the records ever left Dachau. Once Samson and Hannah are officially wed and I get the records back somehow, then I hand them over to the government as instructed by my bishop."

The only plan Luftmann could think of was to have Father Martensen mail them to his Freisinger Strasse house, addressed to Lotte, with a note on the envelope saying to Frau Fanny Hofer's mother, our prayers and intentions from Sankt Angars Kirche for your recovery. After all, Fanny had visited there, had met the Danish priest. Not too unusual, *gell?*"

"That's a pretty thin solution," said Father Goetz. "How would they know in Denmark about Lotte's illness?"

"We don't worry about that. The Gestapo does not check my mail. At least I don't think they do. Besides, can you think of anything better?"

"The Gypsies again?"

"I've told the Gypsies they should never come back to the Reich," said Luftmann.

Father Goetz sighed. "Good advice! Well, we'll try your plan. It's all we have. And Christian, thank you for helping without asking questions."

"Nowadays the less you know the better," said Luftmann, with a chuckle. "Imagine! I never thought I would say something like that."

Samson Gutmann and Hannah Mueller were joined in sacred matrimony in the beautiful red-and-gold brick church with the saints' sculptures surrounding them. Sankt Raphael found the Gutmanns a permanent place in Sweden where he could work as an agricultural consultant, visiting Swedish farms, talking as one farmer to another, having digested all the experimental biodynamics from his reports.

The Gutmanns intended never to return to Germany.

As to the records, when they were returned to Father Goetz. That should have taken care of the M FILE once and for all.

Chapter 57
The M FILE

As instructed, Father Martensen sent back the Mueller baptismal records, the M FILE, by post for Father Goetz, addressed to Frau Lotte Luftmann at the Freisinger Strasse house. Prayers of the Faithful for God's love to help her bear her cross — was scrawled across the back of the envelope.

It arrived at the Luftmann home the day after Father Goetz's arrest.

The old priest's continued critical sermons bothered the Nazis. He had been warned. The damning one, delivered that weekend at Mass, was about the unjust treatment of "our Jewish brethren" and how it causes great pain.

So Father Martinsen's mail was sitting on Luftmann's desk as he tried to sort things out. One move was clear: He had to get the priest out of the camp. He would talk to Sepp. With the SS now in charge of the Dachau KZ, Sepp would have more influence with the Kommandant.

Independently, there was an outcry from Dachau's Roman Catholics, who wrote letters and signed petitions to SS Reichsfuehrer Himmler saying:

> "We know our priest has a loose tongue and doesn't understand
> the good our party does, nevertheless, he is still our priest. We beg
> for his speedy release and kind treatment to an elderly German
> having 72 years in age."

Both Sepp's interference for the gentle priest who helped save his life coupled with the people's vigorous support had weight. Goetz would be released after spending only two weeks in protective custody.

That was enough time for everything to go wrong.

The M FILE fell into Luddy Hofer's hands.

Poking around his grandfather's study, Luddy noticed the postal envelope several times lying on the large desk, unopened. He thought that odd, addressed as it was to his grandmother and unopened. Why unopened? Why didn't his grandfather take it to his ill grandmother, whether she understood it or not? It would have been the right and natural thing to do. He decided to take a peek.

At first he was disappointed. There were indeed prayers for his grandmother to trust in God and hopes for courage and recovery. But there was also inside an envelope addressed to Father Goetz. That set off an alarm! Father Goetz? Why didn't this Father Martensen send it to St. Jakob's, Luddy wondered.

He decided to open it.

He could hardly believe what he read and his luck in finding it, almost peeing his pants in joy. The M FILE, thick with papers, told, in detail, all about the Muellers. There were letters, doctors' reports, and newspaper clips as well. The nuns, in their thorough way, had sent as much information about Hannah as they could to St. Jakob's when she married the Dachau businessman Friedrich Mueller.

Chapter 58
Hannah's Story
Luddy's *Mutprobe*

She was raised by nuns from the Schwaezach Convent near the Black Forest, the order known as Poor Servants of Christ, also called Poor Handmaids of Jesus.

A late child conceived during her mother's change of life, Hannah was an "accident" birth. With grown-up siblings, she was more a family embarrassment than a blessing, cared for at home by servants during the short time she spent there.

There was a name-theft scandal in her family (so prevalent in those times of emancipation) created by her older brothers; it brought her parents ridicule and taunting from their neighbors and was written about, with cartoons, in all the main newspapers throughout the Kaiserreich. Her parents were of moderate wealth. They quickly made plans to emigrate.

The scandal was so prominent that the young child — not even ready for kindergarten — was made an object of ridicule, mistreated by other children of all ages whenever walking with one of the maids in the streets or playing in the parks, where she was shunned as well.

Always fragile, sensing that she had not been wanted, she was traumatized by these unpleasant excursions, and, just before the family left, lost her vision. A nervous breakdown, a neurotic failure, the doctors called it. Authorities, however, thought she could be diseased. She was not permitted to leave the country.

Her parents, tickets purchased, trunks packed, plans made, hastily found the convent outside Berlin, up north where they had lived — who else would take in the sickly child? — made a contribution to the order, and left the child in the sisters' care.

The nuns were loving and kind. They made Hannah feel safe again, and her vision, though imperfect, was somewhat restored. She was a lovely, loving child.

When her parents sent for her, however, upon her recovery, they learned the child no longer was theirs. The nuns had baptized their little ward, telling the family she now belonged to the Roman Catholic Church. Some legal maneuver was attempted by her parents in America, but it was a lost cause. This brief legal battle also made the Prussian and American newspapers.

The sisters raised her well, thoroughly, as if a gift from their Lord. And she was a beauty. So when Friedrich Mueller — a middle-aged bachelor, a good and affluent businessman who never saw what he wanted in his native Dachau and had barely looked, so preoccupied was he with his brewery business — heard on his travels of the convent's ward, her comeliness, some kind of settled controversy, he visited there, asking if perhaps the young girl might be a suitable, childbearing bride for him.

The sisters were glad to make so excellent an arrangement for young Hannah's future. The man was substantial and seemed kind, with an impeccable German Catholic background.

They brought out their Hannah, their dark-haired beauty. Even though she wore the special spectacles they had for her, it was, for Herr Mueller, love at first sight. They married at the Schwaezach Convent. For their honeymoon, he traveled with her to show the world to his shy Berlin bride who knew only the insular convent life, before bringing her back to Dachau.

She joined St. Jakob's Parish upon her arrival. For all those years Father Goetz had kept the marriage certificate and proof of baptism hidden in the church's files.

They read: "NÈE HANNAH ITZIG, BAPTIZED AND CONFIRMED AS HANNAH MARY ELIZABETH ITZIG IN SCHWAEZACH CONVENT IN PRUSSIA. JOINED THERE IN HOLY MATRIMONY WITH FRIEDRICH MUELLER AND BECAME HANNAH MARY ELIZABETH MUELLER."

Wearing a satisfied grin, Luddy whispered, "Grandfather is sloppy — despite what Josef believes — not so smart, after all, to leave this lying around for weeks." He wanted to shout with satisfaction at the treasure he found, but of course he couldn't. In the file there was enough of Hannah's story for him. The facts and the conclusion to which they led.

There was a brief article from the Berlin newspaper that read:

> "Losing their case and rights to their 'accident' child, now a Roman Catholic, her parents in America said Kaddish for her, the prayer for the dead, as was their tradition,"

And that was that. Hannah Mueller was a baptized Jewess.

He would have his revenge on Alf, Bernd, and Fritz Mueller and their kid brother, who would be just like his elder siblings. Their grandmother was a Jew! Their father a half-Jew.

Halfbreeds all! He would take it to the Gestapo. This was documented, not hearsay. This was official. He would be an HJ hero, preventing the crime of Jew race defilement within the Gestapo itself.

Wasn't Herr Mueller a candidate for an important Gestapo job? Yes, it was an heroic act, his *Mutprobe* test of courage demanded by the HJ while the boys were on probation. It would make his acceptance final, getting the coveted HJ dagger, "Blood and Honor" inscribed on it. At least as important, an idea he craved, it could make him feared instead of being one of the fearful.

Marius Mueller's baptismal file revealed that Hannah soon gave Friedrich Mueller a son. When the boy was approaching his second year, Friedrich contracted the cholera while on a financial business trip to a Hamburg bank. Hannah was home with young Marius when Friedrich died in a Hamburg hospital.

There were, however, implications damning Father Goetz, his apparent involvement and intentional deceit by not having the papers mailed directly to St. Jakob's, a point recognized by the Gestapo. Why else would a priest from Copenhagen send it to Herr Luftmann? There had to be collusion between the churchmen. Conspiracy! They would not tolerate that.

Father Goetz was not released from protective custody after all. His stay would be indefinite. With some deliberation, they did not consider Luftmann responsible for what some Danish priest mailed to his wife. After all, it had been unopened and, according to Luddy, on Luftmann's desk for weeks. They did not question him.

After the Nazis with their race laws and use of the Aryan Paragraph, Father Goetz's heavy burden had been knowing he had to submit the M FILE to the authorities for the Marius Mueller background check, dooming Marius's unknowing mother Hannah as non-Aryan, let alone Marius and his children. At least Hannah's painful exposure as a non-Aryan baptized Jewess was resolved when she left the Reich.

He had stalled and delayed until, by the year's end, the cardinal was notified by the government of Goetz's lack of compliance. He scolded the priest, ordering him to deliver the documents at once. But as things turned out, Luddy Hofer had done the job for him.

It was Mueller himself who had filed the angry complaint, brought it to the authorities' attention, causing the cardinal's reprimand, because he felt the unnecessary delay was holding up his promotion to a key position in the Reich.

Chapter 59
Nuremberg: Lebkuchen Upstaged
1935

Because of Luddy's action, the Mueller boys were immediately expelled from the Hitler Youth. Marius Mueller, revealed to be half a Jew, was thrown out of the party and dismissed from any state positions he held and, of course, rejected for the position he coveted so. The Gestapo's standards were as severe as those of the SS, their penalties harsh.

Early in 1935, non-Aryan restrictions intensified. Non-Aryans were forbidden to join the Army, and Nazi racial anti-Semitic slogans appeared in restaurants and shops. It wasn't long after that the Nuremberg Racial Purity Laws uncoiled their venomous heads.

In September, at the annual Nuremberg Nazi rally, the Fuehrer proclaimed the Law for the Protection of German Blood and Honor, banning marriage between Jews and non-Jews, and the Reich Citizenship Laws, rescinding citizenship for German Jews and non-Aryan Christians. By November, the Reich Citizenship Laws were explained in complicated detail, revoking German citizenship from so-called full Jews and *Mischlings*, crossbreeds, half-Jews, and quarter-Jews. "The final nail in the coffin of emancipation, death after only sixty-six years," thought Luftmann, switching off the radio, missing either Lotte or Father Goetz to talk things over with.

Because of the marriage restrictions, Helga Schtreuk quickly divorced Marius Mueller, thinking half a Jew was close enough. 'Who needs him, anyhow," she told her father. "When he called me Frau Schtreuk-Mueller, the Schtreuk was better than Mueller," she said vindictively.

It did not, however, stop the vile treatment of her boys, once popular and important, now outcasts, shunned by their Aryan classmates, not befriended by the non-Aryan classmates they had systematically abused and mistreated.

In school the Mueller boys had to sit on separate "non-Aryan" benches. They were prohibited from games, competitive sports, swimming, and the ever-popular hiking parties and had to withstand the new curriculum that included the most vicious attacks and obscene descriptions of Jews and non-Aryan race strangers.

Helga was beside herself when young Fritz came home from school saying, "I pray to Jesus to make me very ill and let me die. I can bear this no longer."

Schtreuk could do nothing to help. "The children have one Jewish grandparent, Hannah Mueller, four Jewish great-grandparents, a half-Jewish father. The Blood Protection Law applies," he explained. "You must emigrate now while you can, Helga. You are Aryan. I can help you there. There is no future for your children in the Third Reich. Go to America. Some there are sympathetic to the party's cause. There are friends in their German Bund who will help you settle, as well."

"Why do I have to go? I have done nothing wrong. Did I know the swine, was half-Jewish? The Gestapo didn't know until the brat Hofer laid his hands on those papers somehow."

"You have to go, daughter, because of the children. They suffer! And you will be outcast as well, for race defilement. Ignorance is no defense."

She was in tears. Schtreuk, in an unexpected display of affection, embraced her, patting her back with his three-fingered hand, trying to soothe her.

Then Helga said with blatant passion, "Anke! I need Anke! I won't leave without her!"

He stiffened, moved away from his paternal embrace, as if a hateful suspicion was given credibility. Helga and Anke! "If she wishes," he said coldly. "There are no constraints. Anke is an *Alte Kaempfer*."

"And you? What will you do? Benefit? Move into my empty house? My father, who encouraged this race-tainted marriage on me? What do you do?"

"Helga, I was a working man at the brewery who gave my allegiance to a party when all Germans hung their heads in shame; when, mortified, they suffered every kind of hardship and humiliation. As a true German, I honor my oath. I will miss you all. Grieve for the boys. But I will stay in my homeland. That, Helga, is my duty, just as your maternal duty is to rescue your boys from the daily suffering inflicted on them. There is an emigration office in Munich. I will make the arrangements for you, for them, and for your Anke."

In December, after watching from afar as Anke and Helga, arm in arm with his four boys, boarded the train that would take them to the Hamburg port on the Baltic Sea to the ship that would take them to America, Marius Mueller returned to the Burgfrieden home he had acquired from his baptized Jewish mother. There, the once racial specialist for the Munich region hanged himself from an attic rafter with a Swastika banner wrapped around him.

There were many suicides throughout Germany, especially by those struck by lightning, discovering they weren't who they thought they were, with no recourse in courts. Marius had understood that. The justice system was now fully Aryan, from jurors to judges to lawyers.

The Nuremberg Racial Purity laws created a panicked uncertainty in the population. No one could be sure how to assess their backgrounds because of a lack of precision, despite the application of the Mendelian breeding formulas used in American Jim Crow laws. At least in America, skin color could help. There were a multitude of degrees of Jewishness and of non-Aryanness, each having its own restrictions.

Confusion, fear, and shock reigned. Confusion because one-eighth, even one-sixteenth of tainted blood had repercussions. Fear because sixty million Aryan Germans were pledged enemies to non-Aryans of any kind in the Reich. Shock because one day you went to sleep thinking you were one thing and woke up in the morning to learn you were another.

Chapter 60
Another Deal

Father Goetz was still in protective custody. Father Ignatius had taken over the Masses at St. Jakob's, and was in danger himself because of his past outspoken history on the exclusion of Jews preventing the promised Second Coming of the Lord.

Sepp could not interfere with his priest's extended imprisonment. Luftmann, who blamed himself, first for coming up with the plan for the letter to be sent sent to his home, then leaving the envelope unattended, had to make a drastic move to save his friend. Who could be an intermediary? Clearly he could not visit the Gestapo. He felt lucky they had left him alone. Then it came to him. They had worked together in the past. Understood each other.

In Berlin — a different Berlin, cleaned up, shut down, straight-backed, upright, the people tense — a menacing aura engulfed what once had been called the Sodom of Germany. Werner Haupt had the same workplace he had during the Kaiserreich, but no title was bestowed yet on him by the Nazis, and he served more as a remnant showpiece rather than having any active role. He was a conservative, an anti-republic Prussian. And now, a party member.

In his office, Luftmann had to smile when he saw the pragmatist's giant portraits of von Hindenburg, draped in black, and Adolf Hitler, in military garb, hanging on the wall behind the former War Minister's desk.

"If I can help at all, what can you give away this time, Herr Luftmann?" His thin-lipped smile didn't change as he sat straight-backed behind the large dark wood desk.

"Here's what I do to get Father Goetz freed from protective custody — "

"A shorter sentence, then freed. Otherwise we waste time here. He must be taught a lesson. That is their policy, to make examples," Haupt said firmly.

"What I can give helps the party and you, with party insiders," Luftmann pointed out.

"Yes, well, what is this you have they might want and they can't just take?"

"I give them the deed — you take the credit — for the Freisinger Strasse house, my home, substantial, a prestigious address, to establish a Gestapo

Dachau headquarters. Or whatever they wish. Free and clear, just as I gave the Second Reich, the Kaiserreich, the land for the Pumf, which, oddly enough, is where the KZ is holding Father Goetz now."

Haupt snickered. "Hah! Strange how things work out, yes?"

"My wife is ill, Herr Haupt. A bad condition. I am staying at the Karlsfeld farm near my daughter, who cares for her. I try to help. She is a loyal *Alte Kaempfer*, I might add. Her husband, whom you assisted in the past, is in the SS now."

"The SS runs the KZs why not go to your son-in-law?"

"I did once, twice is two times too many."

"I understand," said Haupt, looking interested. "Yes, a Dachau headquarters! A secret headquarters in a residential area. It would enhance my position, making that possible. You know I joined the party. This would show I was ready to act for it as well. Very clever! I commend you. You must be a very good Catholic, my friend, to do such a thing for your priest. I myself have not found religion useful." Here he smiled. "I will take the offer to them in a most compelling way. Anything else?"

Luftmann was prepared for that. He understood this man. "A token gift for you, Herr Haupt, not meant to offend, but to pay for your time and effort."

"Very kind," he took the small, suede drawstring bag filled with gold coins. "In one sense I was repaid already, Herr Luftmann. Mueller's downfall! And you benefited from that, too! He did not wish your daughter and her husband well, as I remember. The Gestapo took care of that fool. Someone turned him in. How dare that upstart Bavarian beer-monger think he could challenge me?" It was the Prussian war lord speaking those words.

Then as Luftmann was walking through the door, he heard a different voice from Werner Haupt, almost the voice of an adviser, a friend. "Like me, you are a survivor, Herr Luftmann. Join the Nazi Party. It is the smart thing to do while you still can."

When Luftmann was about to turn around, the Prussian administrator, back in character, said tersely, "You are dismissed, sir. Good day!"

Dare he wonder what that was all about? A favor for a favor? Luftmann shook the incident from his mind. He had thought about asking Haupt for help with a nursing home for Lotte, but even in desperation Luftmann knew that was foolhardy. Haupt was a Nazi now.

The Freisinger Strasse deal was made, the house with furnishings.

Father Goetz was released a few weeks later, thinner, more age lines in his face. His comment to Luftmann, other than gratitude, "*Dachau — Arbeit macht frei —* is not the innocent place it appears to be, my good friend."

Chapter 61
Fanny's Chance

"I never asked you for anything before, Father-in-law. And you have always been generous and kind to us, and this is a delicate request. But you will understand that it is not for me, but for our dear Fanny."

They were alone, talking privately, walking the path through the farmfields.

"We welcome your move to your farmhouse. Near us. We do need your help at home."

"I'm not a farmer, you know that, Sepp. I'll do what I can. What these old bones allow."

"No, it's not about farming. The Kiembock family runs the farm for us with Gutmann gone. Samson's report was encouraging, I understand. We're using that new farming method."

"So what do you need? Money? Is that what is delicate?"

"I need Fanny to be free from caring for Mother Luftmann. The nursing home is of course the best solution. She makes no progress with us. But if there is none in time, I need for Fanny to be set free. She would never mention it to you, Father-in-law. She is too caring."

"I'll do whatever I can for Fanny. In time for what? Is she ill? Something wrong?" As was his way, Luftmann's thoughts went always to the worst.

"Not ill. But our Fanny has a great opportunity. Herr Harrer wants her to be the poster woman for next year's Berlin Olympics."

Luftmann looked relieved. Then he felt a surge of pride, straightening his stance.

"I thought for sure they would have the *Goldene He*, after she expressed interest in competing for the Reich. But they will not use a Mischling, no matter how Aryan she looks, as a symbol of the new Germany. Father-in-law, I know how much this would mean to Fanny with all of her missed opportunities. But to accept, she needs to travel, do the promotion they want.

This is her last chance to somehow be connected to the Games. It means a great deal, the recognition, to represent the Reich before the world! I think because of her they ask me to be in charge of security. And both of our sons to be special guests of the HJ."

"Fanny on posters all over, representing Germany?" There was awe in Luftmann's voice. For many reasons.

"An extraordinary event, Father Luftmann. Berlin will be declared a no-hate zone. All those racial posters throughout the entire Reich will disappear. Everything befitting a great nation. But she would never relinquish her duty to her mother, and, with Anke gone, there is no one to hire to care for what looks like aged, incurable ballast. People fear going against the Reich's principles just for money."

"Next year's Olympics, you say? She never mentioned anything to me at all."

"She wouldn't, out of loyalty to her mother. But she must give Herr Harrer an answer soon. Whatever happens, I ask you never to say we had this talk."

"That I can promise. I know a medical facility is better for Lotte. I have tried. I will come up with something, Sepp. My daughter should have the opportunity. It was a part of her life unfulfilled through no fault of her own. I am glad you came to me."

"I did not want to offend. I love Mother Luftmann. And want what's best for her also."

"I know that, Sepp. We will figure it out," he said confidently but thinking, what am I to do with Lotte? "How much time does Fanny have?"

"A month at best. They are working now, planning the Games as a showcase for the world to see the new Germany, the Third Reich, and our Fuehrer's leadership."

"Let her accept this honor. I will not let her down."

After the walk, Luftmann stopped by Fanny's home in the compound to visit Lotte. Gretl, whimpering, was at her side, stroking her hand as Fanny was moving Lotte's limbs as best she could. It was a therapy Anke and the doctors had suggested.

"Fanny, I want you to know this. I will find a place for your mother very soon. A place where she can get the intensive treatment she needs."

"Are you sure you can? They are not making room for the very ill. And I hear they are shutting down the facilities that once cared for them, Papa."

"I will find something. Something suitable. Now that Father Goetz is free, I will talk to him again," he promised. Then looking around he asked, "Rolf? I do not see Sepp's dog."

"Oh Papa, he was so old. Everything failing. I don't know how he stayed alive. Josef was brave enough to shoot him for me, put him out of his misery."

"So," he took a deep breath, "That is why your Aunt Gretl whimpers." He paused. "And what about our Josef? How did he feel?"

"HJ teaches that mercy killing is an 'act of courage.' It was his *Mutprobe* test." She hesitated, then added, "But he had tears."

Chapter 62
From Itzig to Itzig

Schtreuk's storm troopers marched into Pastor Siegfried Heinrich's church as he was once again delivering his sermon on the German Christian, Aryan Jesus, national religion movement. The cross in the church, identifying the Pastor's *Deutsche Christen* affiliation, had a Swastika at its center.

He was near the ending, uttering his standard closing prayer. "We pray to God to save our German souls from Jews and the Devil."

His prayer was answered swiftly.

"The service is ended," pushing Heinrich aside from the lectern, Schtreuk told the startled congregation. "We cannot have non-Aryans pastors preaching to true Germans. It is against the law. They must preach and worship with only other mixed breeds like themselves. The new Reich bishop is in full support of this policy. There will be an Aryan preacher for your flock by next week. As for Pastor Heinrich, he will serve other non-Aryan Christans of your religious Confession."

The *Voelkische Beobachter* under News from Dachau, gave the whole story:

> Pastor Heinrich, an active Deutsche Christen minister, was removed from his church, when it was learned his father, Heinrich Hitzig, born Heinrich Itzig, was a baptized Jew. His mother was a baptized Jew from the north as well. Four grandparents Jewish, two fled to America at the end of the 19th-Century. A non-Aryan Christian, though a Lutheran Pastor, he is in violation of the Nuremberg Racial Purity laws by preaching to Aryans. Because he is a Deutsche Christen, he has been transferred and will be allowed to preach only to a non-Aryan congregation.

"Well, I suppose that ends his victory marches," observed Luftmann dryly, discussing the article but hiding his nerves. He and Father Goetz, on their afternoon walk, had stopped at Wittmann's bookstore on Augsberger Strasse, right off Schrannen Square, and were browsing through the shelves.

Luftmann was glad they sent the clergyman elsewhere. Any connection was a bad connection! He and the pastor might be distant relatives. Might?

They had to be, even with many *Itzigs* in the Reich. How could he not be that Jewish Lutheran minister he had joked about with Lotte? The one they had never met when up north. The one who had changed his name again. Too much coincidence!

He sighed. Thanking any God above that he had passed the background checks screening Sepp's appointment to the SS.

"His church did not object to this new segregated congregation policy, only that religion be kept separate from the state. True, the new Neimoeller Evangelicals denounce the cross with the Swastika as a mutation of that principle but, again, not the separate houses of worship for non-Aryan Lutherans. They make only the legal argument of state interference with religion. Whatever happened to Christian martyrdom?" whispered Father Goetz as they left the shop.

"Perhaps practical considerations, Father, like the Vatican Konkordat, *gell*? At least they can still pray to Jesus," Luftmann said glibly.

As they slowly walked the short distance to St. Jakob's in the chilled autumn air, a harbinger of the coming winter, Father Goetz shook his head. There was a pained look on his face, as if acknowledging the hubris of humans. It was time for the I File. Unavoidable! Would his friend be so fluent, so cavalier, when he had to face his own crisis?

He turned to Luftmann, "I had a nursing home near Munich, Sisters of Charity, that agreed to take Lotte — "

"Well, that is good news for both Fanny and Lotte," Luftmann cut in, his voice animated and happy. "Maybe not for Gretl, who is so attached to my wife!"

"I'm sorry, Christian. Let me finish. The facility was closed down by the state. The sisters had to surrender the sick who demanded full-time attention to Eglfing-Haar."

Like water in a sieve, his happiness drained away. "They take care of the very ill at Eglfing-Haar?" he asked in a voice gone dull.

"At that godless place, like the others, I am sure they do what they have to do," said Father Goetz.

Chapter 63
The I File
November 1935

Father Goetz agonized in prayer as to how to warn Christian without violating any obligations to the church. Yet, in these extraordinary times, he argued with himself, were not extraordinary measures called for? Wasn't preparing a family for a crisis important? A duty?

He prayed and came to a decision.

After Mass ended that Sunday, parishioners greeted Father Goetz outside St. Jakob's as they marched out of church. Many told him he was looking better than he had when released from protective custody. Some said they were relieved he didn't provoke the powers that be in his sermon 'God's Will or Ours, a Dilemma.'

"But remember well the warning, we become what we do! The Lord gave us the gift of free will," he had intoned after the Gospel reading. "There is no Volk spirit that makes us who and what we are. What we do is who we are. The Church asks us to bear our crosses as Lord Jesus bore his, telling us not to interfere with the will of God no matter how difficult it is.

"But when do we know whether God or the Devil has set the scene, created the dilemma? And, if Satan, then are we not called to interfere, take action? That is the dilemma. When we pray *Thy will be done*, we ask His help in distinguishing between God's will and Satan's."

The woman who had written the letter of despair a decade ago about Bavaria and not caring anymore, shook the priest's hand and whispered her thank-you for the homily, adding, "You might have omitted Volk, but at least you didn't give the Devil a Munich address, Father. I worry for you. My mother told me one never fights with those on top. The faith, you, and St. Jakob's, are all some of us have."

"Bless you, my daughter," he said. "Trust in God!"

When Luftmann came out, Father Goetz stopped him. "May I ask you to go in the rectory to bring me some pills I left on the corner desk? Look carefully, if you will, Christian, it is the smallest of the bottles there."

Once inside the rectory parlor to retrieve the medication for his friend, Luftmann found no pills at all, let alone the small bottle. However, there was a folder on the otherwise bare corner desk that was labeled ITZIG RECORD.

Next to the folder was an open diocese bulletin dated November 24, 1935, ordering parish priests to continue providing records for the state so they could check racial purity as prescribed under the new citizenship laws. It read:

> As to the records of the deceased, needless to say only those who married and had families of their own should be included in your submissions, unless there is a discrepancy. These must be reported. The Church cannot be accused of concealment or deceit. Any parishioner who has had an ancestry check should be omitted. Exempt also are their children. We must not waste the state's time with unnecessary paperwork.

COMPLIANCE EXPECTED WITHIN THREE WEEKS!

There was a list of the new citizenship guidelines. Scrawled underneath was a hand-written note from the office of his eminence suggesting that, should a priest come across non-Aryan Catholics, he should reach out to them in their time of need.

An icy chill traveled through Luftmann's body, a long-buried apprehension weakened him, awakening a dormant fear. He began to shiver, yet at the same time droplets of perspiration formed on his brow. His hands were clammy.

He sat down, feeling unsteady.

Luftmann understood that he was supposed to read what was inside the folder, the ITZIG RECORD. And he understood that Father Goetz's making it available to him in this manner meant trouble. There never were any pills.

Hands trembling, he opened the folder. One sheet was in it, written by the priest.

> Gretl Luftmann, née Gretl Itzig, baptized by Herr Pfarrer Goetz April 1897 as Gretl Irmgardis Dorothea Luftmann. In the presence of Dachau residents, Christian Luftmann, her brother, as godfather, and Lotte Luftmann, her sister-in-law, both parishioners at St. Jakob's. Her records from Munich were represented as lost during the 19th-century cholera plague.

Glued to the upper right-hand corner of the folder was the nametag, Gretl Itzig, that she had worn during her Munich hospital stay for treatment of the cholera.

He glanced at the diocese bulletin. The instructions. The citizenship guidelines under the new citizenship laws. And as was his lifelong nature, Luftmann realized in a flash all the consequences. What was he going to do?

He could hardly breathe.

While Christian was in the rectory parlor, Father Goetz, in a front pew, sat in the church now emptied of worshipers. The Hofer altar boys were long gone as well.

He had not let Luftmann know what he had known all these years. There was no reason. It was neither right nor wrong. It was Luftmann's secret, not his! It didn't really matter. In those days the Church welcomed converts. But, now, since emancipation was turned inside out with race and blood supreme, it mattered. It was all that mattered.

Gretl was an Itzig; Luftmann was an Itzig, his clever Lutheran ploy notwithstanding. Perhaps Lotte was a full Jew, as well. If so, Fanny would have not a drop of Aryan blood! The boys, Josef and Luddy, were half-breeds. All were non-Aryan Christians.

True, Sepp was cleared of any racial contamination, but, as an SS officer, with their strict and highest loyalty standards to the Reich, what problem would his marriage to a Jewess create? For him to remain married violated The Law for the Protection of German Blood and Honor.

Non-Aryan Christian! Look what it had done to Marius Mueller and his family. A divorce, violating a sacred sacrament, suicide — a mortal sin — children ostracized, emigration.

What would it do to Fanny? Innocent! Thinking she was one person, only to learn, in an instant, by decree, she was another? And that other was despised in the country she loved so? To Sepp? Ignorant! To Josef and Luddy? He knew what happened to the Mueller boys. One of them — was it Fritz? — had hoped he would get sick and die.

He had to submit Gretl's records to the authorities. Gretl, a non-Aryan Minderwertige! Born a Jew, she had no previous background check. Betrayal by the Church, cooperating with the Nazi government, made Father Goetz ill, tormented his soul. What he had known all along, now, he, a Judas priest, had to expose Christian Luftmann's living a lie all these years.

He prostrated himself before the altar, arms akimbo, and prayed for mercy and courage. Once a Luftmann family secret, this masquerade was now a life-changing state offense. Finally, lifting his aged and frail body that had suffered the hardships of Dachau KZ imprisonment, he slowly walked to the rectory. The papers were on the desk. Luftmann was gone.

Disappointed, Father Goetz walked over to retrieve the file. Luftmann probably had to meet one of the Kiembocks, thought the priest. They always drove him back and forth to St. Jakob's. Though he could certainly afford his own, Christian had never gotten the hang of driving an auto.

Father Goetz regretted missing him. He had wanted to assure Christian that Sankt Raphael would be there to help them when they emigrated. But Christian Luftmann had plans of a different kind.

Chapter 64
Deleting The Itzig File

Luftmann's first thought was to get Gretl out of the Reich. Her papers would go with her. Father Goetz would have no obligation. But, even if possible, that would take time.

He was sitting in the farmhouse kitchen, neat, spotless, odorless. No more the fragrant aromas of Lotte's presence — the heavy aroma of deep-fried, doughnuts, the ever-present Lebkuchen, her always freshly brewed coffee. Gone, as well, were the seductive scents of fat-browned pancake soup in pungent stock, the wonderful pork roast stewing on the stove, potato pancakes with cranberries and sweet-smelling stewed fruits. Fanny's kitchen was much the same as his was now, just the sterile smell of cleanliness.

Amazing, with a mother like Lotte, Fanny had never learned to cook or bake, so busy was she with sports, and then the war. She could barely put together cream cheese, baked potatoes, and caraway seeds, a quick and easy meal. Now, Frau Kiembock brought cooked food over for him most of the time. She always had more than enough, feeding her large family.

Fanny could attend to Lotte until he resolved this threatening Gretl issue. This Gretl ambush! It would not interfere with her opportunity at all. He would make sure of that. He could make sure of that. If no nursing home, who knows, maybe the Kiembocks could assist. Frau Kiembock visits Lotte often. What's more, there were plenty of skilled Jewish professionals, doctors and nurses, who had lost their practices under the Aryan Paragraph and the Nuremberg laws, that he could pick and choose from.

He would never tell Fanny the imminent danger lurking over all of them; never tell her that she wasn't who she thought she was. Never! And that he, her father . . . well, that spoke for itself.

He berated himself for rushing Gretl from the hospital directly to the church years ago. Not waiting one day to go over details, to see what was what, his negligence causing this catastrophe, overlooking that hospital tag. What was the rush? Worry? Fear?

Nevertheless, he had to settle the Gretl problem and the ITZIG FILE quickly. Father Goetz had his deadlines. But getting his sister to another place in time? Impossible.

If nations made it hard for healthy people to get in, not filling their own quotas because of economic weakness, why would they want a Minderwertige? Who would take her? Who would stay with her? Maybe Samson and Hannah in Varna? If she could get in! Sweden had its own Nordic pride and racial defenses against inferior specimens. But, the time! the time! Those arrangements would take too long even if they were a possibility.

Resolving the crisis was up to him, him alone. He was solely responsible, had made all the decisions. Running other peoples' lives to suit himself, there had been other choices he could have made.

When he had feared the future — that a Jew could never become a good German because he was a Jew, that emancipation had given them an impossible task — he could have simply left the country with his new wife and started a life elsewhere. He would still be Chaim; she would still be Chaya — maybe not even incapacitated by the repressed inner struggle he imposed on his young bride, the conflicts and stress of living two lives. They could have taken Gretl. She was well enough then, cholera cured! Functional! Luftmann could have changed that offensive surname, Itzig, elsewhere.

There were other choices now. Again, he could choose to emigrate. Allow the truth to come out. Gretl Itzig's truth! Ruin Fanny's life. Sepp's life. His grandchildren's lives. Sabotage everything he had ever worked for. And what about Lotte's medical treatment? It was hard enough now; certainly no one would care at all what happened to an old Jewish invalid. He had to take care of his wife.

Luftmann knew, in the back of his mind, knew what he had to do before he went through the reasoning process. It was acceptable, almost heroic, a *Mutprobe* in this new thousand-year Reich! No one would blame him. No worry about that. (Well, yes, Fanny! But he would deal with that later.) Like Luddy, he might even be a hero.

The reality was good Germans were Nazis now. And being a good German, at least appearing to be, was what he had devoted his life to doing. Besides, despite everything else, hadn't Hitler put the country back on its feet, restored dignity and pride? Even good Christians endorsed his effective policies.

And doctors, Hadn't Father Goetz told him, with disapproval, about the director of a Lutheran asylum in Franconia openly supporting euthanasia for unworthy lives? Saying so in a public speech, that he and his staff were there first to teach people to be good Germans, not to educate them to be children of God.

The state's propaganda machine was at work, as well. Swaying public opinion to adjust to many once unthinkable kinds of solutions in a Christian nation that prided itself for its advanced civilization. Wisely, public opinion was always important to the National Socialist German Workers' Party, now in complete charge.

The state had posters and pamphlets with repugnant pictures of incurable defectives printed saying:

> "Sixty thousand Reichsmarks is the cost for one of these patients.
> Money wasted on the useless, when they can be granted a merciful
> death."

Short propaganda films like *The Inheritance* were shown in cinemas, depicting generations of imbeciles carrying inferior defective genes, a cancer on the nation.

Even though pressed for time, he would be thorough. That afternoon, one of the Kiembock boys was driving him to Eglfing-Haar, just outside Munich. He would take one of the asylum tours, promoted throughout the Reich by the government. They were designed for people to see first hand how their hard-earned dollars were spent on those branded as lives unworthy of life. He had to see Eglfing-Haar for himself.

Once there, Luftmann found himself among SS, SA, HJ, all friendly with new hospital workers who were either party members or sympathizers. The press was invited, always invited, always welcome, armed with notepads and cameras.

The journalist from the *Muenchner Zeitung* was snapping a photo of a uniformed Hitler Youth — Luftmann thanked God it wasn't Luddy or Josef — who had joked about the "looney bin" they were about to see.

The asylum director, Herr Pfanmueller, distributed sheets with references to Binding and Hoche 1920s pro-euthanasia publication. And there was a quotation from the prestigious Psychiatric and Neurological Association:

> "We have spiritual ruins, patients as cost-occasioning ballast that
> should be eradicated in painless fashion — chemical injection, gas,
> experiments ongoing with the new efficient Zyklon B — merciful
> and justifiable in a nation fighting for its very existence."

A staff guide began a standard speech as they passed through the main entrance portals of the sprawling institution.

"Patients are divided among different buildings and wards according to both gender and the seriousness of their condition. There are specific wards for those who need a high degree of attention, for those who befoul themselves, for the agitated and the quiescent, and open wards and secure wards."

"Why secure?" came a question from a reporter.

"For those a danger to themselves and others. There are suicides, too, affecting the morale of staff who do their best serving their ballast patients," he replied.

"Then what?" another asked.

"The incurables and incorrigibles, terminals, are transferred to Eichberg."

"Why there?" the reporter followed up his query.

"They are better equipped to handle such cases. They die of heart failure or pneumonia. They don't last," the guide replied frankly before he went on.

"You should note there are cases where courageous German families call us asking that we mercifully end the lives of their severely afflicted. Those patients are transferred immediately to Eichberg, too. The compassionate laws of the Third Reich allow us to perform this service for families over-burdened by those long-suffering, those no longer truly human, for the survival of race and nation."

Courageous, thought Luftmann, involuntarily shaking his head. To ask that a family member be euthanized was an act of courage? This was the new, good German?

At the tour's end, an SS officer said, "You might as well set up machine guns as a cure for many of your inmates."

Director Pfanmueller had laughed.

In the *Muenchner Zeitung* the next day, a reporter described the experience:

> "Wild eyes stare out of contorted faces. Others glow with a feverish sheen. Grinning grotesques, with no resemblance to human beings. Those who enter are assailed by shrill cries. Fearful screams and mad laughter … Epileptics subject to attacks with jerking bodies, bedridden patients, the sick and insane, skeletons covered with skin. What do time and space mean to them? They vegetate in a twilight day and night. A raving maniac hammers on an iron door."

And the same Munich paper quoted the Catholic theologian and editor of the Roman Catholic *Caritas Journal*, "The Church in Germany has taken a humanist position, but why not in Sweden, Denmark, Switzerland, the United States?"

Did he mean they should, wondered Luftmann? Or did he mean why Germany?

Luftmann had seen all of this. It was accurate. No wonder Fanny had stopped volunteering years ago! Is this what she saw there back then? Was it the beginning?

On the tour when he asked about Eichberg and their transports there, they had said they act swiftly, wasting no time in the interest of mercy. Maybe the final outcome was a blessing, Luftmann thought.

While there he had questioned how *Gnadentod*, mercy killing, merciful killing, better-for the patient killing, worked?

"Injection. Gassing. Painless! It is for the terminally afflicted, suffering souls," he was told, reminding Luftmann of the Grand Inquisitor, Torquemada, believing burning heretics alive purified *their* souls. A good deed, a moral act, not an atrocity!

Gnadentod as a courageous step, the state controlled newspapers congratulating a farmer who had shot his mentally handicapped son! Again a *Mutprobe*, Luftmann thought, like Josef killing Sepp's ancient dog, Rolf. What once was murder is now brave and noble. A compassionate deed! A patriotic act! Being a good German!

Gretl! What did she do, after all? What kind of life did she have? She whimpered for Rolf, stroked Lotte, held her hand, slept with her — a practice that still revolted him — and made barely intelligible sounds. She could have died from the cholera, he reasoned, as his other sister had, instead of being what they now called a non-productive parasite. Or suppose he hadn't taken her in? After all, she would have been in such a place long ago. And who knows what would have happened?

There was a tiny space inside, a residual germ of a different conscience, and Luftmann could not really talk that part of himself into believing any defense, knowing only that it was something he had to do.

Gretl's existence made them Itzigs again. It was the only way to keep her damning baptismal record from being handed over to the state. The only way to make sure the ITZIG FILE was over with, deleted. In the balance, one could look at how all-important it was to him and, really, how little it meant to her.

The family would be safe. And he? He would be an un-Christian Luftmann. So? Was he ever really a Christian one? But he would be a good German. What good Germans had become. Gnadentod was an act of will and courage, like the brave farmer who shot his sleeping son in the middle of the night.

He went into the bathroom, unsteadily, weaving a bit. He locked the door, turned on the water so that no one could hear his wretched, wrenching upheavals, forgetting his house was now empty. Kneeling before the toilet bowl, as if receiving communion, Luftmann emptied his stomach. It did not purge him.

Father Goetz had called the asylum a godless place. All of them godless places. Well, Father Goetz would forgive him. That was a priest's job, forgiving. Then he went to the phone to call Eglfing-Haar.

EPILOGUE
What Next?

Luftmann's mind wandered to that planning place inside him that had always thought about being a good German, a mission he had dedicated himself to all of his life.

There was a next step. A last move.

After all, he had changed his name, his faith, shaved his beard, altered his dress, studied secular subjects, spoke like a German, read like a German, wrote like a German, talked like a German, ate like a German, performed a *Mutprobe* like a good German.

Should he join the Nazi Party like a good German, as Haupt suggested? As Fanny wanted? Sepp had invited? Kiembock had warned? Was he already like the Nazis because of what he had done and knew he would do over again? Everything he did was to save family members, all of whom belonged to the party. It was the only party. There was really no choice, if you thought about it.

Hadn't the Church, the same merciful Church that was absolving him of profound sin, hadn't it made its peace with the Nazi Party? Wasn't that like joining it? What did they call it, an act of omission? By not condemning, therefore approving? Other German Christians embraced the new "world order." Father Goetz had to forgive him, if not respect him. That was his duty.

Do we really become what we do? He was who he was, no matter what. Born that way. Aryans and Jews both would agree!

So, joining the party good Germans seemed to worship, was that the last step, the missing act in his transformation? Something to consider. After all, he could do worse.

The End

CPSIA information can be obtained at www.ICGtesting.com
Printed in the USA
LVOW101253101111

254361LV00002B/66/P